CHILDREN'S CLASSICS

Black Beauty

Anna Sewell

Black Beauty

mustard

Black Beauty
A Parragon Classic

This edition published, 1999
This is a Siena edition of a Mustard Book
Mustard is an imprint of Parragon

First published in 1877

Parragon
Queen Street House
4 Queen Street
Bath BA1 1HE

Printed and bound in the UK

CHAPTER 1

MY EARLY HOME

The first place that I can well remember, was a large, pleasant meadow with a pond of clear water in it. Some trees overshadowed the pond, and rushes and water-lilies grew at the deep end. Over the hedge on one side we looked into a ploughed field; and on the other we looked over a gate at our master's house which stood by the roadside. At the top of the meadow was a plantation of fir-trees; and at the bottom, a running brook overhung by a steep bank.

Whilst I was young I lived upon my mother's milk, as I could not eat grass. In the daytime I ran by her side, and at night I lay down close by her. When it was hot, we used to stand by the pond in the shade of the trees; and when it was cold, we had a nice warm shed near the plantation.

As soon as I was old enough to eat grass, my mother used to go out to work in the daytime, and to come back in the evening.

There were six young colts in the meadow besides me. They were older than I was; some were nearly as large as grown-up horses. I used to run with them, and have great fun. We used to gallop all together round and round the field, as hard as we could go. Sometimes we had rather rough play, for they would frequently bite and kick as well as gallop.

One day when there was a good deal of kicking, my mother whinnied to me to come to her; and then she said: 'I wish you to pay attention to what I am going to say to you. The colts who live here are very good colts, but they are cart-horse colts, and, of course, they have not learned good manners.

'You have been well bred and well born; your father has a great name in these parts, and your grandfather twice won the Cup at the Newmarket races; your grandmother had the sweetest temper of any horse I ever knew, and I think you have never seen me kick or bite.

'I hope you will grow up gentle and good, and never learn bad ways. Do your work with a good will; lift up your feet well when you trot, and never bite or kick even in play.'

I have never forgotten my mother's advice; I knew she was a wise old horse, and our master thought a great deal of her. Her name was Duchess, but he often called her Pet.

Our master was a good, kind man. He gave us good food, good lodging, and kind words; and he spoke as kindly to us as he did to his little children. We were all fond of him, and my mother loved him very much. When she saw him at the gate, she would neigh with joy, and trot up to him. He would pat and stroke her and say, 'Well, old Pet! How is your little Darkie?' I was a dull black, so he called me Darkie.

Then he would give me a piece of bread, which was very good, and sometimes he brought a carrot for my mother. All the horses would come to him, but I think we were his favourites. My mother always took him to the town on a market day in a light gig.

There was a ploughboy, Dick, who sometimes came into our field to pluck blackberries from the hedge. When he had eaten all he wanted he would have, what he called, fun with the colts, throwing sticks and stones at them to make them gallop. We did not much mind him, for we could gallop off; but sometimes a stone would hit and hurt us.

One day he was at this game, and did not know that the master was in the next field; but he was there, watching what was going on. Over the hedge he jumped in a moment, and catching Dick by the arm, gave him such a box on the ear as made him roar with pain. As soon as we saw the master, we trotted up nearer to see what was going on.

'Bad boy!' he said, 'bad boy! to chase the colts. This is not the first time nor the second, but it shall be the last. There, take your money and go home; I shall not want you on my farm again.' So we never saw Dick again.

Old Daniel, the man who looked after the horses, was just as gentle as our master, so we were well off.

Chapter 2

THE HUNT

Before I was two years old, a circumstance happened which I have never forgotten.

It was early in the spring, there had been a little frost in the night, and a light mist still hung over the plantations and meadows.

The other colts and I were feeding in the lower part of the field when we heard, quite in the distance, what sounded like the cry of dogs.

The oldest of the colts raised his head, pricked up his ears, and said, 'There are the hounds!' and immediately cantered off, followed by the rest of us, to the upper part of the field, where we could look over the hedge and see several fields beyond. My mother and an old riding horse of our master were also standing near, and seemed to know all about it.

'They have found a hare,' said my mother, 'and if they come this way, we shall see the hunt.'

Soon the dogs were all tearing down the fields of young wheat next to our meadow. I never heard such a noise as they made. They did not bark, nor howl, nor whine, but kept up a 'Yo! yo, o, o! Yo! yo, o, o!' at the top of their voices. After them came a number of men on horseback, some of them in green coats, all galloping as fast as they could.

The old horse snorted and looked eagerly after them; and we young colts wanted to be galloping with them, but they were soon away into the fields lower down. Here it seemed as if they had come to a stand; the dogs left off barking, and ran about in every direction with their noses to the ground.

'They have lost the scent,' said the old horse; 'perhaps the hare will get off.'

'What hare?' I said.

'Oh! I don't know *what* hare; possibly it may be one of our own hares out of the plantation. Any hare they can find will do for the dogs and men to run after.'

Before long the dogs began their 'Yo! yo, o, o!' again; and back they came all together at full speed, making straight for our meadow at the part where the high bank and hedge overhung the brook.

'Now we shall see the hare,' said my mother; and just then a hare, wild with fright, rushed by, and made for the plantation. On came the dogs, followed by the huntsmen. The dogs burst through the bank, leaped the stream, and came dashing across the field. Six or eight men leaped their horses clean over the hedge and stream, followed close upon the dogs. The hare tried to get through the fence; but it was too thick, and she turned sharp round to make for the road.

Alas! it was too late; the dogs were upon her with their wild cries. We heard one shriek, and that was the end of her. One of the huntsmen rode up and whipped off the dogs, who would soon have torn her to pieces. He held her up by the leg, torn and bleeding; and all the gentlemen seemed well pleased.

As for me, I was so astonished that I did not at first see what was going on by the brook; but when I did look, there was a sad sight. Two fine horses were down; one was struggling in the stream, and the other was groaning on the grass. One of the riders, covered with mud, was getting out of the water; the other lay quite still.

'His neck is broken,' said my mother.

'And serve him right, too,' said one of the colts.

I thought the same, but my mother did not join with us.

'Well, no,' she said, 'you must not say that. But though I am an old horse, and have seen and heard a great deal, I never yet could make out why men are so fond of this sport. They often hurt themselves, spoil good horses, and tear up the fields; and all this for a hare, a fox, or a stag, that they could get more easily some other way. But we are only horses, and don't understand.'

Whilst my mother was saying this we stood and looked on. Many of the riders had gone to the young man; but my master, who had been watching what was going on, was the first to raise him. His head fell back and his arms hung down, and every one looked very serious.

There was no noise now; even the dogs were quiet, and seemed to know that something was wrong. They carried him to our master's house. I heard afterwards that the young fellow was George Gordon, the Squire's only son; a fine, tall young man, and the pride of his family.

People were now riding off in all directions, to the doctor's, to the farrier's, and no doubt to Squire Gordon, to let him know about his son.

When Mr. Bond, the farrier, came to look at the black horse that lay groaning on the grass, he felt him all over and shook his head; one of the horse's legs was broken. Then some one ran to our master's house and came back with a gun. Presently there was a loud bang and a dreadful shriek, and then all was still; the black horse moved no more.

My mother seemed much troubled. She said she had known that horse for years. His name was Rob Roy; a good, bold horse with no vice in him. Afterwards she never would go to that part of the field.

Not many days after, we heard the church bell tolling for a long time; and looking over the gate we saw a long, strange, black coach covered with black cloth and drawn by black horses. After that came another, and another, and another; and all were black. Meanwhile the bell kept tolling, tolling. They were carrying young Gordon to the churchyard to bury him. He would never ride again. What they did with Rob Roy, I never knew; but 'twas all for one little hare.

CHAPTER 3

MY BREAKING IN

I was now beginning to grow handsome; my coat had grown fine and soft, and was glossy black. I had one white foot, and a pretty white star on my forehead.

People thought me very handsome. My master would not sell me till I was four years old; he said lads ought not to work like men, and colts ought not to work like horses till they were quite grown up.

When I was four years old, Squire Gordon came to look at me. He examined my eyes and my mouth, and felt my legs all down. Then I had to walk, trot, and gallop before him. He seemed to like me, and said, 'When he has been well broken in, he will do very well.' My master promised to break me in himself as he would not like me to be frightened or hurt; and he lost no time about it, for the next day the breaking in began.

Every one may not know what breaking in is, so I will describe it. To break in a horse is to teach it to wear a saddle and bridle, and to carry on its back a man, woman, or child; to go just the way the rider wishes, and to do so quietly. Besides this, the horse had to learn to wear a collar, a crupper, and a breeching; and he must learn to stand still whilst these are put on. Then he must be taught to have a cart or a chaise fixed behind him, so that he cannot walk or trot without dragging it after him; and he must learn to go quickly or slowly, just as his driver wishes.

He must never start at what he sees, speak to other horses, bite, kick, or have any will of his own; but must always do his master's will, even though he may be very tired or hungry.

But the worst of all is that when his harness is once on, he may neither jump for joy nor lie down for weariness. So you see this breaking in is a great thing.

Of course, I had long been used to a halter and a headstall, and to be led about in the fields and lanes quietly, but now I was to have a bit and a bridle.

My master gave me some oats as usual, and after a good deal of coaxing, he got the bit into my mouth and fixed the bridle. What a nasty thing the bit was! Those who have never had one in their mouth cannot think how bad it feels. A great piece of cold, hard steel as thick as a man's finger is pushed between your teeth and over your tongue, with the ends coming out at the corners of your mouth, and is held fast there by straps over your head, under your throat, round your nose, and under your chin; so that no way in the world can you get rid of the nasty hard thing. Bad! bad! yes, very bad! At least I thought so; but I knew my mother always wore one when she went out, and that all horses did when they were grown up. And so, what with my master's pats, kind words, and gentle ways, I got to wear my bit and bridle.

Next came the saddle, but that was not half so bad. My master put it on my back very gently, whilst old Daniel held my head. Then, patting and talking to me all the time, he made the girths fast under my body. I had a few oats, then I was led about for a while; and this went on every day till I began to look for the oats and the saddle.

At length, one morning my master got on my back and rode me round the meadow on the soft grass. It certainly did feel queer; but I must say I felt rather proud to carry my master; and, as he continued to ride me a little every day, I soon became accustomed to it.

The next unpleasant business was putting on the iron shoes; that too was very hard at first. My master went with me to the smith's forge to see that I was not hurt or frightened. The blacksmith took my feet in his hand, one after the other, and cut away some of the hoof. It did not pain me, so I stood still on three legs till he had done them all. Then he took a piece of iron the shape of my foot, clapping it on, and drove some nails through the shoe quite into my hoof, so that the shoe was firmly held. My feet were very stiff and heavy, but in time I got used to it.

And now having got so far, my master went on to break me to harness; for this there were more new things to wear. First, they placed a stiff, heavy collar just on my neck, and a bridle with great side-pieces, called blinkers, against my eyes. And blinkers indeed they were, for I could not see on either side, but only straight in front of me. Next there was a small saddle with a nasty stiff strap that went right under my tail; that was the crupper. I hated the crupper—to have my long tail doubled up and poked through that strap was almost as bad as the bit. I never felt more like kicking, but of course, I could not kick such a good master; and so in time I got used to everything, and could do my work as well as my mother.

I must not forget to mention one part of my training which I have always considered a very great advantage. My master sent me for a fortnight to a neighbouring farmer who had a meadow which was skirted on one side by the railway. Here were some sheep and cows, and I was turned in amongst them.

I shall never forget the first train that ran by. I was feeding quietly near the pales which separated the meadow from the railway, when I heard a strange sound at a distance; and before I knew whence it came—with a rush and a clatter, and a puffing out of smoke, a long, black train of something flew by, and was gone almost before I could draw my breath. I turned, and galloped to the farther side of the meadow as fast as I could go; and there I stood snorting with astonishment and fear.

In the course of the day many other trains went by, some more slowly; these drew up at the station close by, and sometimes made an awful shriek and groan before they stopped. I thought it very dreadful, but the cows went on eating very quietly, and hardly raised their heads as the black, frightful thing came puffing and grinding past.

For the first few days I could not feed at peace; but as I found that this terrible creature never came into the field nor did me any harm, I began to disregard it; and very soon I cared as little about the passing of a train as the cows and sheep did.

Since then I have seen many horses much alarmed and restive at the sight or sound of a steam-engine; but thanks to my good master's care, I am as fearless at railway stations as in my own stable.

Now if any one wants to break in a young horse well, that is the way to do it.

My master often drove me in double harness with my mother because she was steady, and could teach me how to go better than a strange horse. She told me the better I behaved, the better I should be treated, and that it was wisest always to do my best to please my master. 'But,' said she, 'there are a great many kinds of men: there are good, thoughtful men like our master, that any horse may be proud to serve; but there are bad, cruel men, who never ought to have a horse or a dog to call their own. Besides these, there are a great many men foolish, vain, ignorant, and careless, who never trouble themselves to think; these spoil more horses than any one, just for want of sense. They don't mean it, but they do it for all that. I hope you will fall into good hands; but a horse never knows who may buy him, or who may drive him. It is all a chance; but still I say, "Do your best wherever it is, and keep up your good name."'

CHAPTER 4

BIRTWICK PARK

At this time I used to stand in the stable, and my coat was brushed every day till it shone like a rook's wing. Early in May there came a man from Squire Gordon's who took me away to the Hall. My master said, 'Good-bye, Darkie; be a good horse, and always do your best.' I could not say 'Good-bye,' so I put my nose into his hand; he patted me kindly, and then I left my first home. As I lived some years with Squire Gordon, I may as well tell you something about the place.

Squire Gordon's park skirted the village of Birtwick. It was entered by a large iron gate, at which stood the first lodge; and then you trotted along on a smooth road between clumps of large old trees. Soon you passed another lodge and another gate, which brought you to the house and the gardens. Beyond this lay the home paddock, the old orchard, and the stables. There was accommodation for many horses and carriages; but I need only describe the stable into which I was taken. This was very roomy, with four good stalls. A large swinging window opened into the yard; this made it pleasant and airy.

The first stall was a large, square one, shut in behind with a wooden gate; the others were common stalls—good stalls, but not nearly so large. My stall had a low rack for hay and a low manger for corn; it was called a loose-box, because the horse that was put into it was not tied up, but left loose to do as he liked. It is a great thing to have a loose-box.

Into this fine box, clean, sweet, and airy, the groom put me. I never in my life was in a better box, and the sides were not so high but that I could see through the iron rails at the top all that went on.

The man gave me some very nice oats, patted me, spoke kindly, and then went away.

When I had eaten my corn, I looked round. In the stall next to mine stood a little fat, grey pony, with a thick mane and tail, a very pretty head, and a pert little nose.

Putting my head up to the iron rails at the top of my box, I said, 'How do you do? What is your name?' He turned round as far as his halter would allow, held up his head, and said: 'My name is Merrylegs. I am very handsome. I carry the young ladies on my back, and sometimes I take our mistress out in the low chair. They think a great deal of me, and so does James. Are you going to live next door to me in the box?'

'Yes,' I replied.

'Well, then,' he said, 'I hope you are good-tempered; next door to me I do not like any one who bites.'

Just then a horse's head looked over from the stall beyond. The ears were laid back, and the eye looked rather ill-tempered. This tall chestnut mare, with a long, handsome neck, looked across to me and said, 'So it is you who have turned me out of my box. Is it not a very strange thing for a colt like you to come and turn a lady out of her own home?'

'I beg your pardon,' I said, 'I have turned no one out. The man who brought me put me here, and I had nothing to do with it. And as to my being a colt, I am turned four years old, and am a grown-up horse. I never yet had words with horse or mare, and it is my wish to live at peace.'

'Well,' she said, 'we shall see. Of course, I do not want to have words with a young thing like you.'

I said no more.

In the afternoon when she went out, Merrylegs told me all about the mare.

'The thing is this,' said Merrylegs. 'Ginger has a bad habit of biting and snapping: that is why she is called Ginger. When she was in the loose-box, she used to snap very much. One day she bit James in the arm and made it bleed, and so Miss Flora and Miss Jessie, who are very fond of me, were afraid to come into the stable. They used to bring me nice things to eat—an apple, or a carrot, or a piece of bread; but after Ginger stood in that box, they dare not come, and I miss them very much. I hope, if you do not bite or snap, that they will now come again.'

I told him I never bit anything but grass, hay, and corn, and could not think what pleasure Ginger found in it.

'Well, I don't think she does find pleasure in it,' said Merrylegs; 'it is just a bad habit. She says no one was ever kind to her, and so why should she not bite? Of course it is a very bad habit; but I am sure, if all she says be true, she must have been very ill-used before she came here. John and James do all they can to please her, and our master never uses a whip if a horse behaves himself; so I think she might be good-tempered here.

'You see,' he said with a wise look, 'I am twelve years old; I know a great deal, and I can tell you there is not a better place for a horse all round the country than this. John is the best groom that ever was; he has been here fourteen years; and you never saw such a kind boy as James is. So it is all Ginger's own fault that she did not stay in that box.'

Chapter 5

A FAIR START

The name of the coachman was John Manly. He had a wife and one little child and they lived in the coachman's cottage very near the stables.

The next morning he took me into the yard and gave me a good grooming. Just as I was going into my box with my coat soft and bright, the Squire came in to look at me, and seemed pleased.

'John,' he said, 'I meant to have tried the new horse this morning, but I have other business. You may as well take him for a round after breakfast. Go by the common and the Highwood, and come back by the water-mill and the river; that will show his paces.'

'I will sir,' said John.

After breakfast he came and fitted me with a bridle. He was very particular in letting out and taking in the straps, to fit my head comfortably. Then he brought the saddle, but it was not broad enough for my back; he saw this in a moment, and went for another, which fitted nicely. He rode me at first slowly, then at a trot, and afterwards at a canter; and when we were on the common he gave me a light touch with his whip, and we had a splendid gallop.

'Ho, ho! my boy,' he said, as he pulled me up, 'you would like to follow the hounds, I think.'

As we came back through the park we met the Squire and Mrs. Gordon walking. They stopped, and John jumped off.

'Well, John, how does he go?'

'First-rate, sir,' answered John. 'He is as fleet as a deer, and has a fine spirit, too; but the lightest touch of the rein will guide him. Down at the end of the common we met one of those travelling carts hung all over with baskets, rugs, and such like. You know, sir, many horses will not pass these carts quietly; but he just took a good look at it, and then went on as quietly and pleasantly as could be.

'Some men were shooting rabbits near the Highwood, and a gun went off close by; he pulled up a little and looked, but did not stir a step to right or left. I just held the rein steady and did not hurry him; it's my opinion he has not been frightened or ill-used while he was young...'

'That's well,' said the Squire. 'I will try him myself tomorrow.'

The next day I was brought up for my master. I remembered my mother's counsel and my good old master's, and I tried to do exactly what the Squire wanted me to do. I found he was a very good rider, and thoughtful for his horse, too. When we came home, the lady was at the hall door as he rode up.

'Well, my dear,' she said, 'how do you like him?'

'He is exactly what John said, my dear. A pleasanter creature I never wish to mount. What shall we call him?'

'Would you like Ebony?' said she; 'he is as black as ebony.'

'No; not Ebony.'

'Will you call him Blackbird, like your uncle's old horse?'

'No; he is far handsomer than old Blackbird ever was.'

'Yes,' she said, 'he is really quite a beauty, and he has such a sweet, good-tempered face and such a fine, intelligent eye—what do you say to calling him Black Beauty?'

'Black Beauty—why, yes, I think that is a very good name. If you like, it shall be so;' and that is how I got my name.

When John went into the stable, he told James that master and mistress had chosen a good sensible English name for me that meant something; not like Marengo, or Pegasus, or Abdullah. They both laughed, and James said: 'If it were not for bringing back the past, I should have named him Rob Roy, for I never saw two horses more alike.'

'That's no wonder,' said John. 'Didn't you know that Farmer Grey's old Duchess was the mother of them both?'

I had never heard that before. So poor Rob Roy who was killed at the hunt was my brother! I do not wonder that my mother was so troubled. It seems that horses have no relations; at least, they never know each other after they are sold.

John seemed very proud of me: he used to make my mane and tail amost as smooth as a lady's hair, and he would talk to me a great deal. Of course, I did not understand all he said, but I learned more and more to know what he *meant*, and what he wanted me to do. I grew very fond of him, because he was so gentle and kind, and seemed to know just how a horse feels; and when he cleaned me, he knew the tender places and the ticklish places; and when he brushed my head, he went as carefully over my eyes as if they were his own, and never stirred up any ill-temper.

James Howard, the stable boy, was just as gentle and pleasant in his way; so I thought myself well off. There was another man who helped in the yard, but he had very little to do with Ginger and me.

A few days after this I had to go in the carriage with Ginger. I wondered how we should get on together; but except laying her ears back when I was led up to her, she behaved very well. She did her work honestly, and did her full share; and I never wish to have a better partner in double harness.

When we came to a hill, instead of slackening her pace, she would throw her weight right into the collar, and pull away straight up. We had both the same sort of courage at our work; and John had more often to hold us in than to urge us forward. He never had to use the whip with either of us. Then our paces were much the same, and I found it very easy to keep step with her when trotting. This made it pleasant, and master always liked us to keep step well, and so did John. After we had been out two or three times together we grew quite friendly and sociable; this made me feel very much at home.

As for Merrylegs, he and I soon became great friends. He was such a cheerful, plucky, good-tempered little fellow that he was a favourite with every one, and especially with Miss Jessie and Miss Flora, who used to ride him about in the orchard and have fine games with him and their little dog Frisky.

Our master had two other horses that stood in another stable. One was Justice, a roan cob, used for riding, or for the luggage cart; the other was an old brown hunter, named Sir Oliver; he was past work now, but was a great favourite with the master, who gave him the run of the park; he sometimes did a little light carting on the estate, or carried one of the young ladies when they rode out with their father; for he was very gentle, and could be trusted with a child as well as Merrylegs. The cob was a strong, well-made, good-tempered horse, and we sometimes had a little chat in the paddock, but of course I could not be so intimate with him as with Ginger, who stood in the same stable.

Chapter 6

LIBERTY

I was quite happy in my new place, and if there was one thing that I missed, it must not be thought I was discontented. All who had to do with me were good, and I had a light, airy stable, and the best of food.

What more could I want? Why, liberty! For three years and a half of my life I had had all the liberty I could wish for; but now, week after week, month after month, and no doubt year after year, I must stand up in a stable night and day except when I am wanted; and then I must be just as steady and quiet as any old horse who has worked twenty years. I must wear straps here and straps there, a bit in my mouth, and blinkers over my eyes.

Now, I am not complaining, for I know it must be so. I mean only to say that for a young horse, full of strength and spirits, who has been used to some large field or plain where he can fling up his head, toss up his tail, gallop away at full speed, and then go round and back again with a snort to his companions—I say that it is hard never now to have a bit more liberty to do as he likes.

Sometimes when I have had less exercise than usual, I have felt so full of life and spring that when John has taken me out to exercise I really could not keep quiet. Do what I would, it seemed as if I must jump, dance, or prance; and many a good shake I know I must have given him, especially at the first, but he was always good and patient.

'Steady, steady, my boy,' he would say; 'wait a while, and we'll have a good swing, and soon get the tickle out of your feet.' Then, as soon as we were out of the village, he would give me a few miles at a spanking trot, and bring me back as fresh as before, only clear of the fidgets, as he called them.

Spirited horses, when not enough exercised, are often called skittish, when in fact it is only play; and some grooms will punish them, but our John did not; he knew it was only high spirits. Still, he had his own ways of making me understand by the tone of his voice or the touch of the rein. If he was very serious and quite determined, I always knew it by his voice, and that had more power over me than anything else, for I was very fond of him.

I ought to say that sometimes we had our liberty for a few hours; this used to be on fine Sundays in the summer-time. The carriage never went out on Sundays, because the church was not far off.

It was a great treat to us to be turned out into the home paddock or the old orchard: the grass was so cool and soft to our feet; the air was so sweet, and the freedom to do as we liked—to gallop, lie down, roll over on our backs, or nibble the sweet grass—was so pleasant. Then, as we stood together under the shade of the large chestnut tree, was a very good time for talking.

Chapter 7

GINGER

One day, when Ginger and I were standing alone in the shade, we had a long talk. She wanted to know all about my bringing up and breaking in; so I told her.

'Well,' she said, 'if I had had your bringing up I might have as good a temper as you; but now I don't believe I ever shall.'

'Why not?' I said.

'Because it has been all so different with me,' she replied. 'I never had anyone, horse or man, that was kind to me, or that I cared to please; for in the first place I was taken from my mother as soon as I was weaned, and put with a lot of other young colts; none of them cared for me, and I cared for none of them. There was no kind master like yours to look after me, talk to me, and bring me nice things to eat.

'The man that had the care of us never gave me a kind word in my life. I do not mean that he ill-used me, but he did not care for us more than to see that we had plenty to eat and were sheltered in the winter.

'A footpath ran through our field, and very often the big boys passing through would fling stones to make us gallop. I was never hit, but one fine young colt was badly cut in the face, and I should think it would leave a scar for life. We did not mind the boys, but of course it made us more wild, and we settled it in our minds that boys were our enemies. We had very good fun in the meadows, either galloping up and down and chasing each other round and round the field, or standing still under the shade of the trees.

'But when it came to breaking in, that was a bad time for me. Several men came to catch me, and when at least they closed me in at one corner of the field, one caught me by the forelock, another took me by the nose, holding it so tight I could hardly draw my breath, and a third, grasping my underjaw in his hard hand, wrenched my mouth open; and so by force they got on the halter and put the bar into my mouth.

'Then one dragged me along by the halter, and another flogged me behind. This was the first experience

I had of man's kindness: it was all force. They did not give me a chance to know what they wanted. I was high bred, with a great deal of spirit, and, no doubt, was very wild and gave them plenty of trouble; but then it was dreadful to be shut up in a stall, day after day, instead of having my liberty. I fretted and pined and wanted to get loose. You know yourself, it's bad enough when you have a kind master and plenty of coaxing; but there was nothing of that sort for me.

'There was one—the old master, Mr. Ryder—who, I think, could soon have brought me round, and have done anything with me; but he had given up all the heavy part of the trade to his son and to another experienced man. My master came only at times to oversee.

'His son was a strong, tall, bold man called Samson; and he used to boast that he had never found a horse that could throw him. There was no gentleness in him as there was in his father, but only hardness: a hard voice, a hard eye, and a hard hand. I felt from the first that what he wanted was to wear all the spirit out of me, and just make me into a quiet, humble, obedient piece of horse-flesh. "Horse-flesh!" Yes, that is all that he thought about;' and Ginger stamped her foot as if the very thought of him made her angry.

Then she went on: 'If I did not do exactly what he wanted he would get put out, and make me run round with that long rein in the training field till he had tired me out. I think he drank a good deal, and I am quite sure that the oftener he drank the worse it was for me.

'One day he had worked me hard in every way he could, and when I lay down I was tired, miserable, and angry; it all seemed so hard. The next morning, he came for me early, and ran me round again for a long time. I had scarcely had an hour's rest when he came again for me with a saddle and bridle and a new kind of bit.

'I could never quite tell how it came about. He had only just mounted me on the training ground, when something I did put him out of temper, and he jerked me hard with the rein. The new bit was very painful, and I reared up suddenly; this angered him still more, and he began to flog me.

'I felt my whole spirit set against him, and I began to kick, and plunge, and rear as I had never done before; we had a regular fight. For a long time he stuck to the saddle and punished me cruelly with his whip and spurs; but my blood was thoroughly up, and I cared for nothing he could do if only I could get him off.

'At last, after a terrible struggle, I threw him off backwards. I heard him fall heavily upon the turf, and, without looking behind me, galloped off to the other end of the field; there I turned round and saw my persecutor slowly rise from the ground and go into the stable. I stood under an oak-tree and watched, but no one came to catch me.

'Time passed; the sun was very hot, the flies swarmed round me and settled on my bleeding flanks where the spurs had dug in. I felt hungry, for I had not eaten since the early morning; but there was not enough grass in that meadow for a goose to live on. I wanted to lie down and rest, but with the saddle strapped tightly on my back there was no comfort, nor was there a drop of water to drink. The afternoon wore on, and the sun got low. I saw the other colts led in, and knew they were having a good feed.

'At last, just as the sun went down, I saw the old master come out with a sieve in his hand. He was a very fine old gentleman with quite white hair, but I should know him by his voice amongst a thousand. It was not high, nor yet low, but full, clear, and kind; and when he gave orders it was so steady and decided that every one, both horses and men, knew that he expected to be obeyed.

'He came quietly along, now and then shaking about the oats that he had in the sieve, speaking cheerfully and gently to me: "Come along, lassie, come along, lassie; come along, come along." I stood still and let him come up.

'He held the oats towards me and I began to eat without fear; his voice took all my fear away. He stood by, patting and stroking me while I was eating, and seeing the clots of blood on my side he seemed very vexed. "Poor lassie, it was a bad business, a bad business!" Then he quietly took the rein and led me to the stable.

'Just at the door stood Samson. I laid my ears back and snapped at him. "Stand back," said the master, "and keep out of her way; you've done a bad day's work for this filly." He growled out something about a vicious brute. "Hark ye," said his father, "a bad-tempered man will never make a good-tempered horse. You've not learned your trade yet, Samson."

'Then he led me into my box, took off the saddle and bridle with his own hands, and tied me up. Calling for a pail of warm water and a sponge, he took off his coat, and while the stable man held the pail, he sponged my sides for some time so tenderly that I was sure he knew how sore and bruised they were. "Whoa! my pretty one," he said; "stand still." His very voice did me good, and the bathing was very comforting.

'The skin was so broken at the corners of my mouth that I could not eat the hay, for the stalks hurt me. He looked closely at my mouth, shook his head, and told the man to fetch me a good bran mash and put some meal into it. How good that mash was! so soft and healing to my mouth. He stood by, stroking me and talking to the man all the time I was eating. "If a high-mettled creature like this," said he, "can't be broken in by fair means, she never will be good for anything."

'After that he often came to see me, and when my mouth was healed, the other breaker, Job, went on training me. As he was steady and thoughtful, I soon learned what he wanted.'

Chapter 8

GINGER'S STORY CONTINUED

The next time that Ginger and I were together in the paddock, she told me about her first place.

'After my breaking in,' she said, 'I was bought by a dealer to match another chestnut horse. For some weeks he drove us together, and then we were sold to a fashionable gentleman, and were sent up to London. I had been driven with a bearing rein by the dealer, and I hated it worse than anything else; but in this place we were reined far tighter, the coachman and his master thinking in this way we looked more stylish. We were often driven about in the Park and other fashionable places. You, who never had a bearing rein on, don't know what it is; but I can tell you it is dreadful.

'I like to toss my head about, and hold it as high as any horse; but you can fancy how it would feel if you tossed your head up high and were obliged to hold it there for hours together, not able to move it at all, except with a jerk still higher; and all this time your neck was aching till you did not know how to bear it.

'Besides this, you have two bits instead of one; and mine was a sharp one. It hurt my tongue and jaw, and the blood from my tongue coloured the froth that kept flying from my lips, as I chafed and fretted at the bits and rein. It was worse when we had to stand by the hour waiting for our mistress at some grand party or entertainment; and if I fretted or stamped with impatience, the whip was laid on. It was enough to drive one mad.'

'Did not your master take any thought for you?' I said.

'No,' said she, 'he cared only to have a stylish turn-out, as they call it. I think he knew very little about horses; he left that to his coachman, who told him that I was of an irritable temper, and that I had not been well broken to the bearing rein, but that I should soon get used to it.

'I grew more and more restless and irritable; I could not help it. Then I began to snap and kick when any one came to harness me, and for this the groom beat me. One day, as they had just buckled us into the carriage and were straining my head up with that rein, I began to plunge and kick with all my might. I soon broke a lot of harness, and kicked myself clear; so my stay there was ended.

'Soon I was sent to Tattersall's to be sold. Of course, I could not be warranted free from vice; so nothing was said about that. My handsome appearance and good paces soon brought a gentleman to bid for me, and I was bought by another dealer. He tried me in all kinds of ways and with different bits, and soon found out what I could bear. At last he drove me quite without a bearing rein, and then sold me as a perfectly quiet horse to a gentleman in the country.

'He was a good master, and I was getting on very well, but his old groom left him and a new one came. This man was as hard-tempered and hard-handed as Samson; he always spoke in a rough, impatient voice, and if I did not move in the stall the moment he wanted me, he would hit me above the hocks with the stable broom or the fork, whichever he might have in his hand. Everything he did was rough, and I began to hate him; he wanted to make me afraid of him, but I was too high-mettled for that.

'One day when he had aggravated me more than usual, I bit him; this of course put him in a great rage, and he began to hit me about the head with a riding whip. After that, he never dared to come into my stall again, either my heels or my teeth were ready for him, and he knew it. I was quite quiet with my master, but of course he listened to what the man said, and so I was sold again.

'The same dealer heard of me, and said he thought he knew of a place where I should do well. "'Twas a pity," he said, "that such a fine horse should go to the bad for want of a real good chance"; and the end of it was that I came here not long before you did. I had now made up my mind that men were my natural enemies, and that I must defend myself. Of course, it is very different here; but who knows how long it will last? I wish I could think about things as you do; but I can't after all I have gone through.'

'Well,' I said, 'I think it would be a real shame if you were to bite or kick John or James.'

'I don't mean to,' she said, 'while they are good to me. I did once bite James pretty sharp, but John said, "Try her with kindness," and instead of punishing me as I expected, James came to me with his arm bound up, and brought me a bran mash and stroked me; and I have never snapped at him since; and I won't again.'

I was sorry for Ginger, but of course I knew very little then, and I thought most likely she made the worst of it. However, I found that as the weeks went on she grew much more gentle and cheerful, and lost the watchful, defiant look that she used to turn on any strange person who came near her. And one day James said, 'I do believe that mare is getting fond of me, she quite whinnied after me this morning when I had been rubbing her forehead.'

'Ay, ay, Jim, 'tis the Birtwick balls,' said John; 'she'll be as good as Black Beauty by-and-by; kindness is all the physic she wants, poor thing!' Master noticed the change too, and one day when he got out of the carriage and came to speak to us, as he often did, he stroked her beautiful neck. 'Well, my pretty one, well, how do things go with you now? You are a good bit happier than when you came to us, I think.'

She put her nose up to him in a friendly, trustful way, while he rubbed it gently.

'We shall make a cure of her, John,' he said.

'Yes, sir, she's wonderfully improved; she's not the same creature that she was. It's the Birtwick balls, sir,' said John, laughing.

This was a little joke of John's; he used to say that a regular course of the Birtwick horse-balls would cure almost any vicious horse. These balls, he said, were made up of patience and gentleness, firmness and petting: one pound of each to be mixed with half a pint of common sense, and given to the horse every day.

Chapter 9

MERRYLEGS

Mr. Blomefield, the Vicar, had a large family of boys and girls, who sometimes came to play with Miss Jessie and Miss Flora. One of the girls was as old as Miss Jessie;

two of the boys were older, and there were several little ones. When they came there was plenty of work for Merrylegs, for nothing pleased them so much as getting on him in turn, and riding him all about the orchard and the home paddock by the hour together.

One afternoon he had been out with them a long time, and when James brought him in and put on his halter, he said:—

'There, you rogue, mind how you behave yourself, or we shall get into trouble.'

'What have you been doing, Merrylegs?' I asked.

'Oh!' said he, tossing his little head, 'I have only been giving these young people a lesson. They did not know when they had had enough, nor when I had had enough; so I just pitched them off backwards: that was the only thing they could understand.'

'What!' said I, 'you threw the children off? I thought you knew better than that! Did you throw Miss Jessie or Miss Flora?'

He looked very much offended, and said:—

'Of course not; I would not do such a thing for the best oats that ever came into the stable. Why I am as careful of our young ladies as the master could be; and as for the little ones, it is I who teach them to ride. When they seemed frightened or a little unsteady on my back, I go as smoothly and as quietly as old pussy when she is after a bird; and when they are all right, I go on again faster, just to use them to it. So don't you trouble yourself preaching to me; I am the best friend and riding-master those children have.

'It is not they; it is the boys. Boys,' said he, shaking his mane, 'are quite different; they must be broken in, as we were broken in when we were colts, and must just be taught what's what.

'The other children had ridden me about for nearly two hours, and then the boys thought it was their turn;

and so it was, and I was quite agreeable. They rode me in turn, and I galloped them about, up and down the fields and all about the orchard for a good hour.

'They had each cut a great hazel stick for a riding-whip, and laid it on a little too hard; but I took it in good part, till at last I thought we had had enough; so I stopped two or three times by way of a hint. Boys, you see, think a horse or pony is like a steam-engine or threshing-machine, that can go on as long and as fast as they please. They never think that a pony can get tired, or have any feelings; so as the one whipping me could not understand, I just rose up on my hind legs and let him slip off behind—that was all. He mounted me again, and I did the same. Then the other boys got up; and as soon as he began to use his stick, I laid him on the grass; and so on, till they were able to understand: that was all.

'They are not bad boys; they don't wish to be cruel. I like them very well; but you see I had to give them a lesson. When they brought me to James and told him, I think he was very angry to see such big sticks. He said they were only fit for drovers or gipsies, and not for young gentlemen.'

'If I had been you,' said Ginger, 'I would have given those boys a good kick, and that would have given them a lesson.'

'No doubt you would,' said Merrylegs; 'but then I am not quite such a fool (begging your pardon) as to anger our master or make James ashamed of me. Besides, those children are under my charge when they are riding; I tell you they are entrusted to me. Why, only the other day I heard our master say to Mrs. Blomefield, "My dear madam, you need not be anxious about the children; my old Merrylegs will take as much care of them as you or I could: I assure you I would not sell that pony for any money, he is so perfectly good-tempered and trustworthy." Do you think I am such an ungrateful brute as to forget all the kind treatment I have had here for five years, and all the trust they place in me, and turn vicious because a couple of ignorant boys used me badly?

'No! no! you never had a good place where they were kind to you, and so you don't know. I'm sorry for you, but I can tell you good places make good horses. I wouldn't vex our people for anything; I love them, I do,' said Merrylegs; and he gave a low 'Ho, ho, ho,' through his nose, as he used to do in the morning when he heard James's footstep at the door.

'Besides,' he went on, 'if I took to kicking, where should I be? Why, sold off in a jiffy with no character; and I might find myself slaved about under a butcher's boy; or worked to death at some seaside place where no one cared for me, except to find out how fast I could go; or flogged along in some cart with three or four great men in it going out for a Sunday spree, as I have often seen in the place I lived in before I came here. No,' said he, shaking his head, 'I hope I shall never come to that.'

Chapter 10.

A TALK IN THE ORCHARD

Ginger and I were not of the regular tall, carriage-horse breed; we had more of the racing blood in us. We stood about fifteen and a half hands high, and were therefore just as good for riding as for driving. Our master used to say that he disliked either horse or man that could do but one thing; and as he did not want to show off in

London parks, he preferred a more active and useful kind of horse.

As for us, our greatest pleasure was when we were saddled for a riding party—the master on Ginger, the mistress on me, and the young ladies on Sir Oliver and Merrylegs. It was so cheerful to be trotting and cantering all together that it always put us in high spirits. I had the best of it, for I always carried the mistress. Her weight was little, her voice sweet, and her hand so light on the rein that I was guided almost without feeling it.

Oh! if people knew what a comfort to horses a light hand is, and how it keeps a good mouth and a good temper, they surely would not chuck, and drag, and pull at the rein as they often do. Our mouths are so tender, that where they have not been spoiled or hardened with bad or ignorant treatment, they feel the slightest movement of the driver's hand, and we know in an instant what is required of us. My mouth had never been spoiled, and I believe that was why the mistress preferred me to Ginger, although her paces were certainly quite as good. She used often to envy me, and said it was all the fault of breaking in, and the gag bit in London, that her mouth was not so perfect as mine; and then old Sir Oliver would say: 'There, there! don't vex yourself; you have the greatest honour; a mare that can carry a tall man of our master's weight, with all your spring and sprightly action, does not need to hold her head down because she does not carry the lady; we horses must take things as they come, and always be contented and willing so long as we are kindly used.'

I had often wondered how it was the Sir Oliver had such a very short tail; it really was only six or seven inches long, with a tassel of hair hanging from it; and on one of our holidays in the orchard I ventured to ask him by what accident he had lost his tail.

'Accident!' he snorted, with a fierce look, 'it was no accident! It was a cruel, shameful, cold-blooded act! When I was young I was taken to a place where these cruel things were done. I was tied up, and made fast so that I could not stir; and then they came and cut my long, beautiful tail through the flesh and through the bone, and took it away.'

'How dreadful' I exclaimed.

'Dreadful! Ah, it was dreadful but it was not only the pain, though that was terrible and lasted a long time; it was not only the indignity of having my best ornament taken from me, though that was bad, but it was this—how could I ever again brush the flies off my side and off my hind legs. You who have tails just whisk the flies off without thinking about it, and you can't tell what a torment it is to have them settle upon you, and sting, and yet have nothing in the world with which to lash them off. I tell you it is a lifelong wrong, and a lifelong loss. But, thank Heaven! men don't do it now.'

'What did they do it for then?' said Ginger.

'For fashion!' said the old horse, with a stamp of his foot. 'For fashion! if you know what that means. There was not a well-bred young horse in my time that had not his tail docked in that shameful way, just as if the good God that made us did not know what we wanted and what looked best.'

'I suppose it is fashion that makes them strap our heads up with those horrid bits that I was tortured with in London,' said Ginger.

'Of course it is,' said he. 'To my mind, fashion is one of the most wicked things in the world. Now look, for instance, at the way they serve dogs, cutting off their tails to make them look plucky, and shearing up their pretty little ears to a point, to make them look sharp, forsooth.

'I had a dear friend once, a brown terrier—"Skye," they called her. She was so fond of me that she would never sleep out of my stall. She made her bed under the manger, and there she had a litter of five as pretty little puppies as need be. None were drowned, for they were a valuable kind, and how pleased she was with them! And when they got their eyes open and crawled about, it was a real pretty sight.

'But one day the men came and took them all away. I thought he might be afraid I should tread upon them: but it was not so. In the evening poor Skye brought them back again, one by one in her mouth; not the happy little things that they were, but bleeding and crying pitifully. They all had a piece of their tails cut off, and the soft flap of their pretty little ears was cut quite off. How their mother licked them, and how troubled she was, poor thing! I never forgot it. The wounds healed in time, and they forgot the pain; but the nice, soft flap, that of course was intended to protect the delicate part of their ears from dust and injury, was gone for ever.

'Why don't they cut their own children's ears into points to make them look sharp? Why don't they cut the end off their noses to make them look plucky? One would be just as sensible as the other. What right have they to torment and disfigure God's creatures?'

Sir Oliver, though he was so gentle, was a fiery old fellow; and what he said was all so new to me and so dreadful, that I found a bitter feeling toward men that I had never had before rise up in my mind. Of course, Ginger was much excited. With flashing eyes and distended nostrils, she flung up her head, declaring that men were both brutes and blockheads.

'Who talks about blockheads?' said Merrylegs, who just came up from the old apple-tree, where he had been rubbing himself against the low branch. 'Who talks about blockheads? I believe that is a bad word.'

'Bad words are made for bad things,' said Ginger; and she told him what Sir Oliver had said.

'It is all true' said Merrylegs sadly, 'and I've seen that about the dogs over and over again where I lived first; but we won't talk about it here. You know that master, John, and James are always good to us; and talking against men in such a place as this doesn't seem fair or grateful. You know there are good masters and good grooms besides ours, though of course ours are the best.'

This wise speech of good little Merrylegs, which we knew was quite true, cooled us all down, especially Sir Oliver, who was dearly fond of his master; and to turn the subject I said, 'Can any one tell me the use of blinkers?'

'No!' said Sir Oliver, shortly, 'because they are no use.'

'They are supposed,' said Justice in his calm way, 'to prevent horses from shying and starting, and getting so frightened as to cause accidents.'

'Then what is the reason they do not put them on riding horses, especially on ladies' horses?' said I.

'There is no reason at all,' said he quietly, 'except the fashion. They say that a horse would be so frightened to see the wheels of his own cart or carriage coming behind him that he would be sure to run away, although of course when he is ridden he sees them all about him if the streets are crowded. I admit they do sometimes come too close to be pleasant, but we don't run away; we are used to it, and understand it. If we never had blinkers put on, we should never want them; we should see what was there, and know what was what, and be much less frightened than by only seeing bits of things that we can't understand.'

Of course there may be some nervous horses which have been hurt or frightened when they were young; these may be the better for them: but as I never was nervous, I can't judge.

'I consider,' said Sir Oliver, 'that blinkers are dangerous things in the night. We horses can see much better in the dark than men can, and many an accident would never have happened if horses might have had the full use of their eyes.

'Some years ago, I remember, there was a hearse with two horses returning one dark night, and just by Farmer Sparrow's house, where the pond is close to the road the wheels were too near the edge, and the hearse was overturned into the water. Both the horses were drowned, and the driver hardly escaped. Of course, after this accident a stout white rail was put up that might easily be seen; but if those horses had not been partly blinded, they would of themselves have kept further from the edge, and no accident would have happened.

'When our master's carriage was overturned, before you came here, it was said that if the lamp on the left side had not gone out, John would have seen the great hole that the road-makers had left; and so he might. But if old Colin had not had blinkers on, he would have seen it, lamp or no lamp, for he was far too knowing an hold horse to run into danger. As it was, he was very much hurt, the carriage was broken, and how John escaped nobody knew.'

'I should say,' said Ginger, curling her nostril, 'that these men who are so wise had better give orders that in future all foals should be born with their eyes set just in the middle of their foreheads, instead of on the side. Men always think they can improve upon Nature and mend what God has made.'

Things were getting rather sore again, when Merrylegs held up his knowing little face and said:—

'I'll tell you a secret—I believe John does not approve of blinkers; I heard him talking to master about it one day. The master said that if horses had been used to them, it might be dangerous in some cases to leave them off; and John said he thought it would be a good thing if all colts were broken in without blinkers, as was done in some foreign countries; so let us cheer up and have a run to the other side of the orchard. I believe the wind has blown down some apples, and we may just as well eat them as for the slugs to have them.'

Merrylegs' suggestion could not be resisted; so we broke off our long conversation and got up our spirits by munching some very sweet apples which lay scattered on the grass.

Chapter 11

PLAIN SPEAKING

The longer I lived at Birtwick, the more proud and happy I felt at having such a place. Our master and mistress were respected and beloved by all who knew them; they were good and kind to everybody and everything; not only to men and women, but to horses and donkeys, to dogs and cats, and to cattle and birds. There was no oppressed or ill-used creature that had not a friend in them, and their servants took the same tone. If any of the village children were known to treat any creature cruelly, they soon heard about it from the Hall.

The Squire and Farmer Grey had worked together, as they said, for more than twenty years to get bearing reins on the cart horses done away with, and in our parts you seldom saw them: but sometimes if mistress met a heavily-laden horse, with his head strained up, she would stop the carriage and get out, and reason with the driver in her sweet, serious voice, and try to show him how foolish and cruel it was.

I don't think any man could withstand our mistress. I wish all ladies were like her.

Our master sometimes used to speak his mind very freely. I remember he was riding me toward home one morning, when he saw a powerful man driving towards us a light pony chaise, with a beautiful little bay pony with slender legs and a high-bred, sensitive head and face. Just as he came to the park gates the little thing turned towards them.

The man, without word or warning, wrenched the creature's head round with such force and suddenness that he nearly threw it on its haunches. Recovering itself, it was going on when he began to lash it furiously. The pony plunged forward, but the strong, heavy hand held the pretty creature back with force almost enough to break its jaw, whilst the whip still cut into him. It was a dreadful sight to me, for I knew what fearful pain it gave that delicate little mouth; but master gave me the word, and we were up with him in a second.

'Sawyer,' he cried in a stern voice, 'is that pony made of flesh and blood?'

'Flesh and blood and temper,' he said. 'He's too fond of his own will, and that won't suit me.'

The man spoke as if he was in a strong passion. He was a builder who had often been to the park on business.

'And do you think,' said master sternly, 'that treatment like this will make him fond of your will?'

'He had no business to make that turn; his road was straight on!' said the man roughly.

'You have often driven that pony up to my place,' said master; 'it only shows the creature's memory and intelligence. How did he know that you were not going there again? But that has little to do with it. I must say, Mr. Sawyer, that more unmanly, brutal treatment of a little pony it was never my painful lot to witness; and by giving way to such a passion, you injure your own character as much, nay more than you injure your horse. And remember, we shall all have to be judged according to our works, whether they be towards man or towards beast.'

Master rode me home slowly, and I could tell by his voice how the thing had grieved him.

He was just as free in speaking to gentlemen of his own rank as those below him; for another day, when we were out, we met a Captain Langley, a friend of our master. He was driving a splendid pair of greys in a kind of brake. After a little conversation the Captain said, 'What do you think of my new team, Mr. Gordon? You know you are the judge of horses in these parts, and I should like your opinion.'

The master backed me a little so as to get a good view of them. 'They are an uncommonly handsome pair,' he said, 'and if they are as good as they look, I am sure you need not wish for anything better: but I see you yet hold to that pet scheme of yours for worrying your horses and lessening their power.'

'What do you mean,' said the other—'the bearing reins? Oh, ah! I know that's a hobby of yours. Well, the fact is, I like to see my horses hold their heads up.'

'So do I,' said master, 'as well as any man, but I don't like to see them *held up*; that takes all the shine out of it. Now you are a military man, Langley, and no doubt like to see your regiment look well on parade, "Heads up," and all that kind of thing. But you would not take much credit for your drill if all your men had their heads tied to a backboard!

'It might not do much harm on parade, except to worry and fatigue them, but how would it be in a bayonet charge against the enemy, when they want the free use of every muscle, and all their strength thrown forward? I would not give much for their chance of victory; and it is just the same with horses; you fret and worry their temper and decrease their power, you will not let them throw their weight against their work, and so they have to do too much with their joints and muscles, and of course it wears them up faster. You may depend upon it, horses were intended to have their heads free, as free as men's are, and if we could act a little more according to common sense, and a good deal less according to fashion, we should find many things work easier; besides, you know as well as I that if a horse makes a false step he has much less chance of recovering himself if his head and neck are fastened back.

'And now,' said the master laughing, 'I have given my hobby a good trot out, can't you make up your mind to mount him too, Captain? Your example would go a long way.'

'I believe you are right in theory,' said the other, 'and that's rather a hard hit about the soldiers; but—well, I'll think about it,' and so they parted.

Chapter 12

A STORMY DAY

One day, late in the autumn, my master had a long journey to go on business. I was put into the dog-cart, and John went with his master. I always liked to go in the dog-cart, it was so light and the high wheels ran along so pleasantly. There had been a great deal of rain, and now the wind was very high and blew the dry leaves across the road in a shower. We went merrily along till we came to the toll-bar and the low wooden bridge. The river banks were rather high, and the bridge, instead of rising, went across just level, so that in the middle, if the river was full, the water would be nearly up to the woodwork and planks; but as there were good substantial rails on each side people did not mind it.

The man at the gate said the river was rising fast, and he feared it would be a bad night. Many of the meadows were under water, and in one low part of the road the water was half-way up to my knees; the bottom was good, and master drove gently, so it was no matter.

When we got to the town, of course, I had a good bait; but as the master's business engaged him a long time, we did not start for home till rather late in the afternoon. The wind was then much higher, and I heard the master say to John he had never been out in such a storm; and so I thought, as we went along the skirts of a wood, where the great branches were swaying about like twigs, and the rushing sound of the wind through the trees was terrible.

'I wish we were well out of this wood,' said my master.

'Yes, sir,' said John, 'it would be rather awkward if one of these branches came down upon us.'

The words were scarcely out of his mouth, when there was a groan, a crack, and a splitting sound, and tearing, crashing down amongst the other trees, came an oak, torn up by the roots, which fell right across the road just before us. I will never say I was not frightened, for I was. I stopped still, and I believe I trembled. Of course, I did not turn round or run away; I was not brought up to do that. John jumped out and in a moment was at my head.

'That was a very near touch,' said my master. 'What's to be done now?'

'Well, sir, we can't drive over that tree nor yet get around it; there will be nothing for it but to go back to the four cross-ways, and that will be a good six miles before we get round to the wooden bridge again. It will make us late, but the horse is fresh.'

So back we went, and round by the cross roads; but by the time we got to the bridge it was very nearly dark, and we could just see that the water was over the middle of it; but as that happened sometimes when floods were out, master did not stop.

We were going along at a good pace, but the moment my feet touched the first part of the bridge, I felt sure there was something wrong. I dare not go forward, and so I made a dead stop. 'Go on, Beauty,' said my master, giving me a touch with the whip; but I dare not stir. He gave me a sharp cut; I jumped, but I dared not go forward.

'There's something wrong, sir,' said John; and he sprang out of the dog-cart and came to my head and looked all about. He tried to lead me forward. 'Come on, Beauty, what's the matter?' Of course I could not tell him, but I knew very well that the bridge was not safe.

Just then the man at the toll-gate on the other side ran out of the house, tossing a torch about like mad.

'Hoy, hoy, hoy, halloo, stop!' he cried.

'What's the matter?' shouted my master.

'The bridge is broken in the middle and part of it is carried away; if you come on you'll be into the river.'

'Thank God!' said my master. 'You Beauty!' said John; and taking the bridle, he gently turned me round to the right-hand road by the river side. The sun has set some time, the wind seemed to have lulled off after that furious blast which tore up the tree. It grew darker and darker, and more and more still. I trotted quietly along, the wheels hardly making a sound on the soft road.

For a good while neither master nor John spoke; and then the master began to speak in a serious voice. I could not understand much of what they said, but I found they thought that if I had gone on as the master wanted me, most likely the bridge would have given way under us, and horse, chaise, master, and man would have fallen into the river; and as the current was flowing very strongly, and there was no light and no help at hand, it was more than likely we should all have been drowned. Master said God had given men reason by which they could find out things for themselves; but He had given animals knowledge which did not depend on reason, much more prompt and perfect in its way, by which they had often saved the lives of men.

John had many stories to tell of dogs and horses, and the wonderful things they had done. He thought people did not value their animals half enough, nor make friends of them as they ought to do. I am sure he makes friends of them if ever man does.

At last we came to the Park gates, and found the gardener looking out for us. He said that mistress had been in a dreadful way ever since dark, fearing some accident had happened, and that she had sent James off on Justice, the roan cob, towards the wooden bridge to make inquiry after us.

We saw a light at the hall door and at the upper windows, and as we came up mistress ran out, saying, 'Are you really safe, my dear? Oh! I have been so anxious, fancying all sorts of things. Have you had no accident?'

'No, my dear; but if your Black Beauty had not been wiser than we were, we should all have been carried down the river at the wooden bridge.' I heard no more, as they went into the house, and John took me to the stable. Oh! what a good supper he gave me that night, a good bran mash and some crushed beans with my oats, and such a thick bed of straw, and I was glad of it, for I was tired.

Chapter 13

THE DEVIL'S TRADE MARK

One day, when John and I had been out on some business for our master, and were returning gently on a long straight road, at some distance we saw a boy trying to leap a pony over a gate. The pony would not take the leap, and the boy cut him with the whip, but he only turned off on one side; he whipped him again, but the pony turned off on the other side; then the boy got off and gave him a hard thrashing, knocking him about the head; then he got up again and tried to make him leap the gate, kicking him all the time shamefully; but still the pony refused.

When we were nearly at the spot, the pony put down his head, threw up his heels, and sent the boy neatly over into a broad quickset hedge; and with the rein danging from his head, he set off home at a full gallop. John laughed out quite loudly. 'Serve him right!' he said.

'Oh! oh! oh!' cried the boy, as he struggled about amongst the thorns; 'I say, come and help me out.'

'Thank ye,' said John, 'I think you are quite in the right place; and maybe a little scratching will teach you not to leap a pony over a gate that is too high for him;' and so with that John rode off.

'It may be,' said he to himself, 'that young fellow is a liar as well as cruel; we'll just go home by Farmer Bushby's, Beauty, and then if anybody wants to know, you and I can tell 'em, ye see.' So we turned off to the right, and soon came up to the stack-yard within sight of the house. The farmer was hurrying out into the road, and his wife was standing at the gate looking very frightened.

'Have you seen my boy?' said Mr. Bushby, as we came up; 'he went out an hour ago on my black pony, and the creature is just come back without a rider.'

'I should think, sir,' said John, 'he had better be without a rider, unless he can be ridden properly.'

'What do you mean?' said the farmer.

'Well, sir, I saw your son whipping, kicking, and knocking that good little pony about shamefully, because he would not leap a gate that was too high for him. The pony behaved well, sir, and showed no vice;

but at last he just threw up his heels and tipped the young gentleman into the thorn hedge. He wanted me to help him out; but—I hope you will excuse me, sir—I did not feel inclined to do so. There are no bones broken, sir; he'll only get a few scratches. I love horses, and it roiles me to see them badly used. It is a bad plan to aggravate an animal till he uses his heels; the first time is not always the last.'

During this time the mother began to cry, 'Oh! my poor Bill, I must go and meet him; he must be hurt.'

'You had better go into the house, wife,' said the farmer; 'Bill wants a lesson about this, and I must see that he gets it. This is not the first time nor the second that he has ill-used that pony, and I shall stop it. I am much obliged to you, Manly. Good-evening.'

So we went on, John chuckling all the way home. He told James about it, who laughed and said, 'Serve him right. I knew that boy at school; he took great airs on himself because he was a farmer's son; he used to swagger about and bully the little boys. Of course we elder ones would not have any of that nonsense, and let him know that in the school and playground farmers' son and labourers' sons were all alike.

'I well remember one day, just before afternoon school, I found him at the large window catching flies and pulling off their wings. He did not see me, and I gave him a box on the ears that laid him sprawling on the floor. Well, angry as I was, I was almost frightened; he roared and bellowed in such a style. The boys rushed in from the playground, and the master ran in from the road to see who was being murdered.

'Of course, I said fair and square at once what I had done, and why; then I showed the master the poor flies, some crushed and some crawling about helpless, and I showed him the wings on the window-sill. I never saw him so angry before; but as Bill was still howling and whining, like the coward that he was, he did not give him any more punishment of that kind, but set him up on a stool for the rest of the afternoon, and said that he should not go out to play for that week.

'Then he talked to all the boys very seriously about cruelty, and said how hard-hearted and cowardly it was to hurt the weak and the helpless. But what stuck in my mind was this—he said that cruelty was the devil's own trade mark, and if we saw any one who took pleasure in cruelty, we might know to whom he belonged, for the devil was a murderer from the beginning and a tormentor to the end. On the other hand, where we saw people who loved their neighbours and were kind to man and beast, we might know that was God's mark; for "God is Love."'

'Your master never taught you a truer thing,' said John; 'there is no religion without love. People may talk as much as they like about their religion, but if it does not teach them to be good and kind to man and beast, it is all a sham—all a sham, James; and it won't stand when things come to be turned inside out and put down for what they are.'

CHAPTER 14

JAMES HOWARD

One morning, early in December, John had just led me into my box after my daily exercise, and was strapping my cloth on. James was coming in from the corn-chamber with some oats, when the master came into the stable. He looked rather serious, and held an open letter in his hand. John fastened the door of my box, touched his cap, and waited for orders.

'Good-morning, John,' said the master; 'I want to know if you have any complaint to make of James?'
'Complaint, sir? No, sir.'
'Is he industrious at his work and respectful to you?'
'Yes, sir, always.'
'You never find he slights his work when your back is turned?'
'Never, sir.'
'That's well; but I must put another question: have you any reason to suspect that when he goes out with the horses to exercise them, or takes a message, he stops about talking to his acquaintance, or goes into houses where he has no business, leaving the horses outside?'
'No, sir, certainly not, and if anybody has been saying that about James, I don't believe it; and I don't mean to believe it unless I have it fairly proved before witnesses. It's not for me to say who has been trying to take away James's character; but I will say this, sir, that a steadier, smarter, more pleasant, honest young fellow I never had in this stable. I can trust his word and I can trust his work.
'He is gentle and clever with the horses, and I would rather have them in his charge than in that of half the young fellows I know in laced hats and liveries; and whoever wants a character of James Howard,' said John, with a decided jerk of his head, 'let them come to John Manly.'
The master stood all this time grave and attentive; but as John finished his speech, a broad smile spread over his face, and looking kindly across at James, who all this time had stood still at the door, he said: 'James, my lad, set down the oats and come here. I am very glad to find that John's opinion of your character agrees so exactly with my own. John is a cautious man,' he said, with a droll smile, 'and it is not always easy to get his opinion about people; so I thought if I beat the bush on this side,

the birds would fly out, and I should learn what I wanted to know quickly; so now we will come to business.

'I have a letter from my brother-in-law, Sir Clifford Williams, of Clifford Hall. He wants me to find him a trustworthy young groom, about twenty or twenty-one, who knows his business. His old coachman, who has lived with him twenty years, is getting feeble, and he wants a man to work with him and get into his ways, so that he would be able, when the old man was pensioned off, to step into his place. He would have eighteen shillings a week at first, a stable suit, a driving suit, a bedroom over the coach-house, and a boy under him. Sir Clifford is a good master, and if you could get the place, it would be a good start for you. I don't want to part with you, and if you left us I know John would lose his right hand.'

'That I should sir,' said John, 'but I would not stand in his light for the world.'

'How old are you, James?' said the master.

'Nineteen next May, sir.'

'That's young. What do you think, John?'

'Well, sir, it's young; but he is as steady as a man, strong, and well grown; and though he has not had much experience in driving, he has a light, firm hand, a quick eye, and is very careful. I am quite sure no horse of his will be ruined for want of having his feet and shoes looked after.'

'Your word will go the farthest, John,' said the master, 'for Sir Clifford adds in a postscript, "If I could find a man trained by your John, I should like him better than any other." So James, lad, think it over; talk to your mother at dinner-time and then let me know what you wish.'

In a few days after this conversation it was fully settled that James should go to Clifford Hall in a month or six weeks, as it best suited his master, and in the meantime he was to get all the practice in driving that could be given him.

Chapter 15

THE OLD OSTLER

After this, my master and mistress decided to pay a visit to some friends who lived about forty-six miles from our home, and James was to drive them. The first day we travelled thirty-two miles; there were some long, heavy hills, but James drove so carefully and thoughtfully that we were not at all harassed. He never forgot to put on the drag as we went downhill, nor to take it off at the right place. He kept our feet on the smoothest part of the road; and if the uphill was very long, he set the wheels a little across the road so that the carriage should not run back, and gave us breathing time. All these little things help a horse very much, particularly if he gets kind words into the bargain.

We stopped once or twice on the road; and just as the sun was going down, we reached the town where we were to spend the night. We stopped at the principal hotel, a very large one in the Market Place. We drove under an archway into a long yard, at the farther end of which were the stables and coach-houses. Two ostlers came to take us out. The head ostler was a pleasant, active little man, with a crooked leg, and a yellow striped waistcoat. I never saw a man unbuckle harness so quickly as he did; and then with a pat and a good word he led me to a long stable with six or eight stalls in it and two or three horses. The other man brought Ginger—James stood by whilst we were rubbed down and cleaned.

I never was cleaned so lightly and quickly as by that little old man. When he had done, James stepped up and felt me over, as if he thought I could not be thoroughly done; but he found my coat as clean and smooth as silk.

'Well,' he said, 'I thought I was pretty quick, and our John quicker still, but you do beat all I ever saw for being quick and thorough at the same time.'

'Practice makes perfect,' said the crooked little ostler, 'and 'twould be a pity if it didn't. Forty years' practice, and not perfect! Ha! ha! that would be a pity. As to being quick, why, bless you! that is only a matter of habit. If you get into the habit of being quick, it is just as easy as being slow—easier, I should say. In fact, it does not agree with my health to be hulking about over a job twice as long as it need take. Bless you! I couldn't whistle if I crawled over my work as some folks do.

'You see I have been about horses ever since I was twelve years old, in hunting-stables and racing-stables. Being small, you see, I was a jockey for several years; but at the Goodwood the turf was very slippery and my poor Larkspur got a fall, and I broke my knee; and so, of course, I was of no more use there.

'But I could not live without horses, of course I couldn't, so I took to the hotels; and I can tell you it is a downright pleasure to handle an animal like this; well-bred, well-mannered, well-cared-for. Bless you! I can tell how a horse is treated. Give me the handling of a horse for twenty minutes, and I'll tell you what sort of a groom he has had.

'Look at this one, pleasant, quiet, turns about just as you want him to do, holds up his feet to be cleaned out, or anything else you please to wish. Then you'll find another fidgety, fretful, won't move the right way, or starts across the stall, tosses up his head as soon as you come near him, lays back his ears, and seems afraid of you, or else squares about at you with his heels.

'Poor things! I know what sort of treatment they have had. If they are timid, the treatment makes them start or shy; if they are high-mettled, it makes them vicious or dangerous; their tempers are mostly made when they are young. Bless you! they are like children; train 'em up in the way they should go, as the good Book says, and when they are old they will not depart from it—if they have a chance, that is.'

Chapter 16

THE FIRE

Later on in the evening, a traveller's horse was brought in by the second ostler, and whilst he was cleaning him a young man with a pipe in his mouth lounged into the stable to gossip.

'I say, Towler,' said the ostler, 'just run up the ladder into the loft and bring down some hay into this horse's rack, will you? Only first lay down your pipe.'

'All right,' said the ostler, and went up through the trap door; and I heard him step across the floor overhead and put down the hay. James came in to look at us the last thing, and the door was locked.

I cannot say how long I had slept, nor what time in the night it was, but I woke up feeling very uncomfortable, though I hardly knew why. I got up; the air seemed all thick and choking. I heard Ginger coughing, and one of the other horses moved about restlessly. It was quite dark, and I could see nothing; but the stable was full of smoke, and I hardly knew how to breathe.

The trap door had been left open, and I thought that was the place from where the smoke came. I listened and heard a soft, rushing sort of noise, and a low crackling and snapping. I did not know what it was, but there was something in the sound so strange that it made me tremble all over. The other horses were now all awake; some were pulling at their halters, others were stamping.

At last I heard steps outside, and the ostler who had put up the traveller's horse burst into the stable with a lantern, and began to untie the horses, and try to lead them out; but he seemed in such a hurry, and was so frightened himself, that he frightened me still more. The first horse would not go with him; he tried the second and third, but they too would not stir. He came to me next and tried to drag me out of the stall by force; of course that was no use. He tried us all by turns and then left the stable.

No doubt we were very foolish, but danger seemed to be all round; there was nobody whom we knew to trust in, and all was strange and uncertain. The fresh air that had come in through the open door made it easier to breathe, but the rushing sound overhead grew louder, and as I looked upward, through the bars of my empty rack, I saw a red light flickering on the wall. Then I heard a cry of 'Fire!' outside, and the old ostler came quietly and quickly in. He got one horse out, and went to another; but the flames were playing round the trap door, and the roaring overhead was dreadful.

The next thing I heard was James's voice, quiet and cheery, as it always was.

'Come, my beauties, it is time for us to be off, so wake

up and come along.' I stood nearest the door, so he came to me first, patting me as he came in.

'Come, Beauty, on with your bridle, my boy, we'll soon be out of this smother.' It was on in no time; then he took the scarf off his neck, and tied it lightly over my eyes, and, patting and coaxing, he led me out of the stable. Safe in the yard, he slipped the scarf off my eyes, and shouted, 'Here somebody! take this horse while I go back for the other.'

A tall, broad man stepped forward and took me, and James darted back into the stable. I set up a shrill whinny as I saw him go. Ginger told me afterwards that whinny was the best thing I could have done for her, for had she not heard me outside, she would never have had courage to come out.

There was much confusion in the yard; the horses were being got out of other stables, and the carriages and gigs were being pulled out of houses and sheds, lest the flames should spread farther. On the other side of the yard windows were thrown open, and people were shouting all sorts of things; but I kept my eye fixed on the stable door, where the smoke poured out thicker than ever, and I could see flashes of red light.

Presently I heard above all the stir and din a loud, clear voice, which I knew was master's:—

'James Howard! James Howard! are you there?' There was no answer, but I heard a crash of something falling in the stable, and the next moment I gave a loud, joyful neigh, for I saw James coming through the smoke, leading Ginger with him; she was coughing violently and he was not able to speak.

'My brave lad!' said master, laying his hand on his shoulder, 'are you hurt?'

James shook his head for he could not speak yet.

'Ay,' said the big man who held me, 'he is a brave lad, and no mistake.'

'And now,' said master, 'when you have got your breath, James, we'll get out of this place as quickly as we can.'

We were moving towards the entry when from the Market Place there came a sound of galloping feet and loud rumbling wheels.

'Tis the fire engine! the fire engine!' shouted two or three voices. 'Stand back, make way!' and clattering and thundering over the stones two horses dashed into the yard with the heavy engine behind them. The firemen leaped to the ground; there was no need to ask where the fire was—it was torching up in a great blaze from the roof.

We got out as fast as we could into the broad, quiet Market Place. The stars were shining, and, except for the noise behind us, all was still. Master led the way to a large hotel on the other side, and as soon as the ostler came, he said, 'James, I must now hasten to your mistress; I trust the horses entirely to you; order whatever you think is needed;' and with that he was gone. The master did not run, but I never saw mortal man walk so fast as he did that night.

There was a dreadful sound before we got into our stalls—the shrieks of those poor horses that were left burning to death in the stable were very terrible! They made both Ginger and me feel very ill. We, however, were taken in and well done by.

The next morning the master came to see how we were and to speak to James. I did not hear much, for the ostler was rubbing me down; but I could see that James looked very happy, and I thought the master was proud of him.

Our mistress had been so much alarmed in the night that the journey was put off till the afternoon; so James had the morning on hand, and went first to the inn to see about our harness and the carriage, and then to hear more about the fire. When he came back, we heard him tell the ostler about it.

At first no one could guess how the fire had been caused; but at last a man said he saw Dick Towler go into the stable with a pipe in his mouth, and when he came out he had not one and went to the tap for another. Then the under-ostler said he had asked Dick to go up the ladder to get down some hay, but told him to lay down his pipe first. Dick denied taking the pipe with him, but no one believed him.

I remember our John Manly's rule, never to allow a pipe in the stable, and thought it ought to be the rule everywhere.

James said the roof and floor had all fallen in and that only the black walls were standing. The two poor horses that could not be got out were buried under the burnt rafters and tiles.

CHAPTER 17

JOHN MANLY'S TALK

The rest of our journey was very easy, and a little after sunset we reached the house of my master's friend. We were taken into a clean, snug stable; there was a kind coachman, who made us very comfortable and who seemed to think a great deal of James when he heard about the fire.

'There is one thing quite clear, young man,' he said. 'Your horses know whom they can trust. It is one of the hardest things in the world to get horses out of a stable when there is either fire or flood. I don't know why they won't come out, but they won't—not one in twenty.'

We stopped two or three days at this place and then returned home. All went well on the journey; we were glad to be in our own stable again, and John was equally glad to see us.

Before James and he left us for the night, James said, 'I wonder who is coming in my place.'

'Little Joe Green at the Lodge,' said John.

'Little Joe Green! Why, he's a child!'

'He is fourteen and a half,' said John.

'But he is such a little chap!'

'Yes, he is small, but he is quick, willing, and kind-hearted too, and wishes very much to come, and his father would like it; and I know the master would like to give him the chance. He said, if I thought he would not do, he would look out for a bigger boy; but I said I was quite agreeable to try him for six weeks.'

'Six weeks!' said James, 'why, it will be six months before he can be of much use! It will make you a deal of work, John.'

'Well,' said John with a laugh, 'work and I are very good friends; I never was afraid of work yet.'

'You are a very good man,' said James; 'I wish I may ever be like you.'

'I don't often speak of myself,' said John, 'but as you are going away from us out into the world to shift for yourself, I'll just tell you how I look on these things. I was just as old as Joseph when my father and mother died of the fever, within ten days of each other, and left me and my crippled sister Nelly, alone in the world, without a relation to whom we could look for help.

'I was a farmer's boy, not earning enough to keep myself, much less both of us, and she must have gone to the workhouse but for our mistress (Nelly calls her her angel, and she has good right to do so). The mistress went and hired a room for her with old Widow Maller, and she gave her knitting and needle-work, when she was able to do it; and when she was ill, she sent her dinners and many nice comfortable things, and was like a mother to her. Then the master took me into the stable under old Norman, the coachman that then was. I had my food at the house and my bed in the loft, and a suit of clothes and three shillings a week, so that I could help Nelly.

'Norman might have turned round and said that at his age he could not be troubled with a raw boy from the plough-tail; but he was like a father to me, and took no end of pains with me. When the old man died some years after, I stepped into his place; and now of course I have top wages, and can lay by for a rainy day or a sunny day as it may happen; and Nelly is as happy as a bird.

'So you see, James, I am not the man that should turn up his nose at a little boy, and vex a good, kind master. No! no! I shall miss you very much, James, but we shall pull through. There's nothing like doing a kindness when 'tis put in your way, and I am glad I can do it.'

'Then,' said James, 'you don't hold with that saying, "Everybody look after himself, and take care of number one"?'

'No, indeed,' said John. 'Where would Nelly and I have been if master and mistress and old Norman had only taken care of number one? Why, she in the workhouse and I hoeing turnips! Where would Black Beauty and Ginger have been if you had only thought of number one? Why, roasted to death! No, Jim, no! that is a selfish, heathenish saying, whoever may use it, and any man who thinks he has nothing to do but take care of number one, why, it's a pity but what he had been drowned like a puppy or a kitten before he got his eyes open; that's what I think,' said John, with a very decided jerk of his head.

James laughed at this; but there was a thickness in his voice when he said, 'You have been my best friend except my mother; I hope you won't forget me.'

'No, lad, no!' said John, 'and if ever I can do you a good turn I hope you won't forget me.'

The next day Joe came to the stables to learn all he could before James left. He learned to sweep the stable, to bring in the straw and hay, and began to clean the harness, and help to wash the carriage. As he was quite too short to do anything in the way of grooming Ginger and me, James taught him upon Merrylegs, for, under John, he was to have full charge of the pony. He was a nice little bright fellow, and always came whistling to his work.

Merrylegs was a good deal put out at being 'mauled about,' as he said, 'by a boy who knew nothing;' but towards the end of the second week he told me confidentially that he thought the boy would turn out well.

At last the day came when James had to leave us; cheerful as he always was, he looked quite downhearted that morning.

'You see,' he said to John, 'I am leaving a great deal behind—my mother and Betsy, you, a good master and mistress, and the horses and my old Merrylegs. At the new place there will not be a soul I shall know. If it were not that I shall get a higher place, and be able to help my mother better, I don't think I should have made up my mind to it; it is a real pinch, John.'

'Ay, James, lad, so it is, but I should not think much of you if you could not leave your home for the first time and not feel it. Cheer up! you'll make friends there, and if you get on well—as I am sure you will—it will be a fine thing for your mother, and she will be proud enough that you have got into such a good place as that.'

So John cheered him up, but every one was sorry to lose James. As for Merrylegs, he pined after him for several days, and went quite off his appetite. So when he had exercised me, John took him out several mornings with a leading rein, and trotting and galloping by my side he got up the little fellow's spirits again, and Merrylegs was soon all right.

Joe's father would often come in and give a little help, as he understood the work, and Joe took a great deal of pains to learn, and John was quite encouraged about him.

Chapter 18

GOING FOR THE DOCTOR

One night, a few days after James had left, I had eaten my hay and was lying down in my straw fast asleep, when I was suddenly awakened by the stable bell ringing very loudly. I heard the door of John's house opened and his feet running up to the Hall. He was back again in no time. He unlocked the stable door and came in, calling out, 'Wake up, Beauty, you must go well now, if ever you did!' and almost before I could think, he had placed the saddle on my back and the bridle on my head. He just ran round for his coat, and then took me at a quick trot up to the Hall door. The Squire stood there with a lamp in his hand.

'Now, John,' he said, 'ride for your life—that is, for your mistress's life; there is not a moment to lose. Give this note to Doctor White. Give your horse a rest at the inn, and be back as soon as you can.'

John said, 'Yes, sir,' and was on my back in a minute. The gardener who lived at the lodge had heard the bell ring, and was ready with the gate open. Away we went through the park, through the village, and down the hill till we came to the toll-gate. John called very loudly and thumped upon the door; the man was soon out and flung open the gate.

'Now,' said John, 'do you keep the gate open for the Doctor; here's the money,' and off we went again.

There was before us a long piece of level road by the riverside. John said to me, 'Now, Beauty, do your best,' and so I did; I wanted neither whip nor spur, and for two miles I galloped as fast as I could lay my feet to the ground. I don't believe that my old grandfather, who won the race at Newmarket, could have gone faster. When we came to the bridge John pulled me up a little and patted my neck. 'Well done, Beauty! good old fellow,' he said. He would have let me go more slowly, but my spirit was up and I was off again as fast as before.

The air was frosty, the moon bright, and it was very pleasant. We went through a village, through a dark wood, then uphill, then downhill, till after an eight miles' run we came to the town. On through the streets we went and into the Market Place. All was quite still except for the clatter of my feet on the stones—everybody was asleep. The church clock struck three as we drew up at Doctor White's door.

John rang the bell twice, and then knocked at the door like thunder. A window was thrown up, and Doctor White, in his nightcap, put his head out and said, 'What do you want?'

'Mrs. Gordon is very ill, sir; master wants you to come at once; he thinks she will die if you cannot get there—here is a note.'

'Wait,' he said, 'I will come.'

He shut the window and was soon at the door.

'The worst of it is,' he said, 'that my horse has been out all day and is quite done up; my son has just been sent for and he has taken the other. What is to be done? Can I have your horse?'

'He has come at a gallop nearly all the way, sir, and I was to give him a rest here, but I think my master would not be against it if you think fit, sir.'

'All right,' he said, 'I will soon be ready.'

John stood by me and stroked my head. I was very hot. The Doctor came out with his riding whip.

'You need not take that, sir,' said John. 'Black Beauty will go till he drops. Take care of him, sir, if you can; I should not like any harm to come to him.'

'No! no! John,' said the Doctor, 'I hope not,' and in a minute we had left John far behind.

I will not describe our way back; the Doctor was a heavier man than John, and not so good a rider; however, I did my very best. The man at the toll-gate had it open. When we came to the hill, the Doctor drew me up. 'Now, my good fellow,' he said, 'take some breath.' I was glad he did, for I was nearly spent; but that breathing helped me on, and soon we were in the park. Joe was at the lodge gate, and my master was at the Hall door, for he had heard us coming. He spoke not a word: the Doctor went into the house with him, and Joe led me to the stable.

I was glad to get home; my legs shook under me, and I could only stand and pant. I had not a dry hair on my body, the water ran down my legs, and I steamed all over—Joe used to say, like a pot on the fire. Poor Joe! he was young and small,and as yet he knew very little, and his father, who would have helped him, had been sent to the next village; but I am sure he did the very best he knew.

He rubbed my legs and my chest, but he did not put

my warm cloth on me; he thought I was so hot I should not like it. Then he gave me a pailful of water to drink. It was cold, and very good, and I drank it all; then he gave me some hay and some corn, and thinking he had done right, he went away.

Soon I began to tremble, and turned deadly cold; my legs, loins, and chest ached, and I felt sore all over. Oh! how I wished for my warm, thick cloth as I stood and trembled. I wished for John, but he had eight miles to walk, so I lay down in my straw and tried to go to sleep.

After a while I heard John at the door; I gave a low moan, for I was in great pain. He was at my side in a moment, stooping down by me. I could not tell him how ill I felt; but he seemed to know it all. He covered me up with two or three warm cloths, and then ran to the house for some hot water; then he made some warm gruel, which I drank; then, I think, I went to sleep.

John seemed to be very much put out. I heard him say to himself, over and over again. 'Stupid boy! stupid boy! No cloth put on, and I dare say the water was cold too; boys are no good;' but Joe was a good boy after all.

I was now very ill; a strong inflammation had attacked my lungs, and I could not draw my breath without pain. John nursed me night and day. He would get up two or three times in the night to come to me; my master, too, often came to see me. 'My poor Beauty,' he said one day, 'my good horse, you saved your mistress's life, Beauty! Yes, you saved her life.'

I was very glad to hear that, for it seems the Doctor had said if we had been a little longer it would have been too late. John told my master he never saw a horse go so fast in his life; it seemed as if the horse knew what was the matter. Of course I did, though John thought I did not; at least, I knew as much as this, that John and I must go at the top of our speed, and that it was for the sake of the mistress.

Chapter 19

ONLY IGNORANCE

I do not know how long I was ill. Mr. Bond, the horse doctor, came every day. One day he bled me, and John held a pail for the blood. I felt very faint after it, and thought I should die. I believe they all thought so too.

Ginger and Merrylegs had been moved into the other stable, so that I might be quiet, for fever made me very quick of hearing; any little noise seemed quite loud, and I could tell every one's footstep going to and from the house. I knew all that was going on. One night John had to give me a draught; Thomas Green came in to help him.

After I had taken it and John had made me as comfortable as he could, he said he should stay half an hour to see how the medicine settled. Thomas said he would stay with him, so they went and sat down on a bench that had been brought into Merrryleg's stall, and put down the lantern at their feet that I might not be disturbed with the light.

For a while both men sat silent, and then Tom Green said in a low voice:—

'I wish, John, you'd say a bit of a kind word to Joe; the boy is quite broken-hearted; he can't eat his meals, and he can't smile. He says he knows it was all his fault, though he is sure he did the best he knew; and he says, if Beauty dies, no one will ever speak to him again. It goes to my heart to hear him; I think you might give him just a word, he is not a bad boy.'

After a short pause, John said slowly: 'You must not be too hard upon me, Tom. I know he meant no harm;

I never said he did. I know he is not a bad boy, but you see I am sore myself. That horse is the pride of my heart, to say nothing of his being such a favourite with the master and mistress; and to think that his life may be flung away in this manner is more than I can bear. But if you think I am hard on the boy, I will try to give him a good word to-morrow—that is, I mean, if Beauty is better.'

'Well, John, thank you! I knew you did not wish to be too hard, and I am glad you see it was only ignorance.'

John's voice almost startled me as he answered, '*Only* ignorance! only *ignorance*! how can you talk about *only* ignorance? Don't you know that ignorance is the worst thing in the world, next to wickedness?—and which does the most mischief Heaven only knows. If people can say, "Oh! I did not know, I did not mean any harm," they think it is all right. I suppose Martha Mulwash did not mean to kill that baby when she dosed it with Dalby and soothing syrups; but she did kill it, and was tried for manslaughter.'

'And serve her right too,' said Tom. 'A woman should not undertake to nurse a tender little child without knowing what is good or what is bad for it.'

'Bill Starkey,' continued John, 'did not mean to frighten his brother into fits when he dressed up like a ghost, and ran after him in the moonlight; but he did; and that bright, handsome little fellow, that might have been the pride of any mother's heart, is just no better than an idiot, and never will be, if he lives to be eighty years old.

'You were a good deal cut up yourself, Tom, two weeks ago, when those young ladies left your hot-house door open, with a frosty east wind blowing right in; you said it killed a good many of your plants.'

'A good many!' said Tom. 'There was not one of the tender cuttings that was not nipped off. I shall have to strike all over again, and the worst of it is, that I don't know where to go to get fresh ones. I was nearly mad when I came in and saw what was done.'

'And yet,' said John, 'I am sure the young ladies did not mean it; it was only ignorance!'

I heard no more of this conversation, for the medicine took effect and sent me to sleep, and in the morning I felt much better; but I often thought of John's words when I came to know more of the world.

Chapter 20

JOE GREEN

Joe Green went on very well; he learned quickly, and was so attentive and careful that John began to trust him in many things; but, as I have said, he was small for his age, and it was seldom that he was allowed to exercise either Ginger or me. But it so happened one morning that John was out with Justice in the luggage-cart, and the master wanted a note to be taken immediately to a gentleman's house about three miles distant, and sent his orders for Joe to saddle me and take it, adding the caution that he was to ride carefully.

The note was delivered, and we were quietly returning till we came to the brickfield. Here we saw a cart heavily laden with bricks. The wheels had stuck fast in the stiff mud of some deep ruts; and the carter was shouting and flogging the two horses unmercifully. Joe pulled up. It was a sad sight. There were the two horses straining and struggling with all their might to drag the cart out, but they could not move it; the sweat streamed from their legs and flanks, their sides heaved, and every muscle was strained, whilst the man, fiercely pulling at the head of the fore-horse, swore and lashed most brutally.

'Hold hard,' said Joe, 'don't go on flogging the horses like that; the wheels are so stuck that they cannot move the cart.' The man took no heed, but went on lashing.

'Stop! pray stop,' said Joe; 'I'll help you to lighten the cart, they can't move it now.'

'Mind your own business, you impudent young rascal, and I'll mind mine.' The man was in a towering passion and the worse for drink; and so he laid on the whip again. Joe turned my head, and the next moment we were going at a round gallop towards the house of the master brickmaker. I cannot say if John would have approved of our pace, but Joe and I were both of one mind, and so angry that we could not go slower.

The house stood close by the roadside. Joe knocked at the door and shouted, 'Hallo! is Mr. Clay at home?' The door was opened, and Mr. Clay himself came out.

'Hallo, young man! you seem in a hurry; any orders from the Squire this morning?'

'No, Mr. Clay; but there's a fellow in your brickyard flogging two horses to death. I told him to stop and he wouldn't. I said I'd help him to lighten the cart, and he wouldn't; so I have come to tell you. Pray, sir, go.' Joe's voice shook with excitement.

'Thank ye, my lad,' said the man, running in for his hat. Then, pausing for a moment—'Will you give evidence of what you saw if I should bring the fellow up before a magistrate?' he asked.

'That I will,' said Joe, 'and glad to.' The man was gone, and we were on our way home at a smart trot.

'Why, what's the matter with you, Joe? you look angry

all over,' said John, as the boy flung himself from the saddle.

'I am angry all over, I can tell you,' said the boy, and then in hurried, excited words, he told all that had happened. Joe was usually such a quiet, gentle, little fellow that it was wonderful to see him so roused.

'Right, Joe! you did right, my boy, whether the fellow gets a summons or not. Many folks would have ridden by and said 'twas not their business to interfere. Now, I say, that with cruelty and oppression it is everybody's business to interfere when they see it; you did right, my boy.'

Joe was quite calm by this time, and proud that John had approved of him. He cleaned out my feet, and rubbed me down with a firmer hand than usual.

They were just going home to dinner when the footman came down to the stable to say that Joe was wanted directly in master's private room; there was a man brought up for ill-using horses, and Joe's evidence was wanted. The boy flushed up to his forehead, and his eyes sparkled. 'They shall have it,' said he.

'Put yourself a bit straight,' said John. Joe gave a pull at his necktie and a twitch at his jacket, and was off in a moment. Our master being one of the country magistrates, cases were often brought to him to settle, or say what should be done.

In the stable we heard no more for some time, as it was the men's dinner-hour. But when Joe came next into the stable I saw he was in high spirits; he gave me a good-natured slap and said, 'We won't see such things done, will we, old fellow?' We heard afterwards that he had given his evidence so clearly, and the horses were in such an exhausted state, bearing marks of such brutal usage, that the carter was committed to take his trial, and might possibly be sentenced to two or three months in prison.

It was wonderful what a change had come over Joe. John laughed, and said he had grown an inch taller in that week; and I believe he had. He was just as kind and gentle as before, but there was more purpose and determination in all that he did—as if he had jumped at once from a boy into a man.

CHAPTER 21

THE PARTING

I had now lived in this happy place three years, but sad changes were about to come over us. We heard from time to time that our mistress was ill. The Doctor was often at the house, and the master looked grave and anxious. Then we heard that she must leave her home at once and go to a warm country for two or three years. The news fell upon the household like the tolling of a death-bell. Everybody was sorry; but the master began directly to make arrangements for breaking up his establishment and leaving England. We used to hear it talked about in our stable; indeed, nothing else was talked about.

John went about his work silent and sad, and Joe scarcely whistled. There was a great deal of coming and going; Ginger and I had full work.

The first to go were Miss Jessie and Miss Flora with their governess. They came to bid us good-bye. They hugged poor Merrylegs like an old friend, and so indeed he was. Then we heard what had been arranged for us. Master had sold Ginger and me to his old friend the Earl of W—, for he thought we should have a good place there. Merrylegs he had given to the Vicar, who was wanting a pony for Mrs. Blomefield; but it was on the condition that he should never be sold, and that when he was past work he should be shot and buried.

Joe was engaged to take care of him, and to help in the house; so I thought that Merrylegs was well off. John had the offer of several good places, but he said he should wait a little and look round.

The evening before they left, the master came into the stable to give some directions and to give his horses the last pat. He seemed very low-spirited; I knew that by his voice. I believe we horses can tell more by the voice than many men can.

'Have you decided what to do, John? he said. 'I find you have not accepted any of these offers.'

'No, sir, I have made up my mind that if I could get a situation with some first-rate colt-breaker and horse-trainer, it would be the right thing for me. Many young animals are frightened and spoiled by wrong treatment, which need not be if the right man took them in hand. I always get on well with horses, and if I could help some of them to a fair start, I should feel as if I was doing some good. What do you think of it, sir?'

'I don't know a man anywhere,' said master, 'that I should think so suitable for it as yourself. You understand horses, and somehow they understand you, and in time you might set up for yourself; I think you could not do better. If in any way I can help you, write to me; I shall speak to my agent in London, and leave your character with him.'

He asked John about his future, and then thanked him for his long and faithful service; but that was too much for John. 'Pray don't, sir, I can't bear it. You and my dear mistress have done so much for me that I could never repay it; but we shall never forget you sir, and please

God we may some day see mistress back again like herself; we must keep up hope, sir.' Master gave John his hand, but he did not speak; and they both left the stable.

The last sad day had come; the footman and the heavy luggage had gone off the day before, and there was only master and mistress and her maid left. Ginger and I brought the carriage up to the hall door for the last time. The servants brought out cushions and rugs and many other things; and when all were arranged, master came down the steps carrying the mistress in his arms (I was on the side next the house and could see all that went on). He placed her carefully in the carriage, while the house servants stood round crying.

'Good-bye again,' he said as he got in; 'we shall not forget any of you—drive on, John.'

Joe jumped up, and we trotted slowly through the park and through the village, where the people were standing at their doors to have a last look and to say, 'God bless them!'

When we reached the railway station, I think mistress walked from the carriage to the waiting-room. I heard her say in her own sweet voice, 'Good-bye, John; God bless you.' I felt the rein twitch, but John made no answer, perhaps he could not speak. As soon as Joe had taken the things out of the carriage, John called him to stand by the horse while he went on the platform. Poor Joe! he stood close up to our heads to hide his tears.

Very soon the train came puffing up into the station. Two or three minutes after the doors were slammed to, the guard whistled, and the train glided away, leaving behind it only clouds of white steam and some very heavy hearts.

When it was quite out of sight, John came back.

'We shall never see her again,' he said—'never.' He took the reins, mounted the box, and drove slowly home with Joe; but it was not our home now.

Chapter 22

EARLSHALL

The next morning after breakfast Joe put Merrylegs into the mistress's low chaise to take him to the vicarage. He came first and said good-bye to us, and Merrylegs neighed to us from the yard. Then John put the saddle on Ginger and the leading rein on me, and rode us across the country about fifteen miles to Earlshall Park, where the Earl of W—lived. Here was a very fine house and a great deal of stabling.

We went into the yard through a stone gateway, and John asked for Mr. York. It was some time before he came. He was a fine-looking, middle-aged man, and his voice said at once that he expected to be obeyed. He was very friendly and polite to John; and after giving us a slight look, he called a groom to take us to our boxes, and invited John to take some refreshment.

We were taken to a light, airy stable and placed in boxes adjoining each other, where we were rubbed down and fed. In about half an hour John and Mr. York, who was to be our new coachman, came in to see us.

'Now, Mr. Manly,' he said, after carefully looking at us both, 'I can see no fault in these horses; but we all know that horses as well as men have their peculiarities, and that sometimes they need different treatment. I should like to know if there is anything particular in either of these that you would like to mention.'

'Well,' said John, 'I don't believe there is a better pair of horses in the country, and right grieved I am to part with them, but they are not alike. The black one is the most perfect temper I ever knew; I suppose he has never known a hard word or a blow since he was foaled, and all his pleasure seems to be what you wish to do.

'But the chestnut I fancy must have had bad treatment; we heard as much from the dealer. She came to us snappish and suspicious, but when she found what sort of place ours was, it all went off by degrees. For three years I have never seen the smallest sign of temper, and if she is well treated there is not a better or more willing animal than she is; but she is naturally of a more irritable constitution than the black horse—flies tease her more; anything wrong in the harness frets her more; and if she were ill-used or unfairly treated, she would not be unlikely to give tit for tat. You know that many high-mettled horses will do so.'

'Of course,' said York, 'I quite understand; but you know it is not easy in stables like these to have all the grooms just what they should be; I do my best, and there I must leave it. I'll remember what you have said about the mare.'

They were going out of the stable, when John stopped and said: 'I had better mention that we have never used the bearing rein with either of them; the black horse never had one on, and the dealer said it was the gag-bit that spoiled the other's temper.'

'Well,' said York, 'if they come here, they must wear the bearing rein. I prefer a loose rein myself, and his lordship is always very reasonable about horses; but my lady—that's another matter. She will have style; and if her carriage horses were not reined up right, she wouldn't look at them. I always stand out against the gag-bit, and shall do so, but the rein must be tight up when my lady rides!'

'I am sorry for it, very sorry,' said John; 'but I must go now, or I shall lose the train.'

He came round to each of us to pat and speak to us for the last time; his voice sounded very sad.

I held my face close to him, as that was all I could do to say good-bye; and then he was gone, and I have never seen him since.

The next day Lord W— came to look at us; he seemed pleased with our appearance.

'I have great confidence in these horses,' he said, 'from the character my friend Mr. Gordon has given me of them. Of course they are not a match in colour, but my idea is that they will do very well for the carriage whilst we are in the country. Before we go to London I must try to match Baron; the black horse, I believe, is perfect for riding.'

York then told him what John had said about us.

'Well,' said he, 'you must keep an eye to the mare, and put the bearing rein easy; I dare say they will do very well with a little humouring at first. I'll mention it to her ladyship.'

In the afternoon we were harnessed and put in the carriage, and as the stable clock struck three we were led round to the front of the house. It was all very grand, and the house three or four times as large as the old one at Birtwick, but not half so pleasant, if a horse may have an opinion. Two footmen, dressed in drab livery, with scarlet breeches and white stockings, were standing ready.

Presently we heard the rustling sound of silk as my lady came down the flight of stone steps. She stepped round to look at us. She was a tall, proud-looking woman, and did not seem pleased about something; but she said nothing, and got into the carriage. This was my first time of wearing a bearing rein, and I must say, though it certainly was a nuisance not to be able to get my head down now and then, it did not pull my head higher than I was accustomed to carry it. I felt anxious about Ginger, but she seemed to be quiet and content.

The next day at three o'clock we were again at the door, and the footmen were there as before. We heard the silk dress rustle as the lady came down the steps, and in an imperious voice she said: 'York, you must put those horses' heads higher; they are not fit to be seen.

York got down and said very respectfully: 'I beg your pardon, my lady, but these horses have not been reined up for three years, and my lord said it would be safer to bring them to it by degrees; but if your ladyship pleases, I can take them up a little more.'

'Do so,' she said.

York came round to our heads and shortened the rein one hole, I think; every little makes a difference, be it for better or worse, and that day we had a steep hill to go up. Then I began to understand what I had heard. Of course I wanted to push my head forward and take the carriage up with a will, as we had been used to do; but no, I had now to pull with my head up, and that took all the spirit out of me, and brought the strain on my back and legs.

When she came in, Ginger said: 'Now you see what it is like; but this is not bad, and if it does not get much worse than this, I shall say nothing about it, for we are very well treated here. But if they strain me up tight, why, let 'em look out! I can't bear it and I won't.'

Day by day, hole by hole, our bearing reins were shortened, and instead of looking forward with pleasure to having my harness put on as I used to do, I began to dread it. Ginger, too, seemed restless, though she said very little. At last I thought the worst was over; for several days there had been no more shortening, and I determined to make the best of it and to do my duty, though now going out was a constant harass instead of a pleasure; but the worse was not come.

Chapter 23

A STRIKE FOR LIBERTY

One day my lady came down later than usual, and the silk rustled more than ever.

'Drive to the Duchess of B—'s,' she said. Then after a pause, she added: 'Are you never going to get those horses' heads up, York? Raise them at once, and let us have no more of this humouring nonsense.'

York came to me first, whilst the groom stood at Ginger's head. He drew my head back and fixed the rein so tight that it was almost intolerable, then he went to Ginger, who was impatiently jerking her head up and down against the bit, as was her way now. She had a good idea of what was coming, and the moment York took the rein off the terret in order to shorten it she took her opportunity and reared up so suddenly that York had his nose roughly hit and his hat knocked off, and the groom was nearly thrown off his legs.

At once they both flew to her head, but she was a match for them, and went on plunging, rearing, and kicking in a most desperate manner. At last she kicked right over the carriage pole and fell down, after giving me a severe blow on my near quarter.

There is no knowing what further mischief she may have done had not York promptly sat himself down flat on her head to prevent her struggling, at the same time calling out, 'Unbuckle the black horse! Run for the winch and unscrew the carriage pole; and somebody cut the trace if you can't unhitch it.'

One of the footmen ran for the winch, and another brought a knife from the house. The groom set me free from Ginger and the carriage, and led me to my box. He just turned me in as I was, and ran back to York.

I was much excited by what had happened, and if I had ever been used to kick or rear, I am sure I should have done it then; but I never had, so there I stood, angry, sore in my leg, my head still strained up to the terret on the saddle, and with no power to get it down. I was very miserable, and felt much inclined to kick the first person who came near me.

Before long, however, Ginger was led in by two grooms, a good deal knocked about and bruised. York came with her and gave his orders, and then came to look at me. In a moment he let down my head.

'Confound these bearing reins!' he said to himself. 'I thought we should have some mischief soon—master will be sorely vexed; but there—if a woman's husband can't rule her, of course a servant can't; so I wash my hands of it, and if she can't get to the Duchesss's garden party, I can't help it.'

York did not say this before the men; he always spoke respectfully when they were by. Now he felt me all over and soon found the place above my hock where I had been kicked. It was swollen and painful; so he ordered it to be sponged with hot water and then some lotion to be rubbed in.

Lord W— was much put out when he learned what had happened. He blamed York for giving way to his mistress, to which York replied that in future he would much prefer to receive his orders only from his lordship. But I think nothing came of it, for things went on the same as before. I thought York might have stood up better for his horses; but perhaps I am no judge.

Ginger was never put into the carriage again, but when her bruises were healed, one of Lord W—'s younger sons said he should like to have her; he was sure she would make a good hunter. As for me, I was obliged still to go in the carriage, and had a fresh partner, called Max, who had always been used to the tight rein. I asked him how it was he bore it.

'Well,' he said, 'I bear it because I must, but it is shortening my life, and it will shorten yours too if you have to stick to it.'

'Do you think,' I said, 'that our masters know how bad it is for us?'

'I can't say,' he replied, 'but the dealers and the horse doctors know it very well. I was at a dealer's once, who was training me and another horse to go as a pair; he was getting our heads up, as he said, a little higher and a little higher every day. A gentleman who was there asked him why he did so; "Because," said he, "people won't buy them unless we do. The London people always want their horses to carry their heads high, and to step high; of course it is very bad for the horses, but then it is good for trade. The horses soon wear up, or get diseased, and they come to another pair." That,' said Max, 'is what he said in my hearing, and you can judge for yourself.'

What I suffered for four long months with that rein it would be hard to describe; but I am quite sure that, had it lasted much longer, either my health or my temper would have given way. Before that, I never knew what it was to foam at the mouth; but now the action of the sharp bit on my tongue and jaw and the constrained position of my head and throat, always caused me to froth more or less at the mouth.

Some people think it very fine to see this, and say, 'What fine, spirited creatures!' But it is just as unnatural for horses as for men to foam at the mouth: it is a sure sign of some discomfort and should be attended to. Besides this, there was a pressure on my windpipe, which often made my breathing very uncomfortable. When I returned from my work, my neck and chest were strained and painful, my mouth and tongue tender, and I felt worn and depressed.

In my old home I always knew that John and my master were my friends; but here, although in many ways I was well treated, I had no friend. York might have known, and very likely did know, how that rein harassed me; but I suppose he took it as a matter of course that could not be helped; at any rate, nothing was done to relieve me.

CHAPTER 24

LADY ANNE, OR A RUNAWAY HORSE

Early in the spring Lord W— and part of his family went up to London and took York with them. Ginger and I and some other horses were left at home for use, and the head groom was left in charge.

The Lady Harriet, who remained at the Hall, was a great invalid, and never went out in the carriage, and the Lady Anne preferred riding on horseback, with her brother or cousins. She was a perfect horsewoman, and as gay and gentle as she was beautiful. She chose me for her horse, and named me Black Auster. I enjoyed very much these rides in the clear, cold air, sometimes with Ginger, sometimes with Lizzie. This Lizzie was a bright bay mare, almost thoroughbred, and a great favourite with the gentlemen on account of her fine action and lively spirit; but Ginger, who knew more of her than I did, told me she was rather nervous.

There was a gentleman of the name of Blantyre staying at the Hall; he always rode Lizzie, and praised her so much that one day Lady Anne ordered the side-saddle to be put on Lizzie and the other saddle on me. When we came to the door, the gentleman seemed very uneasy.

'How is this?' he said; 'are you tired of your good Black Auster?'

'Oh, no, not at all,' she replied, 'but I am amiable enough to let you ride him for once, and I will try your charming Lizzie. You must confess that in size and appearance she is far more like a lady's horse than my own favourite.'

'Do let me advise you not to mount her,' he said; 'she is a charming creature, but she is too nervous for a lady. I assure you she is not perfectly safe; let me beg you to have the saddles changed.'

'My dear cousin,' said Lady Anne, laughing, 'pray do not trouble your good, careful head about me. I have been a horsewoman ever since I was a baby, and I have followed the hounds a great many times, though I know you do not approve of ladies hunting; but still, that is the fact, and I intend to try this Lizzie that you gentlemen are all so fond of; so please help me to mount her the good friend you are.'

There was no more to be said. He placed her carefully on the saddle, looked to the bit and curb, gave the reins gently into her hand and then mounted me. Just as we were moving off, a footman came out with a slip of paper and message from the Lady Harriet—'Would Mr. Blantyre ask this question for her at Dr. Ashley's, and bring the answer?'

The village was about a mile off, and the Doctor's house was the last in it. We went along gaily enough till we came to his gate. There was a short drive up to the house between tall evergreens. Blantyre alighted at the gate and was going to open it for Lady Ann, but she said, 'I will wait for you here; you can hang Auster's rein on the gate.'

He looked at her doubtfully—'I will not be five minutes,' he said.

'Oh, do not hurry yourself; Lizzie and I shall not run away from you.'

He hung my rein on one of the iron spikes, and was soon hidden amongst the trees. By the side of the road, a few paces off, Lizzie was standing quietly with her back to me. My young mistress was sitting easily with a loose rein, humming a little song. I listened to my rider's footsteps until they reached the house, and heard him knock at the door.

There was a meadow on the opposite side of the road, the gate of which stood open. Just then some cart horses and several young colts came trotting out in a very disorderly manner, whilst a boy behind was cracking a great whip. The colts were wild and frolicsome, and one of them bolted across the road and blundered up against Lizzie's hind legs. Whether it was the stupid colt, or the loud cracking of the whip, or both together, I cannot say, but she gave a violent kick and dashed off into a headlong gallop. It was so sudden, that Lady Anne was nearly unseated, but she soon recovered herself.

I gave a loud shrill neigh for help. Again and again I neighed, pawing the ground impatiently, and tossing my head to get the rein loose. I had not long to wait. Blantyre came running to the gate. He looked anxiously about, and just caught sight of the flying figure, now far away on the road. In an instant he sprang into the saddle. I needed no whip or spur, for I was as eager as my rider. He saw it, and giving me a free rein, and leaning a little forward, we dashed after them.

For about a mile and a half the road ran straight, then bent to the right, after which it divided into two roads.

Long before we came to the bend Lady Anne was out of sight. Which way had she turned? A woman was standing at her garden gate, shading her eyes with her hand and looking eagerly up the road. Scarcely drawing the rein, Blantyre shouted, 'Which way?' 'To the right,' cried the woman, pointing with her hand, and away we went up the right-hand road; then for a moment we caught sight of her; another bend and she was hidden again. Several times we caught glimpses, and then lost them. We scarcely seemed to gain ground upon them at all.

An old road-mender was standing near a heap of stones, with shovel dropped and hands raised. As we came near he made a sign to speak. Blantyre drew the rein a little. 'To the common, to the common, sir; she has turned off there.' I knew this common very well. It was for the most part very uneven ground, covered with heather and dark green furze bushes, with here and there a scrubby old thorn-tree. There were also open spaces of fine, short grass, with ant-hills and mole-turns everywhere—the worst place I ever knew for a headlong gallop.

We had hardly turned on the common, when we caught sight again of the green habit flying on before us. My lady's hat was gone, and her long brown hair was streaming behind her. Her head and body were thrown back, as if she were pulling with all her remaining strength, and as if that strength were nearly exhausted. It was clear that the roughness of the ground had very much lessened Lizzie's speed, and there seemed a chance that we might overtake her.

Whilst we were on the high road, Blantyre had given me my head; but now with a light hand and a practised eye, he guided me over the ground in such a masterly manner, that my pace was scarcely slackened, and we were decidedly gaining on them.

About half-way across the heath there had been a wide dyke recently cut, and the earth from the cutting was cast up roughly on the other side. Surely this would stop them! But no; with scarcely a pause Lizzie took the leap, stumbled among the rough clods, and fell. Blantyre groaned, 'Now, Auster, do your best!' He gave me a steady rein, I gathered myself well together, and with one determined leap cleared both dyke and bank.

Motionless among the heather, with her face to the earth, lay my poor your mistress. Blantyre kneeled down and called her name—there was no sound.

Gently he turned her face upward; it was ghastly white, and the eyes were closed. 'Annie, dear Annie, do speak!' but there was no answer. He unbuttoned her habit, loosened her collar, felt her hands and wrists, then started up and looked wildly round for help.

At no great distance were two men cutting turf, who, seeing Lizzie running wild without a rider, had left their work to catch her.

Blantyre's 'Halloo!' soon brought them to the spot. The foremost man seemed much troubled at the sight, and asked what he could do.

'Can you ride?'

'Well, sir, I bean't much of a horseman, but I'd risk my neck for the Lady Anne; she was uncommon good to my wife in the winter.'

'Then mount this horse, my friend; your neck will be quite safe. Ride to the Doctor's and ask him to come instantly; then go on to the Hall; tell them all that you know, and bid them send me the carriage with Lady Anne's maid and other assistance. I shall stay here.'

'All right, sir, I'll do my best, and I pray God the dear young lady may open her eyes soon.' Then seeing the other man, he called out: 'Here Joe, run for some water, and tell my missis to come as quickly as she can to the Lady Anne.'

He then somehow scrambled into the saddle, and with a 'Gee up!' and a clap on my sides with both his legs, he started on his journey, making a little circuit to avoid the dyke. He had no whip, which seemed to trouble him, but my pace soon cured that difficulty, and he found the best thing he could do was to stick to the saddle, and hold me in, which he did manfully. I shook him as little as I could help, but once or twice on the rough ground he called out, 'Steady! Whoa! Steady.' On the high road we were all right; and at the Doctor's and at the Hall he did his errand like a good man and true. They asked him in to take a drop of something. 'No, no!' he said; 'I'll be back to 'em again by a short cut through the fields, and be there before the carriage.'

There was a great deal of hurry and excitement after the news became known. I was just turned into my box, the saddle and bridle were taken off, and a cloth thrown over me.

Ginger was saddled and sent off in great haste for Lord George, and I soon heard the carriage roll out of the yard.

It seemed a long time before Ginger came back and before we were left alone; and then she told me all that she had seen.

'I can't tell much,' she said; 'we went galloping nearly all the way, and got there just as the Doctor rode up. There was a woman sitting on the ground with the lady's head in her lap. The Doctor poured something into her mouth, but all I heard was, "She is not dead." Then I was led off by a man to a little distance. After a while the lady was taken to the carriage, and we came home together. I heard my master say to a gentleman who stopped him to inquire, that he hoped no bones were broken, but that she had not spoken yet.'

When Lord George took Ginger for hunting, York shook his head; he said it ought to be a steady hand to train a horse for the first season, and not a random rider like Lord George.

Ginger used to like it very much, but sometimes when she came back I could see that she had been very much strained, and now and then she gave a short cough. She had too much spirit to complain, but I could not help feeling anxious about her.

Two days after the accident Blantyre paid me a visit. He patted me and praised me very much and told Lord George that he was sure the horse knew of Annie's danger as well as he did. 'I could not have held him in if I would,' said he; 'she ought never to ride any other horse.'

I found by their conversation that my young mistress was now out of danger and would soon be able to ride again. This was good news to me, and I looked forward to a happy life.

Chapter 25

REUBEN SMITH

I must now say a little about Reuben Smith, who was left in charge of the stables when York went to London. No one more thoroughly understood his business than he did, and when he was all right, there could not be a more faithful or valuable man. He was gentle and very clever in his management of horses, and could doctor them almost as well as a farrier, for he had lived two years with a veterinary surgeon. He was a first-rate driver, and could take a four-in-hand, or a tandem, as easily as a pair.

He was a handsome man, a good scholar, and had very pleasant manners. I believe everybody liked him; certainly the horses did. The only wonder was that he should be in an under situation, and not in the place of a head coachman like York: but he had one great fault—the love of drink. He was not like some men, always at it; he used to keep steady for weeks or months together; but then he would break out and have a 'bout' of it, as York called it, and be a disgrace to himself, a terror to his wife, and a nuisance to all that had to do with him. He was, however, so useful that two or three times York had hushed the matter up, and kept it from the Earl's knowledge.

It was now early in April, and the family was expected home some time in May. The light brougham was to be fresh done up, and as Colonel Blantyre was obliged to return to his regiment, it was arranged that Smith should drive him to the town in it, and then ride back; for this purpose he took the saddle with him, and I was chosen for the journey.

At the station the Colonel put some money into Smith's hand and bade him good-bye saying: 'Take care of your young mistress, Reuben, and don't let Black Auster be hacked about by any random young prig that wants to ride him—keep him for the lady.'

We left the carriage at the maker's, and Smith drove me to the White Lion, and ordered the ostler to feed me well and have me ready for him at four o'clock. A nail in one of my front shoes had started as I came along, but the ostler did not notice it till just about four o'clock. Smith did not come into the yard till five, and then he said he should not leave till six, as he had met with some old friends. The man then told him of the nail, and asked if he should have the shoe looked to.

'No,' said Smith, 'that will be all right till we get home.'

He spoke in a very loud, off-hand way, and I thought it was very unlike him not to see about the shoe, as he was generally wonderfully particular about loose nails in our shoes. He came neither at six, seven, nor eight, and it was nearly nine o'clock before he called me, and then it was with a loud, rough voice. He seemed in a very bad temper and abused the ostler, though I could not tell what for.

The landlord stood at the door, and said. 'Have a care, Mr. Smith!' but he answered angrily with an oath; and almost before he was out of the town he began to gallop, frequently giving me a sharp cut with his whip, though I was going at full speed. The moon had not yet risen, and it was very dark. Having been recently mended, the roads were stony, and going over them at this pace made my shoe looser, so that when we were near the turnpike gate it came off.

If Smith had been in his right senses he would have been sensible of something wrong in my pace; but he was too madly drunk to notice anything.

Beyond the turnpike was a long piece of road, upon which some fresh stones had just been laid—large, sharp stones, over which no horse could be driven quickly without risk of danger. Over this road, with one shoe gone, I was forced to gallop at my utmost speed, my rider meanwhile cutting into me with his whip, and with wild curses urging me to go still faster. Of course my shoeless foot suffered dreadfully; the hoof was broken and split down to the quick, and the inside was terribly cut by the sharpness of the stones.

This could not go on; no horse could keep his footing under such circumstances as the pain was too great. I stumbled, and fell with violence on both my knees. Smith was flung off by my fall, and, owing to the speed at which I was going, he must have fallen with great force. I soon recovered my feet and limped to the side of the road, where it was free from stones.

The moon had just risen above the hedge, and by its light I could see Smith lying a few yards beyond me. After making one slight effort to rise, there was a heavy groan. He did not move. I could have groaned too, for I was suffering intense pain both from my foot and knees; but horses are used to bear their pain in silence. I uttered no sound, but stood there and listened.

One more heavy groan from Smith; but though he now lay in the full moonlight, I could see no motion. I could do nothing for him nor for myself. But, oh! how I listened for the sound of horse, or wheels, or footsteps. The road was not much frequented, and at this time of the night we might stay for hours before help came to us.

I stood watching and listening. It was a calm, sweet April night; there were no sounds except a few low notes of a nightingale; and nothing moved but the white clouds near the moon, and a brown owl that flitted over the hedge. It made me think of the summer nights long ago, when I used to lie beside my mother in the green, pleasant meadow at Farmer Grey's.

Chapter 26

HOW IT ENDED

It must have been nearly midnight when I heard at a great distance the sound of a horse's feet. Sometimes the sound died away, then it grew clear again and nearer. The road to Earlshall led through plantations that belonged to the Earl; the sound came in that direction, and I hoped it might be some one coming in search of us. As the sound came nearer and nearer, I was almost sure I could distinguish Ginger's step; a little nearer still, and I could tell she was in the dog-cart. I neighed loudly, and was overjoyed to hear an answering neigh from Ginger and men's voices. They came slowly over the stones, and stopped at the dark figure that lay upon the ground.

One of the men jumped out, and stooped down over it. 'It is Reuben!' he said, 'and he does not stir.'

The other man followed and bent over him. 'He's dead,' he said, 'feel how cold his hands are.'

They raised him up, but there was no life, and his hair was soaked with blood. Laying him down again, they came and looked at me and saw my cut knees.

'Why, the horse has been down and has thrown him! Who would have thought the black horse would have done that? Nobody thought he could fall. Reuben must have been lying here for hours! Odd, too, that the horse has not moved from the place.'

Robert then attempted to lead me forward. I made a step, but almost fell again.

'Hallo! he's bad in his foot as well as his knees. Look here—his hoof is cut all to pieces; he might well come down, poor fellow! I tell you what, Ned, I'm afraid it hasn't been all right with Reuben! Just think of him riding a horse over these stones without a shoe! Why, if he had been in his right senses, he would just as soon have tried to ride him over the moon. I'm afraid it has been the old thing over again.

'Poor Susan! she looked awfully pale when she came to my house to ask if he had come home. She made me believe she was not a bit anxious, and talked of a lot of things that might have kept him. But for all that, she begged me to go and meet him. But what must we do?

There's the horse to get home as well as the body—and that will be no easy matter.'

Then followed a conversation between them, till it was agreed that Robert, the groom, should lead me, and that Ned should take the body; it was a hard job to get it into the dog-cart, for there was no one to hold Ginger; but she knew as well as I did what was going on, and stood as still as a stone. I noticed that, because, if she had a fault it was that she was impatient in standing.

Ned started off very slowly with his sad load, and Robert came and looked at my foot again; then he took his handkerchief and bound it closely round, and so led me home. I shall never forget that night walk; it was more than three miles. Robert led me on very slowly, and I limped and hobbled on as well as I could, suffering great pain. I am sure he was sorry for me, for he often patted and encouraged me, talking to me in a pleasant voice.

At last I reached my own box and had some corn; and after Robert had wrapped up my knees in wet cloths, he tied up my foot in a bran poultice to draw out the heat, and to cleanse it before the horse doctor saw it in the morning. Then I managed to get myself down on the straw and slept in spite of the pain.

The next day, after the farrier had examined my wounds, he said he hoped the joint was not injured, and if so, I should not be spoiled for work, but I should never lose the blemish. I believe they did the best to make a good cure, but it was a long and painful one. Proud flesh, as they called it, came up in my knees, and was burnt out with caustic; and when at last my knees were healed, they put a blistering fluid over the front of both to bring off all the hair; they had some reason for this, and I suppose it was all right.

As Smith's death had been so sudden, and no one was there to see it, there was an inquest held. The landlord and ostler at the White Lion with several other people, gave evidence that he was intoxicated when he started from the inn; the keeper of the toll-gate said he rode at a hard gallop through the gate; and my shoe was picked up amongst the stones; so the case was quite plain to them, and I was cleared of all blame.

Everybody pitied Susan; she was nearly out of her mind, and kept saying over and over again, 'Oh! he was so good—so good! It was all that cursed drink; why will they sell that cursed drink? Oh, Reuben, Reuben!' So she went on till after he was buried; and then, as she had no home or relations, she, with her six little children, were obliged once more to leave the pleasant home by the tall oak-trees, and go into that great gloomy Union House.

Chapter 27

RUINED, AND GOING DOWNHILL

As soon as my knees were sufficiently healed, I was turned into a small meadow for a month or two. No other creature was there, and though I enjoyed the liberty and the sweet grass, yet I had been so long used to society that I felt very lonely. Ginger and I had become fast friends, and now I missed her company extremely.

I often neighed when I heard horses' feet passing in the road, but I seldom got an answer, till one morning the gate was opened, and who should come in but poor old Ginger! The man slipped off her halter and left her there. With a joyful whinny I trotted up to her; we were both glad to meet, but I soon found that it was not for our pleasure that she was brought to be with me. Her story would be too long to tell, but the end of it was that she had been ruined by hard riding, and was now turned off to see what rest would do.

Lord George was young and would take no warning. He was a hard rider, and would hunt whenever he could get a chance, quite careless of his horse. Soon after I left the stable there was a steeplechase, and he determined to ride. Though the groom told him the mare was a little strained, and was not fit for the race, he did not believe it, and on the day of the race he urged Ginger to keep up with the foremost riders. With her high spirit, she strained herself to the utmost and came in with the first three horses; but her wind was touched, besides which, he was too heavy for her, and her back was strained.

'And so,' she said, 'here we are, ruined in the prime of our youth and strength—you by a drunkard, and I by a fool; it is very hard.'

We both felt in ourselves that we were not what we had been. However that did not spoil the pleasure we had in each other's company. We did not gallop about as we once did, but we used to feed and lie down together, and stand for hours under one of the shady lime-trees with our heads close to each other; and so we passed our time till the family returned from town.

One day we saw the Earl come into the meadow, and York was with him. Seeing who it was, we stood still under our lime-tree, and let them come up to us. They examined us carefully. The Earl seemed much annoyed.

'There is three hundred pounds flung away for no earthly use,' said he; 'but what I care most for is, that these horses of my old friend, who thought they would find a good home with me, are ruined. The mare shall have a twelve-months' run, and we shall see what that will do for her; but the black one must be sold; 'tis a great pity, but I could not have knees like these in my stables.'

'No, my lord, of course not,' said York, 'but he might get a place where appearance is not of much consequence, and still be well trained. I know a man in Bath, the master of some livery stables, who often wants a good horse at a low figure; I know he looks well after his horses. The inquest cleared the horse's character, and your lordship's recommendation or mine would be sufficient warrant for him.'

'You had better write to him, York. I should be more particular about the place than the money he would fetch.'

After this they left us.

'They'll soon take you away,' said Ginger, 'and I shall lose the only friend I have, and most likely we shall never see each other again. 'Tis a hard world!'

About a week after this, Robert came into the field with a halter, which he slipped over my head and led me away. There was no leave-taking of Ginger; we neighed to each other as I was led off, and she trotted anxiously along by the hedge, calling to me as long as she could hear the sound of my feet.

Through the recommendation of York, I was bought by the master of the livery stables. I had to go by train, a new experience to me, requiring a good deal of courage the first time; but as I found the puffing, rushing, whistling, and more than all, the trembling of the horse-box in which I stood, did me no real harm, I soon took it quietly.

When I reached the end of my journey, I found myself in a tolerably comfortable stable and well attended to. These stables were not so airy and pleasant as those I had been used to. The stalls were laid on a slope instead of being level, and as my head was kept tied to the manger, I was obliged always to stand on the slope, which was very fatiguing. Men do not seem to know yet that horses can do more work if they can stand comfortably and can turn about.

However, I was well fed and well cleaned, and, on the whole, I think our master took as much care of us as he could. He kept a good many horses and carriages of different kinds, for hire. Sometimes his own men drove them; at others the horse and chaise were let to gentlemen or ladies who drove themselves.

CHAPTER 28

A JOB HORSE AND ITS DRIVERS

Hitherto I had always been driven by people who at least knew how to drive; but in this place I was to get my experience of all the different kinds of bad and ignorant driving to which we horses are subjected; for I was a 'job-horse,' and was let out to all sorts of people who wished to hire me; and as I was good-tempered and gentle, I think I was more often let out to the ignorant drivers than some of the other horses, because I could be depended upon. It would take a long time to tell of all the different styles in which I was driven, but I will mention a few of them.

First, there were the tight-rein drivers—men who seemed to think that all depended on holding the reins as hard as they could, never relaxing the pull on the horse's mouth or giving him the least liberty of movement. These are always talking about 'keeping the horse well in hand,' and 'holding a horse up,' just as if a horse was not made to hold himself up.

Some poor broken-down horses, whose mouths have been made hard and insensible by just such drivers as these, may, perhaps, find some support in it; but for a horse who can depend upon its own legs, has a tender mouth, and is easily guided, it is not only tormenting, but stupid.

Then there are the loose-rein drivers, who let the reins lie easily on our backs and their own hand rest lazily on their knees. Of course, such gentlemen have no control over a horse, if anything happens suddenly. If a horse shies, starts, or stumbles, they are nowhere, and cannot help the horse or themselves till the mischief is done.

Of course, for myself, I had no objection to it, as I was not in the habit of either starting or stumbling, and had only been used to depend on my driver for guidance and encouragement; still, one likes to feel the rein a little in going downhill, and likes to know that one's driver has not gone to sleep.

Besides, a slovenly way of driving gets a horse into bad, and often lazy, habits; and when he changes hands he has to be whipped out of them with more or less pain and trouble. Squire Gordon always kept us to our best pace and our best manners. He said that spoiling a horse and letting him get into bad habits was just as cruel as spoiling a child, and both had to suffer for it afterwards.

Moreover, these drivers are often altogether careless, and will attend to anything else rather than to their horses. I went out in the phaeton one day with one of them; he had a lady and two children behind. He flopped the reins about as we started, and, of course, gave me several unmeaning cuts with the whip, though I was fairly off. There had been a good deal of road-mending going on, and even where the stones were not freshly laid down there was a great many loose ones about. My driver was laughing and joking with the lady and the children, and talking about the country to the right and to the left; but he never thought it worth while to keep an eye on his horse, or to drive on the smoothest parts of the road; and so it easily happened that I got a stone in one of my fore feet.

Now, if Mr. Gordon or John, or, in fact, any good driver, had been there, he would have seen that something was wrong before I had gone three paces. Or, even if it had been dark, a practised hand would have felt by the rein that there was something wrong in the step, and would have got down and picked out the stone. But this man went on laughing and talking, whilst at every step the stone became more firmly wedged between my shoe and the frog of my foot. The stone was sharp on the inside and round on the outside, which, as every one knows, is the most dangerous kind that a horse can pick up, as it cuts his foot and at the same time makes him most liable to stumble and fall.

Whether the man was partly blind or only very careless, I can't say; but he drove me with that stone in my foot for a good half mile before he saw anything was wrong. By that time I was going so lame with the pain that at last he saw it, and called out, 'Well, here's a go! Why, they have sent us out with a lame horse! What a shame!

He then jerked the reins and flipped about with the whip, saying, 'Now, then, it's no use playing the old soldier with me; there's the journey to go, and it's no use turning lame and lazy.'

Just at this time a farmer came riding up on a brown cob; he lifted his hat and pulled up.

'I beg your pardon, sir,' he said, 'but I think there is something the matter with your horse; he goes very much as if he had a stone in his shoe. If you will allow me, I will look at his feet; these loose, scattered stones are very dangerous things for the horses.'

'He's a hired horse,' said the driver. 'I don't know what's the matter with him, but it's a great shame to send out a lame beast like this.'

The farmer dismounted, and, slipping his rein over his arm, at once took up my near foot.

'Bless me, there's a stone. Lame! I should think so!'

At first he tried to dislodge it with his hand, but as it was now very tightly wedged, he drew a stone-pick out of his pocket, and very carefully, and with some trouble, got it out. Then, holding it up, he said, 'there, that's the stone your horse has picked up; it is a wonder he did not fall down and break his knees into the bargain!'

'Well, to be sure!' said my driver. 'That is a queer thing; I never knew before that horses picked up stones.'

'Didn't you?' said the farmer rather contemptuously; 'but they do, though, and the best of them will do it, and can't help it sometimes on such roads as these. And if you don't want to lame your horse, you must look sharp and get them out quickly. This foot is very much bruised,' he said, setting it gently down and patting me. 'If I may advise, sir, you had better drive him gently for a while; the foot is a good deal hurt, and the lameness will not go off directly.'

Then, mounting his cob, and raising his hat to the lady, he drove off.

When he was gone, my driver began to flop the reins about and whip the harness, by which I understood that I was to go on, which of course I did, glad that the stone was gone, but still in a good deal of pain.

This was the sort of experience we job-horses often had.

Chapter 29

COCKNEYS

Then there is the steam-engine style of driving; these drivers were mostly people from towns, who never had a horse of their own, and generally travelled by rail.

They always seemed to think that a horse was something like a steam-engine only smaller. At any rate, they think that if only they pay for it, a horse is bound to go just as far, and just as fast, and with just as heavy a load, as they please. And be the roads heavy and muddy, or dry and good, be they stony or smooth, uphill or downhill, it is all the same—on, on, one must go at the same pace, with no relief and no consideration.

These people never think of getting out to walk up a steep hill. Oh, no, they have paid to ride, and ride they will. The horse? Oh, he's used to it! What were horses made for, if not to drag people uphill? Walk! A good joke, indeed! And so the whip is plied, and the rein is jerked, and often a rough, scolding voice cries out, 'Go along, you lazy beast!' And then comes another slash of the whip, when all the time we are doing our very best to get along, uncomplaining and obedient, though often sorely harassed and down-hearted.

This steam-engine style of driving wears us up faster than any other kind. I would far rather go twenty miles with a good, considerate driver than ten with some of these; it would take less out of me.

Another thing—they scarcely ever put on the drag, however steep the hill may be, and thus bad accidents sometimes happen; or if they do put it on, they often forget to take it off at the bottom of the hill; and more than once I have had to pull half-way up the next hill with one of the wheels lodged fast in the drag-shoe before my driver chose to think about it; and that is a terrible strain on a horse.

Then these cockneys, instead of starting at an easy pace as a gentleman would do, generally set off at full speed from the very stable yard; and when they want to stop, they first whip us and then pull up so suddenly that we are nearly thrown on our haunches, and our mouths are jagged with the bit; they call that pulling up with a dash! And when they turn a corner they do it as sharply as if there was no right side or wrong side of the road.

I well remember one spring evening. Rory and I had been out for the day (Rory was the horse that mostly went with me when a pair was ordered, and a good, honest fellow he was). We had our own driver, and, as he was always considerate and gentle with us, we had a very pleasant day. About twilight we were coming home at a good smart pace. Our road turned sharp to the left; but as we were close to the hedge on our own side, and there was plenty of room to pass, our driver did not pull us in. As we neared the corner I heard a horse and two wheels coming rapidly down the hill towards us. The hedge was high, and I could see nothing; but the next moment we were upon each other. Happily for me, I was on the side next the hedge. Rory was on the right side of the pole, and had not even a shaft to protect him.

The man who was driving was making straight for the corner, and when he came in sight of us he had no time to pull over to his own side. The whole shock came upon Rory. The gig shaft ran right into his chest making him stagger back with a cry that I shall never forget. The other horse was thrown upon its haunches, and one shaft broken. It turned out that it was a horse from our own stables, with the high-wheeled gig that the young men were so fond of.

The driver was one of those random, ignorant fellows, who don't even know which is their own side of the road, or, if they know, don't care. And there was poor Rory, with his flesh torn open and bleeding and the blood streaming down. They said if it had been a little more to one side, it would have killed him; and a good thing for him, poor fellow, if it had.

As it was, it was a long time before the wound healed, and then he was sold for coal carting; and what that is, up and down those steep hills, only horses know. Some of the sights I saw there, where a horse can come downhill with a heavily loaded two-wheeled cart behind him, on which no drag could be placed, make me sad even now to think of.

After Rory was disabled I often went in the carriage with a mare named Peggy, who stood in the stall next to mine. She was a strong, well-made animal, of a bright dun colour, beautifully dappled, and with a dark-brown mane and tail. There was no high-breeding about her, but she was very pretty, and remarkably sweet-tempered and willing. Still, there was an anxious look about her eye, by which I knew that she had some trouble. The first time we went out together I thought she had a very odd pace; she seemed to go partly in a trot, party in a canter—three or four paces, and then to make a little jump forward.

It was very unpleasant for any horse who pulled with her, and made me quite fidgety. When we got home, I asked her what made her go in that odd, awkward way.

'Ah,' she said in a troubled manner, 'I know my paces are very bad, but what can I do? It really is not my fault, it is just because my legs are so short. I stand nearly as high as you, but your legs are a good three inches longer above your knees than mine, and of course you can take a much longer step, and go much faster. You see, I did not make myself; I wish I could have done so, I would have had long legs then; all my troubles come from my short legs,' said Peggy, in a desponding tone.

'But how is it,' I said, 'when you are so strong and good-tempered and willing?'

'Why, you see,' said she, 'men will go so fast, and if one can't keep up to other horses, it is nothing but whip, whip, whip, all the time. And so I have had to keep up as I could, and have got into this ugly, shuffling pace. It was not always so; when I lived with my first master I always went a good regular trot, but then he was not in such a hurry. He was a young clergyman in the country, and a good, kind master he was. He had two churches a good way apart, and a great deal of work, but he never scolded or whipped me for not going fast. He was very fond of me. I only wish I was with him now; but he had to leave and go to a large town, and then I was sold to a farmer.

'Some farmers, you know, are capital masters; but I think this one was a low sort of man. He cared nothing about good horses or good driving; he only cared for going fast. I went as fast as I could, but that would not do, and he was always whipping; so I got into this way of making a spring forward to keep up. On market nights he used to stay very late at the inn, and then drive home at a gallop.

'One dark night he was galloping home as usual when all of a sudden the wheel came against some great, heavy thing in the road, and turned the gig over in a minute. He was thrown out and his arm broken, and some of his ribs, I think. At any rate, it was the end of my living with him, and I was not sorry. But you see it will be the same everywhere for me, if men *must* go so fast. I wish my legs were longer!'

Poor Peggy! I was very sorry for her, and I could not comfort her, for I knew how hard it was upon slow-paced horses to be put with fast ones; all the whipping comes to their share, and they can't help it.

She was often used in the phaeton, and was very much liked by some of the ladies, because she was so gentle; and some time after this she was sold to two ladies who drove themselves and wanted a safe, good horse.

I met her several times out in the country, going a good, steady pace, and looking as gay and contended as a horse could be. I was very glad to see her, for she deserved a good place.

Of course we sometimes came in for good driving here. I remember one morning I was put into the light gig, and taken to a house in Pulteney Street. Two gentlemen came out; the taller of them came round to my head. He looked at the bit and bridle, and just shifted the collar with his hand, to see if it fitted comfortably.

'Do you consider this horse wants a curb?' he said to the ostler.

'Well,' said the man, 'I should say he would go just as well without for he has an uncommonly good mouth, and though he has a fine spirit, he has no vice; but we generally find people like the curb.'

'I don't like it,' said the gentleman; 'be so good as to take it off, and put the rein in at the cheek. An easy mouth is a great thing on a long journey, is it not, old fellow?' he said, patting my neck.

Then he took the reins, and they both got up. I can remember now how quietly he turned me round, and then with a light feel of the rein, and a gentle drawing of the whip across my back, we were off.

I arched my neck and set off at my best pace. I found I had some one behind me who knew how a good horse ought to be driven. It seemed like old times again, and made me feel quite gay.

This gentleman took a great liking to me, and after trying me several times with the saddle, he prevailed upon my master to sell me to a friend of his who wanted a safe, pleasant horse for riding. And so it came to pass that in the summer I was sold to Mr. Barry.

Chapter 30

A THIEF

My new master was an unmarried man. He lived at Bath, and was much engaged in business. His doctor advised him to take horse exercise, and for this purpose he bought me. He hired a stable a short distance from his lodgings, and engaged a man named Filcher as groom. My master knew very little about horses, but he treated me well, and I should have had a good and easy place but for circumstances of which he was ignorant. He ordered the best hay, with plenty of oats, crushed beans, and bran, with vetches or rye grass, as the man might think needful. I heard the master give the order, so I knew there was plenty of good food, and I thought I was well off.

For a few days all went on well; I found that my groom understood his business. He kept the stable clean and airy, groomed me thoroughly, and was never otherwise than gentle. He had been an ostler in one of the great hotels in Bath. This he had given up, and now cultivated fruit and vegetables for the market; and his wife reared and fattened poultry and rabbits for sale.

After a while it seemed to me that my oats became

very short. I had the beans, but bran was mixed with them with a few oats; certainly there were not more than a quarter of the oats there should have been. In two or three weeks this began to tell upon my strength and spirits. The grass food, though very good, was not the thing without corn to keep up my condition. However, I could not complain nor make known my wants. So it went on for about two months; and I wondered my master did not see that something was the matter.

However, one afternoon he rode out into the country to see a friend of his—a gentleman farmer who lived on the road to Wells. This gentleman had a very quick eye for horses; and after he had welcomed his friend, casting his eye over me, he said:—

'It seems to me, Barry, that your horse does not look so well as he did when you first had him: has he been well?'

'Yes, I believe so,' said my master, 'but he is not nearly so lively as he was. My groom tells me that horses are always dull and weak in the autumn, and that I must expect it.'

'Autumn! fiddlestick!' said the farmer; 'why, this is only August; and with your light work and good food, he ought not to go down like this, even if it were autumn. How do you feed him?'

My master told him. The other shook his head slowly, and began to feel me over.

'I can't say who eats your corn, my dear fellow, but I am much mistaken if your horse gets it. Have you ridden very fast?'

'No, very gently.'

'Then just put your hand here,' said he, passing his hand over my neck and shoulders; 'he is as warm and damp as a horse just come up from grass. I advise you to look into your stable a little more. I hate to be suspicious, and, thank Heaven, I have no cause to be, for I can trust my men, present or absent; but there are mean scoundrels wicked enough to rob a dumb beast of his food. You must look into it.' And turning to his man who had come to take me, 'Give this horse a good feed of bruised oats, and don't stint him.'

'Dumb beasts!' yes we are; but if I could have spoken, I could have told my master where his oats went to. My groom used to come every morning about six o'clock with a little boy, who always had a covered basket with him. The boy used to go with his father into the harness-room, where the corn was kept, and I could see them, when the door stood ajar, fill a little bag with oats out of the bin, and then the boy used to be off.

Five or six mornings after this, just as the boy had left the stable, the door was pushed open and a policeman walked in, holding the child tight by the arm. Another policeman followed, and locked the door on the inside, saying, 'Show me the place where your father keeps his rabbits' food.'

The boy looked very frightened and began to cry; but there was no escape; and he led the way to the corn-bin. Here the policeman found another empty bag like that which was found full of oats in the boy's basket.

Filcher was cleaning my feet at the time, but they soon saw him and though he blustered a good deal, they walked him off to the 'lock-up,' and his boy with him. I heard afterwards that the boy was not held to be guilty, but the man was sentenced to prison for two months.

CHAPTER 31

A HUMBUG

My master was not immediately suited, but in a few days my new groom came. He was a tall, good-looking fellow enough; but if ever there was a humbug in the shape of a groom, Alfred Smirk was the man. He was very civil to me, and never used me ill; in fact, he did a great deal of stroking and patting, when his master was there to see it. To make me look smart he always brushed my mane and tail with water, and my hoofs with oil, before he brought me to the door, but as to clearing my feet, looking to my shoes, or grooming me thoroughly, he thought no more of these than if I had been a cow. He left my bit rusty, my saddle damp, and my crupper stiff.

Alfred Smirk considered himself very handsome; he spent a great deal of time before a little looking-glass in the harness-room, attending to his hair, whiskers, and necktie. When his master was speaking to him, it was always, 'Yes, sir; yes, sir,' touching his hat at every word; and every one thought he was a very nice young man, and that Mr. Barry was very fortunate to meet with him. I should say he was the laziest, most conceited fellow I ever came near.

Of course it was a great thing not to be ill-used, but then a horse wants more than that. I had a loose-box, and might have been very comfortable if he had not been too indolent to clean it out. He never took all the straw away, and the smell from what lay underneath was very bad, while the strong vapours that rose up from it made my eyes smart and inflame, and I had not the same appetite for my food.

One day my master came in and said: 'Alfred, the stable smells rather strong; should you not give that stall a good scrub, and throw down plenty of water?'

'Well, sir,' he said, touching his cap, 'I'll do so if you please, sir, but it is rather dangerous, sir, throwing down water in a horse's box; horses are very apt to take cold, sir. I should not like to do him an injury; but I'll do it if you please, sir.'

'Well,' said his master, 'I should not like him to take cold, but I don't like the smell of this stable; do you think the drains are all right?'

'Well, sir, now you mention it, I think the drain does sometimes send back a smell; there may be something wrong, sir.'

'Then send for the bricklayer and have it seen to,' said his master.

'Yes, sir, I will.'

The bricklayer came and pulled up a great many bricks, and found nothing amiss; so he put down some lime and charged the master five shillings; but the smell in my box was as bad as ever. This was not all. Standing as I did on a quantity of moist straw, my feet grew unhealthy and tender and the master used to say:—

'I don't know what is the matter with this horse, he goes very fumble-footed. I am sometimes afraid he will stumble.'

'Yes, sir,' said Alfred, 'I have noticed the same myself, when I have exercised him.'

Now the fact was that he hardly ever did exercise me, and when the master was busy, I often stood for days together without stretching my legs at all, and yet was fed just as high as if I were at hard work. This often disordered by health, and made me sometimes heavy and dull, but more often restless and feverish.

He never even gave me a meal of green meat or a bran mash, which would have cooled me, for he was altogether as ignorant as he was conceited; and then, instead of exercise or change of food, I had to take horse balls and draughts; which, beside the nuisance of having them poured down my throat, used to make me feel ill and uncomfortable.

One day my feet were so tender that, trotting over some fresh stones with my master on my back, I made two such serious stumbles that as we came down Lansdown into the city, master stopped at the farrier's and asked him to see what was the matter with me. The man took up my feet one by one and examined them; then standing up and dusting his hands one against the other, he said:—

'Your horse has got the "thrush," and badly, too; his feet are very tender; it is fortunate that he has not been down. I wonder your groom has not seen to it before. This is the sort of thing we find in foul stables where the litter is never properly cleared out. If you will send him here to-morrow I will attend to the hoof, and I will direct your man how to apply some liniment which I will give him.'

The next day I had my feet thoroughly cleansed and stuffed with tow soaked in some strong lotion, and a very unpleasant business it was.

The farrier ordered all the litter to be taken out of my box day by day, and the floor to be kept very clean. Then I was to have bran mashes, a little green meat, and not so much corn, till my feet were well again. With this treatment I soon regained my spirits, but Mr. Barry was so much disgusted at being twice deceived by his grooms that he determined to give up keeping a horse and to hire when he wanted one. I was therefore kept till my feet were quite sound, and was then sold again.

CHAPTER 32

A HORSE FAIR

No doubt a horse fair is a very amusing place to those who have nothing to lose; at any rate, there is plenty to see—long strings of young horses out of the country, fresh from the marshes; droves of shaggy little Welsh ponies, no higher than Merrylegs; hundreds of cart horses of all sorts, some of them with their long tails braided up and tied with scarlet cord; and a good many, like myself, handsome and high-bred, but fallen into the middle class through some accident or blemish, unsoundness of wind, or some other complaint.

There were some splendid animals quite in their prime and fit for anything, who were throwing out their legs and showing off their paces in high style as they were trotted out with a leading rein, the groom running by the side. But round in the background were a number of poor things, sadly broken down with hard work, their knees knuckling over, and their hind legs swinging out at every step; some were very dejected-looking old horses, with the upper lip hanging down and the ears laying back heavily, as if there was no pleasure in life and no more hope; again, some were so thin you could see all their ribs; and some had old sores on their backs and hips. These were sad sights for a horse who knows not but that he may come to the same sad state.

There was a great deal of bargaining, running up and beating down; and if a horse may speak his mind so far as he understands, I should say there were more lies told and more trickery carried on at that horse fair than a clever man could give an account of. I was put with two or three other strong, useful-looking horses, and a good many people came to look at us. The gentlemen always turned from me when they saw my broken knees, though the man who had me swore it was only a slip in the stall.

To examine me, buyers began to pull my mouth open, then to look at my eyes, next to feel all the way down my legs, and to give me a hard feel of the skin and flesh, and, lastly, to try my paces. What a difference there was in the way these things were done! Some did it in a rough, offhand way, as if one was only a piece of wood; while others would take their hands gently over one's body, with a pat now and then, as much as to say, 'By your leave.' Of course, I judged the buyers a good deal by their manners to myself.

There was one man of whom I thought that if he would buy me I should be happy. He was not a gentleman, nor yet one of the loud, flashy sort that called themselves so. He was a rather small man, but well made, and quick in all his motions. I knew in a moment by the way he handled me that he was used to horses; he spoke gently, and his grey eye had a kindly, cheery look in it. It may seem strange—but it is true all the same—that the clean, fresh smell there was about him made me take to him. There was no smell of old beer and tobacco, which I hated, but a fresh smell as if he had come out of a hay-loft. He offered twenty-three pounds for me; but that was refused, and he walked away. I looked after him, but he was gone.

A very hard-looking, loud-voiced man came next. I was dreadfully afraid he would have me; but he walked off. One or two more came who did not mean business. Then the hard-faced man came back again and offered twenty-three pounds. A very close bargain was being driven, for my salesman began to think he should not get all he asked, and must come down; but just then the grey-eyed man came back again. I could not help reaching out my head towards him. He stroked my face kindly.

'Well, old chap,' he said, 'I think we should suit each other. I'll give twenty-four for him.'

'Say twenty-five and you shall have him.'

'Twenty-four ten,' said my friend, in a very decided tone, 'and not another sixpence—yes or no?'

'Done,' said the salesman, 'and you may depend upon it there's a monstrous deal of quality in that horse, and if you want him for cab work, he's a bargain.'

The money was paid on the spot, and my new master took my halter and led me out of the fair to an inn, where he had a saddle and bridle ready. He gave me a good feed of oats, and stood by whilst I ate it, talking to himself and talking to me. Half an hour after we were on our way to London, through pleasant lanes and country roads, until we came into the great London thoroughfare, on which we travelled steadily till in the twilight we reached the great City. The gas lamps were already lighted; there were streets to the right, streets to the left, and streets crossing each other for mile upon mile. I thought we should never come to the end of them. At last, in passing through one, we came to a long cab-stand, when my rider called out in a cheery voice, 'Good-night, Governor!'

'Hallo!' cried a voice, 'have you got a good one?'

'I think so,' replied my owner.

'I wish you luck with him.'

'Thank ye, Governor'; and he rode on. We soon turned up one of the side streets, and about half-way up turned again into a very narrow one, with rather poor-looking houses on one side and what seemed to be coach-houses and stables on the other.

My owner pulled up at one of the houses and whistled. The door flew open, and a young woman, followed by a little girl and boy, ran out. There was a very lively greeting as my rider dismounted.

'Now, then, Harry, my boy, open the gates, and mother will bring us the lantern.'

The next minute they were all standing round me in a small stable yard.

'Is he gentle, father?'

'Yes, Dolly, as gentle as your own kitten, come and pat him.'

At once the little hand was patting about fearlessly all over my shoulder. How good it felt!

'Let me get him a bran mash while you rub him down,' said the mother.

'Do, Polly, it's just what he wants, and I know you've good a beautiful mash ready for me.'

'Sausage dumpling and apple turnover,' shouted the boy; this set them all laughing. I was led into a comfortable, clean-smelling stall, with plenty of dry straw, and, after a capital supper, I lay down, thinking I was going to be happy.

Chapter 33

A LONDON CAB HORSE

My new master's name was Jeremiah Barker, but as every one called him Jerry, I shall do the same. Polly, his wife, was just as good a match as a man could have. She was a plump, trim, tidy, little woman, with smooth, dark hair, dark eyes, and a merry little mouth. The boy was nearly twelve years old—a tall, frank, good-tempered lad; and little Dorothy (Dolly they called her) was her mother over again at eight years old. They were all wonderfully fond of each other; I never, before or since, knew such a happy, merry family.

Jerry had a cab of his own and two horses, which he drove and attended to himself. His other horse was a tall, white, rather large-boned animal, called Captain. He was old now, but when he was young he must have been splendid; there was still the proud way of holding his head and arching his neck; in fact, he was a high-bred, fine-mannered, noble, old horse, every inch of him.

He told me that in his early youth he went to the Crimean War, for he belonged to an officer in the cavalry, and used to lead the regiment: I will tell more of that hereafter.

The next morning, when I was well groomed, Polly and Dolly came into the yard to see me and to make friends. Harry had been helping his father since the early morning, and had stated his opinion that I should turn out 'a regular brick.' Polly brought me a slice of apple, and Dolly a piece of bread, and they made as much of me as if I had been the 'Black Beauty' of olden time. To be petted again and talked to in a gentle voice was a great treat; and I let them see as well as I could that I wished to be friendly. Polly thought I was very handsome and a great deal too good for a cab, if it was not for the broken knees.

'Of course, there's no one to tell us whose fault that was,' said Jerry, 'and as long as I don't know, I shall give him the benefit of the doubt; for a firmer, neater stepper I never rode. We'll call him "Jack," after the old one—shall we, Polly?'

'Do,' she said, 'for I like to keep a good name going.'

Captain went out in the cab all the morning. Harry came in after school to feed me and give me water. In the afternoon I was put into the cab. Jerry took as much pains to see if the collar and bridle fitted comfortably as if he had been John Manly over again. When the crupper was let out a hole or two, it all fitted well. There was no bearing rein or curb, nothing but a plain ring snaffle. What a blessing that was!

After driving through the side-street we came to the large cab-stand where Jerry had said 'Good-night.' On one side of this wide street were high houses with wonderful shop fronts, and on the other was an old church, and churchyard surrounded by iron palisades. Alongside these iron rails a number of cabs were drawn up, waiting for passengers. Bits of hay were lying about on the ground. Some of the men were standing together talking; others were sitting on their boxes, reading the newspapers; and one or two were feeding their horses with bits of hay and a drink of water. We pulled up in the rank at the back of the last cab. Two or three men came round and began to look at me and to pass their remarks.

'Very good for a funeral,' said one.

'Too smart-looking,' said another, shaking his head in a very wise way; 'you'll find out something wrong one of these fine mornings, or my name isn't Jones.'

'Well,' said Jerry pleasantly, 'I suppose I need not find it out till it finds me out, eh? and, if so, I'll keep up my spirits a little longer.'

Then came up a broad-faced man dressed in a great grey coat with great grey capes and great white buttons, a grey hat, and a blue comforter loosely tied round his neck. His hair was grey too, but he was a jolly-looking fellow, and the other men made way for him. He looked me all over, as if he had been going to buy me; and then straightening himself up, he said with a grunt, 'He's the right sort for you, Jerry; I don't care what you gave for him, he'll be worth it.' Thus my character was established on the stand.

This man's name was Grant, but he was called 'Grey Grant,' or 'Governor Grant.' He had been the longest of any of the men on that stand, and he took it upon himself to settle matters and stop disputes. He was generally a good-humoured, sensible man; but if his temper was a little out, as it was sometimes when he had drunk too much, nobody liked to come too near his fist, for he could deal a very hard blow.

The first week of my life as a cab horse was very trying; I had never been used to London, and the noise, the hurry; the crowds of horses, carts, and carriages through which I had to make my way, made me feel anxious and harassed; but I soon found that I could perfectly trust my driver, and then I made myself easy and got used to it.

Jerry was as good a driver as I had ever known; and, what was better, he took as much thought for his horses as he did for himself. He soon found out that I was willing to work and to do my best; and he never laid the whip on me unless it was to draw the end of it gently over my back when I was to go on. Generally I knew this quite well by the way in which he took up the reins; and I believe his whip was more frequently stuck up by his side than in his hand.

In a short time my master and I understood each other as well as horse and man could do. In the stable, too, he did all that he could for our comfort. The stalls were of the old-fashioned style—too much on the slope; but he had two movable bars fixed across the back of our stalls, so that at night and when we were resting he just took off our halters and put up the bars, and thus we could turn about and stand whichever way we pleased; this is a great comfort.

Jerry kept us very clean, and gave us as much change of food as he could, and always plenty of it; and not only that, but he always gave us plenty of clean, fresh water, which he allowed to stand by us both night and day, except of course when we came in warm.

Some people say that a horse ought not to drink as much as he wishes; but I know if we are allowed to drink when we want it, we drink only a little at a time, and it does us a great deal more good than swallowing it down half a bucketful at a time, as we do if we have been left without water till we are thirsty and miserable.

Some grooms will go home to their beer and leave us for hours with our dry hay and oats, with nothing to moisten them; then, of course, we gulp down too much water at once, which helps to spoil our breathing and sometimes chills our stomachs.

But the best thing that we had here was our Sundays for rest. We worked so hard during the week that I do not think we could have kept up to it but for that day's rest; besides, we then had time to enjoy each other's company. It was on these days that I learned my companion's history.

Chapter 34

AN OLD WAR HORSE

Captain had been broken in and trained for an army horse, his first owner being an officer of cavalry going out to the Crimean War. He said he quite enjoyed the training with all the other horses—trotting together, turning together to the right hand or the left, halting at the word of command, or dashing forward at full speed at the sound of the trumpet, or signal of the officer.

When young, he was a dark, dappled iron grey, and was considered very handsome. His master, a young, high-spirited gentleman, was very fond of him, and from the first treated him with the greatest care and kindness. He told me he thought the life of an army horse was very pleasant; but when it came to being sent abroad in a great ship over the sea, he almost changed his mind.

'That part of it' he said, 'was dreadful! Of course we could not walk off the land into the ship; so they were obliged to put strong straps under our bodies, and then we were lifted off our legs in spite of our struggles, and were swung through the air, over the water, to the deck of the great vessel. There we were placed in small, close stalls, and never for a long time saw the sky, or were we able to stretch our legs. The ship sometimes rolled about in high winds, and we were knocked about, and felt very ill. However, at last it came to an end, and we were hauled up, and swung over again to the land. We were very glad, and snorted and neighed for joy when we once more felt firm ground under our feet.

'We soon found that the country to which we had come was very different from our own, and that we had many hardships to endure besides the fighting; but many of the men were so fond of us that they did everything they could to make us comfortable, in spite of snow, wet, and the fact that all things were out of order.'

'But what about that fighting?' said I; 'was not that worse than anything else?'

'Well,' said he, 'I hardly know. We always liked to hear the trumpet sound, and to be called out, and were impatient to start off, though sometimes we had to stand for hours, waiting for the word of command. But when the word was given we used to spring forward as gaily and eagerly as if there were no cannon-balls, bayonets, or bullets. I believe so long as we felt our rider firm in the saddle, and his hand steady on the bridle, not one of us gave way to fear, not even when the terrible bombshells whirled through the air and burst into a thousand pieces.

'With my noble master, I went into many actions without a wound; and though I saw horses shot down with bullets, others pierced through with lances or gashed with fearful sabre-cuts, though I left them dead on the field, or dying in the agony of their wounds, I don't think I feared for myself. My master's cheery voice as he encouraged his men made me feel as if he and I could not be killed. I had such perfect trust in him, that whilst he was guiding me I was ready to charge up to the very cannon's mouth.

'I saw many brave men cut down, and many fall from their saddles mortally wounded. I have heard the cries and groans of the dying, cantered over ground slippery with blood, and frequently had to turn aside to avoid trampling on a wounded man or horse; but until one dreadful day, I had never felt terror; that day I shall never forget.'

Here old Captain paused for a while and drew a long breath; I waited, and he went on.

'It was one autumn morning, and, as usual, an hour before daybreak our cavalry had turned out ready caparisoned for the day's work, whether fighting or waiting. The men stood waiting for their horses, ready for orders. As the light increased there seemed to be some excitement among the officers; and before the day was well begun we heard the firing of the enemy's guns.

'Then one of the officers rode up and gave the word for the men to mount, and in a second every man was in his saddle, and every horse stood expecting the touch of the reins, or the pressure of his rider's heels—all animated, all eager. But still we had been trained so well, that, except by the champing of our bits, and by the restive tossing of our heads from time to time, it could not be said that we stirred.

'My dear master and I were at the head of the line, and as all sat motionless and watchful, he took a little stray lock of my mane which had turned over the wrong side, laid it over on the right and smoothed it down with his hand; then, patting my neck, he said: "We shall have a day of it today, Bayard, my beauty; but we'll do our duty as we always have done."

'That morning he stroked my neck more, I think, than he had ever done before; quietly on and on, as if he were thinking of something else. I loved to feel his hand on my neck, and arched my crest proudly and happily; but I stood very still, for I knew all his moods, and when he liked me to be quiet, and when gay.

'I cannot tell all that happened that day, but I will tell of the last charge that we made together; it was across a valley right in front of the enemy's cannon. By this time we were well used to the roar of heavy guns, the rattle of musket fire, and the firing of shot near us; but never had I been under such a fire as we rode through that day. From right, left, and front, shot and shell poured in upon us. Many a brave man went down, many a horse fell, flinging his rider to the earth; many a horse without a rider ran wildly out of the ranks; then, terrified at being alone with no hand to guide him, came pressing in amongst his old companions, to gallop with them to the charge.

'Fearful as it was, no one stopped, no one turned back. Every moment the ranks were thinned, but as our comrades fell we closed in to keep the others together; and instead of being shaken or staggered in our pace, our gallop became faster and faster as we neared the cannon, all clouded in white smoke, while the red fire flashed through it.

'My master, my dear master, was cheering on his comrades, with his right arm raised on high, when one of the balls, whizzing close to my head, struck him. I felt him stagger with the shock, though he uttered no cry. I tried to check my speed, but the sword dropped from his right hand, the rein fell loose from the left, and sinking backward from the saddle, he fell to the earth; the other riders swept past us, and by the force of their charge I was driven from the spot where he fell.

'I wanted to keep my place at his side, and not to leave him under that rush of horses' feet, but it was in vain. And now, without a master or a friend, I was alone on that great slaughter-ground. Then fear took hold of me, and I trembled as I had never trembled before. Then I, too, as I had seen others do, tried to join in the ranks and to gallop with them; but I was beaten off by the swords of the soldiers.

'Just then, a soldier whose horse had been killed under him caught at my bridle and mounted me, and with this new master I was again going forward. But our gallant company was cruelly overpowered, and those who remained alive after the fierce fight for the guns came galloping back over the same ground.

'Some of the horses had been so badly wounded that they could scarcely move from loss of blood; other noble creatures were trying on three legs to drag themselves along; and others were struggling to rise on their fore feet when their hind legs had been shattered by shot. Their groans were piteous to hear, and the beseeching look in their eyes as those who escaped passed by and left them to their fate I shall never forget. After the battle, the wounded men were brought in, and the dead were buried.'

'And what about the wounded horses?' I said; 'were they left to die?'

'No, the army farriers went over the field with their

pistols, and shot all that were ruined. Some that had only slight wounds were brought back and attended to, but the greater part of the noble, willing creatures that went out that morning never came back! In our stables there was only about one in four that returned.

'I never saw my dear master again. I believe he fell dead from the saddle. Never did I love any other master so well. I went into many other engagements, but was only once wounded, and then not seriously; and when the war was over I came back again to England, as sound and strong as when I went out.'

I said, 'I have heard people talk about war as if it was a very fine thing.'

'Ah!' said he, 'I should think they have never seen it. No doubt it is very fine when there is no enemy, only just exercise, parade, and sham-fights. Yes, it is very fine then, but when thousands of good, brave men and horses are killed or crippled for life, then it has a very different look.'

'Do you know what they fought about?' said I.

'No,' he said, 'that is more than a horse can understand; but the enemy must have been awfully wicked people if it was right to go all that way over the sea on purpose to kill them.'

Chapter 35

JERRY BARKER

I never knew a better man than my new master—kind and good, as strong for the right as John Manly, and so good-tempered and merry that very few people could pick a quarrel with him. He was very fond of making little songs, which he would sing to himself. His favourite was this:—

'Come, father and mother,
And sister and brother,
Come, all of you, turn to
And help one another.'

And so they did; Harry was as clever at stablework as a much older boy, and always wanted to do what he could. Then Polly and Dolly used to come in the morning to help with the cab—to brush and beat the cushions and rub the glass, while Jerry was giving us a cleaning in the yard and Harry was cleaning the harness. There used to be a great deal of laughing and fun between them, and it put Captain and me in much better spirits than if we had heard scolding and hard words. They were always early in the morning, for Jerry would say:—

'If you in the morning
Throw minutes away,
You can't pick them up
In the course of the day.

You may hurry and skurry,
And flurry and worry,
You've lost them for ever,
For ever and aye.'

He could not bear any careless loitering and waste of time; and nothing was so near making him angry as to find people who were always late wanting a cab horse to be driven hard to make up for their idleness.

One day two wild-looking young men came out of a tavern close by the stand, and called Jerry.

'Here, cabby! look sharp, we are rather late; put on the steam will you, and take us to Victoria in time for the one o'clock train. You shall have a shilling extra.'

'I will take you at the regular pace, gentlemen; shillings don't pay for putting on the steam like that.'

Larry's cab was standing next to ours. He flung open the door and said, 'I'm your man, gentlemen! Take my cab, my horse will get you there all right;' and as he shut them in, with a wink towards Jerry, he said, 'It's against his conscience to go beyond a jog-trot.' Then, slashing his jaded horse, he set off as hard as he could. Jerry patted me on the neck—'No, Jack, a shilling would not pay for that sort of thing, would it, old boy?'

Although Jerry was steadfastly set against hard driving to please careless people, he always went at a good fair pace, and was not against putting on the steam, as he said, if only he knew *why*.

I well remember one morning, as we were on the stand waiting for a fare, that a young man carrying a heavy portmanteau trod on a piece of orange-peel which lay on the pavement and fell down with great force.

Jerry was the first to run and lift him up. He seemed much stunned, and as they had led him into a shop, he walked as if he were in great pain. Jerry, of course, came back to the stand, but in about ten minutes one of the shopmen called him, so he drew up to the pavement.

'Can you take me to the South-Eastern Railway?' said the young man. 'This unlucky fall has made me late, I fear; but it is of great importance that I should not lose the twelve o'clock train. I should be most thankful if you could get me there in time, and will gladly pay you an extra fare.'

'I'll do my very best,' said Jerry heartily, 'if you think

you are well enough, sir,' for he looked dreadfully white and ill.

'I *must* go,' he said earnestly. 'Please open the door, and let us lose no time.'

The next minute Jerry was on the box. He gave a cheery chirrup to me, and a twitch to the rein, that I well understood.

'Now then, Jack, my boy,' said he, 'spin along; we'll show them how we can get over the ground if we only know why.'

Jerry and I were used to the thickest traffic, and no one could beat us at getting through when we were set on it. I was quick and bold, and could always trust my driver; Jerry was quick and patient at the same time, and could trust his horse, which was a great thing too. He very seldom used the whip; I knew by his voice and his click, click, when he wanted to get on fast, and the rein told me where I was to go, so there was no need for whipping.

The streets were very full that day, but we got on pretty well as far as the bottom of Cheapside where there was a block for three or four minutes. The young man put his head out and said anxiously: 'I think I had better get out and walk; I shall never get there if this goes on.'

'I'll do all that can be done, sir,' said Jerry. 'I think we shall be in time; this block-up cannot last much longer, and your luggage is very heavy for you to carry, sir.'

Just then the cart in front of us began to move on, and then we had a good turn. In and out, in and out we went, as fast as horseflesh could do it, and for a wonder, we had a good clear time on London Bridge, for there was a whole train of cabs and carriages all going our way at a quick trot—perhaps wanting to catch that very train. At any rate, with many others, we whirled into the station just as the great clock pointed to eight minutes to twelve.

'Thank God! we are in time,' said the young man; 'and thank you, too, my friend, and your good horse. You have saved me more than money can ever pay for; take this extra half-crown.'

'No, sir, no, thank you all the same. So glad we hit the time, sir; but don't stay now, sir, the bell is ringing. Here, porter! take this gentleman's luggage—Dover line—twelve o'clock train—that's it;' and without waiting for another word, Jerry wheeled me round to make room for other cabs that were dashing up at the last minute, and drew up on one side till the crush was past.

'So glad!' he said, 'so glad! poor young fellow! I wonder what it was that made him so anxious.'

Jerry often talked to himself quite loud enough for me to hear when we were not moving.

On Jerry's return to the rank there was a good deal of laughing and chaffing at him for driving hard to the train for an extra fare, as they said, all against his principles; and they wanted to know how much he had pocketed.

'A good deal more than I generally get,' said he, nodding slyly; 'what he gave me will keep me in little comforts for several days.'

'Gammon!' said one.

'He's a humbug,' said another, 'preaching to us, and then doing the same himself.'

'Look here, mates,' said Jerry. 'The gentleman offered me half a crown extra, but I didn't take it; 'twas quite pay enough for me to see how glad he was to catch that train; and if Jack and I chose to have a quick run now and then to please ourselves, that's our business and not yours.'

'Well,' said Larry, '*you'll* never be a rich man.'

'Most likely not,' said Jerry, 'but I don't know that I shall be the less happy for that. I have heard the commandments read a great many times, and I never noticed that any of them said, "Thou shalt be rich"; and there are a good many curious things said in the New

Testament about rich men that, I think, would make me feel rather queer if I was one of them.'

'If you ever do get rich,' said Governor Grant, looking over his shoulder across the top of his cab, 'you'll deserve it, Jerry, and you won't find a curse come with your wealth. As for you, Larry, you'll die poor, you spend too much in whipcord.'

'Well,' said Larry, 'what is a fellow to do if his horse won't go without it?'

'You never take the trouble to see if he will go without it; your whip is always going as if you had the St. Vitus's dance in your arm; and if it does not wear you out, it wears your horse out. You know you are always changing your horses, and why? because you never given them any peace or encouragement.'

'Well, I have not had good luck,' said Larry, 'that's where it is.'

'And you never will,' said the Governor. 'Good Luck is rather particular with whom she rides, and mostly prefers those who have common sense and a good heart; at least, that is my experience.'

Governor Grant turned round again to his newspaper, and the other men went to their cabs.

CHAPTER 36

THE SUNDAY CAB

One morning, as Jerry had just put me into the shafts and was fastening the traces, a gentleman walked into the yard. 'Your servant, sir,' said Jerry.

'Good-morning, Mr. Barker,' said the gentleman. 'I should be glad to make some arrangements with you for taking Mrs. Briggs regularly to church on Sunday mornings. We go to the New Church now, and that is rather farther than she can walk.'

'Thank you, sir,' said Jerry, 'but I have only taken out a six days' licence,* and therefore I could not take a fare on a Sunday, it would not be legal.'

'Oh!' said the other, 'I did not know yours was a six days' cab; but of course it would be very easy to alter your licence. I would see that you did not lose by it; the fact is, Mrs. Briggs very much prefers you to drive her.'

'I should be glad to oblige the lady, sir, but I had a seven days' licence once, and the work was too hard for me and too hard for my horses. Year in and year out, not a day's rest, never a Sunday with my wife and children, and never able to go to a place of worship, which I had always been used to do before I took to the driving-box; so for the last five years I have taken only a six days' licence, and I find it better all the way round.'

'Well, of course,' replied Mr. Briggs, 'it is very proper that every person should have rest and be able to go to church on Sundays, but I should have thought you would not have minded such a short distance for the horse, and only once a day; you would have all the afternoon and evening for yourself, and we are very good customers, you know.'

'Yes, sir, that is true, and I'm grateful for all favours, I am sure, and anything that I could do to oblige you or the lady, I should be proud and happy to do, but I can't give up my Sundays, sir, indeed I can't. I read that God made man, and He made horses and all the other beasts; and as soon as He made them, He made a rest day, and

*Some years since the annual charge for a cab licence was very much reduced, and the difference between the six and seven days cabs was abolished.

bade that all should rest one day in seven. I think sir, He must have known what was good for them, and I am sure it is good for me. I am stronger and healthier all together now that I have a day of rest; the horses are fresh too, and do not wear up nearly so fast. The six-day drivers all tell me the same, and I have laid more money in the Savings' Bank than ever I did before; and as for my wife and children, sir—why, heart alive! they would not go back to the seven days' work for all they could get by it.'

'Oh, very well,' said the gentleman. 'Don't trouble yourself, Mr. Barker, any further; I will inquire somewhere else;' and he walked away.

'Well,' says Jerry to me, 'we can't help it, Jack, old boy, we must have our Sundays.'

Three weeks had passed away after this conversation, and no order had come from Mrs. Briggs; so there was nothing but taking jobs from the stand. Jerry took it to heart a good deal, for of course the work was harder for horse and man. But Polly would always cheer him up and say, 'Never mind, father, never mind—

Do your best,
And leave the rest,
'Twill all come right
Some day or night.'

It soon became known that Jerry had lost his best customer, and for what reason; most of the men said he was a fool, but two or three took his part.

'If working men don't stick to their Sunday,' said Truman, 'they'll soon have none left; it is every man's right, and every beast's right. By God's law we have a day of rest, and by the law of England we have a day of rest, and I say we ought to hold to the rights these laws give us, and keep them for our children.'

'All very well for you religious chaps to talk so,' said Larry, 'but I'll turn a shilling when I can. I don't believe in religion, for I don't see that your religious people are any better than the rest.'

'If they are not better,' put in Jerry, 'it is because they are not religious. You might as well say that our country's laws are not good because some people break them. If a man gives way to temper, and speaks evil of his neighbour, and does not pay his debts, he is *not* religious; I don't care how much he goes to church. If some men are shams and humbugs, that does not make religion untrue. Real religion is the best and the truest thing in the world, and the only thing that can make a man really happy, or make the world any better.'

'If religion was good for anything,' said Jones, 'it would prevent your religious people from making us work on Sundays, as you know many of them do, and that's why I say religion is nothing but a sham—why, if it was not for the church-and-chapel-goers it would be hardly worth while our coming out on a Sunday; but they have their privileges, as they call them, and I go without. I shall expect them to answer for my soul, if I can't get a chance of saving it.'

Several of the men applauded this, till Jerry said:—

'That may sound well enough, but it won't do; every man must look after his own soul; you can't lay it down at another man's door like a foundling, and expect him to take care of it; and don't you see, if you are always sitting on your box, waiting for a fare, they will say, "If we don't take him, some one else will, and he does not look for any Sunday." Of course they don't go to the bottom of it, or they would see if they never came for a cab, it would be no use your standing there; but people don't always like to go to the bottom of things; it may not be convenient to do it: but if you Sunday drivers would all strike for a day of rest, the thing would be done.'

'And what would all the good people do if they could not get to their favourite preachers?' said Larry.

'Tis not for me to lay down plans for other people,' said Jerry, 'but if they can't walk so far, they can go to what is nearer; and if it should rain they can put on their mackintoshes as they do on a weekday. If a thing is right, it *can* be done, and if it is wrong, it *can be done without*; and a good man will find a way; and that is as true for us cabmen as it is for the churchgoers.'

Chapter 37

THE GOLDEN RULE

Two or three weeks after this, as we came into the yard rather late in the evening, Polly came running across the road with the lantern (she always brought it to him if it was not very wet).

'It has all come right, Jerry; Mrs. Briggs sent her servant this afternoon to ask you to take her out tomorrow at eleven o'clock. I said, yes, I thought you could, but we supposed she employed someone else now.

'"Well," says he, "the real fact is, master was put out because Mr. Barker refused to come out on Sundays, and he has been trying other cabs, but there's something wrong with them all; some drive too fast, and some too slow; and the mistress says there is not a cab so nice and clean as yours; so nothing will suit her but Mr. Barker's cab again."'

Polly was almost out of breath, and Jerry broke out into a merry laugh:—

'All will come right
Some day or night.

You were right, my dear; you generally are. Run in and get the supper, and I'll have Jack's harness off and make him snug and happy in no time.'

After this Mrs. Briggs wanted Jerry's cab quite as often as before; never, however, on a Sunday. But there came a day when we had Sunday work, and this was how it happened.

We had all come home on the Saturday night very tired, and very glad to think that the next day would be all rest; but it was not to be so.

On Sunday morning Jerry was cleaning me in the yard, when Polly stepped up to him, looking very full of something.

'What is it?' said Jerry.

'Well, my dear,' she said, 'poor Dinah Brown has just received a letter to say that her mother is dangerously ill, and that she must go directly if she wishes to see her alive. The place is more than ten miles away from here, right out in the country; and she says if she took the train she should still have four miles to walk; and so weak as she is, and the baby only four weeks old, of course that would be impossible. She wants to know if you would take her in your cab, and she promises to pay you faithfully as soon as she can get the money.'

'Tut, tut, we'll see about that. It was not the money I was thinking about, but of losing our Sunday; the horses are tired, and I am tired too—that's where it pinches.'

'It pinches all round, for that matter,' said Polly, 'for

it's only half Sunday without you. But you know we should do to other people as we would like them to do to us. I know very well what I should like if my mother was dying; and Jerry, dear, I am sure it won't break the Sabbath; for if pulling a poor beast or donkey out of a pit would not spoil the Sabbath, I am quite sure taking poor Dinah would not.'

'Why, Polly, you are as good as the minister; so, as I've had my Sunday morning sermon early to-day, you may go and tell Dinah that I'll be ready for her as the clock strikes ten. But stop—just step round to Butcher Braydon's, with my compliments, and ask him if he would lend me his light trap; I know he never uses it on the Sunday, and it would make a wonderful difference to the horse.'

Away she went, and soon returned, saying that he could have the trap and welcome.

'All right,' said he; 'now put me up a bit of bread and cheese, and I'll be back in the afternoon as soon as I can.'

'And I'll have the meat pie ready for an early tea instead of for dinner,' said Polly. And away she went, whilst he made his preparations to the tune of 'Polly, the woman and no mistake,' of which tune he was very fond.

I was selected for the journey, and at ten o'clock we started in a light, high-wheeled gig, which ran so easily that, after the four-wheeled cab, it seemed like nothing.

It was a fine May day, and soon as we were out of the town the sweet air, the smell of the fresh grass, and the soft country roads were as pleasant as they used to be in the old times, and I soon began to feel quite fresh.

Dinah's family lived in a small farmhouse up a green lane, close by a meadow with some fine shady trees; there were two cows feeding in it. A young man asked Jerry to bring his trap into the meadow, and he would tie me up in the cowshed; he wished he had a better stable to offer.

'If your cows would not be offended,' said Jerry, 'there is nothing my horse would like so well as to have an hour or two in your beautiful meadow. He's quiet, and it would be a rare treat for him.'

'Put him there and welcome,' said the young man. 'The best we have is at your service for your kindness to my sister; we shall be having some dinner in an hour, and I hope you'll come in, though with mother so ill we are all out of sorts in the house.'

Jerry thanked him kindly, but said as he had some dinner with him, there was nothing he should like so well as walking about in the meadow.

When my harness was taken off, I did not know what I should do first—roll over on my back, lie down and rest, or have a gallop across the meadow out of sheer spirits at being free; so I did all by turns. Jerry seemed to be quite as happy as I was. He sat down by a bank under a shady tree, and listened to the birds; then he sang to himself, and read out of the little brown book he is so fond of; next he wandered round the meadow and down by a little brook, where he picked the flowers and the hawthorn, and tied them up with long sprays of ivy; lastly he gave me a good feed of oats which he had brought with him. But the time seemed all too short—I had not been in a field since I left poor Ginger at Earlshall.

We came home at a gentle pace, and Jerry's first words were as we came into the yard, 'Well, Polly, I have not lost my Sunday after all, for the birds were singing hymns in every bush, and I joined in the service; and as for Jack, he was like a young colt.'

When he handed Dolly the flowers she jumped for joy.

CHAPTER 38

DOLLY AND A REAL GENTLEMAN

The winter came in early with a great deal of cold and wet. There was snow, sleet, or rain almost every day for weeks, changing only to keen, driving winds or sharp frosts. We all felt it very much. When it is a dry cold, a couple of good thick rugs will keep the warmth in us; but when it is a soaking rain, they soon get wet through and are no good. Some of the drivers had a waterproof cover to throw over us; this was a fine thing.

But some of the men were so poor that they could not protect either themselves or their horses, and many of them suffered very much that winter. When we horses had worked half the day we went to our dry stables, and could rest; whilst the drivers had to sit on their boxes, sometimes staying out as late as one or two o'clock in the morning if they had to wait for a party.

When the streets were slippery with frost or snow, that was the worst of all for us horses; one mile of such travelling, with a weight to draw and no firm footing, would take more out of us than four on a good road. Every nerve and muscle of our body is on the strain to keep our balance; and added to this, the fear of falling is more exhausting than anything else. If the roads are very bad indeed, our shoes are roughed, but this makes us feel nervous at first.

When the weather was very bad, many of the men would go and sit in the tavern close by, and get someone to watch for them; but they often lost a fare in this way, and could not, as Jerry said, be there without spending money.

He never went to the 'Rising Sun.' There was a coffee-shop near where he now and then went; or he bought off an old man who came to our rank with tins of hot coffee and pies. It was Jerry's opinion that spirits and beer made a man colder afterwards, and that dry clothes, good food, cheerfulness, and a comfortable wife at home were the best things to keep a cabman warm.

Polly always supplied him with something to eat when he could not get home, and sometimes he would see little Dolly peeping from the corner of the street, to make sure if 'Father' was on the stand. If she saw him, she would run off at full speed and soon come back with something in a tin or basket—some hot soup or pudding that Polly had ready.

It was wonderful how such a little thing could get safely across the street, often thronged with horses and carriages; but she was a brave little maid; and felt it quite an honour to bring 'Father's first course,' as he called it. She was a general favourite on the stand, and there was not a man who would not have seen her safely across the street, if Jerry had not been able to do so.

One cold, windy day, Dolly had brought Jerry a basin of something hot, and was standing by him whilst he ate it. He had scarcely begun when a gentleman walking towards us very quickly held up his umbrella. Jerry touched his hat in return, gave the basin to Dolly, and was taking off my cloth, when the gentleman, hastening up, cried out, 'No, no, finish your soup, my friend; I have not much time to spare, but I can wait till you have done, and have set your little girl safely on the pavement.' So saying, he seated himelf in the cab. Jerry thanked him kindly, and came back to Dolly.

'There, Dolly, that's a gentleman; that's a real gentleman, Dolly; he has both time and thought for the comfort of a poor cabman and a little girl.'

Jerry finished his soup, saw the child safely across the road, and then took his orders to drive to Clapham Rise. Several times after this the same gentleman took our cab. I think he was very fond of dogs and horses, for whenever we took him to his own door, two or three dogs would come bounding out to meet him. Sometimes he came round and patted me, saying in his quiet, pleasant way, 'This horse has a good master, and he deserves it.'

It was a very rare thing for any one to notice the horse that had been working for him. I have known ladies do it now and then, and this gentleman and one or two others had given me a pat and a kind word; but ninety-nine out of a hundred would as soon think of patting the steam-engine that drew the train.

This gentleman was not young, and there was a forward stoop in his shoulders, as if he was always going at something. His lips were thin and close shut, though they had a very pleasant smile; his eye was keen, and there was something in his jaw and motion of his head that made one think he was very determined in anything he set about doing. His voice was pleasant and kind; any horse would trust that voice, though it was just as decided as everything else about him.

One day, he and another gentleman took our cab. They stopped at a shop in R— Street, and whilst his friend went in he stood at the door. A little ahead of us, on the other side of the street, a cart with two very fine horses was standing before some wine-vaults; the carter was not with them, and I cannot tell how long they had been standing but they seemed to think they had waited long enough, and began to move off. Before they had gone many paces, the carter came running out and caught them. He seemed furious at their having moved, and with whip and rein punished them brutally, even beating them about the head.

Our gentleman saw it all, and stepping quickly across the street, said in a decided voice, 'If you don't stop that directly, I'll have you summoned for leaving your horses and for brutal conduct.'

The man, who had clearly been drinking, poured forth some abusive language, but he left off knocking the horses about, and taking the reins, got into his cart. Meanwhile our friend had quietly taken a note book from his pocket, and looking at the name and address painted on the cart, he wrote something down.

'What do you want with that?' growled the carter, as he cracked his whip and was moving on. A nod and a grim smile was the only answer he got.

On returning to the cab, our friend was joined by his companion, who said laughingly, 'I should have thought, Wright, you had enough business of your own to look after without troubling yourself about other people's horses and servants.'

Our friend stood still for a moment, and throwing his head a little back, said, 'Do you know why this world is as bad as it is?'

'No,' said the other.

'Then I'll tell you. It is because people think *only* about their own business, and won't trouble themselves to stand up for the oppressed, nor bring the wrongdoer to light. I never see a wicked thing like this without doing what I can, and many a master has thanked me for letting him know how his horses have been used.'

'I wish there were more gentlemen like you, sir,' said Jerry, 'for they are wanted badly enough in this city.'

After this we continued our journey, and as they got out of the cab our friend was saying, 'My doctrine is this, that if we see cruelty or wrong that we have the power to stop, and yet do nothing, we make ourselves sharers in the guilt.'

Chapter 39

SEEDY SAM

I should say that for a cab-horse I was very well off indeed; my driver was my owner, and it was his interest to treat me well and not to overwork me, even had he not been so good a man as he was; but there were a great many horses which belonged to the large cab-owners, who let them out to their drivers for so much money a day. As the horses did not belong to these men, the only thing they thought of was how to get their money out of the horses, first to pay their master, and then to provide their own living; and a dreadful time some of these horses had of it. Of course I understood but little, but it was often talked over on the stand, and the Governor, who was a kind-hearted man and fond of horses, would sometimes speak his mind if a horse came in very much jaded or ill-used.

One day a shabby, miserable-looking driver, who went by the name of 'Seedy Sam,' brought in his horse looking dreadfully beat, and the Governor said, 'You and your horse look more fit for the police-station than for this rank.'

The man flung his tattered rug over the horse, turned full round upon the Governor, and said, in a voice that sounded almost desperate:—

'If the police have any business with the matter, it ought to be the masters who charge us so much, or with the fares that are fixed so low. If a man has to pay eighteen shillings a day for the use of a cab and two horses, as many of us have to do in the season, and must make that up before he earns a penny for himself—I say, 'tis more than hard work. Nine shillings a day to get out of each horse before you begin to get your own living! You know that's true, and if the horses don't work we must starve.

'My children and I have known what that is before now. I've six of 'em, and only one earns anything. I am on the stand fourteen or sixteen hours a day, and I haven't had a Sunday these ten or twelve weeks. You know, Skinner never gives a day if he can help it; and if I don't work hard, tell me who does! I want a warm coat and a mackintosh, but with so many to feed, how can a man get it? I had to pledge my clock a week ago to pay Skinner, and I shall never see it again.'

Some of the other drivers stood round nodding their heads, and saying he was right. The man went on: 'You that have your own horses and cabs, or drive for good masters, have a chance of getting on, and a chance of doing right, I haven't. Within the four-mile radius we can't charge more than sixpence a mile after the first mile.

'This very morning I had to go a clear six miles and took only three shillings. I could not get a return fare, and had to come half the way back; there's twelve miles for the horse and three shillings for me.

'After that I had a three-mile fare, and there were bags and boxes enough to have brought in a good many tuppences if they had been put outside. But you know how people do—all that could be piled up inside on the front seat were put in, and three heavy boxes went on the top—that was sixpence, and the fare one and sixpence. Then I got a return for a shilling; now that makes eighteen miles for the horse and six shillings for me. There's three shillings still for that horse to earn, and nine shillings for the afternoon horse before I touch a penny.

'Of course it is not always as bad as that, but you know it often is; and I say 'tis mockery to tell a man that he must not overwork his horse, for when a beast is downright tired, there's nothing but the whip that will keep his legs going—you can't help yourself. You must put your wife and children before the horse; the masters must look to that, we can't. I don't ill-use my horse for the sake of doing so; none of you can say I do.

'There's wrong lying somewhere—never a day's rest, never a quiet hour with the wife and children. I often feel like an old man, though I'm only forty-five. You know how quick some of the gentry are to suspect us of cheating and overcharging. Why, they stand with their purses in their hands, counting the fare over to a penny, and looking at us as if we were pickpockets. I wish some of 'em had got to sit on my box sixteen hours a day, and had to get a living out of it and eighteen shillings besides, and to do it in all weathers; they would not then be so uncommonly particular never to give us a sixpence over, nor would they then cram all the luggage inside. Of course, some of 'em tip us pretty handsomely now and then, or else we could not live; but we can't *depend* upon that.'

The men who stood round much approved of this speech. One of them said, 'It is desperate hard, and if a man sometimes does what is wrong, it is no wonder; and if he gets a dram too much, who's to blow him up?'

Jerry had taken no part in this conversation, but I never saw his face look so sad before. The Governor had stood with both his hands in his pockets; now he took his handkerchief out of his hat, and wiped his forehead.

'You've beaten me, Sam,' he said, 'for it's all true, and I won't cast it up against you any more about the police. It was the look in that horse's eye that came over me. It is hard lines for both man and beast, and who's to mend it, I don't know; but anyway you might tell the poor beast that you were sorry to take it out of him in that way. Sometimes a kind word is all we can give 'em, poor brutes, and 'tis wonderful what they understand.'

A few mornings after this talk a new man came on the stand with Sam's cab.

'Halloo!' said one, 'what's up with Seedy Sam?'

'He's ill in bed,' said the man; 'he was taken ill last night in the yard, and could scarcely crawl home. His wife sent a boy this morning to say his father was in a high fever and could not get out so I'm here instead.'

The next morning the same man came again.

'How is Sam?' inquired the Governor.

'He's gone,' said the man.

'What! gone? You don't mean to say he's dead?'

'Just snuffed out,' said the other; 'he died at four o'clock this morning. All yesterday he was raving—raving about Skinner and about having no Sundays. "I never had a Sunday's rest," these were his last words.'

No one spoke for a while, and then the Governor said, 'I tell you what, mates, this is a warning to us all.'

Chapter 40

POOR GINGER

One day, whilst our cab and many others were waiting outside one of the parks where a band was playing, a shabby old cab drove up besides ours. The horse was an old worn-out chestnut with an ill-kept coat, and with bones that showed plainly through it. The knees buckled over, and the forelegs were very unsteady.

I had been eating some hay, and the wind rolling a little lock of it that way, the poor creature put out her long, thin neck and picked it up, and then turned round and looked about for more. There was a hopeless look in the dull eye that I could not help noticing; and then, as I was thinking where I had seen that horse before, she looked full at me and said, 'Black Beauty, is that you?'

It was Ginger! but how changed! The beautifully arched and glossy neck was now straight, lank, and fallen in; the clean, straight legs and delicate fetlocks were swollen; the joints were grown out of shape and hard work; the face that was once so full of spirit and life was now full of suffering; and I could tell by the heaving of her sides and by her frequent cough how bad her breath was.

Our drivers were standing together a little way off, so I sidled up to her a step or two that we might have a little quiet talk. It was a sad tale that she had to tell.

After a twelve-months' run off at Earlshall, she was considered to be fit for work again, and was sold to a gentleman. For a little while she got on very well, but after a longer gallop than usual, the old strain returned, and, after being rested and doctored, she was again sold. In this way she changed hands several times, but always getting lower down.

'And so at last,' said she, 'I was bought by a man who keeps a number of cabs and horses, and lets them out. You look well off, and I'm glad of it; but I cannot tell you what my life has been. When they found out my weakness, they said I was not worth what they gave for me, and that I must go into one of the low cabs and just be used up; that is what they are doing—whipping and working me, with never one thought of what I suffer. They paid for me, and must get the money out of me, they say. The man who hires me now pays a deal of money to the dealer every day, and so he has to get it out of me first; and so it goes on all the weeks round, with never a Sunday rest.'

'I said, 'You used to stand up for yourself if you were ill-used.'

'Ah!' she said, 'I did once, but it's no use; men are stronger, and if they are cruel and have no feeling, there is nothing that we can do but just bear it—bear it on and on to the end. I wish the end was come; I wish I was dead. I have seen dead horses and I am sure they do not suffer pain; I hope I may drop down dead at my work, and not be sent off to the knacker's.'

I was very much troubled, and I put my nose up to hers, but I could say nothing to comfort her. I think she was pleased to see me, for she said, 'You are the only friend I ever had.'

Just then her driver came up, and with a tug at her mouth backed her out of the line and drove off, leaving me very sad indeed.

A short time after this a cart with a dead horse in it passed our cab-stand. The head hung out of the cart tail, the lifeless tongue was slowly dropping blood; and the sunken eyes!—but I can't speak of them, the sight was too dreadful. It was a chestnut horse with a long, thin neck. I saw a white streak down the forehead. I believe it was Ginger; I hoped it was, for then her troubles would be over. Oh! if men were more merciful they would shoot us before we come to such misery.

Chapter 41

THE BUTCHER

I saw a great deal of trouble amongst the horses in London, much of which might have been prevented by a little common sense. We horses do not mind hard work if we are treated reasonably; and I am sure there are many driven by quite poor men who have a happier life than I had when, with my silver-mounted harness, I used to go in the Countess of W—'s carriage.

It often went to my heart to see how badly the little ponies were used—straining along with heavy loads, or staggering under heavy blows from some low, cruel boy. Once I saw a little grey pony with a thick mane and a pretty head, and so much like Merrylegs that if I had not been in harness I should have neighed to him. He was doing his best to pull a heavy cart, while a strong rough boy was cutting him under the belly with his whip, and chucking cruelly at his little mouth.

Could it be Merrylegs? It was just like him; but then Mr. Blomefield was never to sell him, and I do not think he would have done so. Yet this may have been quite as good a little fellow, and have had as happy a place when he was young.

I often noticed the great speed at which butchers' horses were made to go, though I did not know why they were driven so fast till one day when we had to wait some time in St. John's Wood. There was a butcher's shop next door, and as we were standing a butcher's cart came dashing up at a great pace. The horse was hot and much exhausted; he hung his head down, while his heaving sides and trembling legs showed how hard he had been driven. The lad jumped out of the cart and was getting the basket when the master came out of the shop much displeased. After looking at the horse, he turned angrily to the lad.

'How many times shall I tell you not to drive in this way? You ruined the last horse and broke his wind, and you are going to ruin this in the same way? If you were not my own son, I would dismiss you on the spot; it is a disgrace to have a horse brought to the shop in such a condition. You are liable to be taken up by the police for furious driving, and if you are, you need not look to me for bail, for I have spoken to you till I'm tired; you must look out for yourself.'

During this speech the boy had stood by, sullen and dogged; but when his father ceased, he broke out angrily, 'It wasn't my fault, and I won't take the blame: I am only going by orders all the time.

'You always say, "Now be quick; now look sharp!" And when I go to the houses, one person wants a leg of mutton for an early dinner, and I must be back with it in a quarter of an hour; another has forgotten to order the beef, and I must go and fetch it and be back in no time or the mistress will scold; the third says they have company coming unexpectedly and must have some chops sent up directly; and the lady at No. 4 in the Crescent *never* orders her dinner till the meat comes in for lunch—it's nothing but hurry, hurry, all the time. If the gentry would think of what they want, and order their meat the day before, there need not be this blow up!'

'I wish to goodness they would,' said the butcher; "twould save me a wonderful deal of harass, and I could suit my customers much better if I knew beforehand. But there—what's the use of talking? Whoever thinks of a butcher's convenience, or a butcher's horse? Now then, take him in, and look to him well. Mind, he does not go out again to-day, and if anything else is wanted, you must carry it yourself in the basket.' With that he went in and the horse was led away.

But all the boys are not cruel. I have seen some as fond of their pony or donkey as if it had been a favourite dog; and the little creatures have worked away as cheerfully and willingly for their young drivers as I work for Jerry. It may be hard work sometimes, but a friends' hand and voice make it easy.

There was a young coster-boy who came up our street with greens and potatoes. He had an old pony, not very handsome, but the most cheerful and plucky little thing I ever saw; and to see how fond those two were of each other was a treat. The pony followed his master like a dog; and when the boy got into his cart, the pony would trot off without a whip or a word and rattle down the street as merrily as if he had come out of the Queen's stables. Jerry liked the boy and called him 'Prince Charlie,' for he said he would make a king of drivers some day.

There was an old man too, who used to come up our street with a little coal cart. He wore a coal-heaver's hat, and looked rough and black. He and his old horse used to plod together along the street like two good partners who understood each other. The horse would stop of his own accord at the doors where they took coal of him. He used to keep one ear bent towards his master. The old man's cry could be heard up the street long before he came near. I never knew what he said, but the children called him 'Old Ba-a-ar Hoo,' for it sounded like that. Polly bought her coal of him, and was very friendly; and Jerry said it was a comfort to think how happy an old horse may be in a poor place.

CHAPTER 42

THE ELECTION

As we came into the yard one afternoon, Polly came out, 'Jerry! I've had Mr. B— here asking about your vote, and he wants to hire your cab for the election; he will call for an answer.'

'Well, Polly, you may say that my cab will be otherwise engaged; I should not like to have it pasted over with their great bills, and as to make Jack and Captain race about to the public-houses to bring up half-drunken voters, why, I think 'twould be an insult to the horses. No, I shan't do it.'

'I suppose you'll vote for the gentleman? He said he was of your politics.'

'So he is in some things, but I shall not vote for him, Polly; you know what his trade is?'

'Yes.'

'Well, a man who gets rich by that trade may be all very well in some ways, but he is blind to what working men want; I could not in my conscience send him up to make the laws. I daresay they'll be angry, but every man must do what he thinks to be the best for his country.'

On the morning before the election Jerry was putting me into the shafts, when Dolly came into the yard sobbing and crying, with her little blue frock and white pinafore spattered all over with mud.

'Why, Dolly, what is the matter?'

'Those naughty boys,' she sobbed, 'have thrown the dirt all over me, and called me a little raga—raga—'

'They called her a little blue ragamuffin, father,' said Harry, who ran in looking very angry; 'but I have given it to them; they won't insult my sister again. I have given them a thrashing they will remember; a set of cowardly, rascally, orange blackguards!'

Jerry kissed the child and said, 'Run in to mother, my pet, and tell her I think you had better stay at home to-day and help her.'

Then, turning gravely to Harry:—

'My boy, I hope you will always defend your sister, and give anybody who insults her a good thrashing—that is as it should be; but mind, I won't have any election blackguarding on my premises. There are as many blue blackguards as there are orange, and as many white as there are purple, or any other colour, and I won't have any of my family mixed up with it. Even women and children are ready to quarrel for the sake of a colour, and not one in ten of them know what it is about.'

'Why, father, I thought blue was for Liberty.'

'My boy, Liberty does not come from colours, they only show party, and all the liberty you can get out of them is liberty to get drunk at other people's expense, liberty to ride to the poll in a dirty old cab, liberty to abuse any one that does not wear your colour, and to shout yourself hoarse at what you only half-understand—that's your liberty!'

'Oh, father, you are laughing.'

'No, Harry, I am serious, and I am ashamed to see how men go on that ought to know better. An election is a very serious thing, at least, it ought to be, and every man ought to vote according to his conscience, and let his neighbour do the same.'

Chapter 43

A FRIEND IN NEED

It was the day of the election. Jerry would not let his cab to either party, but there was no lack of work for us.

First came a stout, puffy gentleman with a carpet-bag, who wanted to go to the Bishopsgate Station; then we were called by a party who wished to be taken to the Regent's Park; and next we were wanted in a side street, where a timid, anxious old lady was waiting to be taken to the Bank. There we had to stop to take her back again; and just as we had set her down, a red-faced gentleman with a handful of papers came running up, out of breath; and before Jerry could get down, he had opened the door, popped himself in, and called out, 'Bow Street Police Station, quick!' So off we went with him; and when after another turn or two we came back, there was no other cab on the stand. Jerry put on my nose-bag, for, as he said, 'We must eat when we can on such days as these; so munch away, Jack, and make the best of your time, old boy.'

I found I had a good feed of crushed oats, wetted with a little bran; this would be a treat any day, but was specially refreshing now. Jerry was so thoughtful and kind—what horse would not do his best for such a master? Then he took out one of Polly's meat pies, and standing near me, he began to eat it.

The streets were very full, and the cabs with the candidates' colours on them were dashing about through the crowd as if life and limb were of no consequence. We saw two people knocked down that day, and one was a woman. The horses were having a bad time of it, poor things! but the voters inside thought nothing of that, for many of them were half drunk, hurrahing out of the cab windows if their own party came by. It was the first election I had seen, and I don't want to be in another, though I have heard things are better now.

Jerry and I had not eaten many mouthfuls before a poor young woman, carrying a heavy child, came along the street. She was looking this way and that way, and seemed quite bewildered. Presently she made her way up to Jerry and asked if he could tell her the way to St. Thomas's Hospital, and how far it was to get there. She had come from the country that morning in a market cart, and did not know it was the election. She was quite a stranger in London, but had got an order for the hospital for her little boy, who was crying with a feeble, pining cry.

'Poor little fellow!' she said, 'he suffers a deal of pain. He is four years old, and can't walk any more than a baby; but the doctor said if I could get him into the hospital, he might get well. Pray, sir, how far is it? and which way must I go?'

'Why missis,' said Jerry, 'you can't get there walking through crowds like this! Why, it is three miles away, and that child is heavy.'

'Yes, bless him, he is, but I am strong, thank God; and if I knew the way, I think I could get on somehow: please tell me the way.'

'You can't do it,' said Jerry; 'you might be knocked down and the child be run over. Now look here, just get into this cab, and I'll drive you safely to the hospital: don't you see the rain is coming on?'

'No, sir, no, I can't do that, thank you; I have only just money enough to get back with. Please tell me the way.'

'Look you here, missis,' said Jerry, 'I've got a wife and dear children at home, and I know a father's feelings. Now get into that cab and I'll take you there for nothing;

I'd be ashamed of myself to let a woman and a sick child run a risk like that.'

'Heaven bless you!' said the woman, and she burst into tears.

'There, there, cheer up, my dear, I'll soon take you there. Come, let me put you inside.'

As Jerry went to open the door, two men with colours in their hats and button-holes ran up, calling out, 'Cab!'

'Engaged!' cried Jerry. But one of the men, pushing past the woman, sprang into the cab, followed by the other. Jerry looked as stern as a policeman: 'This cab is already engaged, gentlemen, by that lady.'

'Lady!' said one of them; 'oh! she can wait: our business is very important; besides, we were in first. It is our right, and we shall stay in.'

A droll smile came over Jerry's face as he shut the door upon them. 'All right, gentlemen; pray stay in as long as it suits you. I can wait while you rest yourselves;' and turning his back upon them, he walked up to the young woman, who was standing near me. 'They'll soon be gone,' he said, laughing; 'don't trouble yourself, my dear.'

And they soon were gone; for when they understood Jerry's dodge, they got out, calling him all sorts of bad names, and blustering about his number and getting a summons. After this little stoppage we were soon on our way to the hospital, going as much as possible through by-streets. Jerry rang the great bell, and helped the young woman out.

'Thank you a thousand times,' she said; 'I could never have got here alone.'

'You're kindly welcome, and I hope the dear child will soon be better.'

He watched her go in at the door, and he said to himself quietly, '"Inasmuch as ye have done it to one of the least of these."' Then he patted my neck; this was always his way when anything pleased him.

The rain was now coming down fast, and just as we were leaving the hospital the door opened again, and the porter called out, 'Cab!' We stopped, and a lady came down the steps. Jerry seemed to know her at once. She put back her veil, and said, 'Barker! Jeremiah Barker! is it you? I am very glad to find you here; you are just the friend I want, for it is very difficult to get a cab in this part of London to-day.'

'I shall be proud to serve you, ma'am; I am right glad I happened to be here. Where may I take you to, ma'am?'

'To the Paddington Station, and then if we are in good time, as I think we shall be, you shall tell me all about Mary and the children.'

We got to the station in good time, and being under shelter, the lady stood a good while talking to Jerry. I found she had been Polly's mistress, and after many inquiries about her, she said, 'How do you find the cab-work suits you in winter? I know Mary was rather anxious about you last year.'

'Yes, ma'am, she was; I had a bad cough that followed me up quite into the warm weather, and when I am kept out late she does worry herself a good deal. You see, ma'am, my work is at all hours and in all weathers, and that does try a man's constitution; but I am getting on pretty well, and I should feel quite lost if I had not horses to look after. I was brought up to it, and I am afraid I should not do as well at anything else.'

'Well, Barker,' she said, 'it would be a great pity that you should seriously risk your health in this work, not only for your own but for Mary's and the children's sake. There are many places where good drivers or good grooms are wanted; and if ever you think you ought to give up this cab-work, let me know.' Then sending some kind messages to Mary, she put something into his hand, saying, 'There are five shillings each for the two children; Mary will know how to spend it.'

Jerry thanked her and seemed much pleased; then, turning out of the station, we at last reached home; I, at least, was tired.

Chapter 44

OLD CAPTAIN AND HIS SUCCESSOR

Captain and I were great friends. He was a noble old fellow, and a very good companion. I never thought that he would have to leave his home and go down the hill, but his turn came; and this is how it happened. I was not there, but I heard all about it.

Jerry and he had taken a party to the great railway station over London bridge, and were coming back, somewhere between the bridge and the Monument, when Jerry saw a brewer's empty dray coming along, drawn by two powerful horses. The drayman was slashing his horses with his heavy whip. The dray was light, and they were going at a furious rate.. The man had no control over them.

The street was full of traffic; one young girl was knocked down and run over, and the next moment the dray dashed up against our cab; both the wheels were torn off, and the cab was thrown over. Captain was dragged down, the shafts splintered, and one of them ran into his side. Jerry, too, was thrown, but was only bruised. Nobody could tell how he escaped; he always said 'twas a miracle.

When poor Captain was got up, he was found to be very much cut and knocked about. Jerry led him home gently, and a sad sight it was to see the blood soaking into his white coat and dropping from his side and shoulder. The drayman being proved to be very drunk, was fined, and the brewer had to pay damages to our master; but there was no one to pay damages to poor Captain.

At first Captain seemed to do well, but he was a very old horse, and it was only his wonderful constitution and Jerry's care that had kept him up at the cab-work so long; now he broke down very much. The farrier said he might mend up enough to sell for a few pounds, but Jerry said, No! a few pounds got by selling a good old servant into hard work and misery would canker all the rest of his money. He thought the kindest thing he could do for the fine old fellow would be to put a sure bullet through his heart, and then he would never suffer more; for he did not know where to find him a kind master for the rest of his days.

The day after this was decided Harry took me to the forge for some new shoes. When I returned Captain was gone. The family and I all felt it very much.

Jerry had now to look out for another horse, and he soon heard of one through an acquaintance who was under-groom in a nobleman's stables. He was a valuable young horse, but he had run away, smashed into another carriage, flung his lordship out, and so cut and blemished himself that he was no longer fit for a gentleman's stables, and the coachman had orders to look round and sell him as well as he could.

'I can do with high spirits,' said Jerry, 'if a horse is not vicious or hard-mouthed.'

'There is not a bit of vice in him,' said the man; 'his mouth is very tender, and I think myself that was the cause of the accident. You see, he had just been clipped, and the weather was bad, and he had not had exercise enough, and when he did go out he was as full of spring as a balloon. Our governor (the coachman, I mean) had him harnessed in as tight and strong as he could, with the martingale, and the bearing rein, a very sharp curb, and the reins, put in at the bottom bar; it is my belief that it made the horse mad, being tender in the mouth and so full of spirit.'

'Likely enough; I'll come and see him,' said Jerry.

The next day, Hotspur—that was his name—came home; he was a fine brown horse, without a white hair in him, as tall as Captain, with a very handsome head, and only five years old. I gave him a friendly greeting by way of good-fellowship, but did not ask him any questions. The first night he was very restless; instead of lying down, he kept jerking his halter rope up and down through the ring, and knocking the block about against the manger so that I could not sleep. However, the next day, after five or six hours in the cab, he came in quiet and sensible. Jerry patted and talked to him a good deal, and very soon they understood each other, and Jerry said that with an easy bit and plenty of work he would be as gentle as a lamb, and that it was an ill wind that blew nobody good, for if his lordship had lost a hundred-guinea favourite, the cabman had gained a good horse with all his strengh in him.

Hotspur thought it a great come-down to be a cab-horse, and was disgusted at standing in the rank, but he confessed to me at the end of the week that an easy mouth and a free head made up for a great deal, and, after all, the work was not so degrading as having one's head and tail fastened to each other at the saddle. In fact, he settled in well, and Jerry liked him very much.

Chapter 45

JERRY'S NEW YEAR

Christmas and the New Year are very merry times for some people; but for cabmen and cabmen's horses these times are no holiday, though they may be a harvest. There are so many parties, balls, and places of amusement open that the work is hard and often late. Sometimes driver and horse, shivering with cold, have to wait for hours in the rain or frost, whilst the merry people within are dancing to the music. I wonder if the beautiful ladies ever think of the weary cabman waiting on his box, and of his patient beast standing till his legs get stiff with cold!

I had now most of the evening work as I was very accustomed to standing, and Jerry was also more afraid of Hotspur, the new horse, taking cold. We had a great deal of late work in the Christmas week, and Jerry's cough was bad, but, however late we were, Polly sat up for him, and, looking anxious and troubled, she came out with the lantern to meet him.

On the evening of the New Year we had to take two gentlemen to a house in one of the West End squares. We set them down at nine o'clock, and were told to come again at eleven. 'But,' said one of them, 'as it is a card party, you may have to wait a few minutes, but don't be late.'

As the clock struck eleven we were at the door, for Jerry was always punctual. The clock chimed the quarters—one, two, three, and then struck twelve; but the door did not open.

The wind had been very changeable, with squalls of

rain during the day, but now it came on sharp, driving sleet, which seemed to come all the way round one; it was very cold, and there was no shelter. Jerry got off his box and came and pulled one of my cloths a little more over my neck; then, stamping his feet, he took a turn or two up and down; then he began to beat his arms, but that set him on coughing; so he opened the cab door and sat at the bottom with his feet on the pavement, and was thus a little sheltered. Still the clock chimed the quarters, but no one came. At half-past twelve he rang the bell, and asked the servant if he would be wanted that night.

'Oh, yes! you'll be wanted safe enough,' said the man; 'you must not go, it will soon be over.' And again Jerry sat down, but his voice was so hoarse I could hardly hear him.

At a quarter past one the door opened, and the two gentlemen came out; they got into the cab without a word, and told Jerry where to drive; it was nearly two miles away. My legs were numb with cold, and I thought I should have stumbled. When the men got out they never said they were sorry to have kept us waiting so long, but were angry at the charge. However, as Jerry never charged more than was his due, he never took less, and so they had to pay for the two hours and a quarter of waiting; but it was hard-earned money to Jerry.

At last we got home. He could hardly speak, and his cough was dreadful. Polly asked no questions, but opened the door and held the lantern for him.

'Can't I do something?' she said.

'Yes; get Jack something warm, and then boil me some gruel.'

This was said in a hoarse whisper. He could hardly get his breath, but he gave me a rub down as usual, and even went up into the hayloft for an extra bundle of straw for my bed. Polly brought me a warm mash that made me comfortable; and then they locked the door.

It was late the next morning before any one came, and then it was only Harry. He cleaned and fed us, and swept out the stalls; then he put the straw back again as if it was Sunday. He was very still, and neither whistled nor sang. At noon he came again and gave us our food and water; this time Dolly came with him. She was crying, and I could gather from what they said that Jerry was dangerously ill and the doctor said it was a bad case. So two days passed, and there was great trouble indoors. We saw only Harry and sometimes Dolly. I think she came for company, for Polly was always with Jerry, who had to be kept very quiet.

On the third day whilst Harry was in the stable, a tap came at the door, and Governor Grant came in.

'I wouldn't go to the house, my boy,' he said, 'but I want to know how your father is.'

'He is very bad,' said Harry, 'he can't be much worse. They call it bronchitis, and the doctor thinks it will turn one way or another to-night.'

'That's bad, very bad,' said Grant, shaking his head. 'I know two men who died of that last week. It takes 'em off in no time but whilst there's life there's hope, so you must keep up your spirits.'

'Yes,' said Harry quickly, 'and the doctor said that father had a better chance than most men, because he didn't drink. He said yesterday the fever was so high that if father had been a drinking man it would have burnt him up like a piece of paper; but I believe he thinks he will get over it; don't you think he will, Mr. Grant?'

The Governor looked puzzled.

'If there's any rule that good men should get over these things, I am sure he will, my boy. He's the best man I know. I'll look in early to-morrow.'

Early next morning he was there.

'Well?' said he.

'Father is better,' said Harry. 'Mother hopes he will get over it.'

'Thank God!' said the Governor; 'and now you must keep him warm, and keep his mind easy. And that brings me to the horses. You see, Jack will be all the better for a rest of a week or two in a warm stable, and you can easily take him a turn up and down the street to stretch his legs; but this young one, if he does not get work, will soon be all up on end as you may say, and will be rather too much for you; and when he does go out, there'll be an accident.'

'He is like that now,' said Harry; 'I have kept him short of corn, but he's so full of spirit I don't know what to do with him.'

'Just so,' said Grant. 'Now, look here. Will you tell your mother that, if she is agreeable, I will come for him every day till something is arranged, and take him for a good spell of work; and whatever he earns, I'll bring your mother half of it, and that will help with the horses' feed. Your father is in a good club, I know, but that won't keep the horses, and they'll be eating their heads off all this time; I'll come at noon to hear what she says,' and without waiting for Harry's thanks, he was gone.

At noon I think he went and saw Polly, for Harry and he came to the stable together, harnessed Hotspur, and took him out.

For a week or more he came for Hotspur, and when Harry thanked him or said anything about his kindness, he laughed it off, saying it was all good luck for him, for his horses were wanting a little rest, which they could not otherwise have had.

Jerry steadily grew better, but the doctor said that he must never go back to the cab-work again if he wished to be an old man. The children had many consultations together about what father and mother would do, and how they could help to earn money.

One afternoon Hotspur was brought in very wet and dirty.

'The streets are nothing but slush,' said the Governor; 'it will give you a good warming, my boy, to get him clean and dry.'

'All right, Governor,' said Harry, 'I shall not leave him till he is; you know I have been trained by my father.'

'I wish all the boys had been trained like you,' said the Governor.

While Harry was sponging off the mud from Hotspur's body and legs, Dolly came in, looking very full of something.

'Who lives at Fairstowe, Harry? Mother has got a letter from Fairstowe; she seemed so glad, and ran upstairs to father with it.'

'Don't you know? Why, it is the name of Mrs. Fowler's place—mother's old mistress, you know—the lady that father met last summer, who sent you and me five shillings each.'

'Oh! Mrs. Fowler; of course I know all about her. I wonder what she is writing to mother about.'

'Mother wrote to her last week,' said Harry. 'You know she told father if ever he gave up the cab-work, she would like to know. I wonder what she says; run in and see, Dolly.'

Harry scrubbed away at Hotspur with a 'huish! huish! like any old ostler.

In a few minutes Dolly came dancing into the stable.

'Oh, Harry! was there ever anything so beautiful? Mrs. Fowler says we are all to go and live near her. There is a cottage now empty that will just suit us, with a garden, a hen-house, apple-trees, and everything! Her coachman is going away in the spring, and then she will want father in his place. And there are good families round, where you can get a place in the garden or stable, or as a page-boy; and there's a good school for me. Mother is laughing and crying in turns, and father does look so happy!'

'That's uncommon jolly,' said Harry, 'and just the right thing, I should say. It will suit father and mother both; but I don't intend to be a page-boy with tight clothes and rows of buttons. I'll be a groom or a gardener.'

It was quickly settled that, as soon as Jerry was well enough, they should remove to the country, and that the cab and horses should be sold as soon as possible.

This was heavy news for me, for I was not young now, and could not look for any improvement in my condition. Since I left Birtwick I had never been so happy as with my dear master Jerry; but three years of cab-work, even under the best conditions, will tell on one's strength, and I felt that I was not the horse that I had been.

Grant said at once that he would take Hotspur. There were men on the stand who would have bought me; but Jerry said I should not go to cab-work again with just anybody, and the Governor promised to find a place for me where I should be comfortable.

The day came for going away. Jerry had not been allowed to go out yet, and I never saw him after that New Year's Eve. Polly and the children came to bid me good-bye. 'Poor old Jack! I wish we could take you with us,' she said; and then, laying her hand on my mane, she put her face close to my neck and kissed me. Dolly was crying, and she kissed me, too. Harry stroked me a great deal, but said nothing, only he seemed very sad; and so I was led away to my new place.

Chapter 46

JAKES AND THE LADY

I was sold to a corn dealer and baker whom Jerry knew, and with him he thought I should have good food and fair work. In the first he was quite right, and if my master had always been on the premises, I do not think I should have been overloaded; but there was a foreman who was always hurrying and driving every one, and frequently, when I had quite a full load, he would order something else to be taken on. My carter, whose name was Jakes, often said it was more than I ought to take, but the other always overruled him saying, ''Tis no use going twice when once will do, and I choose to get business forward.'

Jakes, like the other carters, always had the bearing rein up, which prevented me from drawing easily; and by the time I had been there three or four months, I found the work telling very much on my strength.

One day I was loaded more than usual, and part of the road was up a steep hill: I used all my strength, but I could not get on, and was obliged continually to stop. This did not please my driver, and he laid his whip on badly. 'Get on, you lazy fellow,' he said, 'or I'll make you.'

Again I started the heavy load, and struggled on a few yards; again the whip came down, and again I struggled forward. The pain of that great cart whip was sharp, but my mind was hurt quite as much as my poor sides. To be punished and abused when I was doing my very best was so hard that it took the heart out of me. A third time he was flogging me cruelly, when a lady stepped quickly up to him, and said in a sweet, earnest voice:—

'Oh! pray do not whip your good horse any more; I am sure he is doing all he can. The road is very steep, and I am sure he is doing his best.'

'If doing his best won't get this load up, he must do something more than his best; that's all I know, ma'am,' said Jakes.

'But is it not a very heavy load?' she said.

'Yes, yes, too heavy,' he said; 'but that's not my fault; the foreman came just as we were starting, and would have three hundredweight more put on to save him trouble. I must get on with it as well as I can.'

He was raising the whip again, when the lady said:—

'Pray, stop, I think I can help you if you will let me.'

The man laughed.

'You see,' she said, 'you do not give him a fair chance. He cannot use all his power with his head held back as it is with that bearing rein; if you would take it off, I am sure he would do better—*do* try it,' she said persuasively; 'I should be very glad if you would.'

'Well, well,' said Jakes, with a short laugh, 'anything to please a lady, of course. How far would you wish it down, ma'am?'

'Quite down; give him his head altogether.'

The rein was taken off, and in a moment I put my head down to my very knees. What a comfort it was! Then I tossed it up and down several times to get the aching stiffness out of my neck.

'Poor fellow! that is what you wanted,' said she, patting and stroking me with her gentle hand; 'and now if you will speak kindly to him and lead him on, I believe he will be able to do better.'

Jakes took the rein—'Come on, Blackie.' I put down my head, and threw my whole weight against the collar. I spared no strength; the load moved on, and I pulled it steadily up the hill, and then stopped to take breath.

The lady had walked along the footpath, and now came across into the road. She stroked and patted my neck, as I had not been patted for many a long day.

'You see, he was quite willing when you gave him the chance. I am sure he is a fine-tempered creature, and I daresay has known better days. You won't put that rein on again, will you?' for he was just going to hitch it up on the old plan.

'Well, ma'am, I can't deny that having his head has helped him up the hill, and I'll remember it another time, and thank you, ma'am; but if he went without a bearing rein I should be the laughing-stock of all the carters; it is the fashion, you see.'

'Is it not better,' she said, 'to lead a good fashion than to follow a bad one? A great many gentlemen do not use bearing reins now; our carriage horses have not worn them for fifteen years, and work with much less fatigue than those which have them; besides,' she added in a very serious voice, 'we have no right to distress any of God's creatures without a very good reason; we call them dumb animals, and so they are, for they cannot tell us how they feel, but they do not suffer less because they have no words. But I must not detain you now; I thank you for trying my plan with your good horse, and I am sure you will find it far better than the whip. Good-day.' And with another soft pat on my neck, she stepped lightly across the path, and I saw her no more.

'That was a real lady, I'll be bound for it,' said Jakes to himself; 'she spoke just as politely as if I was a gentleman. I'll try her plan, uphill, at any rate.'

I must do him the justice to say that he let my rein out several holes, and after that, going uphill, he always gave me my head; but the heavy loads went on.

Good food and fair rest will keep up one's strength under full work, but no horse can stand against overloading; and I was getting so thoroughly pulled down from this cause that a younger horse was bought in my place. I may as well mention here what I suffered at this time from another cause. I had heard horses speak of it, but had never myself had experience of the evil of a badly-lighted stable. There was only one very small window at the end, and the consequence was that the stalls were almost dark.

Besides the depressing effect this had on my spirits, it very much weakened my sight, and when I was suddenly brought out of the darkness into the glare of daylight, it was very painful to my eyes. Several times I stumbled over the threshold, and could scarcely see where I was going.

I believe, had I stayed there very long, I should have become purblind, and that would have been a great misfortune; for I have heard men say that a stone-blind horse is safer to drive than one which has imperfect sight, as purblindness generally makes them very timid. However, I escaped without any permanent injury to my sight, and was sold to a large cab-owner.

CHAPTER 47

HARD TIMES

I shall never forget my new master. He had black eyes and a hooked nose; his mouth was as full of teeth as a bull-dog's, and his voice was as harsh as the grinding of cart wheels over gravel-stones. His name was Nicholas Skinner, and I believe he was the same man for whom poor Seedy Sam had driven.

I have heard men say that seeing is believing; but I should say that *feeling* is believing; for much as I had seen before, I never knew till now the utter misery of a cab-horse's life.

Skinner had a low set of cabs and a low set of drivers; he was hard on the men, and the men were hard on the horses. In this place we had no Sunday rest, and it was in the heat of summer.

Sometimes on a Sunday morning a party of fast men would hire a cab for the day—four of them inside and another with the driver, and I had to take them ten or fifteen miles out into the country, and back again; never would any of them get down to walk up a hill, let it be ever so steep or the day ever so hot—unless indeed, when the driver was afraid I should not manage it, and sometimes I was so fevered and worn that I could hardly touch my food. How I used to long for the nice bran mash with nitre in it that Jerry used to give us on Saturday nights in hot weather, that used to cool us down and make us so comfortable. Then we had two nights and a whole day for unbroken rest, and on Monday morning we were as fresh as young horses again; but here there was no rest, and my driver was just as hard as his master.

He had a cruel whip with something so sharp at the end that it sometimes drew blood, and he would even whip me under the belly, and flip out the lash at my head. Indignities like these took the heart out of me terribly, but I still did my best and never hung back; for, as poor Ginger said, it was no use; men are the stronger.

My life was now so utterly wretched that I wished I might, like Ginger, drop down dead at my work, and so be out of my misery; and one day my wish very nearly came to pass.

I went on the stand at eight in the morning, and had done a good share of work when we had to take a fare to the railway. A long train was just expected in, so my driver pulled up at the back of some of the outside cabs to take the chance of a return fare. It was a very heavy train, and as all the cabs were soon engaged, ours was called for.

There was a party of four; a noisy, blustering man with a lady, a little boy, a young girl, and a great deal of luggage. The lady and the boy got into the cab, and while the man ordered about the luggage, the young girl came and looked at me.

'Papa,' she said, 'I am sure this poor horse cannot take us and all our luggage so far; he is so very weak and worn out; do look at him.'

'Oh! he's all right, miss,' said my driver; 'he's strong enough.'

The porter, who was pulling about some heavy boxes, suggested to the gentleman that, as there was so much luggage, he should take a second cab.

'Can your horse do it, or can't he?' said the blustering man.

'Oh! he can do it all right sir. Send up the boxes, porter; he can take more than that.' Saying this, he helped to hand up a box so heavy that I could feel the springs go down.

'Papa, papa, do take a second cab,' said the young girl in a beseeching tone; 'I am sure we are wrong; I am sure it is very cruel.'

'Nonsense, Grace, get in at once, and don't make all this fuss; a pretty thing it would be if a man of business had to examine every cab-horse before he hired it—the man knows his own business of course; there, get in and hold your tongue!'

My gentle friend had to obey; and box after box was dragged up and lodged on top of the cab, or settled by the side of the driver. At last all was ready, and with his usual jerk of the rein and slash of the whip, he drove out of the station.

The load was very heavy, and I had had neither food nor rest since the morning; but I did my best, as I always had done in spite of cruelty and injustice.

I got along fairly till we came to Ludgate Hill; but there, the heavy load and my own exhaustion were too much. I was struggling to keep on, goaded by constant chucks of the rein and use of the whip, when, in a single moment—I cannot tell how—my feet slipped from under me, and I fell heavily to the ground on my side. The suddenness and the force with which I fell seemed to beat all the breath out of my body.

I lay perfectly still; indeed, I had no power to move, and I thought now I was going to die. I heard a sort of confusion round me—loud, angry voices, and the getting down of the luggage; but it was all like a dream. I thought I heard that sweet, pitiful voice saying, 'Oh! that poor horse! it is all our fault.'

Some one came and loosened the throat strap of my bridle, and undid the traces which kept the collar so tight upon me. Some one said, 'He's dead; he'll never get up again.' Then I could hear a policeman giving orders, but I did not even open my eyes; I could only draw a gasping breath now and then. Some cold water was thrown over my head, some cordial was poured into my mouth, and something was covered over me.

I cannot tell how long I lay there, but I found my life coming back, and a kind-voiced man was patting me and encouraging me to rise. After some more cordial had been given me, and after one or two attempts, I staggered to my feet, and was gently led to some stables which were close by. Here I was put into a well-littered stall, and some warm gruel was brought to me; this I drank thankfully.

In the evening I was sufficiently recovered to be led back to Skinner's stables, where I think they did the best for me they could. In the morning Skinner came with a farrier to look at me. He examined me very closely, and said—

'This is a case of overwork more than disease, and if you could give him a run off for six months, he would be able to work again; but now there is not an ounce of strength in him.'

'Then he must just go to the dogs,' said Skinner. 'I have no meadows to nurse sick horses in—he may get well or he may not; that sort of thing does not suit my business. My plan is to work 'em as long as they'll go, and then sell 'em for what they'll fetch at the knacker's or elsewhere.'

'If he was broken-winded,' said the farrier, 'you had better have had him killed out of hand, but he is not; there is a sale of horses coming off in about ten days; if you rest him and feed him up, he may pick up, and you may at any rate get more than his skin is worth.'

Upon this advice, Skinner, rather unwillingly, I think, gave orders that I should be well fed and cared for; and the stableman, happily for me, carried out the orders with a much better will than his master had shown in giving them.

Ten days of perfect rest, plenty of good oats, hay, and bran mashes with boiled linseed mixed in them, did more to get up my condition than anything else could have done. Those linseed mashes were delicious, and I began to think that after all it might be better to live than to go to the dogs. When the twelfth day after the accident came, I was taken to the sale, a few miles out of London. I felt that any change from my present place must be an improvement; so I held up my head, and hoped for the best.

Chapter 48

FARMER THOROUGHGOOD AND HIS GRANDSON WILLIE

At this sale, of course, I found myself in company with the old broken-down horses—some lame, some broken-winded, some old, and some that I am sure it would have been merciful to shoot.

The buyers and sellers, too, many of them, looked not much better off than the poor beasts for which they were bargaining. There were poor old men trying to get a horse or pony for a few pounds to drag about some little wood or coal cart. There were poor men trying to sell a worn-out beast for two or three pounds, rather than have the greater loss of killing him.

Some of them looked as if poverty and hard times had hardened them all over; but there were others for whom I would willingly have used the last of my strength—poor and shabby, but kind and human, with voices that I could trust. There was one tottering old man that took a great fancy to me, and I to him, but I was not strong enough—it was an anxious time!

Coming from the better part of the fair, I noticed a man who looked like a gentleman farmer, with a young boy by his side. He had a broad back and round shoulders, a kind, ruddy face, and he wore a broad-brimmed hat. When he came up to me and my companions, he stood still and gave a pitiful look round upon us. I saw his eye rest on me; I had still a good mane and tail, which did something for my appearance. I pricked up my ears and looked at him.

'There's a horse, Willie, that has known better days.'

'Poor old fellow!' said the boy. 'Do you think, grandpapa, he was ever a carriage-horse?'

'Oh, yes, my boy,' said the farmer, coming closer, 'he might have been anything when he was young. Look at his nostrils and his ears, and the shape of his neck and shoulders; there's a deal of breeding about that horse.' He put out his hand and gave me a kind pat on the neck. I put out my nose in answer to his kindness, and the boy stroked my face.

'Poor old fellow! See, grandpapa, how well he understands kindness. Could you not buy him and make him young again, as you did Ladybird?'

'My dear boy, I can't make all old horses young. Besides, Ladybird was not so old as she was run down and badly used.'

'Well, grandpapa, I don't believe that this one is old; look at his mane and tail. I wish you would look into his mouth, and then you could tell. Though he is so very thin, his eyes are not sunken like some old horses.'

The old gentleman laughed. 'Bless the boy! he is as horsy as his old grandfather.'

'But do look at his mouth, grandpapa, and ask the price; I am sure he would grow young in our meadows.'

The man who had brought me for sale now put in his word.

'The young gentleman's a real knowing one, sir. Now the fact is, this 'ere hoss is just pulled down with overwork in the cabs. He's not an old one, and I heard as how the vet should say that a six months' run off would set him right up, being as how his wind was not broken. I've had the tending of him these ten days past, and a more grateful and pleasant animal I never met. 'Twould be worth a gentleman's while to give a five-pound note for him and let him have a chance. I'll be bound he'd be worth twenty pounds next spring.'

The old gentleman laughed, and the little boy looked up eagerly.

'Oh! grandpapa, did you not say the colt sold for five pounds more than you expected? You would not be poorer if you did buy this one.'

The farmer slowly felt my legs, which were much swollen and strained; then he looked at my mouth—'Thirteen or fourteen, I should say. Just trot him out, will you?'

I arched my poor thin neck, raised my tail a little, and threw out my legs as well as I could, for they were very stiff.

'What is the lowest you will take for him?' said the farmer as I came back.

'Five pounds, sir; that was the lowest price my master set.'

''Tis a speculation,' said the old gentleman, shaking his head, but at the same time slowly drawing out his purse—'quite a speculation! Have you any more business here?' he said, counting the sovereigns into the man's hand.

'No, sir, I can take him for you to the inn if you please.'

'Do so; I am now going there.'

They walked forward, and I was left behind. The boy could hardly control his delight, and the old gentleman seemed to enjoy his pleasure. I had a good feed at the inn, and was then gently ridden home by a servant of my new master and turned into a large meadow with a shed in one corner of it.

Mr. Thoroughgood, for that was the name of my benefactor, gave orders that I should have hay and oats every night and morning, and the run of the meadow during the day. 'You, Willie,' said he, 'must take the oversight of him; I give him into your charge.'

The boy was proud of his charge, and undertook it in all seriousness. There was not a day when he did not pay me a visit, picking me out from among the other horses to give me a bit of carrot or some other good thing, or sometimes to stand by me whilst I ate my oats. He always came with kind words and caresses, and of course I grew very fond of him. He called me Old Crony, as I used to come to him in the field and follow him about. Sometimes he brought his grandfather, who always looked closely at my legs.

'That is our point, Willie,' he would say; 'but he is improving so steadily that I think we shall see a change for the better in the spring.'

The perfect rest, the good food, the soft turf, and gentle exercise soon began to tell on my condition and my spirits. I had a good constitution from my mother, and I was never strained when I was young, so that I had a better chance than many horses who have been worked before they came to their full strength.

During the winter my legs improved so much that I began to feel quite young again. The spring came round, and one day in March Mr. Thoroughgood determined that he would try me in the phaeton. I was well pleased, and he and Willie drove me a few miles. My legs were not stiff now, and I did the work with perfect ease.

'He's growing young, Willie; we must give him a little gentle work now, and by midsummer he will be as good as Ladybird; he has a beautiful mouth and good paces; these could not be better.'

'Oh, grandpapa, how glad I am you bought him!'

'So am I, my boy, but he has to thank you more than me. We must now be looking out for a quiet, genteel place for him where he will be valued.'

CHAPTER 49

MY LAST HOME

One day during the summer the groom cleaned and dressed me with such extraordinary care that I thought some new change must be at hand. He trimmed my fetlocks and legs, passed the tarbrush over my hoofs, and even parted my forelock. I think the harness also had an extra polish. Willie seemed half anxious, half merry, and he got into the chaise with his grandfather.

'If the ladies take to him,' said the old gentleman, 'they'll be suited, and he'll be suited; we can but try.'

At the distance of a mile or two from the village we came to a pretty low house with a lawn and shrubbery at the front and a drive up to the door. Willie rang the bell, and asked if Miss Blomefield or Miss Ellen was at home. Yes, they both were. So whilst Willie stayed with me, Mr. Thoroughgood went into the house.

In about ten minutes he returned, followed by three ladies. One tall, pale lady, wrapped in a white shawl, leaned on a younger lady with dark eyes and a merry face; the third, a very stately-looking person, was Miss Blomefield. They all came to look at me and ask questions. The young lady—this was Miss Ellen—took to me very much; she said she was sure she should like me, for I had such a good face. The tall, pale lady said that she should always be nervous in riding behind a horse that had once been down, as I might come down again; and if I did, she should never get over the fright.

'You see, ladies,' said Mr. Thoroughgood, 'many first-rate horses have their knees broken through the carelessness of their drivers, without any fault of their own; and from what I see of this horse, I should say that is his case; but of course I do not wish to influence you. If you wish, you can have him on trial, and then your coachman will see what he thinks of him.'

'You have always been such a good adviser to us about our horses,' said the stately lady, 'that your recommendation would go a long way with me, and if my sister Lavinia sees no objection, we will accept with thanks your offer of a trial.'

It was then arranged that I should be sent for the next day.

In the morning a smart-looking young man came for me. At first he looked pleased, but when he saw my knees, he said in a disappointed voice: 'I didn't think, sir, you would have recommended my ladies a blemished horse like this.'

'Handsome is that handsome does,' said my master. 'You are only taking him on trial, and I am sure you will do fairly by him, young man; and if he is not as safe as any horse you ever drove, send him back.'

I was led home, placed in a comfortable stable, fed, and left to myself. The next day, when my groom was cleaning my face, he said: 'That is just like the star that Black Beauty had, and he is much the same height, too; I wonder where he is now.'

A little farther on he came to the place in my neck where I was bled, and where a little knot was left in the skin. He almost started, and began to look me over carefully, talking to himself.

'White star in the forehead, one white foot on the off side, this little knot just in that place;' then looking at the middle of my back—'and as I am alive, there is that little patch of white hair that John used to call "Beauty's threepenny-bit." It *must* be Black Beauty! Why, Beauty! Beauty! do you know me, little Joe Green that almost killed you?' And he began patting and patting me as if he was quite overjoyed.

I could not say that I remembered him, for now he was a fine grown young fellow with black whiskers and a man's voice, but I was sure he knew me, and that he was Joe Green; so I was very glad. I put my nose up to him, and tried to say that we were friends. I never saw a man so pleased.

'Give him a fair trial! I should think so indeed! I wonder who the rascal was that broke your knees, my old Beauty! You must have been badly served out somewhere. Well, well, it won't be my fault if you haven't good times of it now. I wish John Manly were here to see you.'

In the afternoon I was put into a low-park chair and brought to the door. Miss Ellen was going to try me, and Green went with her. I soon found that she was a good driver, and she seemed pleased with my paces. I heard Joe telling her about me, and that he was sure I was Squire Gordon's old Black Beauty.

When we returned, the other sister came out to hear how I had behaved myself. She told them what she had just heard, and said, 'I shall certainly write to Mrs. Gordon to tell her that her favourite horse has come to us. How pleased she will be!'

After this I was driven every day for a week or so, and as I appeared to be quite safe, Miss Lavinia at last ventured out in the small close carriage. After this, it was quite decided to keep me and to call me by my old name of 'Black Beauty.'

I have now lived in this happy place a whole year. Joe is the best and kindest of grooms. My work is easy and pleasant, and I feel my strength and spirits all coming back again. Mr. Thoroughgood said to Joe the other day, 'In your place he will last till he is twenty years old—perhaps more.'

Willie always speaks to me when he can, and treats me as his special friend. My ladies have promised that I shall never be sold, and so I have nothing to fear; and here my story ends. My troubles are all over and I am at home; and often before I am quite awake I fancy I am still in the orchard at Birtwick, standing with my old friends under the apple-trees.

CHILDREN'S CLASSICS

KENNETH GRAHAME

The Wind in the Willows

Chapter 1

THE RIVER BANK

The Mole had been working very hard all the morning, spring-cleaning his little home. First with brooms, then with dusters; then on ladders and steps and chairs, with a brush and a pail of whitewash; till he had dust in his throat and eyes, and splashes of whitewash all over his black fur, and an aching back and weary arms. Spring was moving in the air above and in the earth below and around him, penetrating even his dark and lowly little house with its spirit of divine discontent and longing. It was small wonder, then, that he suddenly flung down his brush on the floor, said "Bother!" and "O blow!" and also "Hang spring-cleaning!" and bolted out of the house without even waiting to put on his coat. Something up above was calling him imperiously, and he made for the steep little tunnel which answered in his case to the gravelled carriage-drive owned by animals whose residences are nearer to the sun and air. So he scraped and scratched and scrabbled and scrooged, and then he scrooged again and scrabbled and scratched and scraped, working busily with his little paws and muttering to himself, "Up we go! Up we go!" till at last, pop! his snout came out into the sunlight, and he found himself rolling in the warm grass of a great meadow.

"This is fine!" he said to himself: "This is better than whitewashing!" The sunshine struck hot on his fur, soft breezes caressed his heated brow, and after the seclusion of the cellarage he had lived in so long the carol of happy birds fell on his dulled hearing almost like a shout. Jumping off all his four legs at once, in the joy of living and the delight of spring without its cleaning, he pursued his way across the meadow till he reached the hedge on the further side.

"Hold up!" said an elderly rabbit at the gap. "Sixpence for the privilege of passing by the private road!" He was bowled over in an instant by the impatient and contemptuous Mole, who trotted along the side of the hedge chaffing the other rabbits as they peeped hurriedly from their holes to see what the row was about. "Onion-sauce! Onion-sauce!" he remarked jeeringly, and was gone before they could think of a thoroughly satisfactory reply. Then they all started grumbling at each other. "How *stupid* you are! Why didn't you tell him—" "Well, why didn't *you say*—" "You might have reminded him—" and so on, in the usual way; but of course, it was then much too late, as is always the case.

It all seemed too good to be true. Hither and thither through the meadows he rambled busily, along the hedgerows, across the copses, finding everywhere birds building, flowers budding, leaves thrusting—everything happy, and progressive, and occupied. And instead of having an uneasy conscience pricking him and whispering "Whitewash!" he somehow could only feel how jolly it was to be the only idle dog among all these busy citizens. After all, the best part of a holiday is perhaps not so much to be resting yourself, as to see all the other fellows busy working.

He thought his happiness was complete when, as he meandered aimlessly along, suddenly he stood by the edge of a full-fed river. Never in his life had he seen a river before—this sleek, sinuous, bodied animal, chasing and chuckling, gripping things with a gurgle and leaving them with a laugh, to fling itself on fresh playmates that shook themselves free, and were caught and held again. All was a-shake and a-shiver—glints and gleams and sparkles, rustle and swirl, chatter and bubble. The Mole was bewitched, entranced, fascinated. By the side of the river he trotted as one trots, when very small, by the side of a man, who holds one spellbound by exciting stories; and when tired at last, he sat on the bank, while the river still chattered on to him, a babbling procession of the best stories in the world, sent from the heart of the earth to be told at last to the insatiable sea.

As he sat on the grass and looked across the river, a dark hole in the bank opposite, just above the water's edge, caught his eye, and dreamily he fell to considering what a nice snug dwelling-place it would make for an animal with few wants and fond of a bijou riverside residence, above flood-level and remote from noise and dust. As he gazed, something bright and small seemed to twinkle down in the heart of it, vanished, then twinkled once more like a tiny star. But it could hardly be a star in such an unlikely situation; and it was too glittering and small for a glow-worm. Then, as he looked, it winked at him, and so declared itself to be an eye; and a small face began gradually to grow up round it, like a frame round a picture.

A brown little face, with whiskers.

A grave round face, with the same twinkle in its eye that had first attracted his notice.

Small neat ears and thick silky hair.

It was the Water Rat! Then the two animals stood and regarded each other cautiously.

"Hullo, Mole!" said the Water Rat.

"Hullo, Rat!" said the Mole.

"Would you like to come over?" inquired the Rat presently.

"Oh, it's all very well to *talk*," said the Mole, rather pettishly, he being new to a river and riverside life and its ways.

The Rat said nothing, but stooped and unfastened a rope and hauled on it; then lightly stepped into a little boat which the Mole had not observed. It was painted blue outside and white within, and was just the size for two animals; and the Mole's whole heart went out to it at once, even though he did not yet fully understand its uses.

The Rat sculled smartly across and made fast. Then he held up his fore-paw as the Mole stepped gingerly down. "Lean on that!" he said. "Now then, step lively!" and the Mole to his surprise and rapture found himself actually seated in the stern of a real boat.

"This has been a wonderful day!' said he, as the Rat shoved off and took to the sculls again. "Do you know, I've never been in a boat before in all my life."

"What?" cried the Rat, open-mouthed. "Never been in a—you never—well, I—what have you been doing, then?"

"Is it so nice as all that?" asked the Mole shyly, though he was quite prepared to believe it as he leant back in his seat and surveyed the cushions, the oars, the rowlocks, and all the fascinating fittings, and felt the boat sway lightly under him.

"Nice? It's the *only* thing," said the Water Rat solemnly, as he leant forward for his stroke. "Believe me, my young friend, there is *nothing*—absolutely nothing—half so much worth doing as simply messing about in boats. Simply messing," he went on dreamily: "messing—about—in—boats; messing—"

"Look ahead, Rat" cried the Mole suddenly.

It was too late. The boat struck the bank full tilt. The dreamer, the joyous oarsman, lay on his back at the bottom of the boat, his heels in the air.

"—about in boats—or *with* boats," the Rat went on composedly, picking himself up with a pleasant laugh. "In or out of 'em, it doesn't matter. Nothing seems really to matter, that's the charm of it. Whether you get away, or whether you don't; whether you arrive at your destination or whether you reach somewhere else, or whether you never get anywhere at all, you're always busy, and you never do anything in particular; and when you've done it there's always something else to do, and you can do it if you like, but you'd much better not. Look here ! If you've really nothing else on hand this morning, supposing we drop down the river together, and have a long day of it?"

The Mole waggled his toes from sheer happiness, spread his chest with a sigh of full contentment, and leaned back blissfully into the soft cushions. "*What* a day I'm having!" he said. "Let us start at once!"

"Hold hard a minute, then!" said the Rat. He looped the painter through a ring in his landing-stage, climbed up into his hole above, and after a short interval reappeared staggering under a fat, wicker luncheon-basket.

"Shove that under your feet," he observed to the Mole, as he passed it down into the boat. Then he untied the painter and took the sculls again.

"What's inside it?" asked the Mole, wriggling with curiosity.

"There's cold chicken inside it," replied the Rat briefly; "coldtonguecoldhamcoldbeefpickledgherkinssalad-frenchrollscressandwichespottedmeatgingerbeerlemon-adesodawater—" "O stop, stop," cried the Mole in ecstasies: "This is too much!"

"Do you really think so?" inquired the Rat seriously. "It's only what I always take on these little excursions; and the other animals are always telling me that I'm a mean beast and cut it very fine!"

The Mole never heard a word he was saying. Absorbed in the new life he was entering upon, intoxicated with the sparkle, the ripple, the scents and the sounds and the sunlight, he trailed a paw in the water and dreamed long waking dreams. The Water Rat, like the good little fellow he was, sculled steadily on and forbore to disturb him.

"I like your clothes awfully, old chap," he remarked after some half an hour or so had passed. "I'm going to get a black velvet smoking-suit myself some day, as soon as I can afford it."

"I beg your pardon," said the Mole, pulling himself together with an effort. "You must think me very rude; but all this is so new to me. So—this—is—a—River!"

"*The* River," corrected the Rat.

"And you really live by the river? What a jolly life!"

"By it and with it and on it and in it," said the Rat. "It's brother and sister to me, and aunts, and company, and food and drink, and (naturally) washing. It's my world, and I don't want any other. What it hasn't got is not worth having, and what it doesn't know is not worth knowing. Lord! the times we've had together! Whether in winter or summer, spring or autumn, it's always got its fun and its excitements. When the floods are on in February, and my cellars and basement are brimming with drink that's no good to me, and the brown water runs by my best bedroom window; or again when it all drops away and shows patches of mud that smells like plum-cake, and the rushes and weed clog the channels, and I can potter about dry-shod over most of the bed of it and find fresh food to eat, and things careless people have dropped out of boats!"

"But isn't it a bit dull at times?" the Mole ventured to ask. "Just you and the river, and no one else to pass a word with?"

"No one else to—well, I mustn't be hard on you," said the Rat with forbearance. "You're new to it, and of course you don't know. The bank is so crowded nowadays that many people are moving away altogether. O no, it isn't what it used to be, at all. Otters, kingfishers, dabchicks, moorhens, all of them about all day long and always wanting you to *do* something—as if a fellow had no business of his own to attend to!"

"What lies over *there*?" asked the Mole, waving a paw towards a background of woodland that darkly framed the water-meadows on one side of the river.

"That? O, that's just the Wild Wood," said the Rat shortly. "We don't go there very much, we river bankers."

"Aren't they—aren't they very *nice* people in there?" said the Mole a trifle nervously.

"W-e-ll," replied the Rat, "let me see. The squirrels are all right. *And* the rabbits—some of 'em, but rabbits are a mixed lot. And then there's Badger, of course. He lives right in the heart of it; wouldn't live anywhere else, either, if you paid him to do it. Dear old Badger! Nobody interferes with *him*. They'd better not," he added significantly.

"Why, who *should* interfere with him?" asked the Mole.

"Well, of course—there—are others," explained the Rat in a hesitating sort of way. "Weasels—and stoats—and foxes—and so on. They're all right in a way—I'm very good friends with them—pass the time of day when we meet, and all that—but they break out sometimes, there's no denying it, and then—well, you can't really trust them, and that's the fact."

The Mole knew well that it is quite against animal-etiquette to dwell on possible trouble ahead, or even to allude to it; so he dropped the subject.

"And beyond the Wild Wood again?" he asked: "Where it's all blue and dim, and one sees what may be hills or perhaps they mayn't, and something like the smoke of towns, or is it only clouddrift."

"Beyond the Wild Wood comes the Wide World," said the Rat. "And that's something that doesn't matter, either to you or me. I've never been there, and I'm never going, nor you either, if you've got any sense at all. Don't ever refer to it again, please. Now then! Here's our backwater at last, where we're going to lunch."

Leaving the main stream, they now passed into what seemed at first sight like a little landlocked lake. Green turf sloped down to either edge, brown snaky tree-roots gleamed below the surface of the quiet water, while ahead of them the silvery shoulder and foamy tumble of a weir, arm-in-arm with a restless dripping mill-wheel, that held up in its turn a grey-gabled mill-house, filled the air with a soothing murmur of sound, dull and smothery, yet with little clear voices speaking up cheerfully out of it at intervals. It was so very beautiful that the Mole could only hold up both forepaws and gasp, "O my! O my! O my!"

The Rat brought the boat alongside the bank, made her fast, helped the still awkward Mole safely ashore, and swung out the luncheon-basket. The Mole begged as a favour to be allowed to unpack it all by himself; and the Rat was very pleased to indulge him, and to sprawl at full length on the grass and rest, while his excited friend shook out the table-cloth and spread it, took out all the mysterious packets one by one and arranged their contents in due order, still gasping, "O my! O my!" at each fresh revelation. When all was ready, the Rat said, "Now, pitch in, old fellow!" and the Mole was indeed very glad to obey, for he had started his spring-cleaning at a very early hour that morning, as people *will* do, and had not paused for bite or sup; and he had been through a very great deal since that distant time which now seemed so many days ago.

"What are you looking at?" said the Rat presently, when the edge of their hunger was somewhat dulled, and the Mole's eyes were able to wander off the table-cloth a little.

"I am looking," said the Mole, "at a streak of bubbles that I see travelling along the surface of the water. That is a thing that strikes me as funny."

"Bubbles? Oho!" said the Rat, and chirruped cheerily in an inviting sort of way.

A broad glistening muzzle showed itself above the edge of the bank, and the Otter hauled himself out and shook the water from his coat.

"Greedy beggars!" he observed, making for the provender.

"Why didn't you invite me, Ratty?"

"This was an impromptu affair," explained the Rat. "By the way—my friend, Mr Mole."

"Proud, I'm sure," said the Otter, and the two animals were friends forthwith.

"Such a rumpus everywhere!" continued the Otter. "All the world seems out on the river today. I came up this backwater to try and get a moment's peace, and then stumble upon you fellows! At least—I beg pardon—I don't exactly mean that, you know."

There was a rustle behind them, proceeding from a hedge wherein last year's leaves still clung thick, and a stripy head, with high shoulders behind it, peered forth on them.

"Come on, old Badger!" shouted the Rat.

The Badger trotted forward a pace or two; then grunted, "H'm! Company," and turned his back and disappeared from view.

"That's *just* the sort of fellow he is" observed the disappointed Rat. "Simply hates Society! Now we shan't see any more of him today. Well, tell us *who's* out on the river?"

"Toad's out, for one," replied the Otter. "In his brand-new wager-boat; new togs, new everything!"

The two animals looked at each other and laughed.

"Once, it was nothing but sailing," said the Rat. "Then he tired of that and took to punting. Nothing would please him but to punt all day and every day, and a nice mess he made of it. Last year it was house-boating, and we all had to go and stay with him in his house-boat, and pretend we liked it. He was going to spend the rest of his life in a house-boat. It's all the same, whatever he takes up; he gets tired of it, and starts on something fresh."

"Such a good fellow, too," remarked the Otter reflectively. "But no stability—especially in a boat!"

From where they sat they could get a glimpse of the main stream across the island that separated them; and just then a wager-boat flashed into view, the rower—a short, stout figure—splashing badly and rolling a good deal, but working his hardest. The Rat stood up and hailed him, but Toad—for it was he—shook his head and settled sternly to his work.

"He'll be out of the boat in a minute if he rolls like that," said the Rat, sitting down again.

"Of course he will," chuckled the Otter. Did I ever tell you that good story about Toad and the lock-keeper? It happened this way. Toad . . ."

An errant May-fly swerved unsteadily athwart the current in the intoxicated fashion affected by young bloods of May-flies seeing life. A swirl of water and a "cloop!" and the May-fly was visible no more.

Neither was the Otter.

The Mole looked down. The voice was still in his ears, but the turf whereon he had sprawled was clearly vacant. Not an Otter to be seen, as far as the distant horizon.

But again there was a streak of bubbles on the surface of the river.

The Rat hummed a tune, and the Mole recollected that animal-etiquette forbade any sort of comment on the sudden disappearance of one's friends at any moment, for any reason or no reason whatever.

"Well, well," said the Rat, "I suppose we ought to be moving. I wonder which of us had better pack the luncheon-basket?" He did not speak as if he was frightfully eager for the treat.

"O, please let me," said the Mole. So, of course, the Rat let him.

Packing the basket was not quite such pleasant work as unpacking the basket. It never is. But the Mole was bent on enjoying everything, and although just when he had got the basket packed and strapped up rightly he saw a plate staring up at him from the grass, and when the job had been done again the Rat pointed out a fork which anybody ought to have seen, and last of all, behold! the mustard-pot, which he had been sitting on without knowing it—still, somehow, the thing got finished at last, without much loss of temper.

The afternoon sun was getting low as the Rat sculled gently homewards in a dreamy mood, murmuring poetry-things over to himself, and not paying much attention to Mole. But the Mole was very full of lunch, and self-satisfaction, and pride, and already quite at home in a boat (so he thought) and was getting a bit restless besides: and presently he said, "Ratty! Please, *I* want to row, now!"

The Rat shook his head with a smile. "Not yet, my young friend," he said—"wait till you've had a few lessons. It's not so easy as it looks."

The Mole was quiet for a minute or two. But he began to feel more and more jealous of Rat, sculling so strongly and so easily along, and his pride began to whisper that he could do it every bit as well He jumped up and seized the sculls, so suddenly, that the Rat, who was gazing out over the water and saying more poetry-things to himself, was taken by surprise and fell backwards off his seat with his legs in the air for the second time, while the triumphant Mole took his place and grabbed the sculls with entire confidence.

"Stop it, you *silly* ass" cried the Rat, from the bottom of the boat. "You can't do it! You'll have us over."

The Mole flung his sculls back with a flourish, and made a great dig at the water. He missed the surface altogether, his legs flew up above his head, and he found himself lying on the top of the prostrate Rat. Greatly alarmed, he made a grab at the side of the boat, and the next moment—Sploosh!

Over went the boat, and he found himself struggling in the river.

O my, how cold the water was, and O, how *very* wet it felt. How it sang in his ears as he went down, down, down! How bright and welcome the sun looked as he rose to the surface coughing and spluttering! How black was his despair when he felt himself sinking again! Then a firm paw gripped him by the back of his neck. It was the Rat, and he was evidently laughing—the Mole could *feel* him laughing, right down his arm and through his paw, and so into his—the Mole's—neck.

The Rat got hold of a scull and shoved it under the Mole's arm; then he did the same by the other side of him and, swimming behind, propelled the helpless animal to shore, hauled him out, and set him down on the bank, a squashy, pulpy lump of misery.

When the Rat had rubbed him down a bit, and wrung some of the wet out of him, he said, "Now then, old fellow! Trot up and down the towing-path as hard as you can, till you're warm and dry again, while I dive for the luncheon-basket."

So the dismal Mole, wet without and ashamed within, trotted about till he was fairly dry, while the Rat plunged into the water again, recovered the boat, righted her and made her fast, fetched his floating property to shore by degrees, and finally dived successfullly for the luncheon-basket and struggled to land with it.

When all was ready for a start once more, the Mole, limp and dejected, took his seat in the stern of the boat; and as they set off, he said in a low voice, broken with emotion, "Ratty, my generous friend! I am very sorry indeed for my foolish and ungrateful conduct. My heart quite fails me when I think how I might have lost that beautiful luncheon-basket. Indeed, I have been a complete ass, and I know it. Will you overlook it this once and forgive me, and let things go on as before?"

"That's all right, bless you!" responded the Rat cheerily. "What's a little wet to a Water Rat? I'm more in the water than out of it most days. Don't you think any more about it; and, look here! I really think you had better come and stop with me for a little time. It's very plain and rough, you know—not like Toad's house at all— but you haven't seen that yet; still, I can make you comfortable. And I'll teach you to row, and to swim, and you'll soon be as handy on the water as any of us."

The Mole was so touched by his kind manner of speaking that he could find no voice to answer him; and he had to brush away a tear or two with the back of his paw. But the Rat kindly looked in another direction, and presently the Mole's spirits revived again, and he was even able to give some straight back-talk to a couple of moorhens who were sniggering to each other about his bedraggled appearance.

When they got home, the Rat made a bright fire in the parlour, and planted the Mole in an arm-chair in front of it, having fetched down a dressing-gown and slippers for him, and told him river stories till supper-time. Very thrilling stories they were, too, to an earth-dwelling animal like Mole. Stories about weirs, and sudden floods, and leaping pike, and steamers that flung hard bottles—at least bottles were certainly flung, and *from* steamers, so presumably *by* them; and about herons, and how particular they were whom they spoke to; and about adventures down drains, and night-fishings with Otter, or excursions far afield with Badger. Supper was a most cheerful meal; but very shortly afterwards a terribly sleepy Mole had to be escorted upstairs by his considerate host, to the best bedroom, where he soon laid his head on his pillow in great peace and contentment, knowing that his new-found friend the River was lapping the sill of his window.

This day was only the first of many similar ones for the emancipated Mole, each of them longer and fuller of interest as the ripening summer moved onward. He learnt to swim and to row, and entered into the joy of running water; and with his ear to the reed-stems he caught, at intervals, something of what the wind went whispering so constantly among them.

CHAPTER 2

THE OPEN ROAD

"Ratty," said the Mole suddenly, one bright summer morning, "if you please, I want to ask you a favour."

The Rat was sitting on the river bank, singing a little song. He had just composed it himself, so he was very taken up with it, and would not pay proper attention to Mole or anything else. Since early morning he had been swimming in the river, in company with his friends the ducks. And when the ducks stood on their heads suddenly, as ducks will, he would dive down and tickle their necks, just under where their chins would be if ducks had chins, till they were forced to come to the surface again in a hurry, spluttering and angry and shaking their feathers at him, for it is impossible to say quite *all* you feel when your head is under water. At last they implored him to go away and attend to his own affairs and leave them to mind theirs. So the Rat went away, and sat on the river bank in the sun, and made up a song about them, which he called

"DUCKS' DITTY"

All along the backwater,
'Through the rushes tall
Ducks are a-dabbling,
Up tails all!

Ducks' tails, drakes' tails,
Yellow feet a-quiver,
Yellow bills all out of sight
Busy in the river?

Slushy green undergrowth
Where the roach swim—
Here we keep our larder,
Cool and full and dim.

Every one for what he likes!
We like to be
Heads down, tails up
Dabbling free!

High in the blue above
Swifts whirl and call—
We are down a-dabbling,
Up tails all!

"I don't know that I think so *very* much of that little song, Rat," observed the Mole cautiously. He was no poet himself and didn't care who knew it; and he had a candid nature.

"Nor don't the ducks neither," replied the Rat cheerfully. "They say, '*Why* can't fellows be allowed to do what they like *when* they like and *as* they like, instead of other fellows sitting on banks and watching them all the time and making remarks and poetry and things about them? What *nonsense* it all is!' That's what the ducks say."

"So it is, so it is," said the Mole, with great heartiness.

"No, it isn't!" cried the Rat indignantly.

"Well then, it isn't, it isn't," replied the Mole soothingly. "But what I wanted to ask you was, won't you take me to call on Mr Toad? I've heard so much about him, and I do so want to make his acquaintance."

"Why, certainly," said the good-natured Rat, jumping to his feet and dismissing poetry from his mind for the day. "Get the boat out, and we'll paddle up there at once. It's never the wrong time to call on Toad. Early or late he's always the same fellow. Always good-tempered, always glad to see you, always sorry when you go!"

"He must be a very nice animal," observed the Mole, as he got into the boat and took the sculls, while the Rat settled himself comfortably in the stern.

"He is indeed the best of animals," replied Rat. "So simple, so good-natured, and so affectionate. Perhaps he's not very clever—we can't all be geniuses; and it may be that he is both boastful and conceited. But he has got some great qualities, has Toady."

Rounding a bend in the river, they came in sight of a handsome, dignified old house of mellowed red brick, with well-kept lawns reaching down to the water's edge.

"There's Toad Hall," said the Rat; "and that creek on the left, where the notice-board says 'Private. No landing allowed', leads to his boat-house, where we'll leave the boat. The stables are over there to the right. That's the banqueting-hall you're looking at now—very old, that is. Toad is rather rich, you know, and this is really one of the nicest houses in these parts, though we never admit as much to Toad."

They glided up the creek, and the Mole shipped his sculls as they passed into the shadow of a large boat-house. Here they saw many handsome boats, slung from the cross-beams or hauled up on a slip, but none in the water; and the place had an unused and a deserted air.

The Rat looked around him. "I understand," said he. "Boating is played out. He's tired of it, and done with it. I wonder what new fad he has taken up now? Come along and let's look him up. We shall hear all about it quite soon enough."

They disembarked, and strolled across the gay flower-decked lawns in search of Toad, whom they presently happened upon resting in a wicker garden-chair, with a preoccupied expression of face, and a large map spread out on his knees.

"Hooray" he cried, jumping up on seeing them, "this is splendid!" He shook the paws of both of them warmly, never waiting for an introduction to the Mole. "How *kind* of you!" he went on, dancing round them. "I was just going to send a boat down the river for you, Ratty, with strict orders that you were to be fetched up here at once, whatever you were doing. I want you badly—both of you. Now what will you take? Come inside and have something! You don't know how lucky it is, your turning up just now!"

"Let's sit quiet a bit, Toady!" said the Rat, throwing himself into an easy chair, while the Mole took another by the side of him and made some civil remark about Toad's "delightful residence".

"Finest house on the whole river," cried Toad boisterously. "Or anywhere else, for that matter," he could not help adding.

Here the Rat nudged the Mole. Unfortunately the Toad saw him do it, and turned very red. There was a moment's painful silence. Then Toad burst out laughing. "All right, Ratty," he said "It's only my way, you know. And it's not such a very bad house, is it? You know you rather like it yourself. Now, look here. Let's be sensible. You are the very animals I wanted. You've got tc help me. It's most important!"

"It's about your rowing, I suppose," said the Rat, with an innocent air. "You're getting on fairly well, though you splash a good bit still. With a great deal of patience, and any quantity of coaching, you may—"

"O, pooh! boating?" interrupted the Toad, in great disgust. "Silly boyish amusement. I've given that up *long* ago. Sheer waste of time, that's what it is. It makes me downright sorry to see you fellows, who ought to know better, spending all your energies in that aimless manner. No, I've discovered the real thing, the only genuine occupation for a lifetime. I propose to devote the remainder of mine to it, and can only regret the wasted years that lie behind me, squandered in trivialities. Come with me, dear Ratty, and your amiable friend also, if he will be so very good, just as far as the stable-yard, and you shall see what you shall see!"

He led the way to the stable-yard accordingly, the Rat following with a most mistrustful expression; and there, drawn out of the coach-house into the open, they saw a gipsy caravan, shining with newness, painted a canary-yellow picked out with green and red wheels.

"There you are!" cried the Toad, straddling and expanding himself "There's real life for you, embodied in that little cart. The open road, the dusty highway, the heath, the common, the hedgerows, the rolling downs! Camps, villages, towns, cities! Here to-day, up and off to somewhere else to-morrow! Travel, change, interest, excitement! The whole world before you, and a horizon that's always changing! And mind, this is the very finest cart of its sort that was ever built, without exception. Come inside and look at the arrangements. Planned 'em all myself, I did!"

The Mole was tremendously interested and excited, and followed him eagerly up the steps and into the interior of the caravan. The Rat only snorted and thrust his hands deep into his pockets, remaining where he was.

It was indeed very compact and comfortable. Little sleeping-bunks—a little table that folded up against the wall—a cooking-stove, lockers, bookshelves, a bird cage with a bird in it; and pots, pans, jugs and kettles of every size and variety.

"All complete!" said the Toad triumphantly, pulling open a locker. "You see—biscuits, potted lobster, sardines—everything you can possibly want. Soda-water here—baccy there—letter-paper, bacon, jam, cards and dominoes—you'll find," he continued, as they descended the steps again, "you'll find that nothing whatever has been forgotten, when we make our start this afternoon."

"I beg your pardon," said the Rat slowly, as he chewed a straw, "but did I overhear you say something about '*we*', and '*start*', and '*this afternoon*'?"

"Now, you dear good old Ratty," said Toad imploringly, "don't begin talking in that stiff and sniffy sort of way, because you know you've *got* to come. I can't possibly manage without you, so please consider it settled, and don't argue—it's the one thing I can't stand. You surely don't mean to stick to your dull fusty old river all your life, and just live in a hole in a bank, and *boat*? I want to show you the world! I'm going to make an *animal* of you, my boy!"

"I don't care," said the Rat doggedly. "I'm not coming, and that's flat. And I *am* going to stick to my old river, *and* live in a hole, *and* boat, as I've always done. And what's more, Mole's going to stick to me and do as I do, aren't you, Mole?"

"Of course I am," said the Mole loyally. "I'll always stick to you, Rat, and what you say is to be—has got to be. All the same, it sounds as if it might have been—well, rather fun, you know!" he added wistfully. Poor Mole! The Life Adventurous was so new a thing to him and so thrilling; and this fresh aspect of it was so tempting; and he had fallen in love at first sight with the canary-coloured cart and all its little fitments.

The Rat saw what was passing in his mind, and wavered. He hated disappointing people, and he was fond of the Mole, and would do almost anything to oblige him. Toad was watching both of them closely.

"Come along in and have some lunch," he said diplomatically, "and we'll talk it over. We needn't decide anything in a hurry. Of course, *I* don't really care. I only want to give pleasure to you fellows. 'Live for others!' That's my motto in life."

During luncheon—which was excellent, of course, as everything at Toad Hall always was—the Toad simply let himself go. Disregarding the Rat, he proceeded to play upon the inexperienced Mole as on a harp. Naturally a voluble animal, and always mastered by his imagination, he painted the prospects of the trip and the joys of the open life and the road-side in such glowing colours that the Mole could hardly sit in his chair for excitement. Somehow, it soon seemed taken for granted by all three of them that the trip was a settled thing; and the Rat, though still unconvinced in his mind, allowed his good-nature to over-ride his personal objections. He could not bear to disappoint his two friends, who were already deep in schemes and anticipations, planning out each day's separate occupation for several weeks ahead.

When they were quite ready, the now triumphant Toad led his companions to the paddock and set them to capture the old grey horse, who, without having been consulted, and to his own extreme annoyance, had been told off by Toad for the dustiest job in this dusty expedition. He frankly preferred the paddock, and took a deal of catching. Meantime Toad packed the lockers still tighter with necessaries, and hung nose-bags, nets of onions, bundles of hay, and baskets from the bottom of the cart. At last the horse was caught and harnessed, and they set off, all talking at once, each animal either trudging by the side of the cart or sitting on the shaft, as the humour took him. It was a golden afternoon. The smell of the dust they kicked up was rich and satisfying; out of thick orchards on either side of the road, birds called and whistled to them cheerily; good-natured wayfarers, passing them, gave them "Good day", or stopped to say nice things about their beautiful cart; and rabbits, sitting at their front doors in the hedgerows, held up their forepaws, and said, "O my! O my! O my!"

Late in the evening, tired and happy and miles from home, they drew up on a remote common far from habitations, turned the horse loose to graze, and ate their simple supper sitting on the grass by the side of the cart. Toad talked big about all he was going to do in the days to come, while stars grew fuller and larger all around them, and a yellow moon, appearing suddenly and silently from nowhere in particular, came to keep them company and listen to their talk. At last they turned into their little bunks in the cart; and Toad, kicking out his legs, sleepily said, "Well, good night, you fellows! This is the real life for a gentleman! Talk about your old river!"

"I *don't* talk about my river," replied the patient Rat. "You know I don't, Toad. But I *think* about it," he added pathetically, in a lower tone: "I think about it—all the time!"

The Mole reached out from under his blanket, felt for the Rat's paw in the darkness, and gave it a squeeze. "I'll do whatever you like, Ratty," he whispered. "Shall we run away to-morrow morning, quite early—*very* early—and go back to our dear old hole on the river?"

"No, no, we'll see it out," whispered back the Rat. "Thanks awfully, but I ought to stick by Toad till this trip is ended. It wouldn't be safe for him to be left to himself It won't take very long. His fads never do. Good night!"

The end was indeed nearer than even the Rat suspected.

After so much open air and excitement the Toad slept very soundly, and no amount of shaking could rouse him out of bed next morning. So the Mole and Rat turned to, quietly and manfully, and while the Rat saw to the horse, and lit a fire, and cleaned last night's cups and platters, and got things ready for breakfast, the Mole trudged off to the nearest village, a long way off, for milk and eggs and various necessaries the Toad had, of course, forgotten to provide. The hard work had all been done, and the two animals were resting, thoroughly exhausted, by the time Toad appeared on the scene, fresh and gay, remarking what a pleasant easy life it was they were all leading now, after the cares and worries and fatigues of house-keeping at home.

They had a pleasant ramble that day over grassy downs and along narrow by-lanes, and camped, as before, on a common, only this time the two guests took care that Toad should do his fair share of work. In consequence, when the time came for starting next morning, Toad was by no means so rapturous about the simplicity of the primitive life, and indeed attempted to resume his place in his bunk, whence he was hauled by force. Their way lay, as before, across country by narrow lanes, and it was not till the afternoon that they came out on the high road their first high road; and there disaster, fleet and unfore-seen, sprang out on them—disaster momentous indeed to their expedition, but simply overwhelming in its effect on the after-career of Toad.

They were strolling along the high road easily, the Mole by the horse's head, talking to him, since the horse had complained that he was being frightfully left out of it, and nobody considered him in the least; the Toad and the Water Rat walking behind the cart talking together—at least Toad was talking, and Rat was saying at intervals, "Yes, precisely; and what did *you* say to *him*?"—and thinking all the time of something very different, when far behind them they heard a faint warning hum, like the drone of a distant bee. Glancing back, they saw a small cloud of dust, with a dark centre of energy advancing on them at incredible speed, while from out of the dust a faint "Poop-poop!" wailed like an uneasy animal in pain. Hardly regarding it, they turned to resume their conver-sation, when in an instant (as it seemed) the peaceful scene was changed, and with a blast of wind and a whirl of sound that made them jump for the nearest ditch, it was on them! The "poop-poop" rang with a brazen shout in their ears, they had a moment's glimpse of an interior of glittering plate-glass and rich morocco, and the magnificent motor-car, immense, breath-snatching, passionate, with its pilot tense and hugging his wheel, possessed all earth and air for the fraction of a second, flung an enveloping cloud of dust that blinded and enwrapped them utterly, and then dwindled to a speck in the far distance, changed back into a droning bee once more.

The old grey horse, dreaming, as he plodded along, of his quiet paddock, in a new raw situation such as this simply abandoned himself to his natural emotions. Rearing, plunging, backing steadily, in spite of all the Mole's efforts at his head, and all the Mole's lively language directed at his better feelings, he drove the cart backwards towards the deep ditch at the side of the road. It wavered an instant—then there was a heartrending crash—and the canary-coloured cart, their pride and their joy, lay on its side in the ditch, an irredeemable wreck.

The Rat danced up and down in the road, simply transported with passion. "You villains!" he shouted, shaking both fists, "You scoundrels, you highwaymen, you—you—road-hogs!—I'll have the law on you! I'll report you! I'll take you through all the Courts!" His home-sickness had quite slipped away from him, and for the moment he was the skipper of the canary-coloured vessel driven on a shoal by the reckless jockeying of rival mariners, and he was trying to recollect all the fine and biting things he used to say to masters of steam-launches when their wash, as they drove too near the bank, used to flood his parlour carpet at home.

Toad sat straight down in the middle of the dusty road, his legs stretched out before him, and stared fixedly in the direction of the disappearing motor-car. He breathed short, his face wore a placid, satisfied expression, and at intervals he faintly murmured "Poop-poop!"

The Mole was busy trying to quiet the horse, which he succeeded in doing after a time. Then he went to look at the cart, on its side in the ditch. It was indeed a sorry sight. Panels and windows smashed, axles hopelessly bent, one wheel off, sardine-tins scattered over the wide world, and the bird in the bird-cage sobbing pitifully and calling to be let out.

The Rat came to help him, but their united efforts were not sufficient to right the cart. "Hi! Toad!" they cried. "Come and bear a hand, can't you!"

The Toad never answered a word, or budged from his seat in the road; so they went to see what was the matter with him. They found him in a sort of trance, a happy smile on his face, his eyes still fixed on the dusty wake of their destroyer. At intervals he was still heard to murmur "Poop-poop!"

The Rat shook him by the shoulder. "Are you coming to help us, Toad?" he demanded sternly.

"Glorious, stirring sight!" murmured Toad, never offering to move. "The poetry of motion! The *real* way to travel! The *only* way to travel! Here to-day—in next week to-morrow! Villages skipped, towns and cities jumped—always somebody else's horizon! O bliss! O poop-poop! O my! O my!"

"O *stop* being an ass, Toad!" cried the Mole despairingly.

"And to think I never *knew*!" went on the Toad in a dreamy monotone. "All those wasted years that lie behind me. I never knew, never even *dreamt*! But now—but *now* that I know, now that I fully realize! O what a flowery track lies spread before me, hence-forth! What dust-clouds shall spring up behind me as I speed on my reckless way! What carts I shall fling carelessly into the ditch in the wake of my magnificent onset! Horrid little carts—common carts—canary-coloured carts!"

"What are we to do with him?" asked the Mole of the Water Rat.

"Nothing at all," replied the Rat firmly. "Because there is really nothing to be done. You see, I know him from of old. He is now possessed. He has got a new craze, and it always takes him that way, in its first stage. He'll continue like that for days now, like an animal walking in a happy dream, quite useless for all practical purposes. Never mind him. Let's go and see what there is to be done about the cart."

A careful inspection showed them that, even if they succeeded in righting it by themselves, the cart would travel no longer. The axles were in a hopeless state, and the missing wheel was shattered into pieces.

The Rat knotted the horse's reins over his back and took him by the head, carrying the bird-cage and its hysterical occupant in the other hand. "Come on!" he said grimly to the Mole. "It's five or six miles to the nearest town, and we shall just have to walk it. The sooner we make a start the better."

"But what about Toad?" asked the Mole anxiously, as they set off together. "We can't leave him here, sitting in the middle of the road by himself, in the distracted state he's in! It's not safe. Supposing another Thing were to come along?"

"O, *bother* Toad," said the Rat savagely; "I've done with him." They had not proceeded very far on their way, however, when there was a pattering of feet behind them, and Toad caught them up and thrust a paw inside the elbow of each of them; still breathing short and staring into vacancy.

"Now, look here, Toad!" said the Rat sharply: "as soon as we get to the town, you'll have to go straight to the police-station, and see if they know anything about that motor-car and who it belongs to, and lodge a complaint against it. And then you'll have to go to a blacksmith's or a wheelwright's and arrange for the cart to be fetched and mended and put to rights. It'll take time, but it's not quite a hopeless smash. Meanwhile, the Mole and I will go to an inn and find comfortable rooms where we can stay till the cart's ready, and till your nerves have recovered their shock."

"Police-station! Complaint!" murmured Toad dreamily. "Me *complain* of that beautiful, that heavenly vision that has been vouchsafed me! *Mend* the *cart*! I've done with carts for ever. I never want to see the cart, or to hear of it again. O Ratty! You can't think how obliged I am to you for consenting to come on this trip! I wouldn't have gone without you, and then I might never have seen that—that swan, that sunbeam, that thunderbolt! I might never have heard that entrancing sound, or smelt that bewitching smell! I owe it all to you, my best of friends!"

The Rat turned from him in despair. "You see what it is?" he said to the Mole, addressing him across Toad's head: "He's quite hopeless. I give it up—when we get to the town we'll go to the railway station, and with luck we may pick up a train there that'll get us back to River Bank to-night. And if ever you catch me going a-pleasuring with this provoking animal again"—He snorted, and during the rest of that weary trudge addressed his remarks exclusively to Mole.

On reaching the town they went straight to the station and deposited Toad in the second-class waiting-room, giving a porter twopence to keep a strict eye on him. They then left the horse at an inn stable, and gave what directions they could about the cart and its contents. Eventually, a slow train having landed them at a station not very far from Toad Hall, they escorted the spellbound, sleep-walking Toad to his door, put him inside it, and instructed his house-keeper to feed him, undress him, and put him to bed. Then they got out their boat from the boat-house, sculled down the river home, and at a very late hour sat down to supper in their own cosy riverside parlour, to the Rat's great joy and contentment.

The following evening the Mole, who had risen late and taken things very easy all day, was sitting on the bank fishing, when the Rat, who had been looking up his friends and gossiping, cane strolling along to find him. "Heard the news?" he said. "There's nothing else being talked about, all along the river bank. Toad went up to Town by an early train this morning. And he has ordered a large and very expensive motor-car."

Chapter 3

THE WILD WOOD

The Mole had long wanted to make the acquaintance of the Badger. He seemed, by all accounts, to be such an important personage and, though rarely visible, to make his unseen influence felt by everybody about the place. But whenever the Mole mentioned his wish to the Water Rat he always found himself put off. "It's all right," the Rat would say. "Badger'll turn up some day or other—he's always turning up—and then I'll introduce you. The best of fellows! But you must not only take him as you find him, but *when* you find him."

"Couldn't you ask him here—dinner or something?" said the Mole.

"He wouldn't come," replied the Rat simply. "Badger hates Society, and invitations, and dinner, and all that sort of thing."

"Well, then, supposing we go and call on *him*?" suggested the Mole.

"O, I'm sure he wouldn't like that at *all*," said the Rat, quite alarmed. "He's so very shy, he'd be sure to be offended. I've never even ventured to call on him at his own home myself, though I know him so well. Besides, we can't. It's quite out of the question, because he lives in the very middle of the Wild Wood."

"Well, supposing he does," said the Mole. "You told me the Wild Wood was all right, you know."

"Oh, I know, I know, so it is," replied the Rat evasively. "But I think we won't go there just now. Not *just* yet. It's a long way, and he wouldn't be at home at this time of year anyhow, and he'll be coming along some day, if you'll wait quietly."

The Mole had to be content with this. But the Badger never came along, and every day brought its amusements, and it was not till summer was long over, and cold and frost and miry ways kept them much indoors, and the swollen river raced past outside their windows with a speed that mocked at boating of any sort or kind, that he found his thoughts dwelling again with much persistence on the solitary grey Badger, who lived his own life by himself, in his hole in the middle of the Wild Wood.

In the winter time the Rat slept a great deal, retiring early and rising late. During his short day he sometimes scribbled poetry or did other small domestic jobs about the house; and, of course, there were always animals dropping in for a chat, and consequently there was a good deal of story-telling and comparing notes on the past summer and all its doings.

Such a rich chapter it had been, when one came to look back on it all! With illustrations so numerous and so very highly coloured! The pageant of the river bank had marched steadily along, unfolding itself in scene-pictures that succeeded each other in stately procession. Purple loosestrife arrived early, shaking luxuriant tangled locks along the edge of the mirror whence its own face laughed back at it. Willow-herb, tender and wistful, like a pink sunset cloud was not slow to follow. Comfrey, the purple hand-in-hand with the white, crept forth to take its place in the line; and at last one morning the diffident and delaying dog-rose stepped delicately on the stage, and one knew, as if string music had announced it in stately chords that strayed into a gavotte, that June at last was here. One member of the company was still awaited; the shepherd-boy for the nymphs to woo, the knight for whom the ladies waited at the window, the prince that was to kiss the sleeping summer back to life and love. But when meadow-sweet, debonair and odorous in amber jerkin, moved graciously to his place in the group, then the play was ready to begin.

And what a play it had been! Drowsy animals, snug in their holes while wind and rain were battering at their doors, recalled still keen mornings an hour before sunrise, when the white mist, as yet undispersed, clung closely along the surface of the water; then the shock of the early plunge, the scamper along the bank, and the radiant transformation of earth, air, and water, when suddenly the sun was with them again, and grey was gold and colour was born and sprang out of the earth once more. They recalled the languorous siesta of hot midday, deep in green undergrowth, the sun striking through in tiny golden shafts and spots; the boating and bathing of the afternoon, the rambles along dusty lanes and through yellow cornfields; and the long cool evening at last, when so many threads were gathered up, so many friendships rounded, and so many adventures planned for the morrow. There was plenty to talk about on those short winter days when the animals found themselves round the fire; still, the Mole had a good deal of spare time on his hands, and so one afternoon, when the Rat in his arm-chair before the blaze was alternately dozing and trying over rhymes that wouldn't fit, he formed the resolution to go out by himself and explore the Wild Wood, and perhaps strike up an acquaintance with Mr Badger.

It was a cold still afternoon with a hard steely sky overhead, when he slipped out of the warm parlour into the open air. The country lay bare and entirely leafless around him, and he thought that he had never seen so far and so intimately into the insides of things as on that winter day when Nature was deep in her annual slumber and seemed to have kicked the clothes off. Copses, dells, quarries and all hidden places, which had been mysterious mines for exploration in leafy summer, now exposed themselves and their secrets pathetically, and seemed to ask him to overlook their shabby poverty for a while, till they could riot in rich masquerade as before, and trick and entice him with the old deceptions. It was pitiful in a way, and yet cheering—even exhilarating. He was glad that he liked the country undecorated, hard, and stripped of its finery. He had got down to the bare bones of it, and they were fine and strong and simple. He did not want the warm clover and the play of seeding grasses; the screens of quickset, the billowy drapery of beech and elm seemed best away; and with great cheerfulness of spirit he pushed on towards the Wild Wood, which lay before him low and threatening, like a black reef in some still southern sea.

There was nothing to alarm him at first entry. Twigs crackled under his feet, logs tripped him, funguses on stumps resembled caricatures, and startled him for the moment by their likeness to something familiar and far away; but that was all fun, and exciting. It led him on, and he penetrated to where the light was less, and trees crouched nearer and nearer, and holes made ugly mouths at him on either side.

Everything was very still now. The dusk advanced on him steadily, rapidly, gathering in behind and before; and the light seemed to be draining away like flood-water.

Then the faces began.

It was over his shoulder, and indistinctly, that he first thought he saw a face: a little evil wedge-shaped face, looking out at him from a hole. When he turned and confronted it, the thing had vanished. He quickened his pace, telling himself cheerfully not to begin imagining things, or there would be simply no end to it. He passed another hole, and another, and another; and then—yes!—no!—yes! certainly a little narrow face, with hard eyes, had flashed up for an instant from a hole, and was gone. He hesitated—braced himself up for an effort and strode on. Then suddenly, and as if it had been so all the time, every hole, far and near, and there were hundreds of them, seemed to possess its face, coming and going rapidly, all fixing on him glances of malice and hatred: all hard-eyed and evil and sharp.

If he could only get away from the holes in the banks, he thought, there would be no more faces. He swung off the path and plunged into the untrodden places of the wood.

Then the whistling began.

Very faint and shrill it was, and far behind him, when first he heard it; but somehow it made him hurry forward. Then, still very faint and shrill, it sounded far ahead of him, and made him hesitate and want to go back. As he halted in indecision it broke out on either side, and seemed to be caught up and passed on throughout the whole length of the wood to its furthest limit. They were up and alert and ready, evidently, whoever they were! And he—he was alone, and unarmed, and far from any help; and the night was closing in.

Then the pattering began.

He thought it was only falling leaves at first, so slight and delicate was the sound of it. Then as it grew it took a regular rhythm, and he knew it for nothing else but the pat-pat-pat of little feet, still a very long way off. Was it in front or behind? It seemed to be first one, then the other, then both. It grew and it multiplied, till from every quarter as he listened anxiously, leaning this way and that, it seemed to be closing in on him. As he stood still to hearken, a rabbit came running hard towards him through the trees. He waited, expecting it to slacken pace, or to swerve from him into a different course. Instead, the animal almost brushed him as it dashed past, his face set and hard, his eyes staring. "Get out of this, you fool, get out," the Mole heard him mutter as he swung round a stump and disappeared down a friendly burrow.

The pattering increased till it sounded like sudden hail on the dry-leaf carpet spread around him. The whole wood seemed running now, running hard, hunting, chasing, closing in round something or—somebody? In panic, he began to run too, aimlessly, he knew not whither. He ran up against things, he fell over things and into things, he darted under things and dodged round things. At last he took refuge in the dark deep hollow of an old beech tree, which offered shelter, concealment—perhaps even safety, but who could tell? Anyhow, he was too tired to run any further, and could only snuggle down into the dry leaves which had drifted into the hollow and hope he was safe for the time. and as he lay there panting and trembling, and listened to the whistlings and the patterings outside, he knew it at last, in all its fullness, that dread thing which other little dwellers in field and hedgerow had encountered here, and known as their darkest moment—that thing which the Rat had vainly tried to shield him from—the Terror of the Wild Wood!

Meantime the Rat, warm and comfortable, dozed by his fireside. His paper of half-finished verses slipped from his knee, his head fell back, his mouth opened, and he wandered by the verdant banks of dream-rivers. Then a coal slipped, the fire crackled and sent up a spurt of flame, and he woke with a start. Remembering what he had been engaged upon, he reached down to the floor for his verses, pored over them for a minute, and then looked round for the Mole to ask him if he knew a good rhyme for something or other.

But the Mole was not there.

He listened for a time. The house seemed very quiet.

Then he called "Moly!" several times, and, receiving no answer, got up and went out into the hall.

The Mole's cap was missing from its accustomed peg. His goloshes, which always lay by the umbrella-stand, were also gone.

The Rat left the house and carefully examined the muddy surface of the ground outside, hoping to find the Mole's tracks. There they were, sure enough. The goloshes were new, just bought for the winter, and the pimples on their soles were fresh and sharp. He could see the imprints of them in the mud, running along straight and purposeful, leading direct to the Wild Wood.

The Rat looked very grave, and stood in deep thought for a minute or two. Then he re-entered the house, strapped a belt round his waist, shoved a brace of pistols into it, took up a stout cudgel that stood in a corner of the hall, and set off for the Wild Wood at a smart pace.

It was already getting towards dusk when he reached the first fringe of trees and plunged without hesitation into the wood, looking anxiously on either side for any sign of his friend. Here and there wicked little faces popped out of holes, but vanished immediately at sight of the valorous animal, his pistols, and the great ugly cudgel in his grasp; and the whistling and pattering, which he had heard quite plainly on his first entry, died away and ceased, and all was very still. He made his way manfully through the length of the wood, to its furthest edge; then, forsaking all paths, he set himself to traverse it, laboriously working over the whole ground, and all the time calling out cheerfully, "Moly, Moly, Moly! Where are you? It's me—it's old Rat!"

He had patiently hunted through the wood for an hour or more, when at last to his joy he heard a little answering cry. Guiding himself by the sound, he made his way through the gathering darkness to the foot of an old beech tree, with a hole in it, and from out of the hole came a feeble voice, saying, "Ratty! Is that really you?"

The Rat crept into the hollow, and there he found the Mole, exhausted and still trembling. "O, Rat!" he cried, "I've been so frightened, you can't think!"

"Oh, I quite understand," said the Rat soothingly. "You shouldn't really have gone and done it, Mole. I did my best to keep you from it. We river-bankers, we hardly ever come here by ourselves. If we have to come, we come in couples, at least; then we're generally all right. Besides, there are a hundred things one has to know, which we understand all about and you don't, as yet. I mean pass-words, and signs, and sayings which have power and effect, and plants you carry in your pocket, and verses you repeat, and dodges and tricks you practise; all simple enough when you know them, but they've got to be known if you're small, or you'll find yourself in trouble. Of course if you were Badger or Otter, it would be quite another matter."

"Surely the brave Mr Toad wouldn't mind coming here by himself, would he?" inquired the Mole.

"Old Toad?" said the Rat, laughing heartily. "He wouldn't show his face here alone, not for a whole hatful of golden guineas, Toad wouldn't."

The Mole was greatly cheered by the sound of the Rat's careless laughter, as well as by the sight of his stick and his gleaming pistols, and he stopped shivering and began to feel bolder and more himself again.

"Now then," said the Rat presently, "we really must pull ourselves together and make a start for home while there's still a little light left. It will never do to spend the night here, you understand. Too cold, for one thing."

"Dear Ratty," said the poor Mole, "I'm dreadfully sorry, but I'm simply dead beat and that's a solid fact. You *must* let me rest here a while longer, and get my strength back, if I'm to get home at all."

"O, all right," said the good-natured Rat, "rest away. It's pretty nearly pitch dark now, anyhow; and there ought to be a bit of a moon later."

So the Mole got well into the dry leaves and stretched himself out, and presently dropped off into sleep, though of a broken and troubled sort; while the Rat covered himself up, too, as best he might, for warmth, and lay patiently waiting, with a pistol in his paw.

When at last the Mole woke up, much refreshed and in his usual spirits, the Rat said, "Now then! I'll just take a look outside and see if everything's quiet, and then we really must be off."

He went to the entrance of their retreat and put his head out. Then the Mole heard him saying quietly to himself, "Hullo! hullo! here—*is*—a—go!"

"What's up, Ratty?" asked the Mole.

"*Snow* is up," replied the Rat briefly; "or rather, *down*. It's snowing hard."

The Mole came and crouched beside him, and, looking out, saw the wood that had been so dreadful to him in quite a changed aspect. Holes, hollows, pools, pitfalls, and other black menaces to the wayfarer were vanishing fast, and a gleaming carpet of faery was springing up everywhere, that looked too delicate to be trodden upon by rough feet. A fine powder filled the air and caressed the cheek with a tingle in its touch, and the black boles of the trees showed up in a light that seemed to come from below.

"Well, well, it can't be helped," said the Rat after pondering. "We must make a start, and take our chance, I suppose. The worst of it is, I don't exactly know where we are. And now this snow makes everything look so very different."

It did indeed. The Mole would not have known that it was the same wood. However, they set out bravely, and took the line that seemed most promising, holding on to each other and pretending with invincible cheerfulness that they recognized an old friend in every fresh tree that grimly and silently greeted them, or saw openings, gaps, or paths with a familiar turn in them, in the monotony of white space and black tree-trunks that refused to vary.

An hour or two later—they had lost all count of time—they pulled up, dispirited, weary, and hopelessly at sea, and sat down on a fallen tree-trunk to recover their breath and consider what was to be done. They were aching with fatigue and bruised with tumbles; they had fallen into several holes and got wet through; the snow was getting so deep that they could hardly drag their little legs through it, and the trees were thicker and more like each other than ever. There seemed to be no end to this wood, and no beginning, and no difference in it, and, worst of all, no way out.

"We can't sit here very long," said the Rat. "We shall have to make another push for it, and do something or other. The cold is too awful for anything, and the snow will soon be too deep for us to wade through." He peered about him and considered. "Look here," he went on, "this is what occurs to me; There's a sort of dell down there in front of us, where the ground seems all hilly and humpy and hummocky. Well make our way down into that, and try and find some sort of shelter, a cave or hole with a dry floor to it, out of the snow and the wind, and there we'll have a good rest before we try again, for we're both of us pretty dead beat. Besides, the snow may leave off, or something may turn up."

So once more they got on their feet, and struggled down into the dell, where they hunted about for a cave or some corner that was dry and a protection from the keen wind and the whirling snow. They were investigating one of the hummocky bits the Rat had spoken of, when suddenly the Mole tripped up and fell forward on his face with a squeal.

"O, my leg!" he cried. "O, my poor shin!" and he sat upon the snow and nursed his leg in both his front paws.

"Poor old Mole!" said the Rat kindly. "You don't seem to be having much luck to-day, do you? Let's have a look at the leg. Yes," he went on, going down on his knees to look, "you've cut your shin, sure enough. Wait till I get at my handkerchief, and I'll tie it up for you."

"I must have tripped over a hidden branch or a stump," said the Mole miserably. "O my! O my!"

"It's a very clean cut," said the Rat, examining it again attentively. "That was never done by a branch or a stump.

Looks as if it was made by a sharp edge of something in metal. Funny!" He pondered a while, and examined the humps and slopes that surrounded them.

"Well, never mind what done it," said the Mole, forgetting his grammar in his pain. "It hurts just the same, whatever done it."

But the Rat, after carefully tying up the leg with his handkerchief, had left him and was busy scraping in the snow. He scratched and shovelled and explored, all four legs working busily, while the Mole waited impatiently, remarking at intervals, "O, *come* on, Rat!"

Suddenly the Rat cried "Hooray" and then "Hooray-oo-ray-oo-ray-oo-ray!" and fell to executing a feeble jig in the snow.

"What *have* you found, Ratty?" asked the Mole, still nursing his leg.

"Come and see!" said the delighted Rat, as he jigged on.

The Mole hobbled up to the spot and had a good look.

"Well," he said at last, slowly, "I *see* it right enough. Seen the same sort of thing before, lots of times. Familiar object, I call it. A door-scraper! Well, what of it? Why dance jigs round a door-scraper?"

"But don't you see what it *means,* you—you dull-witted animal?" cried the Rat impatiently.

"Of course I see what it means," replied the Mole. "It simply means that some *very* careless and forgetful person has left his door-scraper lying about in the middle of the Wild Wood, *just* where it's *sure* to trip *everybody* up. Very thoughtless of him, I call it. When I get home I shall go and complain about it to—to somebody or other, see if I don't!"

"O dear! O dear!" cried the Rat, in despair at his obtuseness.

"Here, stop arguing and come and scrape!" And he set to work again and made the snow fly in all directions around him.

After some further toil his efforts were rewarded, and a very shabby door-mat lay exposed to view.

"There, what did I tell you?" exclaimed the Rat in great triumph.

"Absolutely nothing whatever," replied the Mole, with perfect truthfulness. "Well now," he went on, "you seem to have found another piece of domestic litter, done for and thrown away, and I suppose you're perfectly happy. Better go ahead and dance your jig round that if you've got to, and get it over, and then perhaps we can go on and not waste any more time over rubbish-heaps. Can we *eat* a door-mat? Or sleep under a door-mat? Or sit on a door-mat and sledge home over the snow on it, you exasperating rodent?"

"Do—you—mean—to—say," cried the excited Rat, "that this door-mat doesn't *tell* you anything?"

"Really, Rat," said the Mole quite pettishly, "I think we've had enough of this folly. Who ever heard of a door-mat telling any one anything? They simply don't do it. They are not that sort at all. Door-mats know their place."

"Now look here, you—you thick-headed beast," replied the Rat, really angry, "this must stop. Not another word, but scrape—scrape and scratch and dig and hunt round, especially on the sides of the hummocks, if you want to sleep dry and warm tonight, for it's our last chance!"

The Rat attacked a snow-bank beside them with ardour, probing with his cudgel everywhere and then digging with fury; and the Mole scraped busily too, more to oblige the Rat than for any other reason, for his opinion was that his friend was getting light-headed.

Some ten minutes' hard work, and the point of the Rat's cudgel struck something that sounded hollow. He worked till he could get a paw through and feel; then called the Mole to come and help him. Hard at it went the two animals, till at last the result of their labours stood full in view of the astonished and hitherto incredulous Mole.

In the side of what had seemed to be a snow-bank stood a solid-looking little door, painted a dark green. An iron bell-pull hung by the side, and below it, on a small brass plate, neatly engraved in square capital letters, they could read by the aid of moonlight:

MR BADGER

The Mole fell backwards on the snow from sheer surprise and delight. "Rat!" he cried in penitence, "you're a wonder! A real wonder, that's what you are. I see it all now! You argued it out, step by step, in that wise head of yours, from the very moment that I fell and cut my shin, and you looked at the cut, and at once your majestic mind said to itself, 'Door-scraper!' And then you turned to and found the very door-scraper that done it! Did you stop there? No. Some people would have been quite satisfied; but not you. Your intellect went on working. 'Let me only just find a door-mat,' says you to yourself, 'and my theory is proved!' And of course you found your door-mat. You're so clever, I believe you could find anything you liked. 'Now,' says you, 'that door exists, as plain as if I saw it. There's nothing else remains to be done but to find it!' Well, I've read about that sort of thing in books, but I've never come across it before in real life. You ought to go where you'll be properly appreciated. You're simply wasted here, among us fellows. If I only had your head, Ratty—"

"But as you haven't," interrupted the Rat rather unkindly, "I suppose you're going to sit on the snow all night and talk? Get up at once and hang on to that bell-pull you see there, and ring hard, as hard as you can, while I hammer!"

While the Rat attacked the door with his stick, the Mole sprang up at the bell-pull, clutched it and swung there, both feet well off the ground, and from quite a long way off they could faintly hear a deep-toned bell respond.

CHAPTER 4

MR BADGER

They waited patiently for what seemed a very long time, stamping in the snow to keep their feet warm. At last they heard the sound of slow shuffling footsteps approaching the door from the inside. It seemed, as the Mole remarked to the Rat, like some one walking in carpet slippers that were too large for him and down at heel; which was intelligent of Mole, because that was exactly what it was.

There was the noise of a bolt shot back, and the door opened a few inches, enough to show a long snout and a pair of sleepy blinking eyes.

"Now, the *very* next time this happens," said a gruff and suspicious voice, "I shall be exceedingly angry. Who is it *this* time, disturbing people on such a night? Speak up!"

"O, Badger," cried the Rat, "let us in, please. It's me, Rat, and my friend Mole, and we've lost our way in the snow."

"What, Ratty, my dear little man!" exclaimed the Badger, in quite a different voice. "Come along in, both of you, at once. Why, you must be perished. Well I never! Lost in the snow! And in the Wild Wood too, and at this time of night! But come in with you."

The two animals tumbled over each other in their eagerness to get inside, and heard the door shut behind them with great joy and relief.

The Badger, who wore a long dressing-gown, and whose slippers were indeed very down-at-heel, carried a flat candlestick in his paw and had probably been on his way to bed when their summons sounded. He looked kindly down on them and patted both their heads. "This is not the sort of night for small animals to be out," he said paternally. "I'm afraid you've been up to some of your pranks again, Ratty. But come along; come into the kitchen. There's a first-rate fire there, and supper and everything."

He shuffled on in front of them, carrying the light, and they followed him, nudging each other in an anticipating sort of way, down a long, gloomy, and to tell the truth, decidedly shabby passage, into a sort of a central hall, out of which they could dimly see other long tunnel-like passages branching, passages mysterious and without apparent end. But there were doors in the hall as well—stout oaken comfortable-looking doors. One of these the Badger flung open, and at once they found themselves in all the glow and warmth of a large fire-lit kitchen.

The floor was well-worn red brick, and on the wide hearth burnt a fire of logs, between two attractive chimney-corners tucked away in the wall, well out of any suspicion of draught. A couple of high-backed settles, facing each other on either side of the fire, gave further sitting accommodation for the sociably disposed. In the middle of the room stood a long table of plain boards placed on trestles, with benches down each side. At one end of it, where an arm-chair stood pushed back, were spread the remains of the Badger's plain but ample supper. Rows of spotless plates winked from the shelves of the dresser at the far end of the room, and from the rafters overhead hung hams, bundles of dried herbs, nets of onions, and baskets of eggs. It seemed a place where heroes could fitly feast after victory, where weary harvesters could line up in scores along the table and keep their Harvest Home with mirth and song, or where two or three friends of simple tastes could sit about as they pleased and eat and smoke and talk in comfort and contentment. The ruddy brick floor smiled up at the smoky ceiling; the oaken settles, shiny with long wear, exchanged cheerful glances with each other; plates on the dresser grinned at pots on the shelf, and the merry firelight flickered and played over everything without distinction.

The kindly Badger thrust them down on a settle to toast themselves at the fire, and bade them remove their wet coats and boots. Then he fetched them dressing-gowns and slippers, and himself bathed the Mole's shin with warm water and mended the cut with sticking-plaster till the whole thing was just as good as new, if not better. In the embracing light and warmth, warm and dry at last, with weary legs propped up in front of them, and a suggestive clink of plates being arranged on the table behind, it seemed to the storm-driven animals, now in safe anchorage, that the cold and trackless Wild Wood just left outside was miles and miles away, and all that they had suffered in it a half-forgotten dream.

When at last they were thoroughly toasted, the Badger summoned them to the table, where he had been busy laying a repast. They had felt pretty hungry before, but when they actually saw at last the supper that was spread for them, really it seemed only a question of what they should attack first where all was so attractive, and whether the other things would obligingly wait for them till they had time to give them attention. Conversation was impossible for a long time; and when it was slowly resumed, it was that regrettable sort of conversation that results from talking with your mouth full. The Badger did not mind that sort of thing at all, nor did he take any notice of elbows on the table, or everybody speaking at once. As he did not go into Society himself, he had got an idea that these things belonged to the things that didn't really matter. (We know of course that he was wrong, and took too narrow a view; because they do matter very much, though it would take too long to explain why.) He sat in his arm-chair at the head of the table, and nodded gravely at intervals as the animals told their story; and he did not seem surprised or shocked at anything, and he never said, "I told you so," or, "Just what I always said," or remarked that they ought to have done so-and-so, or ought not to have done something else. The Mole began to feel very friendly towards him.

When supper was really finished at last, and each animal felt that his skin was now as tight as was decently safe, and that by this time he didn't care a hang for anybody or anything, they gathered round the glowing embers of the great wood fire, and thought how jolly it was to be sitting up so late, and so independent, and so full; and after they had chatted for a time about things in general, the Badger said heartily, "Now then! tell us the news from your part of the world. How's old Toad going on?"

"O, from bad to worse," said the Rat gravely, while the Mole, cocked up on a settle and basking in the firelight, his heels higher than his head, tried to look properly mournful. "Another smash-up only last week, and a bad one. You see, he will insist on driving himself, and he's hopelessly incapable. If he'd only employ a decent, steady, well-trained animal, pay him good wages, and leave everything to him, he'd get on all right. But no; he's convinced he's a heaven-born driver, and nobody can teach him anything; and all the rest follows."

"How many has he had?" inquired the Badger gloomily.

"Smashes, or machines?" asked the Rat. "O, well, after all, it's the same thing—with Toad. This is the seventh. As for the others—you know that coach-house of his? Well, it's piled up—literally piled up to the roof—with fragments of motor-cars, none of them bigger than your hat! That accounts for the other six—so far as they can be accounted for."

"He's been in hospital three times," put in the Mole; "and as for the fines he's had to pay, it's simply awful to think of."

"Yes, and that's part of the trouble," continued the Rat. "Toad's rich, we all know; but he's not a millionaire. And he's a hopelessly bad driver, and quite regardless of law and order. Killed or ruined—it's got to be one of the two things, sooner or later. Badger! we're his friends—oughtn't we to do something?"

The Badger went through a bit of hard thinking. "Now look here!" he said at last, rather severely; "of course you know I can't do anything *now*?"

His two friends assented, quite understanding his point. No animal, according to the rules of animal-etiquette, is ever expected to do anything strenuous, or heroic, or even moderately active during the off-season of winter. All are sleepy—some actually asleep. All are weather-bound, more or less; and all are resting from arduous days and nights, during which every muscle in them has been severely tested, and every energy kept at full stretch.

"Very well then!" continued the Badger. "*But*, when once the year has really turned, and the nights are shorter, and half-way through them one rouses and feels fidgety and wanting to be up and doing by sunrise, if not before—*you* know—!"

Both animals nodded gravely. *They* knew!

"Well, *then*," went on the Badger, "we—that is, you and me and our friend the Mole here—we'll take Toad seriously in hand. We'll stand no nonsense whatever. We'll bring him back to reason, by force if need be. We'll *make* him be a sensible Toad. We'll—you're asleep, Rat!"

"Not me!" said the Rat, waking up with a jerk.

"He's been asleep two or three times since supper," said the Mole laughing. He himself was feeling quite wakeful and even lively, though he didn't know why. The reason was, of course, that he being naturally an underground animal by birth and breeding, the situation of Badger's house exactly suited him and made him feel at home; while the Rat, who slept every night in a bedroom the windows of which opened on a breezy river, naturally felt the atmosphere still and oppressive.

"Well, it's time we were all in bed," said the Badger, getting up and fetching flat candlesticks. "Come along, you two, and I'll show you your quarters. And take your time to-morrow morning— breakfast at any hour you please!"

He conducted the two animals to a long room that seemed half bedchamber and half loft. The Badger's winter stores, which indeed were visible everywhere, took up half the room—piles of apples, turnips, and potatoes, baskets full of nuts, and jars of honey; but the two little white beds on the remainder of the floor looked soft and inviting, and the linen on them, though coarse, was clean and smelt beautifully of lavender; and the Mole and the Water Rat, shaking off their garments in some thirty seconds, tumbled in between the sheets in great joy and contentment.

In accordance with the kindly Badger's injunctions, the two tired animals came down to breakfast very late next morning, and found a bright fire burning in the kitchen, and two young hedgehogs sitting on a bench at the table, eating oatmeal porridge out of wooden bowls. The hedgehogs dropped their spoons, rose to their feet, and ducked their heads respectfully as the two entered.

"There, sit down, sit down," said the Rat pleasantly, "and go on with your porridge. Where have you youngsters come from? Lost your way in the snow, I suppose?"

"Yes, please, sir," said the elder of the two hedgehogs respectfully. "Me and little Billy here, we was trying to find our way to school—mother *would* have us go, was the weather ever so—and of course we lost ourselves, sir, and Billy he got frightened and took and cried, being young and faint-hearted. And at last we happened up against Mr Badger's back door, and made so bold as to knock, sir, for Mr Badger he's a kind-hearted gentleman, as everyone knows—"

"I understand," said the Rat, cutting himself some rashers from a side of bacon, while the Mole dropped some eggs into a saucepan. "And what's the weather like outside? You needn't 'sir' me quite so much," he added.

"O, terrible bad, sir, terrible deep the snow is," said the hedgehog. "No getting out for the likes of you gentlemen to-day."

"Where's Mr Badger?" inquired the Mole, as he warmed the coffee-pot before the fire.

"The master's gone into his study, sir," replied the hedgehog, "and he said as how he was going to be particular busy this morning, and on no account was he to be disturbed."

This explanation, of course, was thoroughly understood by everyone present. The fact is, as already set forth, when you live a life of intense activity for six months in the year, and of comparative or actual somnolence for the other six, during the latter period you cannot be continually pleading sleepiness when there are people about or things to be done. The excuse gets monotonous. The animals well knew that Badger, having eaten a hearty breakfast, had retired to his study and settled himself in an arm-chair with his legs up on another and a red cotton handkerchief over his face, and was being "busy" in the usual way at this time of the year.

The front-door bell clanged loudly, and the Rat, who was very greasy with buttered toast, sent Billy, the smaller hedgehog, to see who it might be. There was a sound of much stamping in the hall, and presently Billy returned in front of the Otter, who threw himself on the Rat with an embrace and a shout of affectionate greeting.

"Get off!" spluttered the Rat, with his mouth full.

"Thought I should find you here all right," said the Otter cheerfully. "They were all in a great state of alarm along River Bank when I arrived this morning. Rat never been home all night—nor Mole either—something dreadful must have happened, they said; and the snow had covered up all your tracks, of course. But I knew that when people were in any fix they mostly went to Badger, or else Badger got to know of it somehow, so I came straight off here, through the Wild Wood and the snow! My! it was fine, coming through the snow as the red sun was rising and showing against the black tree-trunks! As you went along in the stillness, every now and then masses of snow slid off the branches suddenly with a flop! making you jump and run for cover. Snow-castles and snow-caverns had sprung up out of nowhere in the night—and snow bridges, terraces, ramparts—I could have stayed and played with them for hours. Here and there great branches had been torn away by the sheer weight of the snow, and robins perched and hopped on them in their perky conceited way, just as if they had done it themselves. A ragged string of wild geese passed overhead, high on the grey sky, and a few rooks whirled over the trees, inspected, and flapped off homewards with a disgusted expression; but I met no sensible being to ask the news of. About half-way across I came on a rabbit sitting on a stump, cleaning his silly face with his paws. He was a pretty scared animal when I crept up behind him and placed a heavy forepaw on his shoulder. I had to cuff his head once or twice to get any sense out of it at all. At last I managed to extract from him that Mole had been seen in the Wild Wood last night by one of them. It was the talk of the burrows, he said, how Mole, Mr Rat's particular friend, was in a bad fix; how he had lost his way, and 'They' were up and out hunting, and were chivvying him round and round. 'Then why didn't any of you *do* something?' I asked. 'You mayn't be blest with brains, but there are hundreds and hundreds of you, big, stout fellows, as fat as butter, and your burrows running in all directions, and you could have taken him in and made him safe and comfortable, or tried to, at all events.' 'What, *us*?' he merely said: '*do* something? us rabbits?' So I cuffed him again and left him. There was nothing else to be done. At any rate, I had learnt something; and if I had had the luck to meet any of 'Them' I'd have learnt something more—or *they* would."

"Weren't you at all—er—nervous?" asked the Mole, some of yesterday's terror coming back to him at the mention of the Wild Wood.

"Nervous?" The Otter showed a gleaming set of strong white teeth as he laughed. "I'd give 'em nerves if any of them tried anything on with me. Here, Mole, fry me some slices of ham, like the good little chap you are. I'm frightfully hungry, and I've got any amount to say to Ratty here. Haven't seen him for an age."

So the good-natured Mole, having cut some slices of ham, set the hedgehogs to fry it, and returned to his own breakfast, while the Otter and the Rat, their heads together, eagerly talked river-shop, which is long shop and talk that is endless, running on like the babbling river itself.

A plate of fried ham had just been cleared and sent back for more, when the Badger entered, yawning and rubbing his eyes, and greeted them all in his quiet, simple way, with kind inquiries for every one. "It must be getting on for luncheon time," he remarked to the Otter. "Better stop and have it with us. You must be hungry, this cold morning."

"Rather!" replied the Otter, winking at the Mole. "The sight of these greedy young hedgehogs stuffing themselves with fried ham makes me feel positively famished."

The hedgehogs, who were just beginning to feel hungry again after their porridge, and after working so hard at their frying, looked timidly up at Mr Badger, but were too shy to say anything.

"Here, you two youngsters be off home to your mother," said the Badger kindly. "I'll send some one with you to show you the way. You won't want any dinner to-day, I'll be bound."

He gave them sixpence apiece and a pat on the head, and they went off with much respectful swinging of caps and touching of forelocks.

Presently they all sat down to luncheon together. The Mole found himself placed next to Mr Badger, and, as the other two were still deep in river-gossip from which nothing could divert them, he took the opportunity to tell Badger how comfortable and homelike it all felt to him. "Once well underground," he said, "you know exactly where you are. Nothing can happen to you, and nothing can get at you. You're entirely your own master, and you don't have to consult anybody or mind what they say. Things go on all the same overhead, and you let 'em, and don't bother about 'em. When you want to, up you go, and there the things are, waiting for you."

The Badger simply beamed on him. "That's exactly what I say," he replied. "There's no security, or peace and tranquillity, except underground. And then, if your ideas get larger and you want to expand—why, a dig and a scrape, and there you are! If you feel your house is a bit too big, you stop up a hole or two, and there you are again! No builders, no tradesmen, no remarks passed on you by fellows looking over your wall, and, above all, no weather. Look at Rat, now. A couple of feet of flood-water, and he's got to move into hired lodgings; uncomfortable, inconveniently situated, and horribly expensive. Take Toad. I say nothing against Toad Hall; quite the best house in these parts, *as* a house. But supposing a fire breaks out—where's Toad? Supposing tiles are blown off, or walls sink or crack, or windows get broken—where's Toad? Supposing the rooms are draughty—I *hate* a draught myself—where's Toad? No, up and out of doors is good enough to roam about and get one's living in; but underground to come back to at last—that's my idea of *home*!"

The Mole assented heartily; and the Badger in consequence got very friendly with him. "When lunch is over," he said, "I'll take you all round this little place of mine. I can see you'll appreciate it. You understand what domestic architecture ought to be, you do."

After luncheon, accordingly, when the other two had settled themselves into the chimney-corner and had started a heated argument on the subject of *eels*, the Badger lighted a lantern and bade the Mole follow him. Crossing the hall, they passed down one of the principal tunnels, and the wavering light of the lantern gave glimpses on either side of rooms both large and small, some mere cupboards, others nearly as broad and imposing as Toad's dining-hall. A narrow passage at right angles led them into another corridor, and here the same thing was repeated. The Mole was staggered at the size, the extent, the ramifications of it all; at the length of the dim passages, the solid vaultings of the crammed store-chambers, the masonry everywhere, the pillars, the arches, the pavements. "How on earth, Badger," he said at last, "did you ever find time and strength to do all this? It's astonishing!"

"It *would* be astonishing indeed," said the Badger simply, "if I had done it. But as a matter of fact I did none of it—only cleaned out the passages and chambers, as far as I had need of them. There's lots more of it, all round about. I see you don't understand, and I must explain it to you. Well, very long ago, on the spot where the Wild Wood waves now, before ever it had planted itself and grown up to what it now is, there was a city—a city of people, you know. Here, where we are standing, they lived, and walked, and talked, and slept, and carried on their business. Here they stabled their horses and feasted, from here they rode out to fight or drove out to trade. They were a powerful people, and rich, and great builders. They built to last, for they thought their city would last for ever."

"But what has become of them all?" asked the Mole.

"Who can tell?" said the Badger. "People come—they stay for a while, they flourish, they build—and they go. It is their way. But we remain. There were badgers here, I've been told, long before that same city ever came to be. And now there are badgers here again. We are an enduring lot, and we may move out for a time, but we wait, and are patient, and back we come. And so it will ever be."

"Well, and when they went at last, those people?" said the Mole.

"When they went," continued the Badger, "the strong winds and persistent rains took the matter in hand, patiently, ceaselessly, year after year. Perhaps we badgers too, in our small way, helped a little—who knows? It was all down, down, down, gradually—ruin and levelling and disappearance. Then it was all up, up, up, gradually, as seeds grew to saplings, and saplings to forest trees, and bramble and fern came creeping in to help. Leaf-mould rose and obliterated, streams in their winter freshets brought sand and soil to clog and to cover, and in course of time our home was ready for us again, and we moved in. Up above us, on the surface, the same thing happened. Animals arrived, liked the look of the place, took up their quarters, settled down, spread, and flourished. They didn't bother themselves about the past—they never do; they're too busy. The place was a bit humpy and hillocky, naturally, and full of holes; but that was rather an advantage. And they don't bother about the future, either—the future when perhaps the people will move in again—for a time—as may very well be. The Wild Wood is pretty well populated by now; with all the usual lot, good, bad, and indifferent—I name no names. It takes all sorts to make a world. But I fancy you know something about them yourself by this time."

"I do indeed," said the Mole, with a slight shiver.

"Well, well," said the Badger, patting him on the shoulder, it was your first experience of them, you see. They're not so bad really; and we must all live and let live. But I'll pass the word round to-morrow, and I think you'll have no further trouble. Any friend of *mine* walks where he likes in this country, or I'll know the reason why!"

When they got back to the kitchen again, they found the Rat walking up and down, very restless. The underground atmosphere was oppressing him and getting on his nerves, and he seemed really to be afraid that the river would run away if he wasn't there to look after it. So he had his overcoat on, and his pistols thrust into his belt again. "Come along, Mole," he said anxiously, as soon as he caught sight of them. "We must get off while it's daylight. Don't want to spend another night in the Wild Wood again."

"It'll be all right, my fine fellow," said the Otter. "I'm coming along with you, and I know every path blindfold; and if there's a head that needs to be punched, you can confidently rely upon me to punch it."

"You really needn't fret, Ratty," added the Badger placidly. "My passages run further than you think, and I've bolt-holes to the edge of the wood in several directions, though I don't care for everybody to know about them. When you really have to go, you shall leave by one of my short cuts. Meantime, make yourself easy, and sit down again."

The Rat was nevertheless still anxious to be off and attend to his river, so the Badger, taking up his lantern again, led the way along a damp and airless tunnel that wound and dipped, part vaulted, part hewn through solid rock, for a weary distance that seemed to be miles. At last daylight began to show itself confusedly through tangled growth overhanging the mouth of the passage; and the Badger, bidding them a hasty good-bye, pushed them hurriedly through the opening, made everything look as natural as possible again, with creepers, brushwood, and dead leaves, and retreated.

They found themselves standing on the very edge of the Wild Wood. Rocks and brambles and tree-roots behind them, confusedly heaped and tangled; in front, a great space of quiet fields, hemmed by lines of hedges black on the snow, and, far ahead, a glint of the familiar old river, while the wintry sun hung red and low on the horizon. The Otter, as knowing all the paths, took charge of the party, and they trailed out on a bee-line for a distant stile. Pausing there a moment and looking back, they saw the whole mass of the Wild Wood, dense, menacing, compact, grimly set in vast white surroundings; simultaneously they turned and made swiftly for home, for firelight and the familiar things it played on, for the voice, sounding cheerily outside their window, of the river that they knew and trusted in all its moods, that never made them afraid with any amazement.

As he hurried along, eagerly anticipating the moment when he would be at home again among the things he knew and liked, the Mole saw clearly that he was an animal of tilled field and hedgerow, linked to the ploughed furrow, the frequented pasture, the lane of evening lingerings, the cultivated garden-plot. For others the asperities, the stubborn endurance, or the clash of actual conflict, that went with Nature in the rough; he must be wise, must keep to the pleasant places in which his lines were laid and which held adventure enough, in their way, to last for a lifetime.

Chapter 5

DULCE DOMUM

The sheep ran huddling together against the hurdles, blowing out thin nostrils and stamping with delicate forefeet, their heads thrown back and a light steam rising from the crowded sheep-pen into the frosty air, as the two animals hastened by in high spirits, with much chatter and laughter. They were returning across country after a long day's outing with Otter, hunting and exploring on the wide uplands where certain streams tributary to their own river had their first small beginnings; and the shades of the short winter day were closing in on them, and they had still some distance to go. Plodding at random across the plough, they had heard the sheep and had made for them; and now, leading from the sheep-pen, they found a beaten track that made walking a lighter business, and responded, moreover, to that small inquiring something which all animals carry inside them, saying unmistakably, "Yes, quite right; *this* leads home!"

"It looks as if we're coming to a village," said the Mole somewhat dubiously, slackening his pace, as the track, that had in time become a path and then had developed into a lane, now handed them over to the charge of a well-metalled road. The animals did not hold with villages, and their own highways, thickly frequented as they were, took an independent course, regardless of church, post office, or public-house.

"Oh, never mind!" said the Rat. "At this season of the year they're all safe indoors by this time, sitting round the fire; men, women, and children, dogs and cats and all. We shall slip through all right, without any bother or unpleasantness, and we can have a look at them through their windows if you like, and see what they're doing."

The rapid nightfall of mid-December had quite beset the little village as they approached it on soft feet over a first thin fall of powdery snow. Little was visible but squares of a dusky orange-red on either side of the street, where the firelight or lamplight of each cottage overflowed through the casements into the dark world without. Most of the low latticed windows were innocent of blinds, and to the lookers-in from outside, the inmates, gathered round the tea-table, absorbed in handiwork, or talking with laughter and gesture, had each that happy grace which is the last thing the skilled actor shall capture—the natural grace which goes with perfect unconsciousness of observation. Moving at will from one theatre to another, the two spectators, so far from home themselves, had something of wistfulness in their eyes as they watched a cat being stroked, a sleepy child picked up and huddled off to bed, or a tired man stretch and knock out his pipe on the end of a smouldering log.

But it was from one little window, with its blind drawn down, a mere blank transparency on the night, that the sense of home and the little curtained world within walls—the larger stressful world of outside Nature shut out and forgotten—most pulsated. Close against the white blind hung a bird-cage, clearly silhouetted, every wire, perch, and appurtenance distinct and recognisable, even to yesterday's dull-edged lump of sugar. On the middle perch the fluffy occupant, head tucked well into feathers, seemed so near to them as to be easily stroked, had they tried; even the delicate tips of his plumped-out plumage pencilled plainly on the illuminated screen. As they looked, the sleepy little fellow stirred uneasily, woke, shook himself and raised his head. They could see the gape of his tiny beak as he yawned in a bored sort of way, looked round, and then settled his head into his back again, while the ruffled feathers gradually subsided into perfect stillness. Then a gust of bitter wind took them in the back of the neck, a small sting of frozen sleet on the skin woke them as from a dream, and they knew their toes to be cold and their legs tired and their own home distant a weary way.

Once beyond the village, where the cottages ceased abruptly, on either side of the road they could smell through the darkness the friendly fields again; and they braced themselves for the last long stretch, the home stretch, the stretch that we know is bound to end, some time, in the rattle of the door-latch, the sudden firelight, and the sight of familiar things greeting us as long-absent travellers from far oversea. They plodded along steadily and silently, each of them thinking his own thoughts. The Mole's ran a good deal on supper, as it was pitch dark, and it was all a strange country to him as far as he knew, and he was following obediently in the wake of the Rat, leaving the guidance entirely to him. As for the Rat, he was walking a little way ahead, as his habit was, his shoulders humped, his eyes fixed on the straight grey road in front of him; so he did not notice poor Mole when suddenly the summons reached him, and took him like an electric shock.

We others, who have long lost the more subtle of the physical senses, have not even proper terms to express an animal's intercommunications with his surroundings, living or otherwise, and have only the word "smell", for instance, to include the whole range of delicate thrills which murmur in the nose of the animal night and day, summoning, warning, inciting, repelling. It was one of these mysterious fairy calls from out the void that suddenly reached Mole in the darkness, making him tingle through and through with its very familiar appeal, even while as yet he could not clearly remember what it was. He stopped dead in his tracks, his nose searching hither and thither in its efforts to recapture the fine filament, the telegraphic current, that had so strongly moved him. A moment, and he had caught it again; and with it this time came recollection in fullest flood.

Home! That was what they meant, those caressing appeals, those soft touches wafted through the air, those invisible little hands pulling and tugging, all one way! Why, it must be quite close by him at that moment, his old home that he had hurriedly forsaken and never sought again, that day when he first found the river! And now it was sending out its scouts and its messengers to capture him and ring him in. Since his escape on that bright morning he had hardly given it a thought, so absorbed had he been in his new life, in all its pleasures, its surprises, its fresh and captivating experiences. Now, with a rush of old memories, how clearly it stood up before him, in the darkness! Shabby indeed, and small and poorly furnished, and yet his, the home he had made for himself, the home he had been so happy to get back to after his day's work. And the home had been happy with him, too, evidently, and was missing him, and wanted him back, and was telling him so, through his nose, sorrowfully, reproachfully, but with no bitterness or anger; only with plaintive reminder that it was there, and wanted him.

The call was clear, the summons was plain. He must obey it instantly, and go. "Ratty!" he called, full of joyful excitement, "hold on! Come back! I want you, quick!"

"O, *come* along, Mole, do!" replied the Rat cheerfully, still plodding along.

"*Please* stop, Ratty!" pleaded the poor Mole, in anguish of heart. "You don't understand! It's my home, my old home! I've just come across the smell of it, and it's close by here, really quite close. And I *must* go to it, I must, I must! O, come back, Ratty! Please, please come back!"

The Rat was by this time very far ahead, too far to hear clearly what the Mole was calling, too far to catch the sharp note of painful appeal in his voice. And he was much taken up with the weather, for he too could smell something—something suspiciously like approaching snow.

"Mole, we mustn't stop now, really!" he called back. "We'll come for it tomorrow, whatever it is you've found. But I daren't stop now—it's late, and the snow's coming on again, and I'm not sure of the way! And I want your nose, Mole, so come on quick, there's a good fellow!" And the Rat pressed forward on his way without waiting for an answer.

Poor Mole stood alone in the road, his heart torn asunder, and a big sob gathering, gathering, somewhere low down inside him, to leap up to the surface presently, he knew, in passionate escape. But even under such a test as this his loyalty to his friend stood firm. Never for a moment did he dream of abandoning him. Meanwhile, the wafts from his old home pleaded, whispered, conjured, and finally claimed him imperiously. He dared not tarry longer within their magic circle. With a wrench that tore his very heartstrings he set his face down the road and followed submissively in the track of the Rat, while faint, thin little smells, still dogging his retreating nose, reproached him for his new friendship and his callous forgetfullness.

With an effort he caught up the unsuspecting Rat, who began chattering cheerily about what they would do when they got back, and how jolly a fire of logs in the parlour would be, and what a supper he meant to eat; never noticing his companion's silence and distressful state of mind At last, however, when they had gone some considerable way further, and were passing some tree-stumps at the edge of a copse that bordered the road, he stopped and said kindly, "Look here, Mole, old chap, you seem dead tired. No talk left in you, and your feet dragging like lead. We'll sit down here for a minute and rest. The snow has held off so far, and the best part of our journey is over."

The Mole subsided forlornly on a tree-stump and tried to control himself, for he felt it surely coming. The sob he had fought with so long refused to be beaten. Up and up, it forced its way to the air, and then another, and another, and others thick and fast; till poor Mole at last gave up the struggle, and cried freely and helplessly and openly, now that he knew it was all over and he had lost what he could hardly be said to have found.

The Rat, astonished and dismayed at the violence of Mole's paroxysm of grief, did not dare to speak for a while. At last he said, very quietly and sympathetically, "What is it, old fellow? Whatever can be the matter? Tell us your trouble, and let me see what I can do."

Poor Mole found it difficult to get any words out between the upheavals of his chest that followed one upon another so quickly and held back speech and choked it as it came. "I know it's a— shabby, dingy little place," he sobbed forth at last, brokenly: "not like—your cosy quarters—or Toad's beautiful hall—or Badger's great house—but it was my own little home—and I was fond of it— and I went away and forgot all about it—and then I smelt it suddenly—on the road, when I called and you wouldn't listen, Rat— and everything came back to me with a rush—and I *wanted* it!—O dear, O dear—and when you *wouldn't* turn back, Ratty—and I had to leave it, though I was smelling it all the time—I thought my heart would break.—We might have just gone and had one look at it, Ratty—only one look—it was close by—but you wouldn't turn back, Ratty, you wouldn't turn back! O dear, O dear!"

Recollection brought fresh waves of sorrow, and sobs again took full charge of him, preventing further speech.

The Rat stared straight in front of him, saying nothing, only patting Mole gently on the shoulder. After a time he muttered gloomily, "I see it all now! What a *pig* I have been! A pig—that's me! Just a pig—a plain pig."

He waited till Mole's sobs became gradually less stormy and more rhythmical; he waited till at last sniffs were frequent and sobs only intermittent. Then he rose from his seat, and, remarking carelessly, "Well, now we'd really better be getting on, old chap!" set off up the road again, over the toilsome way they had come.

"Wherever are you (hic) going to (hic), Ratty?" cried the tearful Mole, looking up in alarm.

"We're going to find that home of yours, old fellow," replied the Rat pleasantly; "so you had better come along, for it will take some finding, and we shall want your nose."

"O, come back, Ratty, do!" cried the Mole, getting up and hurrying after him. "It's no good, I tell you! It's too late, and too dark, and the place is to far off, and the snow's coming! And—and I never meant to let you know I was feeling that way about it—it was all an accident and a mistake! And think of River Bank, and your supper!"

"Hang River Bank, and supper too!" said the Rat heartily. "I tell you, I'm going to find this place now, if I stay out all night. So cheer up, old chap, and take my arm, and we'll very soon be back there again."

Still snuffling, pleading, and reluctant, Mole suffered himself to be dragged back along the road by his imperious companion, who by a flow of cheerful talk and anecdote endeavoured to beguile his spirits back and make the weary way seem shorter. When at last it seemed to the Rat that they must be nearing that part of the road where the Mole had been "held up", he said, "Now, no more talking. Business! Use your nose, and give your mind to it."

They moved on in silence for some little way, when suddenly the Rat was conscious, through his arm that was linked in Mole's, of a faint sort of electric thrill that was passing down that animal's body. Instantly he disengaged himself, fell back a pace, and waited, all attention.

The signals were coming through!

Mole stood a moment rigid, while his uplifted nose, quivering slightly, felt the air.

Then a short, quick run forward—a fault—a check—a try back; and then a slow, steady, confident advance.

The Rat, much excited, kept close to his heels as the Mole, with something of the air of a sleep-walker, crossed a dry ditch, scrambled through a hedge, and nosed his way over a field open and trackless and bare in the faint starlight.

Suddenly, without giving warning, he dived; but the Rat was on the alert, and promptly followed him down the tunnel to which his unerring nose had faithfully led him.

It was close and airless, and the earthy smell was strong, and it seemed a long time to Rat ere the passage ended and he could stand erect and stretch and shake himself. The Mole struck a match, and by its light the Rat saw that they were standing in an open space, neatly swept and sanded underfoot, and directly facing them was Mole's little front door, with "Mole End" painted, in Gothic lettering, over the bell-pull at the side.

Mole reached down a lantern from a nail on the wall and lit it, and the Rat, looking round him, saw that they were in a sort of fore-court. A garden-seat stood on one side of the door, and on the other, a roller; for the Mole, who was a tidy animal when at home, could not stand having his ground kicked up by other animals into little runs that ended in earth-heaps. On the walls hung wire baskets with ferns in them, alternating with brackets carrying plaster statuary—Garibaldi, and the infant

Samuel, and Queen Victoria, and other heroes of modern Italy. Down one side of the fore-court ran a skittle-alley, with benches along it and little wooden tables marked with rings that hinted at beer-mugs. In the middle was a small round pond containing goldfish and surrounded by a cockleshell border. Out of the centre of the pond rose a fanciful erection clothed in more cockle-shells and topped by a large silvered glass ball that reflected everything all wrong and had a very pleasing effect.

Mole's face beamed at the sight of all these objects so dear to him, and he hurried Rat through the door, lit a lamp in the hall, and took one glance round his old home. He saw the dust lying thick on everything, saw the cheerless, deserted look of the long-neglected house, and its narrow, meagre dimensions, its worn and shabby contents—and collapsed again on a hall-chair, his nose in his paws. "O, Ratty!" he cried dismally, "why ever did I do it? Why did I bring you to this poor, cold little place, on a night like this, when you might have been at River Bank by this time, toasting your toes before a blazing fire, with all your own nice things about you!"

The Rat paid no heed to his doleful self-reproaches. He was running here and there, opening doors, inspecting rooms and cupboards, and lighting lamps and candles and sticking them up everywhere. "What a capital little house this is!" he called out cheerily. "So compact! So well planned! Everything here and everything in its place! We'll make a jolly night of it. The first thing we want is a good fire; I'll see to that—I always know where to find things. So this is the parlour? Splendid! Your own idea, those little sleeping-bunks in the wall? Capital! Now, I'll fetch the wood and the coals, and you get a duster, Mole—you'll find one in the drawer of the kitchen table—and try and smarten things up a bit. Bustle about, old chap!"

Encouraged by his inspiriting companion, the Mole roused himself and dusted and polished with energy and heartiness, while the Rat, running to and fro with armfuls of fuel, soon had a cheerful blaze roaring up the chimney. He hailed the Mole to come and warm himself; but Mole promptly had another fit of the blues, dropping down on a couch in dark despair and burying his face in his duster.

"Rat," he moaned, "how about your supper, you poor, cold, hungry, weary animal? I've nothing to give you—nothing—not a crumb!"

"What a fellow you are for giving in!" said the Rat reproachfully.

"Why, only just now I saw a sardine-opener on the kitchen dresser, quite distinctly; and everybody knows that means there are sardines about somewhere in the neighbourhood. Rouse yourself! pull yourself together, and come with me and forage."

They went and foraged accordingly, hunting through every cupboard and turned out every drawer. The result was not so very depressing after all, though of course it might have been better; a tin of sardines—a box of captain's biscuits, nearly full—and a German sausage encased in silver paper.

"There's a banquet for you!" observed the Rat, as he arranged the table. "I know some animals who would give their ears to be sitting down to supper with us to-night!"

"No bread!" groaned the Mole dolorously; "no butter, no—"

"No *pâté de foie gras*, no champagne!" continued the Rat, grinning. "And that reminds me—what's that little door at the end of the passage? Your cellar, of course! Every luxury in this house! Just you wait a minute."

He made for the cellar door, and presently reappeared, somewhat dusty, with a bottle of beer in each paw and another under each arm. "Self-indulgent beggar you seem to be, Mole," he observed. "Deny yourself nothing. This is really the jolliest little place I ever was in. Now, wherever did you pick up those prints? Make the place look so home-like, they do. No wonder you're so fond of it, Mole. Tell us all about it, and how you came to make it what it is."

Then, while the Rat busied himself fetching plates, and knives and forks, and mustard which he mixed in an egg-cup, the Mole, his bosom still heaving with the stress of his recent emotion, related—somewhat shyly at first, but with more freedom as he warmed to his subject—how this was planned, and how that was thought out, and how this was got through a windfall from an aunt, and that was a wonderful find and a bargain, and this other thing was bought out of laborious savings and a certain amount of "going without". His spirits finally quite restored, he must needs go and caress his possessions, and take a lamp and show off their points to his visitor, and expatiate on them, quite forgetful of the supper they both so much needed; Rat, who was desperately hungry but strove to conceal it, nodding seriously, examining with a puckered brow, and saying, "Wonderful", and "Most remarkable", at intervals, when the chance for an observation was given him.

At last the Rat succeeded in decoying him to the table, and had just got seriously to work with the sardine-opener when sounds were heard from the forecourt without—sounds like the scuffling of small feet in the gravel and a confused murmur of tiny voices, while broken sentences reached them—"Now, all in a line—hold the lantern up a bit, Tommy—clear your throats first—no coughing after I say one, two, three.—Where's young Bill?—Here, come on, do, we're all a-waiting—"

"What's up?" inquired the Rat, pausing in his labours.

"I think it must be the field-mice," replied the Mole, with a touch of pride in his manner. "They go round carol-singing regularly at this time of the year. They're quite an institution in these parts. And they never pass me over—they come to Mole End last of all; and I used to give them hot drinks, and supper too sometimes, when I could afford it. It will be like old times to hear them again."

"Let's have a look at them!" cried the Rat, jumping up and running to the door.

It was a pretty sight, and a seasonable one, that met their eyes when they flung the door open. In the fore-court, lit by the dim rays of a horn lantern, some eight or ten little field-mice stood in a semicircle, red worsted comforters round their throats, their forepaws thrust deep into their pockets, their feet jigging for warmth. With bright beady eyes they glanced shyly at each other, sniggering a little, sniffing and applying coat-sleeves a good deal. As the door opened, one of the elder ones that carried the lantern was just saying, "Now then, one, two, three!" and forthwith their shrill little voices uprose on the air, singing one of the old-time carols that their fore-fathers composed in fields that were fallow and held by frost, or when snow-bound in chimney corners, and handed down to be sung in the miry street to lamp-lit windows at Yule-time.

CAROL

Villagers all this frosty tide,
Let your doors swing open wide,
Though wind may follow, and snow beside,
Yet draw us in by your fire to bide;
Joy shall be yours in the morning!

Here we stand in the cold and the sleet,
Blowing fingers and stamping feet,
Come from far away you to greet—
You by the fire and we in the street—
Bidding you joy in the morning!

For here one half of the night was gone,
Sudden a star has led us on,
Raining bliss and benison—
Bliss to-morrow and more anon
Joy for every morning!

Good man Joseph toiled through the snow—
Saw the star o'er a stable low;
Mary she might not further go—
Welcome thatch, and litter below!
Joy was hers in the morning!

And then they heard the angels tell
"Who were the first to cry Nowell?
Animals all as it befell,
In the stable where they did dwell!
Joy shall be theirs in the morning."

The voices ceased, the singers, bashful but smiling, exchanged sidelong glances, and silence succeeded—but for a moment only. Then, from up above and far away, down the tunnel they had so lately travelled was borne to their ears in a faint musical hum the sound of distant bells ringing a joyful and clangorous peal.

"Very well sung, boys!" cried the Rat heartily. "And now come along in, all of you, and warm yourselves by the fire, and have something hot!"

"Yes, come along, field-mice," cried the Mole eagerly. "This is quite like old times! Shut the door after you. Pull up that settle to the fire. Now, you just wait a minute, while we—O, Ratty!" he cried in despair, plumping down on a seat, with tears impending. "Whatever are we doing? We've nothing to give them!"

"You leave all that to me," said the masterful Rat. "Here, you with the lantern! Come over this way. I want to talk to you. Now, tell me, are there any shops open at this hour of the night?"

"Why, certainly, sir," replied the field-mouse respectfully. "At this time of the year our shops keep open to all sorts of hours."

"Then look here!" said the Rat. "You go off at once, you and your lantern, and you get me—"

Here much muttered conversation ensued, and the Mole only heard bits of it, such as—"Fresh, mind!—no, a pound of that will do—see you get Buggins's, for I won't have any other—no, only the best—if you can't get it there, try somewhere else—yes, of course, home-made, no tinned stuff—well then, do the best you can!" Finally, there was a chink of coin passing from paw to paw, the field-mouse was provided with an ample basket for his purchases, and off he hurried, he and his lantern.

The rest of the field-mice, perched in a row on the settle, their small legs swinging, gave themselves up to enjoyment of the fire, and toasted their chilblains till they tingled; while the Mole, failing to draw them into easy conversation, plunged into family history and made each of them recite the names of his numerous brothers, who were too young, it appeared, to be allowed to go out a-carolling this year, but looked forward very shortly to winning the parental consent

The Rat, meanwhile, was busy examining the label on one of the beer-bottles. "I perceive this to be Old Burton," he remarked approvingly. "*Sensible* Mole! The very thing! Now we shall be able to mull some ale! Get the things ready, Mole, while I draw the corks."

It did not take long to prepare the brew and thrust the tin heater well into the red heart of the fire; and soon every field-mouse was sipping and coughing and choking (for a little mulled ale goes a long way) and wiping his eyes and laughing and forgetting he had ever been cold in all his life.

"They act plays too, these fellows," the Mole explained to the Rat. "Make them up all by themselves, and act them afterwards. And very well they do it, too! They gave us a capital one last year, about a field-mouse who was captured at sea by a Barbary corsair, and made to row in a galley; and when he escaped and got home again, his lady-love had gone into a convent. Here, you! You were in it, I remember. Get up and recite a bit."

The field-mouse addressed got up on his legs, giggled shyly, looked round the room, and remained absolutely tongue-tied. His comrades cheered him on, Mole coaxed and encouraged him, and the Rat went so far as to take him by the shoulders and shake him; but nothing could overcome his stage-fright. They were all busily engaged on him like watermen applying the Royal Humane Society's regulations to a case of long submersion, when the latch clicked, the door opened, and the field-mouse with the lantern reappeared, staggering under the weight of his basket.

There was no more talk of play-acting once the very real and solid contents of the basket had been tumbled out on the table. Under the generalship of Rat, everybody was set to do something or to fetch something. In a very few minutes supper was ready, and Mole, as he took the head of the table in a sort of dream, saw a lately barren board set thick with savoury comforts; saw his little friends' faces brighten and beam as they fell to without delay; and then let himself loose—for he was famished indeed—on the provender so magically provided, thinking what a happy home-coming this had turned out, after all. As they ate, they talked of old times, and the field-mice gave him the local gossip up to date, and answered as well as they could the hundred questions he had to ask them. The Rat said little or nothing, only taking care that each guest had what he wanted, and plenty of it, and that Mole had no trouble or anxiety about anything.

They clattered off at last, very grateful and showering wishes of the season, with their jacket pockets stuffed with remembrances for the small brothers and sisters at home. When the door had closed on the last of them and the chink of the lanterns had died away, Mole and Rat kicked the fire up, drew their chairs in, brewed themselves a last nightcap of mulled ale, and discussed the events of the long day. At last the Rat, with a tremendous yawn, said, "Mole, old chap, I'm ready to drop. Sleepy is simply not the word. That your own bunk over on that side? Very well, then, I'll take this. What a ripping little house this is! Everything so handy!"

He clambered into his bunk and rolled himself well up in the blankets, and slumber gathered him forthwith, as a swath of barley is folded into the arms of the reaping-machine.

The weary Mole also was glad to turn in without delay, and soon had his head on his pillow, in great joy and contentment. But ere he closed his eyes he let them wander round his old room, mellow in the glow of the firelight that played or rested on familiar and friendly things which had long been unconsciously a part of him, and now smilingly received him back, without rancour. He was now in just the frame of mind that the tactful Rat had quietly worked to bring about in him. He saw clearly how plain and simple—how narrow, even—it all was; but clearly, too, how much it all meant to him, and the special value of some such anchorage in one's existence. He did not at all want to abandon the new life and its splendid spaces, to turn his back on sun and air and all they offered him and creep home and stay there; the upper world was all too strong, it called to him still, even down there, and he knew he must return to the larger stage. But it was good to think he had this to come back to, this place which was all his own, these things which were so glad to see him again and could always be counted upon for the same simple welcome.

CHAPTER 6

MR TOAD

It was a bright morning in the early part of summer; the river had resumed its wonted banks and its accustomed pace, and a hot sun seemed to be pulling everything green and bushy and spiky up out of the earth towards him, as if by strings. The Mole and the Water Rat had been up since dawn, very busy on matters connected with boats and the opening of the boating season; painting and varnishing, mending paddles, repairing cushions, hunting for missing boat-hooks, and so on; and were finishing breakfast in their little parlour and eagerly discussing their plans for the day, when a heavy knock sounded at the door.

"Bother!" said the Rat, all over egg. "See who it is, Mole, like a good chap, since you've finished."

The Mole went to attend the summons, and the Rat heard him utter a cry of surprise. Then he flung the parlour door open, and announced with much importance, "Mr Badger!"

This was a wonderful thing, indeed, that the Badger should pay a formal call on them, or indeed on anybody. He generally had to be caught, if you wanted him badly, as he slipped quietly along a hedgerow of an early morning or a late evening, or else hunted up in his own house in the middle of the wood, which was a serious undertaking.

The Badger strode heavily into the room, and stood looking at the two animals with an expression full of seriousness. The Rat let his egg-spoon fall on the table-cloth, and sat open-mouthed.

"The hour has come!" said the Badger at last with great solemnity.

"What hour?" asked the Rat uneasily, glancing at the clock on the mantelpiece.

"*Whose* hour, you should rather say," replied the Badger. "Why, Toad's hour! The hour of Toad! I said I would take him in hand as soon as the winter was well over, and I'm going to take him in hand to-day!"

"Toad's hour, of course!" cried the Mole delightedly. "Hooray! I remember now! *We'll* teach him to be a sensible Toad!"

"This very morning," continued the Badger, taking an arm-chair, "as I learnt last night from a trustworthy source, another new and exceptionally powerful motor-car will arrive at Toad Hall on approval or return. At this very moment, perhaps, Toad is busily arranging himself in those singularly hideous habiliments so dear to him, which transform him from a (comparatively) good-looking Toad into an Object which throws any decent-minded animal that comes across it into a violent fit We must be up and doing, ere it is too late. You two animals will accompany me instantly to Toad Hall, and the work of rescue shall be accomplished."

"Right you are!" cried the Rat, starting up. "We'll rescue the poor unhappy animal! We'll convert him! He'll be the most converted Toad that ever was before we've done with him!"

They set off up the road on their mission of mercy, Badger leading the way. Animals when in company walk in a proper and sensible manner, in single file, instead of sprawling all across the road and being of no use or support to each other in case of sudden trouble or danger.

They reached the carriage-drive of Toad Hall to find, as the Badger had anticipated, a shiny new motor-car, of great size, painted a bright red (Toad's favourite colour), standing in front of the house. As they neared the door it was flung open, and Mr Toad, arrayed in goggles, cap, gaiters, and enormous overcoat, came swaggering down the steps, drawing on his gauntleted gloves.

"Hullo! come on, you fellows!" he cried cheerfully on catching sight of them. "You're just in time to come with me for a jolly—to come for a jolly—for a—er jolly—"

His hearty accents faltered and fell away as he noticed the stern unbending look on the countenances of his silent friends, and his invitation remained unfinished.

The Badger strode up the steps. "Take him inside," he said sternly to his companions. Then, as Toad was hustled through the door, struggling and protesting, he turned to the chauffeur in charge of the new motor-car.

"I'm afraid you won't be wanted to-day," he said. "Mr Toad has changed his mind. He will not require the car. Please understand that this is final. You needn't wait." Then he followed the others inside and shut the door.

"Now, then!" he said to the Toad, when the four of them stood together in the hall, "first of all, take those ridiculous things off!"

"Shan't!" replied Toad, with great spirit. "What is the meaning of this gross outrage? I demand an instant explanation."

"Take them off him, then, you two," ordered the Badger briefly.

They had to lay Toad out on the floor, kicking and calling all sorts of names, before they could get to work properly. Then the Rat sat on him, and the Mole got his motor-clothes off him bit by bit, and they stood him up on his legs again. A good deal of his blustering spirit seemed to have evaporated with the removal of his fine panoply. Now that he was merely Toad, and no longer the Terror of the Highway, he giggled feebly and looked from one to the other appealingly, seeming quite to understand the situation.

"You knew it must come to this, sooner or later, Toad," the Badger explained severely. You've disregarded all the warnings we've given you, you've gone on squandering the money your father left you, and you're getting us animals a bad name in the district by your furious driving and your smashes and your rows with the police. Independence is all very well, but we animals never allow our friends to make fools of themselves beyond a certain limit; and that limit you've reached. Now, you're a good fellow in many respects, and I don't want to be too hard on you. I'll make one more effort to bring you to reason. You will come with me into the smoking-room, and there you will hear some facts about yourself; and we'll see whether you come out of that room the same Toad that you went in."

He took Toad firmly by the arm, led him into the smoking-room, and closed the door behind them.

"That's no good!" said the Rat contemptuously. "*Talking* to Toad'll never cure him. He'll *say* anything."

They made themselves comfortable in arm-chairs and waited patiently. Through the closed door they could just hear the long continuous drone of the Badger's voice, rising and falling in waves of oratory; and presently they noticed that the sermon began to be punctuated at intervals by long-drawn sobs, evidently proceeding from the bosom of Toad, who was a soft-hearted and affectionate fellow, very easily converted—for the time being—to any point of view.

After some three-quarters of an hour the door opened, and the Badger reappeared, solemnly leading by the paw a very limp and dejected Toad. His skin hung baggily about him, his legs wobbled, and his cheeks were furrowed by the tears so plentifully called forth by the Badger's moving discourse.

"Sit down there Toad," said the Badger kindly, pointing to a chair. "My friends," he went on, "I am pleased to inform you that Toad has at last seen the error of his ways. He is truly sorry for his misguided conduct in the past, and he has undertaken to give up motor-cars entirely and for ever. I have his solemn promise to that effect."

"That is very good news," said the Mole gravely.

"Very good news indeed," observed the Rat dubiously, "if only—*if* only—"

He was looking very hard at Toad as he said this, and could not help thinking he perceived something vaguely resembling a twinkle in that animal's still sorrowful eye.

"There's only one thing more to be done," continued the gratified Badger. "Toad, I want you solemnly to repeat, before your friends here, what you fully admitted to me in the smoking-room just now. First, you are sorry for what you've done, and you see the folly of it all?"

There was a long, long pause. Toad looked desperately this way and that, while the other animals waited in grave silence. At last he spoke.

"No!" he said a little sullenly, but stoutly; "I'm *not* sorry. And it wasn't folly at all! It was simply glorious!"

"What?" cried the Badger, greatly scandalized. "You backsliding animal, didn't you tell me just now, in there—"

"O, yes, yes, in *there*," said Toad impatiently. "I'd have said anything in there. You're so eloquent, dear Badger, and so moving, and so convincing, and put all your points so frightfully well—you can do what you like with me in *there*, and you know it. But I've been searching my mind since, and going over things in it, and I find that I'm not a bit sorry or repentant really, so it's no earthly good saying I am; now, is it?"

"Then you don't promise," said the Badger, "never to touch a motor-car again?"

"Certainly not"' replied Toad emphatically. "On the contrary, I faithfully promise that the very first motor-car I see, poop-poop! off I go in it!"

"Told you so, didn't I?" observed the Rat to the Mole.

"Very well, then," said the Badger firmly, rising to his feet. "Since you won't yield to persuasion, we'll try what force can do. I feared it would come to this all along. You've often asked us three to come and stay with you, Toad, in this handsome house of yours; well, now we're going to. When we've converted you to a proper point of view we may quit, but not before. Take him upstairs, you two, and lock him úp in his bedroom, while we arrange matters between ourselves."

"It's for your own good, Toady, you know," said the Rat kindly, as Toad, kicking and struggling, was hauled up the stairs by his two faithful friends. "Think what fun we shall all have together, just as we used to, when you've quite got over this—this painful attack of yours!"

"We'll take great care of everything for you till you're well, Toad," said the Mole; "and we'll see your money isn't wasted, as it has been."

"No more of those regrettable incidents with the police, Toad," said the Rat, as they thrust him into his bedroom.

"And no more weeks in hospital, being ordered about by female nurses, Toad," added the Mole, turning the key on him.

They descended the stair, Toad shouting abuse at them through the keyhole; and the three friends then met in conference on the situation.

"It's going to be a tedious business," said the Badger, sighing. "I've never seen Toad so determined. However, we will see it out. He must never be left an instant unguarded. We shall have to take it in turns to be with him, till the poison has worked itself out of his system."

They arranged watches accordingly. Each animal took it in turns to sleep in Toad's room at night, and they divided the day up between them. At first Toad was undoubtedly very trying to his careful guardians. When his violent paroxysms possessed him he would arrange bedroom chairs in rude resemblance of a motor-car and would crouch on the foremost of them, bent forward and staring fixedly ahead, making uncouth and ghastly noises, till the climax was reached, when, turning a complete somersault, he would lie prostrate amidst the ruins of the chairs, apparently completely satisfied for the moment. As time passed, however, these painful seizures grew gradually less frequent, and his friends strove to divert his mind into fresh channels. But his interest in other matters did not seem to revive, and he grew apparently languid and depressed.

One fine morning the Rat, whose turn it was to go on duty, went upstairs to relieve Badger, whom he found fidgeting to be off and stretch his legs in a long ramble round his wood and down his earths and burrows. "Toad's still in bed," he told the Rat, outside the door. "Can't get much out of him, except, 'O, leave him alone, he wants nothing, perhaps he'll be better presently, it may pass off in time, don't be unduly anxious,' and so on. Now, you look out, Rat! When Toad's quiet and submissive, and playing at being the hero of a Sunday-School prize, then he's at his artfullest. There's sure to be something up. I know him. Well, now I must be off."

"How are you to-day, old chap?" inquired the Rat cheerfully, as he approached Toad's bedside.

He had to wait some minutes for an answer. At last a feeble voice replied, "Thank you so much, dear Ratty! So good of you to inquire! But first tell me how you are yourself, and the excellent Mole?"

"O, *we're* all right," replied the Rat. "Mole," he added incautiously, "is going out for a run round with Badger. They'll be out till luncheon-time, so you and I will spend a pleasant morning together, and I'll do my best to amuse you. Now jump up, there's a good fellow, and don't lie moping there on a fine morning like this!"

"Dear, kind Rat," murmured Toad, "how little you realize my condition, and how very far I am from 'jumping up' now—if ever! But do not trouble about me. I hate being a burden to my friends, and I do not expect to be one much longer. Indeed, I almost hope not."

"Well, I hope not, too," said the Rat heartily. "You've been a fine bother to us all this time, and I'm glad to hear it's going to stop. And in weather like this, and the boating season just beginning! It's too bad of you, Toad! It isn't the trouble we mind, but you're making us miss such an awful lot."

"I'm afraid it *is* the trouble you mind, though," replied the Toad languidly. "I can quite understand it. It's natural enough. You're tired of bothering about me. I mustn't ask you to do anything further. I'm a nuisance, I know."

"You are, indeed," said the Rat "But I tell you, I'd take any trouble on earth for you, if only you'd be a sensible animal."

"If I thought that, Ratty," murmured Toad, more feebly than ever, "then I would beg you—for the last time, probably—to step round to the village as quickly as possible—even now it may be too late—and fetch the doctor. But don't you bother. It's only a trouble, and perhaps we may as well let things take their course."

"Why, what do you want a doctor for?" inquired the Rat, coming closer and examining him. He certainly lay very still and flat, and his voice was weaker and his manner much changed.

"Surely you have noticed of late—" murmured Toad. "But no—why should you? Noticing things is only a trouble. To-morrow, indeed, you may be saying to yourself, 'O, if only I had noticed sooner! If only I had done something!' But no; it's a trouble. Never mind—forget that I asked."

"Look here, old man," said the Rat, beginning to get rather alarmed, "of course I'll fetch a doctor to you, if you really think you want him. But you can hardly be bad enough for that yet. Let's talk about something else."

"I fear, dear friend," said Toad, with a sad smile, "that 'talk' can do little in a case like this—or doctors either, for that matter; still, one must grasp at the slightest straw. And, by the way—while you are about it—I *hate* to give you additional trouble, but I happen to remember that you will pass the door—would you mind at the same time asking the lawyer to step up? It would be a convenience to me, and there are moments—perhaps I should say there is a moment—when one must face disagreeable tasks, at whatever cost to exhausted nature!"

"A lawyer! O, he must be really bad!" the affrighted Rat said to himself, as he hurried from the room, not forgetting, however, to lock the door carefully behind him.

Outside, he stopped to consider. The other two were far away, and he had no one to consult.

"It's best to be on the safe side," he said, on reflection. "I've known Toad fancy himself frightfully bad before, without the slightest reason; but I've never heard him ask for a lawyer! If there's nothing really the matter, the doctor will tell him he's an old ass, and cheer him up; and that will be something gained. I'd better humour him and go; it won't take very long." So he ran off to the village on his errand of mercy.

The Toad, who had hopped lightly out of bed as soon as he heard the key turned in the lock, watched him eagerly from the window till he disappeared down the carriage-drive. Then, laughing heartily, he dressed as quickly as possible in the smartest suit he could lay hands on at the moment, filled his pockets with cash which he took from a small drawer in the dressing-table, and next, knotting the sheets from his bed together and tying one end of the improvised rope round the central mullion of the handsome Tudor window which formed such a feature of his bedroom, he scrambled out, slid lightly to the ground, and, taking the opposite direction to the Rat, marched off light-heartedly, whistling a merry tune.

It was a gloomy luncheon for Rat when the Badger and the Mole at length returned, and he had to face them at table with his pitiful and unconvincing story. The Badger's caustic, not to say brutal, remarks may be imagined, and therefore passed over; but it was painful to the Rat that even the Mole, though he took his friend's side as far as possible, could not help saying, "You've been a bit of a duffer this time, Ratty! Toad, too, of all animals!"

"He did it awfully well," said the crestfallen Rat.

"He did *you* awfully well!" rejoined the Badger hotly. "However, talking won't mend matters. He's got clear away for the time, that's certain; and the worst of it is, he'll be so conceited with what he'll think is his cleverness that he may commit any folly. One comfort is, we're free now, and needn't waste any more of our precious time doing sentry-go. But we'd better continue to sleep at Toad Hall for a while longer. Toad may be brought back at any moment—on a stretcher, or between two policemen."

So spoke the Badger, not knowing what the future held in store, or how much water, and of how turbid a character, was to run under bridges before Toad should sit at ease again in his ancestral Hall.

Meanwhile, Toad, gay and irresponsible, was walking briskly along the high road, some miles from home. At first he had taken by-paths, and crossed many fields, and changed his course several times, in case of pursuit; but now, feeling by this time safe from recapture, and the sun smiling brightly on him, and all nature joining in a chorus of approval to the song of self-praise that his own heart was singing to him, he almost danced along the road in his satisfaction and conceit.

"Smart piece of work that!" he remarked to himself, chuckling. "Brain against brute force—and brain came out on the top—as it's bound to do. Poor old Ratty! My! won't he catch it when the Badger gets back! A worthy fellow, Ratty, with many good qualities, but very little intelligence and absolutely no education. I must take him in hand some day, and see if I can make something of him."

Filled full of conceited thoughts such as these he strode along, his head in the air, till he reached a little town, where the sign of "The Red Lion", swinging across the road half-way down the main street, reminded him that he had not breakfasted that day, and that he was exceedingly hungry after his long walk. He marched into the inn, ordered the best luncheon that could be provided at so short a notice, and sat down to eat it in the coffee-room.

He was about half-way through his meal when an only too familiar sound, approaching down the street, made him start and fall a-trembling all over. The poop-poop! drew nearer and nearer, the car could be heard to turn into the inn-yard and come to a stop, and Toad had to hold on to the leg of the table to conceal his over-mastering emotion. Presently the party entered the coffee-room, hungry, talkative and gay, voluble on their experiences of the morning and the merits of the chariot that had brought them along so well. Toad listened eagerly, all ears, for a time; at last he could stand it no longer. He slipped out of the room quietly, paid his bill at the bar, and as soon as he got outside sauntered round quietly to the inn-yard. "There cannot be any harm," he said to himself, "in my only just *looking* at it!"

The car stood in the middle of the yard, quite unattended, the stable-helps and other hangers-on being all at their dinner. Toad walked slowly round it, inspecting, criticizing, musing deeply.

"I wonder," he said to himself presently, "I wonder if this sort of car *starts* easily?"

Next moment, hardly knowing how it came about, he found he had hold of the handle and was turning it. As the familiar sound broke forth, the old passion seized on Toad and completely mastered him, body and soul. As if in a dream he found himself, somehow, seated in the driver's seat; as if in a dream, he pulled the lever and swung the car round the yard and out through the archway; and, as if in a dream, all sense of right and wrong, all fear of obvious consequences, seemed temporarily suspended. He increased his pace, and as the car devoured the street and leapt forth on the high road through the open country, he was only conscious that he was Toad once more, Toad at his best and highest, Toad the terror, the traffic-queller, the Lord of the lone trail, before whom all must give way or be smitten into nothingness and everlasting night. He chanted as he flew, and the car responded with sonorous drone; the miles were eaten up under him as he sped he knew not whither, fulfilling his instincts, living his hour, reckless of what might come to him.

"To my mind," observed the Chairman of the Bench of Magistrates cheerfully, "the *only* difficulty that presents itself in this otherwise very clear case is, how we can possibly make it sufficiently hot for the incorrigible rogue and hardened ruffian whom we see cowering in the dock before us. Let me see: he has been found guilty, on the clearest evidence, first, of stealing a valuable motor-car; secondly, of driving to the public danger; and, thirdly, of gross impertinence to the rural police. Mr Clerk, will you tell us, please, what is the very stiffest penalty we can impose for each of these offences? Without, of course, giving the prisoner the benefit of any doubt, because there isn't any."

The Clerk scratched his nose with his pen. "Some people would consider," he observed, "that stealing the motor-car was the worst offence; and so it is. But cheeking the police undoubtedly carries the severest penalty, and so it ought. Supposing you were to say twelve months for the theft, which is mild; and three years for the furious driving, which is lenient; and fifteen years for the cheek, which was pretty bad sort of cheek, judging by what we've heard from the witness-box, even if you only believe one-tenth part of what you heard, and I never believe more myself—those figures, if added together correctly, tot up to nineteen years—"

"First rate" said the Chairman.

"—So you had better make it a round twenty years and be on the safe side," concluded the Clerk.

"An excellent suggestion!" said the Chairman approvingly. "Prisoner! Pull yourself together and try and stand up straight. It's going to be twenty years for you this time. And mind, if you appear before us again, upon any charge whatever, we shall have to deal with you very seriously!"

Then the brutal minions of the law fell upon the hapless Toad; loaded him with chains, and dragged him from the Court House, shrieking, praying, protesting; across the market-place, where the playful populace, always as severe upon detected crime as they are sympathetic and helpful when one is merely "wanted", assailed him with jeers, carrots, and popular catch-words; past hooting school children, their innocent faces lit up with the pleasure they ever derive from the sight of a gentleman in difficulties; across the hollow-sounding drawbridge, below the spiky portcullis, under the frowning archway of the grim old castle, whose ancient towers soared high overhead; past guardrooms full of grinning soldiery off duty, past sentries who coughed in a horrid sarcastic way, because that is as much as a sentry on his post dare do to show his contempt and abhorrence of crime; up time-worn winding stairs, past men-at-arms in casquet and corselet of steel, darting threatening looks through their vizards; across courtyards, where mastiffs strained at their leash and pawed the air to get at him; past ancient warders, their halberds leant against the wall, dozing over a pasty and a flagon of brown ale; on and on, past the rack-chamber and the thumbscrew-room, past the turning that led to the private scaffold, till they reached the door of the grimmest dungeon that lay in the heart of the inner-most keep. There at last they paused, where an ancient gaoler sat fingering a bunch of mighty keys.

"Oddsbodikin," said the sergeant of police, taking off his helmet and wiping his forehead. "Rouse thee, old loon, and take over from us this vile Toad, a criminal of deepest guilt and matchless artfulness and resource. Watch and ward him with all thy skill; and mark thee well, grey-beard, should aught untoward befall, thy old head shall answer for his—and a murrain on both of them!"

The gaoler nodded grimly, laying his withered hand on the shoulder of the miserable Toad. The rusty key creaked in the lock, the great door clanged behind them; and Toad was a helpless prisoner in the remotest dungeon of the best-guarded keep of the stoutest castle in all the length and breadth of Merry England.

CHAPTER 7

THE PIPER AT THE GATES OF DAWN

The Willow-Wren was twittering his thin little song, hidden himself, in the dark selvedge of the river bank. Though it was past ten o'clock at night, the sky still clung to and retained some lingering skirts of light from the departed day; and the sullen heats of the torrid afternoon broke up and rolled away at the dispersing touch of the cool fingers of the short midsummer night. Mole lay stretched on the bank, still panting from the stress of the fierce day that had been cloudless from dawn to late sunset, and waited for his friend to return. He had been on the river with some companions, leaving the Water Rat free to keep an engagement of long standing with Otter; and he had come back to find the house dark and deserted, and no sign of Rat, who was doubtless keeping it up late with his old comrade. It was still too hot to think of staying indoors, so he lay on some cool dock-leaves, and thought over the past day and its doings, and how very good they all had been.

The Rat's light footfall was presently heard approaching over the parched grass. "O, the blessed coolness!" he said, and sat down, gazing thoughtfully into the river, silent and preoccupied.

"You stayed to supper, of course?" said the Mole presently.

"Simply had to," said the Rat. "They wouldn't hear of my going before. You know how kind they always are. And they made things as jolly for me as ever they could, right up to the moment I left. But I felt a brute all the time, as it was clear to me they were very unhappy, though they tried to hide it. Mole, I'm afraid they're in trouble. Little Portly is missing again; and you know what a lot his father thinks of him, though he never says much about it."

"What, that child?" said the Mole lightly. "Well, suppose he is; why worry about it? He's always straying off and getting lost, and turning up again; he's so adventurous. But no harm ever happens to him. Everybody hereabouts knows him and likes him, just as they do old Otter, and you may be sure some animal or other will come across him and bring him back again all right. Why, we've found him ourselves, miles from home, and quite self-possessed and cheerful!"

"Yes; but this time it's more serious," said the Rat gravely. "He's been missing for some days now, and the Otters have hunted everywhere, high and low, without finding the slightest trace. And they've asked every animal, too, for miles around, and no one knows anything about him. Otter's evidently more anxious than he'll admit. I got out of him that young Portly hasn't learnt to swim very well yet, and I can see he's thinking of the weir. There's a lot of water coming down still, considering the time of year, and the place always had a fascination for the child. And then there are—well, traps and things—*you* know. Otter's not the fellow to be nervous about any son of his before it's time. And now he *is* nervous. When I left, he came out with me—said he wanted some air, and talked about stretching his legs. But I could see it wasn't that, so I drew him out and pumped him, and got it all from him at last. He was going to spend the night watching by the ford. You know the place where the old ford used to be, in bygone days before they built the bridge?"

"I know it well," said the Mole. "But why should Otter choose to watch there?"

"Well, it seems that it was there he gave Portly his first swimming lesson," continued the Rat. "From that shallow, gravelly spit near the bank. And it was there he used to teach him fishing, and there young Portly caught his first fish, of which he was so very proud. The child loved the spot, and Otter thinks that if he came wandering back from wherever he is—if he *is* anywhere by this time, poor little chap—he might make for the ford he was so fond of; or if he came across it he'd remember it well, and stop there and play, perhaps. So Otter goes there every night and watches—on the chance, you know, just on the chance!"

They were silent for a time, both thinking of the same thing—the lonely, heart-sore animal, crouched by the ford, watching and waiting, the long night through—on the chance.

"Well, well," said the Rat presently, "I suppose we ought to be thinking about turning in." But he never offered to move.

"Rat," said the Mole, "I simply can't go and turn in, and go to sleep, and *do* nothing, even though there doesn't seem to be anything to be done. We'll get the boat out, and paddle upstream. The moon will be up in an hour or so, and then we will search as well as we can—anyhow, it will be better than going to bed and doing *nothing*."

"Just what I was thinking myself," said the Rat. "It's not the sort of night for bed anyhow; and daybreak is not so very far off, and then we may pick up some news of him from early risers as we go along."

They got the boat out, and the Rat took the sculls, paddling with caution. Out in midstream there was a clear, narrow track that faintly reflected the sky; but wherever shadows fell on the water from bank, bush, or tree, they were as solid to all appearance as the banks themselves, and the Mole had to steer with judgment accordingly. Dark and deserted as it was, the night was full of small noises, song and chatter and rustling, telling of the busy little population who were up and about, plying their trades and vocations through the night till sunshine should fall on them at last and send them off to their well-earned repose. The water's own noises, too, were more apparent than by day, its gurglings and "cloops" more unexpected and near at hand; and constantly they started at what seemed a sudden clear call from an actual articulate voice.

The line of the horizon was clear and hard against the sky, and in one particular quarter it showed black against a silvery climbing phosphorescence that grew and grew. At last, over the rim of the waiting earth the moon lifted with slow majesty till it swung clear of the horizon and rode off, free of moorings; and once more they began to see surfaces—meadows widespread, and quiet gardens, and the river itself from bank to bank, all softly disclosed, all washed clean of mystery and terror, all radiant again as by day, but with a difference that was tremendous. Their old haunts greeted them again in other raiment, as if they had slipped away and put on this pure new apparel and come quietly back, smiling as they shyly waved to see if they would be recognized again under it.

Fastening their boat to a willow, the friends landed in this silent, silver kingdom, and patiently explored the hedges, the hollow trees, the runnels and their little culverts, the ditches and dry water-ways. Embarking again and crossing over, they worked their way up the stream in this manner, while the moon, serene and detached in a cloudless sky, did what she could, though so far off, to help them in their quest; till her hour came and she sank; earthwards reluctantly, and left them, and mystery once more held field and river.

Then a change began slowly to declare itself. The horizon became clearer, field and tree came more into sight, and somehow with a different look; the mystery began to drop away from them. A bird piped suddenly, and was still; and a light breeze sprang up and set the reeds and bulrushes rustling. Rat, who was in the stern of the boat while Mole sculled, sat up suddenly and listened with a passionate intentness. Mole, who with gentle strokes was just keeping the boat moving while he scanned the banks with care, looked at him with curiosity.

"It's gone!" sighed the Rat, sinking back in his seat again. "So beautiful and strange and new! Since it was to end so soon, I almost wish I had never heard it. For it has roused a longing in me that is pain, and nothing seems worth while but just to hear that sound once more and go on listening to it for ever. No! There it is again!" he cried, alert once more. Entranced, he was silent for a long space, spellbound.

"Now it passes on and I begin to lose it," he said presently. "O, Mole! the beauty of it! The merry bubble and joy, the thin, clear happy call of the distant piping! Such music I never dreamed of, and the call in it is stronger even than the music is sweet! Row on, Mole, row! For the music and the call must be for us."

The Mole, greatly wondering, obeyed. "I hear nothing myself," he said, "but the wind playing in the reeds and rushes and osiers."

The Rat never answered, if indeed he heard. Rapt, transported, trembling, he was possessed in all his senses by this new divine thing that caught up his helpless soul and swung and dandled it, a powerless but happy infant in a strong sustaining grasp.

In silence Mole rowed steadily, and soon they came to a point where the river divided, a long backwater branching off to one side. With a slight movement of his head Rat, who had long dropped the rudder-lines, directed the rower to take the backwater. The creeping tide of light gained and gained, and now they could see the colour of the flowers that gemmed the water's edge.

"Clearer and nearer still," cried the Rat joyously. "Now you must surely hear it! Ah—at last—I see you do!"

Breathless and transfixed the Mole stopped rowing as the liquid run of that glad piping broke on him like a wave, caught him up, and possessed him utterly. He saw the tears on his comrade's cheeks, and bowed his head and understood. For a space they hung there, brushed by the purple loosestrife that fringed the bank; then the clear imperious summons that marched hand-in-hand with the intoxicating melody imposed its will on Mole, and mechanically he bent to his oars again. And the light grew steadily stronger, but no birds sang as they were wont to do at the approach of dawn; and but for the heavenly music all was marvellously still.

On either side of them, as they glided onwards, the rich meadow-grass seemed that morning of a freshness and a greenness unsurpassable. Never had they noticed the roses so vivid, the willow-herb so riotous, the meadow-sweet so odorous and pervading. Then the murmur of the approaching weir began to hold the air, and they felt a consciousness that they were nearing the end, whatever it might be, that surely awaited their expedition.

A wide half-circle of foam and glinting lights and shining shoulders of green water, the great weir closed the backwater from bank to bank, troubled all the quiet surface with twirling eddies and floating foam-streaks, and deadened all other sounds with its solemn and soothing rumble. In midmost of the stream, embraced in the weir's shimmering arm-spread, a small island lay anchored, fringed close with willow and silver birch and alder. Reserved, shy, but full of significance, it hid whatever it might hold behind a veil, keeping it till the hour should come, and, with the hour, those who were called and chosen.

Slowly, but with no doubt or hesitation whatever, and in something of a solemn expectancy, the two animals passed through the broken, tumultuous water and moored their boat at the flowery margin of the island. In silence they landed, and pushed through the blossom and scented herbage and undergrowth that led up to the level ground, till they stood on a little lawn of a marvellous green, set round with Nature's own orchard-trees—crab-apple, wild cherry, and sloe.

"This is the place of my song-dream, the place the music played to me," whispered the Rat, as if in a trance. "Here, in this holy place, here if anywhere, surely we shall find Him!"

Then suddenly the Mole felt a great Awe fall upon him, an awe that turned his muscles to water, bowed his head, and rooted his feet to the ground. It was no panic terror—indeed he felt wonderfully at peace and happy—but it was an awe that smote and held him and, without seeing, he knew it could only mean that some august Presence was very, very near. With difficulty he turned to look for his friend, and saw him at his side cowed, stricken, and trembling violently. And still there was utter silence in the populous bird-haunted branches around them; and still the light grew and grew.

Perhaps he would never have dared to raise his eyes, but that, though the piping was now hushed, the call and the summons seemed still dominant and imperious. He might not refuse, were Death himself waiting to strike him instantly, once he had looked with mortal eye on things rightly kept hidden. Trembling he obeyed, and raised his humble head; and then, in that utter clearness of the imminent dawn, while Nature, flushed with fullness of incredible colour, seemed to hold her breath for the event, he looked in the very eyes of the Friend and Helper; saw the backward sweep of the curved horns, gleaming in the growing daylight; saw the stern, hooked nose between the kindly eyes that were looking down on them humorously, while the bearded mouth broke into a half-smile at the corners; saw the rippling muscles on the arm that lay across the broad chest, the long supple hand still holding the pan-pipes only just fallen away from the parted lips; saw the splendid curves of the shaggy limbs disposed in majestic ease on the sward; saw, last of all, nestling between his very hooves, sleeping soundly in entire peace and contentment, the little, round, podgy, childish form of the baby otter. All this he saw, for one moment breathless and intense, vivid on the morning sky; and still, as he looked, he lived; and still, as he lived, he wondered.

"Rat!" he found breath to whisper, shaking. "Are you afraid?"

"Afraid?" murmured the Rat, his eyes shining with unutterable love. "Afraid! Of *Him*? O, never, never! And yet—and yet—O, Mole, I am afraid!" Then the two animals, crouching to the earth, bowed their heads and did worship.

Sudden and magnificent, the sun's broad golden disc showed itself over the horizon facing them; and the first rays, shooting across the level water-meadows, took the animals full in the eyes and dazzled them. When they were able to look once more, the Vision had vanished, and the air was full of the carol of birds that hailed the dawn.

As they stared blankly, in dumb misery deepening as they slowly realized all they had seen and all they had lost, a capricious little breeze, dancing up from the surface of the water, tossed the aspens, shook the dewy roses, and blew lightly and caressingly in their faces, and with its soft touch came instant oblivion. For this is the last best gift that the kindly demi-god is careful to bestow on those to whom he has revealed himself in their helping: the gift of forgetfulness. Lest the awful remembrance should remain and grow, and overshadow mirth and pleasure, and the great haunting memory should spoil all the afterlives of little animals helped out of difficulties, in order that they should be happy and light-hearted as before.

Mole rubbed his eyes and stared at Rat, who was looking about him in a puzzled sort of way. "I beg your pardon; what did you say, Rat?" he asked.

"I think I was only remarking," said Rat slowly, "that this was the right sort of place, and that here, if anywhere, we should find him. And look! Why, there he is, the little fellow!" And with a cry of delight he ran towards the slumbering Portly.

But Mole stood still a moment, held in thought. As one wakened suddenly from a beautiful dream, who struggles to recall it, and can recapture nothing but a dim sense of the beauty of it, the beauty! Till that, too, fades away in its turn, and the dreamer bitterly accepts the hard, cold waking and all its penalties; so Mole, after struggling with his memory for a brief space, shook his head sadly and followed the Rat.

Portly woke up with a joyous squeak, and wriggled with pleasure at the sight of his father's friends, who had played with him so often in past days. In a moment, however, his face grew blank, and he fell to hunting round in a circle with pleading whine. As a child that has fallen happily asleep in its nurse's arms, and wakes to find itself alone and laid in a strange place, and searches corners and cupboards, and runs from room to room, despair growing silently in its heart, even so Portly searched the island and searched, dogged and unwearying, till at last the black moment came for giving it up, and sitting down and crying bitterly.

The Mole ran quickly to comfort the little animal; but Rat, lingering, looked long and doubtfully at certain hoof-marks deep in the sward.

"Some—great—animal—has been here," he murmured slowly and thoughtfully; and stood musing, musing; his mind strangely stirred.

"Come along, Rat!" called the Mole. "Think of poor Otter, waiting up there by the ford!"

Portly had soon been comforted by the promise of a treat—a jaunt on the river in Mr Rat's real boat; and the two animals conducted him to the water's side, placed him securely between them in the bottom of the boat, and paddled off down the backwater. The sun was fully up by now, and hot on them, birds sang lustily and without restraint, and flowers smiled and nodded from either bank, but somehow—so thought the animals—with less of richness and blaze of colour than they seemed to remember seeing quite recently somewhere—they wondered where.

The main river reached again, they turned the boat's head up stream, towards the point where they knew their friend was keeping his lonely vigil. As they drew near the familiar ford, the Mole took the boat in to the bank, and they lifted Portly out and set him on his legs on the tow-path, gave him his marching orders and a friendly farewell pat on the back, and shoved out into mid-stream. They watched the little animal as he waddled along the path contentedly and with importance; watched him till they saw his muzzle suddenly lift and his waddle break into a clumsy amble as he quickened his pace with shrill whines and wriggles of recognition. Looking up the river, they could see Otter start up, tense and rigid, from out of the shallows where he crouched in dumb patience, and could hear his amazed and joyous bark as he bounded up through the osiers on to the path. Then the Mole, with a strong pull on one oar, swung the boat round and let the full stream bear them down again whither it would, their quest now happily ended.

"I feel strangely tired, Rat," said the Mole, leaning wearily over his oars as the boat drifted. "It's being up all night, you'll say, perhaps; but thats nothing. We do as much half the nights of the week, at this time of the year. No; I feel as if I had been through something very exciting and rather terrible, and it was just over; and yet nothing particular has happened."

"Or something very surprising and splendid and beautiful," murmured the Rat, leaning back and closing his eyes. "I feel just as you do, Mole; simply dead tired, though not body-tired. It's lucky we've got the stream with us, to take us home. Isn't it jolly to feel the sun again, soaking into one's bones! And hark to the wind playing in the reeds!"

"It's like music—far-away music," said the Mole, nodding drowsily.

"So I was thinking," murmured the Rat, dreamful and languid. "Dance-music—the lilting sort that runs on without a stop—but with words in it, too—it passes into words and out of them again—I catch them at intervals then it is dance-music once more, and then nothing but the reeds' soft thin whispering."

"You hear better than I," said the Mole sadly. "I cannot catch the words."

"Let me try and give you them," said the Rat softly, his eyes still closed. "Now it is turning into words again—faint but clear—*Lest the awe should dwell—And turn your frolic to fret—You shall look on my power at the helping hour—But then you shall forget!* Now the reeds take it up—*forget, forget,* they sigh, and it dies away in a rustle and a whisper. Then the voice returns—

Lest limbs be reddened and rent—I spring the trap that is set—As I loose the snare you may glimpse me there—For surely you shall forget! Row nearer, Mole, nearer to the reeds! It is hard to catch, and grows each minute fainter.

"*Helper and healer, I cheer—Small waifs in the woodland wet— Strays I find in it, wounds I bind in it—Bidding them all forget!* Nearer, Mole, nearer! No, it is no good; the song has died away into reed-talk."

"But what do the words mean?" asked the wondering Mole.

"That I do not know," said the Rat simply. "I passed them on to you as they reached me. Ah! now they return again, and this time full and clear! This time, at last, it is the real, the unmistakable thing, simple—passionate—perfect—"

"Well, let's have it, then," said the Mole, after he had waited patiently for a few minutes, half dozing in the hot sun.

But no answer came. He looked, and understood the silence. With a smile of much happiness on his face, and something of a listening look still lingering there, the weary Rat was fast asleep.

Chapter 8

TOAD'S ADVENTURES

When Toad found himself immured in a dank and noisome dungeon, and knew that all the grim darkness of a medieval fortress lay between him and the outer world of sunshine and well-metalled high roads where he had lately been so happy, disporting himself as if he had bought up every road in England, he flung himself at full length on the floor, and shed bitter tears, and abandoned himself to dark despair. "This is the end of everything" (he said), "at least it is the end of the career of Toad, which is the same thing; the popular and handsome Toad, the rich and hospitable Toad, the Toad so free and careless and debonair! How can I hope to be ever set at large again" (he said), "who have been imprisoned so justly for stealing so handsome a motor-car in such an audacious manner; and for such lurid and imaginative cheek, bestowed upon such a number of fat, red-faced policemen!" (Here his sobs choked him.) "Stupid animal that I was" (he said), "now I must languish in this dungeon, till people who were proud to say they knew me, have forgotten the very name of Toad! O wise old Badger!" (he said), "O clever, intelligent Rat and sensible Mole! What sound judgments, what a knowledge of men and matters you possess! O unhappy and forsaken Toad!" With lamentations such as these he passed his days and nights for several weeks, refusing his meals or intermediate light refreshments, though the grim and ancient gaoler, knowing that Toad's pockets were well lined, frequently pointed out that many comforts, and indeed luxuries, could by arrangement be sent in—at a price—from outside.

Now the gaoler had a daughter, a pleasant wench and good-hearted, who assisted her father in the lighter duties of his post. She was particularly fond of animals, and, besides her canary, whose cage hung on a nail in the massive wall of the keep by day, to the great annoyance of prisoners who relished an after-dinner nap, and was shrouded in an antimacassar on the parlour table at night, she kept several piebald mice and a restless revolving squirrel. This kind-hearted girl, pitying the misery of Toad, said to her father one day, "Father! I can't bear to see that poor beast so unhappy, and getting so thin! You let me have the managing of him. You know how fond of animals I am. I'll make him eat from my hand, and sit up, and do all sorts of things."

Her father replied that she could do what she liked with him. He was tired of Toad, and his sulks and his airs and his meanness. So that day she went on her errand of mercy, and knocked at the door of Toad's cell.

"Now, cheer up, Toad," she said coaxingly, on entering, "and sit up and dry your eyes and be a sensible animal. And do try and eat a bit of dinner. See, I've brought you some of mine, hot from the oven!"

It was bubble-and-squeak, between two plates, and its fragrance filled the narrow cell. The penetrating smell of cabbage reached the nose of Toad as he lay prostrate in his misery on the floor, and gave him the idea for a moment that perhaps life was not such a blank and desperate thing as he had imagined. But still he wailed, and kicked with his legs, and refused to be comforted. So the wise girl retired for the time, but, of course, a good deal of the smell of hot cabbage remained behind, as it will do, and Toad, between his sobs, sniffed and reflected, and gradually began to think new and inspiring thoughts: of chivalry, and poetry, and deeds still to be done; of broad meadows, and cattle browsing in them, raked by sun and wind; of kitchen-gardens, and straight herb-borders, and warm snap-dragon beset by bees; and of the comforting clink of dishes set down on the table at Toad Hall, and the scrape of chair-legs on the floor as every one pulled himself close up to his work. The air of the narrow cell took on a rosy tinge; he began to think of his friends, and how they would surely be able to do something; of lawyers, and how they would have enjoyed his case, and what an ass he had been not to get in a few; and lastly, he thought of his own great cleverness and resource, and all that he was capable of if he only gave his great mind to it; and the cure was almost complete.

When the girl returned, some hours later, she carried a tray, with a cup of fragrant tea steaming on it; and a plate piled up with very hot buttered toast, cut thick, very brown on both sides, with the butter running through the holes in it in great golden drops, like honey from the honey-comb. The smell of that buttered toast simply talked to Toad, and with no uncertain voice; talked of warm kitchens, of breakfasts on bright frosty mornings, of cosy parlour firesides on winter evenings, when one's ramble was over and slippered feet were propped on the fender; of the purring of contented cats, and the twitter of sleepy canaries. Toad sat up on end once-more, dried his eyes, sipped his tea and munched his toast, and soon began talking freely about himself, and the house he lived in, and his doings there, and how important he was, and what a lot his friends thought of him.

The gaoler's daughter saw that the topic was doing him as much good as the tea, as indeed it was, and encouraged him to go on.

"Tell me about Toad Hall," said she. "It sounds beautiful."

"Toad Hall," said the Toad proudly, "is an eligible self-contained gentleman's residence, very unique; dating in part from the fourteenth century, but replete with every modern convenience. Up-to-date sanitation. Five minutes from church, post office, and golf-links. Suitable for—"

"Bless the animal," said the girl, laughing, "I don't want to *take* it. Tell me something *real* about it. But first wait till I fetch you some more tea and toast."

She tripped away, and presently returned with a fresh trayful; and Toad, pitching into the toast with avidity, his spirits quite restored to their usual level, told her about the boat-house, and the fish-pond, and the old walled kitchen-garden; and about the pig-styes, and the stables, and the pigeon-house, and the hen-house; and about the dairy, and the wash-house, and the china-cupboards, and the linen-presses (she liked that bit especially); and about the banqueting-hall, and the fun they had there when the other animals were gathered round the table and Toad was at his best, singing songs, telling stories, carrying on generally. Then she wanted to know about his animal-friends, and was very interested in all he had to tell her about them and how they lived, and what they did to pass their time. Of course, she did not say she was fond of animals as *pets*, because she had the sense to see that Toad would be extremely offended. When she said good night, having filled his water jug and shaken up his straw for him, Toad was very much the same sanguine, self-satisfied animal that he had been of old. He sang a little song or two, of the sort he used to sing at his dinner-parties, curled himself up in the straw, and had an excellent night's rest and the pleasantest of dreams.

They had many interesting talks together, after that, as the dreary days went on; and the gaoler's daughter grew very sorry for Toad, and thought it a great shame that a poor little animal should be locked up in prison for what seemed to her a very trivial offence. Toad, of course, in his vanity, thought that her interest in him proceeded from a growing tenderness; and he could not help half regretting that the social gulf between them was so very wide, for she was a comely lass, and evidently admired him very much.

One morning the girl was very thoughtful, and answered at random, and did not seem to Toad to be paying proper attention to his witty sayings and sparkling comments.

"Toad," she said presently, "just listen, please. I have an aunt who is a washerwoman."

"There, there," said Toad graciously and affably, "never mind; think no more about it. *I* have several aunts who *ought* to be washerwomen."

"Do be quiet a minute, Toad," said the girl. "You talk too much, that's your chief fault, and I'm trying to think, and you hurt my head. As I said, I have an aunt who is a washerwoman; she does the washing for all the prisoners in this castle—we try to keep any paying business of that sort in the family, you understand. She takes out the washing on Monday morning, and brings it in on Friday evening. This is a Thursday. Now, this is what occurs to me: you're very rich—at least you're always telling me so—and she's very poor. A few pounds wouldn't make any difference to you, and it would mean a lot to her. Now, I think if she were properly approached— squared, I believe, is the word you animals use—you could come to some arrangement by which she would let you have her dress and bonnet and so on, and you could escape from the castle as the official washerwoman. You're very alike in many respects—particularly about the figure."

"We're *not*," said the Toad in a huff. "I have a very elegant figure—for what I am."

"So has my aunt," replied the girl, "for what *she* is. But have it your own way. You horrid, proud, ungrateful animal, when I'm sorry for you, and trying to help you!"

"Yes, yes, that's all right; thank you very much indeed," said the Toad hurriedly. "But look here! you wouldn't surely have Mr Toad, of Toad Hall, going about the country disguised as a washerwoman!"

"Then you can stop here as a Toad," replied the girl with much spirit. "I suppose you want to go off in a coach-and-four!"

Honest Toad was always ready to admit himself in the wrong. "You are a good, kind, clever girl," he said, "and I am indeed a proud and a stupid toad. Introduce me to your worthy aunt, if you will be so kind, and I have no doubt that the excellent lady and I will be able to arrange terms satisfactory to both parties."

Next evening the girl ushered her aunt into Toad's cell, bearing his week's washing pinned up in a towel. The old lady had been prepared beforehand for the interview, and the sight of certain golden sovereigns that Toad had thoughtfully placed on the table in full view practically completed the matter and left little further to discuss. In return for his cash, Toad received a cotton print gown, an apron, a shawl, and a rusty black bonnet; the only stipulation the old lady made being that she should be gagged and bound and dumped down in a corner. By this not very convincing artifice, she explained, aided by picturesque fiction which she could supply herself, she hoped to retain her situation, in spite of the suspicious appearance of things.

Toad was delighted with the suggestion. It would enable him to leave the prison in some style, and with his reputation for being a desperate and dangerous fellow untarnished; and he readily helped the gaoler's daughter to make her aunt appear as much as possible the victim of circumstances over which she had no control.

"Now it's your turn, Toad," said the girl. "Take off that coat and waistcoat of yours; you're fat enough as it is."

Shaking with laughter, she proceeded to "hook-and-eye" him into the cotton print gown, arranged the shawl with a professional fold, and tied the strings of the rusty bonnet under his chin.

"You're the very image of her," she giggled, "only I'm sure you never looked half so respectable in all your life before. Now, goodbye, Toad, and good luck. Go straight down the way you came up; and if any one says anything to you, as they probably will, being but men, you can chaff back a bit, of course, but remember you're a widow woman, quite alone in the world, with a character to lose."

With a quaking heart, but as firm a footstep as he could command, Toad set forth cautiously on what seemed to be a most hare-brained and hazardous undertaking; but he was soon agreeably surprised to find how easy everything was made for him, and a little humbled at the thought that both his popularity, and the sex that seemed to inspire it, were really another's. The washerwoman's squat figure in its familiar cotton print seemed a passport for every barred door and grim gateway; even when he hesitated, uncertain as to the right turning to take, he found himself helped out of his difficulty by the warder at the next gate, anxious to be off to his tea, summoning him to come along sharp and not keep him waiting there all night. The chaff and the humorous sallies to which he was subjected, and to which, of course, he had to provide prompt and effective reply, formed, indeed, his chief danger; for Toad was an animal with a strong sense of his own dignity, and the chaff was mostly (he thought) poor and clumsy, and the humour of the sallies entirely lacking. However, he kept his temper, though with great difficulty, suited his retorts to his company and his supposed character, and did his best not to overstep the limits of good taste.

It seemed hours before he crossed the last courtyard, rejected the pressing invitations from the last guardroom, and dodged the outspread arms of the last warder, pleading with simulated passion for just one farewell embrace. But at last he heard the wicket-gate in the great outer door click behind him, felt the fresh air of the outer world upon his anxious brow, and knew that he was free!

Dizzy with the easy success of his daring exploit, he walked quickly towards the lights of the town, not knowing in the least what he should do next, only quite certain of one thing, that he must remove himself as quickly as possible from a neighbourhood where the lady he was forced to represent was so well-known and so popular a character.

As he walked along, considering, his attention was caught by some red and green lights a little way off, to one side of the town, and the sound of the puffing and snorting of engines and the banging of shunted trucks fell on his ear. "Aha!" he thought, "this is a piece of luck! A railway-station is the thing I want most in the whole world at this moment; and what's more, I needn't go through the town to get to it, and shan't have to support this humiliating character by repartees which, though thoroughly effective, do not assist one's sense of self-respect."

He made his way to the station accordingly, consulted a time-table, and found that a train, bound more or less in the direction of his home, was due to start in half an hour. "More luck!" said Toad, his spirits rising rapidly, and went off to the booking-office to buy his ticket.

He gave the name of the station that he knew to be nearest to the village of which Toad Hall was the principal feature, and mechanically put his fingers, in search of the necessary money, where his waistcoat pocket should have been. But here the cotton gown, which had nobly stood by him so far, and which he had basely forgotten, intervened, and frustrated his efforts. In a sort of nightmare he struggled with the strange uncanny thing that seemed to hold his hands, turn all muscular strivings to water, and laugh at him all the time; while other travellers, forming up in a line behind, waited with impatience, making suggestions of more or less value and comments of more or less stringency and point. At last—somehow—he never rightly understood how—he burst the barriers, attained the goal, arrived at where all waistcoat pockets are eternally situated, and found—not only no money, but no pocket to hold it, and no waistcoat to hold the pocket!

To his horror he recollected that he had left both coat and waistcoat behind him in his cell, and with them his pocket-book, money, keys, watch, matches, pencil-case—all that makes life worth living, all that distinguishes the many-pocketed animal, the lord of creation, from the inferior one-pocketed or no-pocketed productions that hop or trip about permissively, unequipped for the real contest.

In his misery he made one desperate effort to carry the thing off, and, with a return to his fine old manner—a blend of the Squire and the College Don—he said, "Look here! I find I've left my purse behind. Just give me that ticket, will you, and I'll send the money on to-morrow. I'm well-known in these parts."

The clerk stared at him and the rusty black bonnet a moment, and then laughed. "I should think you were pretty well-known in these parts," he said, "if you've tried this game on often. Here, stand away from the window, please, madam; you're obstructing the other passengers!"

An old gentleman who had been prodding him in the back for some moments here thrust him away, and, what was worse, addressed him as his good woman, which angered Toad more than anything that had occurred that evening.

Baffled and full of despair, he wandered blindly down the platform where the train was standing, and tears trickled down each side of his nose. It was hard, he thought, to be within sight of safety and almost of home, and to be baulked by the want of a few wretched shillings and by the pettifogging mistrustfulness of paid officials. Very soon his escape would be discovered, the hunt would be up, he would be caught, reviled, loaded with chains, dragged back again to prison and bread-and-water and straw; his guards and penalties would be doubled; and O, what sarcastic remarks the girl would make! What was to be done? He was not swift of foot; his figure was unfortunately recognizable. Could he not squeeze under the seat of a carriage? He had seen this method adopted by schoolboys, when the journey-money provided by thoughtful parents had been diverted to other and better ends. As he pondered, he found himself opposite the engine, which was being oiled, wiped, and generally caressed by its affectionate driver, a burly man with an oil-can in one hand and a lump of cotton-waste in the other.

"Hullo, mother!" said the engine-driver, "what's the trouble? You don't look particularly cheerful."

"O, sir!" said Toad, crying afresh, "I am a poor unhappy washerwoman, and I've lost all my money, and can't pay for a ticket, and I must get home tonight somehow, and whatever I am to do I don't know. O dear, O dear!"

"That's a bad business, indeed," said the engine-driver reflectively. "Lost your money—and can't get home—and got some kids, too, waiting for you, I dare say?"

"Any amount of 'em," sobbed Toad. "and they'll be hungry—and playing with matches—and upsetting lamps, the little innocents!—and quarrelling, and going on generally. O dear, O dear!"

"Well, I'll tell you what I'll do," said the good engine-driver. "You're a washerwoman to your trade, says you. Very well, that's that. And I'm an engine-driver, as you well may see, and there's no denying it's terribly dirty work. Uses up a power of shirts, it does, till my missus is fair tired of washing of 'em. If you'll wash a few shirts for me when you get home, and send 'em along, I'll give you a ride on my engine. It's against the Company's regulations, but we're not so very particular in these out-of-the-way parts."

The Toad's misery turned into rapture as he eagerly scrambled up into the cab of the engine. Of course, he had never washed a shirt in his life, and couldn't if he tried and, anyhow, he wasn't going to begin; but he thought: "When I get safely home to Toad Hall, and have money again, and pockets to put it in, I will send the engine-driver enough to pay for quite a quantity of washing, and that will be the same thing, or better."

The guard waved his welcome flag, the engine-driver whistled in cheerful response, and the train moved out of the station. As the speed increased, and the Toad could see on either side of him real fields, and trees, and hedges, and cows, and horses, all a-flying past him, and as he thought how every minute was bringing him nearer to Toad Hall and sympathetic friends, and money to chink in his pocket, and a soft bed to sleep in, and good things to eat, and praise and admiration at the recital of his adventures and his surpassing cleverness, he began to skip up and down and shout and sing snatches of song, to the great astonishment of the engine-driver, who had come across washerwomen before, at long intervals, but never one at all like this.

They had covered many and many a mile, and Toad was already considering what he would have for supper as soon as he got home, when he noticed that the engine-driver, with a puzzled expression on his face, was leaning over the side of the engine and listening hard. Then he saw him climb on to the coals and gaze out over the top of the train; then he returned and said to Toad: "It's very strange; we're the last train running in this direction to-night, yet I could be sworn that I heard another following us!"

Toad ceased his frivolous antics at once. He became grave and depressed, and a dull pain in the lower part of his spine, communicating itself to his legs, made him want to sit down and try desperately not to think of all the possibilities.

By this time the moon was shining brightly, and the engine-driver, steadying himself on the coal, could command a view of the line behind them for a long distance.

Presently he called out, "I can see it clearly now! It is an engine, on our rails, coming along at a great pace! It looks as if we were being pursued!"

The miserable Toad, crouching in the coal-dust, tried hard to think of something to do, with dismal want of success.

"They are gaining on us fast!" cried the engine-driver. "And the engine is crowded with the queerest lot of people! Men like ancient warders, waving halberds; policemen in their helmets, waving truncheons; and shabbily dressed men in pot-hats, obvious and unmistakable plain-clothes detectives even at this distance, waving revolvers and walking-sticks; all waving, and all shouting the same thing—'Stop, stop, stop!'"

Then Toad fell on his knees among the coals and, raising his clasped paws in supplication, cried, "Save me, only save me, dear kind Mr Engine-driver, and I will confess everything! I am not the simple washerwoman I seem to be! I have no children waiting for me, innocent or otherwise! I am a toad—the well-known and popular Mr Toad, a landed proprietor; I have just escaped, by my great daring and cleverness, from a loathsome dungeon into which my enemies had flung me; and if those fellows on that engine recapture me, it will be chains and bread-and-water and straw and misery once more for poor, unhappy, innocent Toad!"

The engine-driver looked down upon him very sternly, and said, "Now tell the truth; what were you put in prison for?"

"It was nothing very much," said poor Toad, colouring deeply. "I only borrowed a motor-car while the owners were at lunch; they had no need of it at the time. I didn't mean to steal it, really; but people—especially magistrates—take such harsh views of thoughtless and high-spirited actions."

The engine-driver looked very grave and said, "I fear that you have been indeed a wicked toad, and by rights I ought to give you up to offended justice. But you are evidently in sore trouble and distress, so I will not desert you. I don't hold with motor-cars, for one thing; and I don't hold with being ordered about by policemen when I'm on my own engine, for another. And the sight of an animal in tears always makes me feel queer and soft-hearted. So cheer up, Toad! I'll do my best, and we may beat them yet!"

They piled on more coals, shovelling furiously; the furnace roared, the sparks flew, the engine leapt and swung, but still their pursuers slowly gained. The engine-driver, with a sigh, wiped his brow with a handful of cotton-waste, and said, "I'm afraid it's no good, Toad. You see, they are running light, and they have the better engine. There's just one thing left for us to do, and it's your only chance, so attend very carefully to what I tell you. A short way ahead of us is a long tunnel, and on the other side of that the line passes through a thick wood. Now, I will put on all the speed I can while we are running through the tunnel but the other fellows will slow down a bit, naturally, for fear of an accident. When we are through, I will shut off steam and put on brakes as hard as I can, and the moment it's safe to do so you must jump and hide in the wood, before they get through the tunnel and see you. Then I will go full speed ahead again, and they can chase me if they like, for as long as they like, and as far as they like. Now mind and be ready to jump when I tell you!"

They piled on more coals, and the train shot into the tunnel, and the engine rushed and roared and rattled, till at last they shot out at the other end into fresh air and the peaceful moonlight, and saw the wood lying dark and helpful upon either side of the line. The driver shut off steam and put on brakes, the Toad got down on the step, and as the train slowed down to almost a walking pace he heard the driver call out, "Now, jump!"

Toad jumped, rolled down a short embankment, picked himself up unhurt, scrambled into the wood and hid.

Peeping out, he saw his train get up speed again and disappear at a great pace. Then out of the tunnel burst the pursuing engine, roaring and whistling, her motley crew waving their various weapons and shouting, "Stop! stop! stop!" When they were past, the Toad had a hearty laugh—for the first time since he was thrown into prison.

But he soon stopped laughing when he came to consider that it was now very late and dark and cold, and he was in an unknown wood, with no money and no chance of supper, and still far from friends and home; and the dead silence of everything, after the roar and rattle of the train, was something of a shock. He dared not leave the shelter of the trees, so he struck into the wood, with the idea of leaving the railway as far as possible behind him.

After so many weeks within walls, he found the wood strange and unfriendly and inclined, he thought, to make fun of him. Nightjars, sounding their mechanical rattle, made him think that the wood was full of searching warders, closing in on him. An owl, swooping noiselessly towards him, brushed his shoulder with its wing, making him jump with the horrid certainty that it was a hand; then flitted off, moth-like, laughing its low ho! ho! ho! which Toad thought in very poor taste. Once he met a fox, who stopped, looked him up and down in a sarcastic sort of way, and said, "Hullo, washerwoman! Half a pair of socks and a pillow-case short this week! Mind it doesn't occur again!" and swaggered off, sniggering. Toad looked about for a stone to throw at him, but could not succeed in finding one, which vexed him more than anything. At last, cold, hungry, and tired out, he sought the shelter of a hollow tree, where with branches and dead leaves he made himself as comfortable a bed as he could, and slept soundly till the morning.

Chapter 9

WAYFARERS ALL

The Water Rat was restless, and he did not exactly know why. To all appearances the summer's pomp was still at fullest height, and although in the tilled acres green had given way to gold, though rowans were reddening, and the woods were dashed here and there with a tawny fierceness, yet light and warmth and colour were still present in undiminished measure, clean of any chilly premonitions of the passing year. But the constant chorus of the orchards and hedges had shrunk to a casual evensong from a few yet unwearied performers; the robin was beginning to assert himself once more; and there was a feeling in the air of change and departure. The cuckoo, of course, had long been silent; but many another feathered friend, for months a part of the familiar landscape and its small society, was missing too, and it seemed that the ranks thinned steadily day by day. Rat, ever observant of all winged movement, saw that it was taking daily a southing tendency; and even as he lay in bed at night he thought he could make out, passing in the darkness overhead, the beat and quiver of impatient pinions, obedient to the peremptory call.

Nature's Grand Hotel has its Season, like the others. As the guests one by one pack, pay, and depart, and the seats at the *table d'hôte* shrink pitifully at each succeeding meal; as suites of rooms are closed, carpets taken up, and waiters sent away; those boarders who are staying on, *en pension*, until the next year's full reopening, cannot help being somewhat affected by all these flittings and farewells, this eager discussion of plans, routes, and fresh quarters, this daily shrinkage in the stream of comradeship. One gets unsettled, depressed, and inclined to be querulous. Why this craving for change? Why not stay on quietly here, like us, and be jolly? You don't know this hotel out of the season, and what fun we have among ourselves, we fellows who remain and see the whole interesting year out. All very true, no doubt, the others always reply; we quite envy you—and some other year perhaps—but just now we have engagements—and there's the bus at the door—our time is up! So they depart, with a smile and a nod, and we miss them, and feel resentful. The Rat was a self-sufficing sort of animal, rooted to the land, and, whoever went, he stayed; still, he could not help noticing what was in the air, and feeling some of its influence in his bones.

It was difficult to settle down to anything seriously, with all this flitting going on. Leaving the water-side, where rushes stood thick and tall in a stream that was becoming sluggish and low, he wandered country-wards, crossed a field or two of pasturage already looking dusty and parched, and thrust into the great realm of wheat, yellow, wavy, and murmurous, full of quiet motion and small whisperings. Here he often loved to wander, through the forest of stiff strong stalks that carried their own golden sky away over his head—a sky that was always dancing, shimmering, softly talking; or swaying strongly to the passing wind and recovering itself with a toss and a merry laugh. Here, too, he had many small friends, a society complete in itself, leading full and busy lives, but always with a spare moment to gossip and exchange news with a visitor. To-day, however, though they were civil enough, the field-mice and harvest-mice seemed preoccupied. Many were digging and tunnelling busily; others, gathered together in small groups, examined plans and drawings of small flats, stated to be desirable and compact, and situated conveniently near the

Stores. Some were hauling out dusty trunks and dress-baskets, others were already elbow-deep packing their belongings; while everywhere piles and bundles of wheat, oats, barley, beech-mast and nuts, lay about ready for transport.

"Here's old Ratty!" they cried as soon as they saw him. "Come and bear a hand, Rat, and don't stand about idle!"

"What sort of games are you up to?" said the Water Rat severely. "You know it isn't time to be thinking of winter quarters yet, by a long way!"

"O yes, we know that" explained a field-mouse rather shamefacedly; "but it's always as well to be in good time, isn't it? We really *must* get all the furniture and baggage and stores moved out of this before those horrid machines begin clicking round the fields; and then, you know, the best flats get picked up so quickly nowadays, and if you're late you have to put up with *anything,* and they want such a lot of doing up, too, before they're fit to move into. Of course, we're early, we know that; but we're only just making a start."

"O, bother *starts,*" said the Rat. 'It's a splendid day. Come for a row, or a stroll along the hedges, or a picnic in the woods, or something."

"Well, I *think* not *to-day,* thank you," replied the field-mouse hurriedly. "Perhaps some *other* day—when we've more *time*"—

The Rat, with a snort of contempt, swung round to go, tripped over a hat-box, and fell, with undignified remarks.

"If people would be more careful," said a field-mouse rather stiffly "and look where they're going, people wouldn't hurt themselves and forget themselves. Mind that hold-all, Rat! You'd better sit down somewhere. In an hour or two we may be more free to attend to you."

"You won't be 'free,' as you call it, much this side of Christmas, I can see that," retorted the Rat grumpily, as he picked his way out of the field.

He returned somewhat despondently to his river again—his faithful, steady-going old river, which never packed up, flitted, or went into winter quarters.

In the osiers which fringed the bank he spied a swallow sitting. Presently it was joined by another, and then by a third; and the birds, fidgeting restlessly on their bough, talked together earnestly and low.

"What, *already*?" said the Rat, strolling up to them. "What's the hurry? I call it simply ridiculous."

"O, we're not off yet, if that's what you mean," replied the first swallow. "We're only making plans and arranging things. Talking it over, you know—what route we're taking this year, and where we'll stop, and so on. That's half the fun!"

"Fun?" said the Rat; "now that's just what I don't understand. If you've *got* to leave this pleasant place, and your friends who will miss you, and your snug homes that you've just settled into, why, when the hour strikes I've no doubt you'll go bravely, and face all the trouble and discomfort and change and newness, and make believe that you're not very unhappy. But to want to talk about it, or even think about it, till you really need—"

"No, you don't understand, naturally," said the second swallow. "First, we feel it stirring within us, a sweet unrest; then back come the recollections one by one, like homing pigeons. They flutter through our dreams at night, they fly with us in our wheelings and circlings by day. We hunger to inquire of each other, to compare notes and assure ourselves that it was all really true, as one by one the scents and sounds and names of long-forgotten places come gradually back and beckon to us."

"Couldn't you stop on for just this year" suggested the Water Rat wistfully. "We'll all do our best to make you feel at home. You've no idea what good times we have here, while you are far away."

"I tried 'stopping on' one year," said the third swallow. "I had grown so fond of the place that when the time came I hung back and let the others go on without me. For a few weeks it was all well enough, but afterwards, O the weary length of the nights! The shivering, sunless days! The air so clammy and chill, and not an insect in an acre of it! No, it was no good; my courage broke down, and one cold, stormy night I took wing, flying well inland on account of the strong easterly gales. It was snowing hard as I beat through the passes of the great mountains, and I had a stiff fight to win through; but never shall I forget the blissful feeling of the hot sun again on my back as I sped down to the lakes that lay so blue and placid below me, and the taste of my first fat insect! The past was like a bad dream; the future was all happy holiday as I moved Southwards week by week, easily, lazily, lingering as long as I dared, but always heeding the call! No, I had had my warning; never again did I think of disobedience."

"Ah, yes, the call of the South, of the South!' twittered the other two dreamily. "Its songs, its hues, its radiant air! O, do you remember—" and, forgetting the Rat, they slid into passionate reminiscence, while he listened fascinated, and his heart burned within him. In himself, too, he knew that it was vibrating at last, that chord hitherto dormant and unsuspected. The mere chatter of these southern-bound birds, their pale and second-hand reports, had yet power to awaken this wild new sensation and thrill him through and through with it; what would one moment of the real thing work in him—one passionate touch of the real southern sun, one waft of the authentic odour? With closed eyes he dared to dream a moment in full abandonment, and when he looked again the river seemed steely and chill, the green fields grey and lightless. Then his loyal heart seemed to cry out on his weaker self for its treachery.

"Why do you ever come back, then, at all?" he demanded of the swallows jealously. "What do you find to attract you in this poor drab little country?"

"And do you think," said the first swallow, "that the other call is not for us too, in its due season? The call of lush meadow-grass, wet orchards, warm, insect-haunted ponds, of browsing cattle, of haymaking, and all the farm-buildings clustering round the House of the perfect Eaves?"

"Do you suppose," asked the second one, "that you are the only living thing that craves with a hungry longing to hear the cuckoo's note again?"

"In due time," said the third, "we shall be homesick once more for quiet water-lilies swaying on the surface of an English stream. But to-day all that seems pale and thin and very far away. Just now our blood dances to other music."

They fell a-twittering among themselves once more, and this time their intoxicating babble was of violet seas, tawny sands, and lizard-haunted walls.

Restlessly the Rat wandered off once more, climbed the slope that rose gently from the north bank of the river, and lay looking out towards the great ring of Downs that barred his vision further southwards—his simple horizon hitherto, his Mountains of the Moon, his limit behind which lay nothing he had cared to see or to know. To-day, to him gazing south with a new-born need stirring in his heart, the clear sky over their long low outline seemed to pulsate with promise; to-day, the unseen was everything, the unknown the only real fact of life. On this side of the hills was now the real blank, on the other lay the crowded and coloured panorama that his inner eye was seeing so clearly. What seas lay beyond, green, leaping, and crested! What sun-bathed coasts, along which the white villas glittered against the olive woods! What quiet harbours, thronged with gallant shipping bound for purple islands of wine and spice, islands set low in languorous waters!

He rose and descended river-wards once more; then changed his mind and sought the side of the dusty lane. There, lying half-buried in the thick, cool under-hedge tangle that bordered it, he could muse on the metalled road and all the wondrous world that it led to; on all the wayfarers, too, that might have trodden it, and the fortunes and adventures they had gone to seek or found unseeking—out there, beyond—beyond!

Footsteps fell on his ear, and the figure of one that walked somewhat wearily came into view; and he saw that it was a Rat, and a very dusty one. The wayfarer, as he reached him, saluted with a gesture of courtesy that had something foreign about it—hesitated a moment—then with a pleasant smile turned from the track and sat down by his side in the cool herbage. He seemed tired, and the Rat let him rest unquestioned, understanding something of what was in his thoughts; knowing, too, the value all animals attach at times to mere silent companionship, when the weary muscles slacken and the mind marks time.

The wayfarer was lean and keen-featured, and somewhat bowed at the shoulders; his paws were thin and long, his eyes much wrinkled at the corners, and he wore small gold earrings in his neatly-set, well-shaped ears. His knitted jersey was of a faded blue, his breeches, patched and stained, were based on a blue foundation, and his small belongings that he carried were tied up in a blue cotton handkerchief.

When he had rested awhile the stranger sighed, snuffed the air, and looked about him.

"That was clover, that warm whiff on the breeze!" he remarked; "and those are cows we hear cropping the grass behind us and blowing softly between mouthfuls. There is a sound of distant reapers, and yonder rises a blue line of cottage smoke against the woodland. The river runs somewhere close by, for I hear the call of a moorhen, and I see by your build that you're a freshwater mariner. Everything seems asleep, and yet going on all the time. It is a goodly life that you lead, friend; no doubt the best in the world, if only you are strong enough to lead it!"

"Yes, it's *the* life, the only life, to live," responded the Water Rat dreamily, and without his usual whole-hearted conviction.

"I did not say exactly that," replied the stranger cautiously; "but no doubt it's the best. I've tried it, and I know. And because I've just tried it—six months of it—and know it's the best, here am I, footsore and hungry, tramping away from it, tramping southward, following the old call, back to the old life, *the* life which is mine and which will not let me go."

"Is this, then, yet another of them?" mused the Rat. "And where have you just come from?" he asked. He hardly dared to ask where he was bound for; he seemed to know the answer only too well.

"Nice little farm," replied the wayfarer briefly. "Up along in that direction"—he nodded northwards. "Never mind about it. I had everything I could want—everything I had any right to expect of life, and more; and here I am! Glad to be here all the same, though, glad to be here! So many miles further on the road, so many hours nearer to my heart's desire!"

His shining eyes held fast to the horizon, and he seemed to be listening for some sound that was wanting from that inland acreage, vocal as it was with the cheerful music of pasturage and farmyard.

"You are not one of *us*," said the Water Rat, "nor yet a farmer; nor even, I should judge, of this country."

"Right," replied the stranger. "I'm a seafaring rat, I am, and the port I originally hail from is Constantinople, though I'm a sort of a foreigner there too, in a manner of speaking. You will have heard of Constantinople, friend? A fair city, and an ancient and glorious one. And you may have heard, too, of Sigurd, King of Norway, and how he sailed thither with sixty ships, and how he and his men rode up through streets all canopied in their honour with purple and gold; and how the Emperor and Empress came down and banqueted with him on board his ship. When Sigurd returned home, many of his Northmen remained behind and entered the Emperor's body-guard, and my ancestor, a Norwegian born, stayed behind too, with the ships that Sigurd gave the Emperor. Seafarers we have ever been, and no wonder; as for me, the city of my birth is no more my home than any pleasant port between there and the London River. I know them all, and they know me. Set me down on any of their quays or foreshores, and I am home again."

"I suppose you go on great voyages," said the Water Rat with growing interest. "Months and months out of sight of land, and provisions running short, and allowanced as to water, and your mind communing with the mighty ocean, and all that sort of thing?"

"By no means," said the Sea Rat frankly. "Such life as you describe would not suit me at all. I'm in the coasting trade, and rarely out of sight of land. It's the jolly times on shore that appeal to me, as much as any seafaring. O, those southern seaports! The smell of them, the riding-lights at night, the glamour!"

"Well, perhaps you have chosen the better way," said the Water Rat, but rather doubtfully. "Tell me something of your coasting, then, if you have a mind to, and what sort of harvest an animal of spirit might hope to bring home from it to warm his latter days with gallant memories by the fireside; for my life, I confess to you, feels to me to-day somewhat narrow and circumscribed."

"My last voyage," began the Sea Rat, "that landed me eventually in this country, bound with high hopes for my inland farm, will serve as a good example of any of them, and, indeed, as an epitome of my highly-coloured life. Family troubles, as usual, began it. The domestic storm-cone was hoisted, and I shipped myself on board a small trading vessel bound from Constantinople, by classic seas whose every wave throbs with a deathless memory, to the Grecian Islands and the Levant. Those were golden days and balmy nights! In and out of harbour all the time—old friends everywhere—sleeping in some cool temple or ruined cistern during the heat of the day—feasting and song after sundown, under great stars set in a velvet sky! Thence we turned and coasted up the Adriatic, its shores swimming in an atmosphere of amber, rose, and aquamarine; we lay in wide land-locked harbours, we roamed through ancient and noble cities, until at last one morning, as the sun rose royally behind us, we rode into Venice down a path of gold. O, Venice is a fine city, wherein a rat can wander at his ease and take his pleasure! Or,when weary of wandering, can sit at the edge of the Grand Canal at night, feasting with his friends, when the air is full of music and the sky fill of stars, and the lights flash and shimmer on the polished steel prows of the swaying gondolas, parked so that you could walk across the canal on them from side to side! And then the food—do you like shell-fish? Well, well, we won't linger over that now."

He was silent for a time; and the Water Rat, silent too and enthralled, floated on dream-canals and heard a phantom song pealing high between vaporous grey wave-lapped walls.

"Southwards we sailed again at last," continued the Sea Rat, "coasting down the Italian shore, till finally we made Palermo, and there I quitted for a long, happy spell on shore. I never stick too long to one ship; one gets narrow-minded and prejudiced. Besides, Sicily is one of my happy hunting-grounds. I know everybody there, and their ways just suit me. I spent many jolly weeks in the island, staying with friends up country. When I grew restless again I took advantage of a ship that was trading to Sardinia and Corsica; and very glad I was to feel the fresh breeze and the sea-spray in my face once more."

"But isn't it very hot and stuffy, down in the—hold, I think you call it?" asked the Water Rat.

The seafarer looked at him with the suspicion of a wink. "I'm an old hand," he remarked with much simplicity. "The captain's cabin's good enough for me."

"It's a hard life, by all accounts," murmured the Rat, sunk deep in thought.

"For the crew it is," replied the seafarer gravely, again with the ghost of a wink.

"From Corsica," he went on, "I made use of a ship that was taking wine to the mainland. We made Alassio in the evening, lay to, hauled up our wine-casks, and hove them overboard, tied one to the other by a long line. Then the crew took to the boats and rowed shorewards, singing as they went, and drawing after them the long bobbing procession of casks, like a mile of porpoises. On the sands they had horses waiting, which dragged the casks up the steep street of the little town with a fine rush and clatter and scramble. When the last cask was in, we went and refreshed and rested, and sat late into the night, drinking with our friends; and next morning I was off to the great olive-woods for a spell and a rest. For now I had done with islands for the time, and ports and shipping were plentiful; so I led a lazy life among the peasants, lying and watching them work, or stretched high on the hillside with the blue Mediterranean far below me. And so at length, by easy stages, and partly on foot, partly by sea, to Marseilles, and the meeting of old shipmates, and the visiting of great ocean-bound vessels, and feasting once more. Talk of shell-fish! Why, sometimes I dream of the shell-fish of Marseilles, and wake up crying!"

"That reminds me," said the polite Water Rat; "you happened to mention that you were hungry, and I ought to have spoken earlier. Of course you will stop and take your midday meal with me? My hole is close by; it is some time past noon, and you are very welcome to whatever there is."

"Now I call that kind and brotherly of you," said the Sea Rat. "I was indeed hungry when I sat down, and ever since I inadvertently happened to mention shell-fish, my pangs have been extreme. But couldn't you fetch it along out here? I am none too fond of going under hatches, unless I'm obliged to; and then, while we eat, I could tell you more concerning my voyages and the pleasant life I lead—at least, it is very pleasant to me, and by your attention I judge it commends itself to you; whereas if we go indoors it is a hundred to one that I shall presently fall asleep."

"That is indeed an excellent suggestion," said the Water Rat, and hurried off home. There he got out the luncheon-basket and packed a simple meal, in which, remembering the stranger's origin and preferences, he took care to include a yard of long French bread, a sausage out of which the garlic sang, some cheese which lay down and cried, and a long-necked straw-covered flask containing bottled sunshine shed and garnered on far Southern slopes. Thus laden, he returned with all speed, and blushed for pleasure at the old seaman's commendations of his taste and judgment, as together they unpacked the basket and laid out the contents on the grass by the roadside.

The Sea Rat, as soon as his hunger was somewhat assuaged, continued the history of his latest voyage, conducting his simple hearer from port to port of Spain, landing him at Lisbon, Oporto, and Bordeaux, introducing him to the pleasant harbours of Cornwall and Devon, and so up the Channel to that final quayside, where, landing after winds long contrary, storm-driven and weather-beaten, he had caught the first magical hints and heraldings of another Spring, and, fired by these, had sped on a long tramp inland, hungry for the experiment of life on some quiet farmstead, very far from the weary beating of any sea.

Spellbound and quivering with excitement, the Water Rat followed the Adventurer league by league, over stormy bays, through crowded roadsteads, across harbour bars on a racing tide, up winding rivers that hid their busy little towns round a sudden turn, and left him with a regretful sigh planted at his dull inland farm, about which he desired to hear nothing.

By this time their meal was over, and the Seafarer, refreshed and strengthened, his voice more vibrant, his eye lit with a brightness that seemed caught from some far-away sea-beacon, filled his glass with the red and glowing vintage of the South, and, leaning towards the Water Rat, compelled his gaze and held him, body and soul, while he talked. Those eyes were of the changing foam-streaked grey-green of leaping Northern seas; in the glass shone a hot ruby that seemed the very heart of the South, beating for him who had courage to respond to its pulsation. The twin lights, the shifting grey and the steadfast red, mastered the Water Rat and held him bound, fascinated, powerless. The quiet world outside their rays receded far away and ceased to be. And the talk, the wonderful talk flowed on—or was it speech entirely, or did it pass at times into song—shanty of the sailors weighing the dripping anchor, sonorous hum of the shrouds in a tearing North-Easter, ballad of the fisherman hauling his nets at sundown against an apricot sky, chords of guitar and mandoline from gondola or caique? Did it change into the cry of the wind, plaintive at first, angrily shrill as it freshened, rising to a tearing whistle, sinking to a musical trickle of air from the leech of the bellying sail? All these sounds the spellbound listener seemed to hear, and with them the hungry complaint of the gulls and the sea-mews, the soft thunder of the breaking wave, the cry of the protesting shingle. Back into speech again it passed, and with beating heart he was following the adventures of a dozen seaports, the fights, the escapes, the rallies, the comradeships, the gallant undertakings; or he searched islands for treasure, fished in still lagoons and dozed day-long on warm white sand. Of deep-sea fishings he heard tell, and mighty silver gatherings of the mile-long net; of sudden perils, noise of breakers on a moonless night, or the tall bows of the great liner taking shape overhead through the fog; of the merry home-coming, the headland rounded, the harbour lights opened out: the groups seen dimly on the quay, the cheery hail, the splash of the hawser; the trudge up the steep little street towards the comforting glow of red-curtained windows.

Lastly, in his waking dream it seemed to him that the Adventurer had risen to his feet, but was still speaking, still holding him fast with his sea-grey eyes.

"And now," he was softly saying, "I take to the road again, holding on south-westwards for many a long and dusty day; till at last I reach the little grey sea town I know so well, that clings along one steep side of the harbour. There through dark doorways you look down flights of stone steps, overhung by great pink tufts of valerian and ending in a patch of sparkling blue water. The little boats that lie tethered to the rings and stanchions of the old sea-wall are gaily painted as those I clambered in and out of in my own childhood; the salmon leap on the flood tide, schools of mackerel flash and play past quay-sides and foreshores, and by the windows the great vessels glide, night and day, up to their moorings or forth to the open sea. There, sooner or later, the ships of all seafaring nations arrive; and there, at its destined hour, the ship of my choice will let go its anchor. I shall take my time, I shall tarry and bide, till at last the right one lies waiting for me, warped out into midstream, loaded low, her bowsprit pointing down harbour. I shall slip on board, by boat or along hawser; and then one morning I shall wake to the song and tramp of the sailors, the clink of the capstan, and the rattle of the anchor-chain coming merrily in. We shall break out the jib and the foresail, the white houses on the harbour side will glide slowly past us as she gathers steering-way, and the voyage will have begun! As she forges towards the headland she will clothe herself with canvas; and then, once outside, the sounding slap of great green seas as she heels to the wind, pointing South!

"And you, you will come too, young brother; for the days pass, and never return, and the South still waits for you. Take the Adventure, heed the call, now 'ere the irrevocable moment passes! 'Tis but a banging of the door behind you, a blithesome step forward, and you are out of the old life and into the new! Then some day, some day long hence, jog home here if you will, when the cup has been drained and the play has been played, and sit down by your quiet river with a store of goodly memories for company. You can easily overtake me on the road, for you are young, and I am ageing and go softly. I will linger, and look back; and at last I will surely see you coming. eager and light-hearted, with all the South in your face!"

The voice died away and ceased, as an insect's tiny trumpet dwindles swiftly into silence; and the Water Rat, paralysed and staring, saw at last but a distant speck on the white surface of the road.

Mechanically he rose and proceeded to repack the luncheon-basket, carefully and without haste. Mechanically he returned home, gathered together a few small necessaries and special treasures he was fond of, and put them in a satchel; acting with slow deliberation, moving about the room like a sleep-walker; listening ever with parted lips. He swung the satchel over his shoulder, carefully selected a stout stick for his wayfaring, and with no haste, but with no hesitation at all, he stepped across the threshold just as the Mole appeared at the door.

"Why, where are you off to, Ratty" asked the Mole in great surprise, grasping him by the arm.

"Going South, with the rest of them," murmured the Rat in a dreamy monotone, never looking at him. "Seawards first and then on shipboard, and so to the shores that are calling me!"

He pressed resolutely forward, still without haste, but with dogged fixity of purpose; but the Mole, now thoroughly alarmed, placed himself in front of him, and looking into his eyes saw that they were glazed and set and turned a streaked and shifting grey— not his friend's eyes, but the eyes of some other animal! Grappling with him strongly he dragged him inside, threw him down, and held him.

The Rat struggled desperately for a few moments, and then his strength seemed suddenly to leave him, and he lay still and exhausted, with closed eyes, trembling. Presently the Mole assisted him to rise and placed him in a chair, where he sat collapsed and shrunken into himself, his body shaken by a violent shivering, passing in time into an hysterical fit of dry sobbing. Mole made the door fast, threw the satchel into a drawer and locked it, and sat down quietly on the table by his friend, waiting for the strange seizure to pass. Gradually the Rat sank into a troubled doze, broken by starts and confused murmurings of things strange and wild and foreign to the unenlightened Mole; and from that he passed into a deep slumber.

Very anxious in mind, the Mole left him for a time and busied himself with household matters; and it was getting dark when he returned to the parlour and found the Rat where he had left him, wide awake indeed, but listless, silent, and dejected. He took one hasty glance at his eyes; found them, to his great gratification, clear and dark and brown again as before; and then sat down and tried to cheer him up and help him to relate what had happened to him.

Poor Ratty did his best, by degrees, to explain things; but how could he put into cold words what had mostly been suggestion? How recall, for another's benefit, the haunting sea voices that had sung to him, how reproduce at second-hand the magic of the Seafarer's hundred reminiscences? Even to himself, now the spell was broken and the glamour gone, he found it difficult to account for what had seemed, some hours ago, the inevitable and only thing. It is not surprising, then, that he failed to convey to the Mole any clear idea of what he had been through that day.

To the Mole this much was plain: the fit, or attack, had passed away, and had left him sane again, though shaken and cast down by the reaction. But he seemed to have lost all interest for the time in the things that went to make up his daily life, as well as in all pleasant forecastings of the altered days and doings that the changing season was surely bringing.

Casually, then, and with seeming indifference, the Mole turned his talk to the harvest that was being gathered in, the towering wagons and their straining teams, the growing ricks, and the large moon rising over bare acres dotted with sheaves. He talked of the reddening apples around, of the browning nuts, of jams and preserves and the distilling of cordials; till by easy stages such as these he reached mid-winter, its hearty joys and its snug home life, and then he became simply lyrical.

By degrees the Rat began to sit up and to join in. His dull eye brightened, and he lost some of his listless air.

Presently the tactful Mole slipped away and returned with a pencil and a few half-sheets of paper, which he placed on the table at his friend's elbow.

"It's quite a long time since you did any poetry," he remarked. "You might have a try at it this evening, instead of—well, brooding over things so much. I've an idea that you'll feel a lot better when you've got something jotted down—if it's only just the rhymes."

The Rat pushed the paper away from him wearily, but the discreet Mole took occasion to leave the room, and when he peeped in again some time later, the Rat was absorbed and deaf to the world; alternately scribbling and sucking the top of his pencil. It is true that he sucked a good deal more than he scribbled; but it was joy to the Mole to know that the cure had at least begun.

CHAPTER 10

THE FURTHER ADVENTURES OF TOAD

The front door of the hollow tree faced eastwards, so Toad was called at an early hour; partly by the bright sunlight streaming in on him, partly by the exceeding coldness of his toes, which made him dream that he was at home in bed in his own handsome room with the Tudor window, on a cold winter's night, and his bedclothes had got up, grumbling and protesting they couldn't stand the cold any longer, and had run downstairs to the kitchen fire to warm themselves; and he had followed on bare feet, along miles and miles of icy stone-paved passages, arguing and beseeching them to be reasonable. He would probably have been aroused much earlier, had he not slept for some weeks on straw over stone flags, and almost forgotten the friendly feeling of thick blankets pulled well up round the chin.

Sitting up, he rubbed his eyes first and his complaining toes next, wondered for a moment where he was, looking round for the familiar stone wall and little barred window; then, with a leap of the heart, remembered everything—his escape, his flight, his pursuit; remembered, first and best thing of all, that he was free!

Free! The word and the thought alone were worth fifty blankets. He was warm from end to end as he thought of the jolly world outside, waiting eagerly for him to make his triumphal entrance, ready to serve him and play up to him, anxious to help him and to keep him company, as it always had been in days of old before misfortune fell upon him. He shook himself and combed the dry leaves out of his hair with his fingers; and,. his toilet complete, marched forth into the comfortable morning sun, cold but confident, hungry but hopeful, all nervous terrors of yesterday dispelled by rest and sleep and frank and heartening sunshine.

He had the world all to himself that early summer morning. The dewy woodland, as he threaded it, was solitary and still; the green fields that succeeded the trees were his own to do as he liked with; the road itself, when he reached it, in that loneliness that was everywhere, seemed, like a stray dog, to be looking anxiously for company. Toad, however, was looking for something that could talk, and tell him clearly which way he ought to go. It is all very well, when you have a light heart, and a clear conscience, and money in your pocket, and nobody scouring the country for you to drag you off to prison again, to follow where the road beckons and points, not caring whither. The practical Toad cared very much indeed, and he could have kicked the road for its helpless silence when every minute was of importance to him.

The reserved rustic road was presently joined by a shy little brother in the shape of a canal, which took its hand and ambled along by its side in perfect confidence, but with the same tongue-tied, uncommunicative attitude towards strangers. "Bother them!" said Toad to himself. "But, anyhow, one thing's clear. They must both be coming *from* somewhere, and going *to* somewhere. You can't get over that, Toad, my boy!" So he marched on patiently by the water's edge.

Round a bend in the canal came plodding a solitary horse, stooping forward as if in anxious thought. From rope traces attached to his collar stretched a long line, taut, but dipping with his stride, the further part of it dripping pearly drops. Toad let the horse pass, and stood waiting for what the fates were sending him.

With a pleasant swirl of quiet water at its blunt bow the barge slid up alongside of him, its gaily painted gunwale level with the towing-path, its sole occupant a big stout woman wearing a linen sun-bonnet, one brawny arm laid along the tiller.

"A nice morning, ma'am!" she remarked to Toad, as she drew up level with him.

"I dare say it is, ma'am!" responded Toad politely, as he walked along the tow-path abreast of her. "I dare say it is a nice morning to them that's not in sore trouble, like what I am. Here's my married daughter, she sends off to me post-haste to come to her at once; so off I comes, not knowing what may be happening or going to happen, but fearing the worst, as you will understand, ma'am, if you're a mother, too. And I've left my business to look after itself—I'm in the washing and laundering line, you must know, ma'am—and I've left my young children to look after themselves, and a more mischievous and troublesome set of young imps doesn't exist, ma'am; and I've lost all my money, and lost my way, and as for what may be happening to my married daughter, why, I don't like to think of it, ma'am!"

"Where might your married daughter be living, ma'am?" asked the barge-woman.

"She lives near to the river, ma'am," replied Toad "Close to a fine house called Toad Hall, that's somewheres hereabouts in these parts. Perhaps you may have heard of it."

"Toad Hall? Why, I'm going that way myself," replied the barge-woman. This canal joins the river some miles further on, a little above Toad Hall; and then it's an easy walk. You come along in the barge with me, and I'll give you a lift."

She steered the barge close to the bank, and Toad, with many humble and grateful acknowledgments, stepped lightly on board and sat down with great satisfaction.

"Toad's luck again!" thought he. "I always come out on top!"

"So you're in the washing business, ma'am?" said the barge-woman politely, as they glided along. "And a very good business you've got too, I dare say, if I'm not making too free in saying so."

"Finest business in the whole county," said Toad airily. "All the gentry come to me—wouldn't go to any one else if they were paid, they know me so well. You see, I understand my work thoroughly, and attend to it all myself. Washing, ironing, clear-starching, making up gents' fine shirts for evening wear—everything's done under my own eye!"

"But surely you don't *do* all that work yourself, ma'am?" asked the barge-woman respectfully.

"O, I have girls," said Toad lightly: "twenty girls or thereabouts, always at work. But you know what *girls* are, ma'am! Nasty little hussies, that's what *I* call 'em!"

"So do I, too," said the barge-woman with great heartiness. "But I dare say you set yours to rights, the idle trollops! And are you *very* fond of washing?"

"I love it," said Toad. "I simply dote on it. Never so happy as when I've got both arms in the wash-tub. But, then, it comes so easy to me! No trouble at all! A real pleasure, I assure you, ma'am!"

"What a bit of luck, meeting you!" observed the barge-woman thoughtfully. "A regular piece of good fortune for both of us."

"Why, what do you mean?" asked Toad nervously.

"Well, look at me, now," replied the barge-woman. "*I* like washing, too, just the same as you do; and for that matter, whether I like it or not I have got to do all my own, naturally, moving about as I do. Now my husband, he's such a fellow for shirking his work and leaving the barge to me, that never a moment do I get for seeing to my own affairs. By rights he ought to be here now, either steering or attending to the horse, though luckily the horse has sense enough to attend to himself. Instead of which, he's gone off with the dog, to see if they can't pick up a rabbit for dinner somewhere. Says he'll catch me up at the next lock. Well, that's as may be—I don't trust him, once he gets off with that dog, who's worse than he is. But, meantime, how am I to get on with my washing?"

"O, never mind about the washing," said Toad, not liking the subject "Try and fix your mind on that rabbit. A nice fat young rabbit, I'll be bound. Got any onions?"

"I can't fix my mind on anything but my washing," said the barge-woman, "and I wonder you can be talking of rabbits, with such a joyful prospect before you. There's a heap of things of mine that you'll find in a corner of the cabin. If you'll just take one or two of the most necessary sort—I won't venture to describe them to a lady like you, but you'll recognize 'em at a glance—and put them through the wash-tub as we go along, why, it'll be a pleasure to you, as you rightly say, and a real help to me. You'll find a tub handy, and soap, and a kettle on the stove, and a bucket to haul up water from the canal with. Then I shall know you're enjoying yourself, instead of sitting here idle, looking at the scenery and yawning your head off."

"Here, you let me steer!" said Toad, now thoroughly frightened, "and then you can get on with your washing your own way. I might spoil your things, or not do 'em as you like. I'm more used to gentlemen's things myself. It's my special line."

"Let you steer?" replied the barge-woman, laughing. "It takes some practice to steer a barge properly. Besides, it's dull work, and I want you to be happy. No, you shall do the washing you are so fond of and I'll stick to the steering that I understand. Don't try and deprive me of the pleasure of giving you a treat!"

Toad was fairly cornered. He looked for escape this way and that, saw that he was too far from the bank for a flying leap, and sullenly resigned himself to his fate. "If it comes to that," he thought in desperation, "I suppose any fool can *wash*!"

He fetched tub, soap, and other necessaries from the cabin, selected a few garments at random, tried to recollect what he had seen in casual glances through laundry windows, and set to.

A long half-hour passed, and every minute of it saw Toad getting crosser and crosser. Nothing that he could do to the things seemed to please them or do them good. He tried coaxing, he tried slapping, he tried punching; they smiled back at him out of the tub unconverted, happy in their original sin. Once or twice he looked nervously over his shoulder at the barge-woman, but she appeared to be gazing out in front of her, absorbed in her steering. His back ached badly, and he noticed with dismay that his paws were beginning to get all crinkly. Now Toad was very proud of his paws. He muttered under his breath words that should never pass the lips of either washerwomen or Toads; and lost the soap, for the fiftieth time.

A burst of laughter made him straighten himself and look round. The barge-woman was leaning back and laughing unrestrainedly, till the tears ran down her cheeks.

"I've been watching you all the time," she gasped. "I thought you must be a humbug all along, from the conceited way you talked. Pretty washerwoman you are! Never washed so much as a dish-clout in your life, I'll lay!"

Toad's temper, which had been simmering viciously for some time, now fairly boiled over, and he lost all control of himself.

"You common, low, *fat* barge-woman!" he shouted; "don't you dare to talk to your betters like that! Washerwoman indeed! I would have you to know that I am a Toad, a very well-known respected, distinguished Toad! I may be under a bit of a cloud at present, but I will *not* be laughed at by a barge-woman!"

The woman moved nearer to him and peered under his bonnet keenly and closely. "Why, so you are!" she cried. "Well, I never! A horrid, nasty, crawly Toad! And in my nice clean barge, too! Now that is a thing that I will *not* have."

She relinquished the tiller for a moment. One big mottled arm shot out and caught Toad by a fore-leg, while the other gripped him fast by a hind-leg. Then the world turned suddenly upside down, the barge seemed to flit lightly across the sky, the wind whistled in his ears, and Toad found himself flying through the air, revolving rapidly as he went.

The water, when he eventually reached it with a loud splash, proved quite cold enough for his taste, though its chill was not sufficient to quell his proud spirit, or slake the heat of his furious temper. He rose to the surface spluttering, and when he had wiped the duckweed out of his eyes the first thing he saw was the fat barge-woman looking back at him over the stern of the retreating barge and laughing; and he vowed, as he coughed and choked, to be even with her.

He struck out for the shore, but the cotton gown greatly impeded his efforts, and when at length he touched land he found it hard to climb up the steep bank unassisted. He had to take a minute or two's rest to recover his breath; then, gathering his wet skirts well over his arms, he started to run after the barge as fast as his legs would carry him, wild with indignation, thirsting for revenge.

The barge-woman was still laughing when he drew up level with her. "Put yourself through your mangle, washerwoman," she called out, "and iron your face and crimp it, and you'll pass for quite a decent-looking Toad!"

Toad never paused to reply. Solid revenge was what he wanted, not cheap, windy, verbal triumphs, though he had a thing or two in his mind that he would have liked to say. He saw what he wanted ahead of him. Running swiftly on he overtook the horse, unfastened the tow-rope and cast off, jumped lightly on the horse's back, and urged it to a gallop by kicking it vigorously in the sides. He steered for the open country, abandoning the tow-path, and swinging his steed down a rutty lane. Once he looked back, and saw that the barge had run aground on the other side of the canal, and the barge-woman was gesticulating wildly and shouting, "Stop, stop, stop!" "I've heard that song before," said Toad, laughing, as he continued to spur his steed onward in its wild career.

The barge-horse was not capable of any very sustained effort, and its gallop soon subsided into a trot, and its trot into an easy walk; but Toad was quite contented with this, knowing that he, at any rate, was moving, and the barge was not. He had quite recovered his temper, now that he had done something he thought really clever; and he was satisfied to jog along quietly in the sun, taking advantage of any by-ways and bridle-paths, and trying to forget how very long it was since he had had a square meal, till the canal had been left very far behind him.

He had travelled some miles, his horse and he, and he was feeling drowsy in the hot sunshine, when the horse stopped, lowered his head, and began to nibble the grass; and Toad, waking up, just saved himself from falling off by an effort. He looked about him and found he was on a wide common, dotted with patches of gorse and bramble as far as he could see. Near him stood a dingy gipsy caravan, and beside it a man was sitting on a bucket turned upside down, very busy smoking and staring into the wide world. A fire of sticks was burning near by, and over the fire hung an iron pot, and out of that pot came forth bubblings and gurglings, and a vague suggestive steaminess. Also smells—warm, rich, and varied smells—that twined and twisted and wreathed themselves at last into one complete, voluptuous, perfect smell that seemed like the very soul of Nature taking form and appearing to her children, a true Goddess, a mother of solace and comfort. Toad now knew well that he had not been really hungry before. What he had felt earlier in the day had been a mere trifling qualm. This was the real thing at last, and no mistake; and it would have to be dealt with speedily, too, or there would be trouble for somebody or something. He looked the gipsy over carefully, wondering vaguely whether it would be easier to fight him or cajole him. So there he sat, and sniffed and sniffed, and looked at the gipsy; and the gipsy sat and smoked, and looked at him.

Presently the gipsy took his pipe out of his mouth and remarked in a careless way, "Want to sell that there horse of yours?"

Toad was completely taken aback. He did not know that gipsies were very fond of horse-dealing, and never missed an opportunity, and he had not reflected that caravans were always on the move and took a deal of drawing. It had not occurred to him to turn the horse into cash, but the gipsy's suggestion seemed to smooth the way towards the two things he wanted so badly—ready money and a solid breakfast.

"What?" he said, "me sell this beautiful young horse of mine? O no; it's out of the question. Who's going to take the washing home to my customers every week? Besides, I'm too fond of him, and he simply dotes on me."

"Try and love a donkey," suggested the gipsy. "Some people do."

"You don't seem to see," continued Toad, "that this fine horse of mine is a cut above you altogether. He's a blood horse, he is, partly; not the part you see, of course—another part. And he's been a Prize Hackney, too, in his time—that was the time before you knew him, but you can still tell it on him at a glance if you understand anything about horses. No, it's not to be thought of for a moment. All the same, how much might you be disposed to offer me for this beautiful young horse of mine?"

The gipsy looked the horse over, and then he looked Toad over with equal care, and looked at the horse again. "Shillin' a leg," he said briefly, and turned away, continuing to smoke and try to stare the wide world out of countenance.

"A shilling a leg?" cried Toad. "If you please, I must take a little time to work that out, and see just what it comes to."

He climbed down off his horse, and left it to graze, and sat down by the gipsy, and did sums on his fingers, and at last he said, "A shilling a leg? Why, that comes to exactly four shillings, and no more. O no; I could not think of accepting four shillings for this beautiful young horse of mine."

"Well," said the gipsy, "I'll tell you what I will do. I'll make it five shillings, and that's three-and-six-pence more than the animal's worth. And that's my last word."

Then Toad sat and pondered long and deeply. For he was hungry and quite penniless, and still some way—he knew not how far—from home, and enemies might still be looking for him. To one in such a situation, five shillings may very well appear a large sum of money. On the other hand, it did not seem very much to get for a horse. But then, again, the horse hadn't cost him anything; so whatever he got was all clear profit. At last he said firmly, "Look here, gipsy! I tell you what we will do; and this is my last word. You shall hand me over six shillings and sixpence, cash down; and further, in addition thereto, you shall give me as much breakfast as I can possibly eat, at one sitting of course, out of that iron pot of yours that keeps sending forth such delicious and exciting smells. In return, I will make over to you my spirited young horse, with all the beautiful harness and trappings that are on him, freely thrown in. If that's not good enough for you, say so, and I'll be getting on. I know a man near here who's wanted this horse of mine for years."

The gipsy grumbled frightfully, and declared if he did a few more deals of that sort he'd be ruined. But in the end he lugged a dirty canvas bag out of the depths of his trouser-pocket, and counted out six shillings and sixpence into Toad's paw. Then he disappeared into the caravan for an instant, and returned with a large iron plate and a knife, fork, and spoon. He tilted up the pot, and a glorious stream of hot rich stew gurgled into the plate. It was, indeed, the most beautiful stew in the world, being made of partridges, and pheasants, and chickens, and hares, and rabbits, and pea-hens, and guinea-fowls, and one or two other things. Toad took the plate on his lap, almost crying, and stuffed, and stuffed, and stuffed, and kept asking for more, and the gipsy never grudged it him. He thought that he had never eaten so good a breakfast in all his life.

When Toad had taken as much stew on board as he thought he could possibly hold, he got up and said good-bye to the gipsy, and took an affectionate farewell of the horse; and the gipsy, who knew the riverside well, gave him directions which way to go, and he set forth on his travels again in the best possible spirits. He was, indeed, a very different Toad from the animal of an hour ago. The sun was shining brightly, his wet clothes were quite dry again, he had money in his pockets once more, he was nearing home and friends and safety, and, most and best of all, he had had a substantial meal, hot and nourishing, and felt big, and strong, and careless, and self-confident.

As he tramped along gaily, he thought of his adventures and escapes, and how when things seemed at their worst he had always managed to find a way out; and his pride and conceit began to swell within him. "Ho, ho!" he said to himself as he marched along with his chin in the air, "what a clever Toad I am! There is surely no animal equal to me for cleverness in the whole world! My enemies shut me up in prison, encircled by sentries, watched night and day by warders; I walk out through them all, by sheer ability coupled with courage. They pursue me with engines, and policemen, and revolvers; I snap my fingers at them, and vanish, laughing, into space. I am, unfortunately, thrown into a canal by a woman, fat of body and very evil-minded. What of it? I swim ashore, I seize her horse, I ride off in triumph, and I sell the horse for a whole pocketful of money and an excellent breakfast! Ho, ho! I am The Toad, the handsome, the popular, the successful Toad!" He got so puffed up with conceit that he made up a song as he walked in praise of himself, and sang it at the top of his voice, though there was no one to hear it but him. It was perhaps the most conceited song that any animal ever composed:

The world has held great Heroes,
As history-books have showed;
But never a name to go down to fame
Compared with that of Toad!

The clever men at Oxford
Know all that there is to be knowed.
But they none of them know one half as much
As intelligent Mr Toad!

The animals sat in the Ark and cried,
Their tears in torrents flowed.
Who was it said, "There's land ahead"?
Encouraging Mr Toad!

The Army all saluted
As they marched along the road.

Was it the King? Or Kitchener?
No It was Mr Toad.

The Queen and her Ladies-in-waiting
Sat at the window and sewed
She cried, "Look! who's that handsome man?"
They answered, "Mr Toad."

There was a great deal more of the same sort, but too dreadfully conceited to be written down. These are some of the milder verses.

He sang as he walked, and he walked as he sang, and got more inflated every minute. But his pride was shortly to have a severe fall.

After some miles of country lanes he reached the high road, and as he turned into it and glanced along its white length, he saw approaching him a speck that turned into a dot and then into a blob, and then into something very familiar; and a double note of warning, only too well known, fell on his delighted ear.

"This is something like!" said the excited Toad. "This is real life again, this is once more the great world from which I have been missed so long! I will hail them, my brothers of the wheel, and pitch them a yarn, of the sort that has been so successful hitherto; and they will give me a lift, of course, and then I will talk to them some more; and, perhaps, with luck, it may even end in my driving up to Toad Hall in a motor-car! That will be one in the eye for Badger!"

He stepped confidently out into the road to hail the motor-car, which came along at an easy pace, slowing down as it neared the lane; when suddenly he became very pale, his heart turned to water, his knees shook and yielded under him, and he doubled up and collapsed with a sickening pain in his interior. And well he might, the unhappy animal; for the approaching car was the very one he had stolen out of the yard of the Red Lion Hotel on that fatal day when all his troubles began! And the people in it were the very same people he had sat and watched at luncheon in the coffee-room!

He sank down in a shabby, miserable heap in the road, murmuring to himself in his despair, "It's all up! It's all over now! Chains and policemen again! Prison again! Dry bread and water again! O, what a fool I have been! What did I want to go strutting about the country for, singing conceited songs, and hailing people in broad day on the high road, instead of hiding till nightfall and slipping home quietly by back ways! O hapless Toad! O ill-fated animal!"

The terrible motor-car drew slowly nearer and nearer, till at last he heard it stop just short of him. Two gentlemen got out and walked round the trembling heap of crumpled misery lying in the road, and one of them said, "O dear! this is very sad! Here is a poor old thing—a washerwoman apparently—who has fainted in the road! Perhaps she is overcome by the heat, poor creature; or possibly she has not had any food to-day. Let us lift her into the car and take her to the nearest village, where doubtless she has friends."

They tenderly lifted Toad into the motor-car and propped him up with soft cushions, and proceeded on their way.

When Toad heard them talk in so kind and sympathetic a manner, he knew that he was not recognized, his courage began to revive, and he cautiously opened first one eye and then the other.

"Look!" said one of the gentlemen, "she is better already. The fresh air is doing her good. How do you feel now, ma'am?"

"Thank you kindly, sir," said Toad in a feeble voice, "I'm feeling a great deal better!"

"That's right," said the gentleman. "Now keep quite still, and, above all, don't try to talk."

"I won't," said Toad "I was only thinking, if I might sit on the front seat there, beside the driver, where I could get the fresh air full in my face, I should soon be all right again."

"What a very sensible woman!" said the gentleman. "Of course you shall." So they carefully helped Toad into the front seat beside the driver, and on they went once more.

Toad was almost himself again by now. He sat up, looked about him, and tried to beat down the tremors, the yearnings, the old cravings that rose up and beset him and took possession of him entirely.

"It is fate!" he said to himself "Why strive? why struggle?" and he turned to the driver at his side.

"Please, sir," he said, "I wish you would kindly let me try and drive the car for a little. I've been watching you carefully, and it looks so easy and so interesting, and I should like to be able to tell my friends that once I had driven a motor-car!"

The driver laughed at the proposal, so heartily that the gentleman inquired what the matter was. When he heard, he said, to Toad's delight, "Bravo, ma'am! I like your spirit. Let her have a try, and look after her. She won't do any harm."

Toad eagerly scrambled into the seat vacated by the driver, took the steering-wheel in his hands, listened with affected humility to the instructions given him, and set the car in motion, but very slowly and carefully at first, for he was determined to be prudent.

The gentlemen behind clapped their hands and applauded, and Toad heard them saying, "How well she does it! Fancy a washerwoman driving a car as well as that, the first time!"

Toad went a little faster; then faster still, and faster.

He heard the gentlemen call out warningly, "Be careful, washerwoman!" And this annoyed him, and he began to lose his head.

The driver tried to interfere, but he pinned him down in his seat with one elbow, and put on full speed. The rush of air in his face, the hum of the engine, and the light jump of the car beneath him intoxicated his weak brain. "Washerwoman, indeed!" he shouted recklessly. "Ho, ho! I am the Toad, the motor-car snatcher, the prison-breaker, the Toad who always escapes! Sit still, and you shall know what driving really is, for you are in the hands of the famous, the skilful, the entirely fearless Toad!"

With a cry of horror the whole party rose and flung themselves on him. "Seize him!" they cried, "seize the Toad, the wicked animal who stole our motor-car! Bind him, chain him, drag him to the nearest police-station! Down with the desperate and dangerous Toad!"

Alas! they should have thought, they ought to have been more prudent, they should have remembered to stop the motor-car somehow before playing any pranks of that sort. With a half-turn of the wheel the Toad sent the car crashing through the low hedge that ran along the roadside. One mighty bound, a violent shock, and the wheels of the car were churning up the thick mud of a horse-pond.

Toad found himself flying through the air with the strong upward rush and delicate curve of a swallow. He liked the motion, and was just beginning to wonder whether it would go on until he developed wings and turned into a Toad-bird, when he landed on his back with a thump, in the soft rich grass of a meadow. Sitting up, he could just see the motor-car in the pond, nearly submerged; the gentlemen and the driver, encumbered by their long coats, were floundering helplessly in the water.

He picked himself up rapidly and set off running across country as hard as he could, scrambling through hedges, jumping ditches, pounding across fields, till he was breathless and weary, and had to settle down into an easy walk. When he had recovered his breath somewhat, and was able to think calmly, he began to giggle, and from giggling he took to laughing, and he laughed till he had to sit down under a hedge. "Ho, ho" he cried, in ecstasies of self-admiration. "Toad again! Toad, as usual comes out on the top! Who was it got them to give him a lift? Who managed to get on the front seat for the sake of fresh air? Who persuaded them into letting him see if he could drive? Who landed them all in a horse-pond? Who escaped, flying gaily and unscathed through the air, leaving the narrow-minded, grudging, timid excursionists in the mud where they should rightly be? Why, Toad, of course; clever Toad, great Toad, *good* Toad!"

Then he burst into song again, and chanted with uplifted voice:

The motor-car went Poop-poop-poop,
As it raced along the road.
Who was it steered it into a pond?
Ingenious Mr Toad!

"O, how clever I am! How clever, how clever, how very clev—"

A slight noise at a distance behind him made him turn his head and look. O horror! O misery! O despair!

About two fields off, a chauffeur in his leather gaiters and two large rural policemen were visible, running towards him as hard as they could go!

Poor Toad sprang to his feet and pelted away again, his heart in his mouth "O my!" he gasped, as he panted along, "what an ass I am! What a *conceited* and heedless ass! Swaggering again! Shouting and singing songs again! Sitting still and gassing again! O my! O my! O my!"

He glanced back, and saw to his dismay that they were gaining on him. On he ran desperately, but kept looking back, and saw that they still gained steadily. He did his best, but he was a fat animal, and his legs were short, and still they gained. He could hear them close behind him now. Ceasing to heed where he was going, he struggled on blindly and wildly, looking back over his shoulder at the now triumphant enemy, when suddenly the earth failed under his feet, he grasped at the air, and, splash! he found himself head over ears in deep water, rapid water, water that bore him along with a force he could not contend with; and he knew that in his blind panic he had run straight into the river!

He rose to the surface and tried to grasp the reeds and the rushes that grew along the water's edge close under the bank, but the stream was so strong that it tore them out of his hands. "O my!" gasped poor Toad, "if ever I steal a motor-car again! If ever I sing another conceited song"—then down he went, and came up breathless and spluttering. Presently he saw that he was approaching a big dark hole in the bank, just above his head, and as the stream bore him past he reached up with a paw and caught hold of the edge and held on. Then slowly and with difficulty he drew himself up out of the water, till at last he was able to rest his elbows on the edge of the hole. There he remained for some minutes, puffing and panting, for he was quite exhausted.

As he sighed and blew and stared before him into the dark hole, some bright small thing shone and twinkled in its depths, moving towards him. As it approached, a face grew up gradually around it, and it was a familiar face!

Brown and small, with whiskers.

Grave and round, with neat ears and silky hair.

It was the Water Rat!

Chapter 11

"LIKE SUMMER TEMPESTS CAME HIS TEARS"

The Rat put out a neat little brown paw, gripped Toad firmly by the scruff of the neck, and gave a great hoist and a pull; and the water-logged Toad came up slowly but surely over the edge of the hole, till at last he stood safe and sound in the hall, streaked with mud and weed to be sure, and with the water streaming off him, but happy and high-spirited as of old, now that he found himself once more in the house of a friend, and dodgings and evasions were over, and he could lay aside a disguise that was unworthy of his position and wanted such a lot of living up to.

"O Ratty!" he cried. "I've been through such times since I saw you last, you can't think! Such trials, such sufferings, and all so nobly borne! Then such escapes, such disguises, such subterfuges, and all so cleverly planned and carried out! Been in prison—got out of it, of course! Been thrown into a canal—swam ashore! Stole a horse sold him for a large sum of money! Humbugged everybody—made 'em all do exactly what I wanted! O, I *am* a smart Toad, and no mistake! What do you think my last exploit was? Just hold on till I tell you—"

"Toad," said the Water Rat, gravely and firmly, "you go off upstairs at once, and take off that old cotton rag that looks as if it might formerly have belonged to some washerwoman, and clean yourself thoroughly, and put on some of my clothes, and try and come down looking like a gentleman if you *can*; for a more shabby, bedraggled, disreputable-looking object than you are I never set eyes on in my whole life! Now, stop swaggering and arguing, and be off! I'll have something to say to you later!"

Toad was at first inclined to stop and do some talking back at him. He had had enough of being ordered about when he was in prison, and here was the thing being begun all over again, apparently; and by a Rat, too! However, he caught sight of himself in the looking-glass over the hat-stand with the rusty black bonnet perched rakishly over one eye, and he changed his mind and went very quickly and humbly upstairs to the Rat's dressing-room. There he had a thorough wash and brush-up, changed his clothes, and stood for a long time before the glass, contemplating himself with pride and pleasure, and thinking what utter idiots all the people must have been to have ever mistaken him for one moment for a washer-woman.

By the time he came down again luncheon was on the table, and very glad Toad was to see it, for he had been through some trying experiences and had taken much hard exercise since the excellent breakfast provided for him by the gipsy. While they ate Toad told the Rat all his adventures, dwelling chiefly on his own cleverness, and presence of mind in emergencies, and cunning in tight places; and rather making out that he had been having a gay and highly-coloured experience. But the more he talked and boasted, the more grave and silent the Rat became.

When at last Toad had talked himself to a standstill, there was silence for a while; and then the Rat said, "Now, Toady, I don't want to give you pain, after all you've been through already; but, seriously, don't you see what an awful ass you've been making of yourself? On your own admission you have been handcuffed, imprisoned, starved, chased, terrified out of your life, insulted, jeered at, and ignominiously flung into the water—by a woman, too! Where's the amusement in that? Where does the fun come in? And all because you must needs go and steal a motor-car. You know that you've never had anything but trouble from motor-cars from the moment you first set eyes on one. But if you *will* be mixed up with them—as you generally are, five minutes after you've started—why *steal* them? Be a cripple, if you think it's exciting; be a bankrupt, for a change, if you've set your mind on it; but why choose to be a convict? When are you going to be sensible, and think of your friends, and try and be a credit to them? Do you suppose it's any pleasure to me, for instance, to hear animals saying, as I go about, that I'm the chap that keeps company with gaol-birds?"

Now, it was a very comforting point in Toad's character that he was a thoroughly good-hearted animal, and never minded being jawed by those who were his real friends. And even when most set upon a thing he was always able to see the other side of the question. So although, while the Rat was talking so seriously, he kept saying to himself mutinously, "But it *was* fun, though! Awful fun!" and making strange suppressed noises inside him, k-i-ck-ck-ck, and poop-p-p, and other sounds resembling stifled snorts, or the opening of soda-water bottles, yet when the Rat had quite finished, he heaved a deep sigh and said, very nicely and humbly, "Quite right, Ratty! How *sound* you always are! Yes, I've been a conceited old ass, I can quite see that; but now I'm going to be a good Toad, and not do it any more. As for motor-cars, I've not been at all so keen about them since my last ducking in that river of yours. The fact is, while I was hanging on to the edge of your hole and getting my breath, I had a sudden idea—a really brilliant idea—connected with motor-boats—there, there! don't take on so, old chap, and stamp, and upset things, it was only an idea, and we won't talk any more about it now. We'll have our coffee, *and* a smoke, and a quiet chat, and then I'm going to stroll gently down to Toad Hall, and get into clothes of my own, and set things going again on the old lines. I've had enough of adventures. I shall lead a quiet, steady, respectable life, pottering about my property, and improving it, and doing a little landscape gardening at times. There will always be a bit of dinner for my friends when they come to see me; and I shall keep a pony-chaise to jog about the country in, just as I used to in the good old days, before I got restless, and wanted to *do* things."

"Stroll gently down to Toad Hall!" cried the Rat, greatly excited. "What are you talking about? Do you mean to say you haven't *heard*?"

"Heard what?" said Toad, turning rather pale. "Go on, Ratty! Quick! Don't spare me! What haven't I heard?"

"Do you mean to tell me," shouted the Rat, thumping with his little fist upon the table, "that you've heard nothing about the Stoats and Weasels?"

"What, the Wild Wooders?" cried Toad, trembling in every limb. "No, not a word! What have they been doing?"

"—And how they've been and taken Toad Hall?" continued the Rat.

Toad leaned his elbows on the table, and his chin on his paws; and a large tear welled up in each of his eyes, overflowed and splashed on the table, plop! plop!

"Go on, Ratty," he murmured presently; "tell me all. The worst is over. I am an animal again. I can bear it."

"When you—got—into that—that—trouble of yours," said the Rat slowly and impressively; "I mean, when you—disappeared from society for a time, over that misunderstanding about a—a machine, you know—"

Toad merely nodded.

"Well, it was a good deal talked about down here, naturally," continued the Rat, "not only along the river-side, but even in the Wild Wood. Animals took sides, as always happens. The River-Bankers stuck up for you, and said you had been infamously treated, and there was no justice to be had in the land nowadays. But the Wild Wood animals said hard things, and served you right, and it was time this sort of thing was stopped. And they got very cocky, and went about saying you were done for this time! You would never come back again, never, never!"

Toad nodded once more, keeping silence.

"That's the sort of little beasts they are," the Rat went on. "But Mole and Badger, they stuck out, through thick and thin, that you would come back again soon, somehow. They didn't know exactly how, but somehow!"

Toad began to sit up in his chair again, and to smirk a little.

"They argued from history," continued the Rat. "They said that no criminal laws had ever been known to prevail against cheek and plausibility such as yours, combined with the power of a long purse. So they arranged to move their things into Toad Hall, and sleep there, and keep it aired, and have it all ready for you when you turned up. They didn't guess what was going to happen, of course; still, they had their suspicions of the Wild Wood animals. Now I come to the most painful and tragic part of my story. One dark night—it was a *very* dark night, and blowing hard, too, and raining simply cats and dogs—a band of weasels, armed to the teeth, crept silently up the carriage-drive to the front entrance. Simultaneously, a body of desperate ferrets, advancing through the kitchen-garden, possessed themselves of the backyard and offices; while a company of skirmishing stoats who stuck at nothing occupied the conservatory and the billiard-room, and held the French windows opening on to the lawn.

"The Mole and the Badger were sitting by the fire in the smoking-room, telling stories and suspecting nothing, for it wasn't a night for any animals to be out in, when those blood-thirsty villains broke down the doors and rushed in upon them from every side. They made the best fight they could, but what was the good? They were unarmed, and taken by surprise, and what can two animals do against hundreds? They took and beat them severely with sticks, those two poor faithful creatures, and turned them out into the cold and the wet, with many insulting and uncalled-for remarks!"

Here the unfeeling Toad broke into a snigger, and then pulled himself together and tried to look particularly solemn.

"And the Wild Wooders have been living in Toad Hall ever since," continued the Rat; "and going on simply anyhow! Lying in bed half the day, and breakfast at all hours, and the place in such a mess (I'm told) it's not fit to be seen! Eating your grub, and drinking your drink, and making bad jokes about you, and singing vulgar songs, about—well, about prisons, and magistrates, and policemen; horrid personal songs, with no humour in them. And they're telling the tradespeople and everybody that they've come to stay for good."

"O, have they!" said Toad, getting up and seizing a stick. "I'll jolly soon see about that!"

"It's no good, Toad!" called the Rat after him. "You'd better come back and sit down; you'll only get into trouble."

But the Toad was off, and there was no holding him. He marched rapidly down the road, his stick over his shoulder, frowning and muttering to himself in his anger, till he got near his front gate, when suddenly there popped up from behind the palings a long yellow ferret with a gun.

"Who comes there?" said the ferret sharply.

"Stuff and nonsense!" said Toad very angrily. "What do you mean by talking like that to me? Come out of it at once, or I'll—"

The ferret said never a word, but he brought his gun up to his shoulder. Toad prudently dropped flat in the road, and *Bang!* a bullet whistled over his head.

The startled Toad scrambled to his feet and scampered off down the road as hard as he could; and as he ran he heard the ferret laughing, and other horrid thin little laughs taking it up and carrying on the sound.

He went back, very crestfallen and told the Water Rat.

"What did I tell you?" said the Rat. "It's no good. They've got sentries posted, and they are all armed. You must just wait."

Still, Toad was not inclined to give in all at once. So he got out the boat, and set off rowing up the river to where the garden front of Toad Hall came down to the water-side.

Arriving within sight of his old home, he rested on his oars and surveyed the land cautiously. All seemed very peaceful and deserted and quiet. He could see the whole front of Toad Hall, glowing in the evening sunshine, the pigeons settling by twos and threes along the straight line of the roof; the garden, a blaze of flowers; the creek that led up to the boat-house, the little wooden bridge that crossed it; all tranquil, uninhabited, apparently waiting for his return. He would try the boat-house first, he thought. Very warily he paddled up to the mouth of the creek, and was just passing under the bridge, when... *Crash!*

A great stone, dropped from above, smashed through the bottom of the boat. It filled and sank, and Toad found himself struggling in deep water. Looking up, he saw two stoats leaning over the parapet of the bridge and watching him with great glee. "It will be your head next time, Toady!" they called out to him. The indignant Toad swam to shore, while the stoats laughed and laughed, supporting each other, and laughed again, till they nearly had two fits—that is, one fit each, of course.

The Toad retraced his weary way on foot, and related his disappointing experiences to the Water Rat once more.

"Well, *what* did I tell you?" said the Rat very crossly. "And, now, look here! See what you've been and done! Lost me my boat that I was so fond of, that's what you've done! And simply ruined that nice suit of clothes that I lent you! Really, Toad, of all the trying animals—I wonder you manage to keep any friends at all!"

The Toad saw at once how wrongly and foolishly he had acted. He admitted his errors and wrong-headedness and made a full apology to Rat for losing his boat and spoiling his clothes. And he wound up by saying, with that frank self-surrender which always disarmed his friends' criticism and won them back to his side, "Ratty! I see that I have been a headstrong and a wilful Toad! Henceforth, believe me, I will be humble and submissive, and will take no action without your kind advice and full approval."

"If that is really so," said the good-natured Rat, already appeased, "then my advice to you is, considering the lateness of the hour, to sit down and have your supper, which will be on the table in a minute, and be very patient. For I am convinced that we can do nothing until we have seen the Mole and the Badger, and heard their latest news, and held conference and taken their advice in this difficult matter."

"O, ah, yes, of course, the Mole and the Badger," said Toad lightly. "What's become of them, the dear fellows? I had forgotten all about them."

"Well may you ask!" said the Rat reproachfully. "While you were riding about the country in expensive motor-cars, and galloping proudly on blood-horses, and breakfasting on the fat of the land, those two poor devoted animals have been camping out in the open, in every sort of weather, living very rough by day and lying very hard by night; watching over your house, patrolling your boundaries, keeping a constant eye on the stoats and the weasels, scheming and planning and contriving how to get your property back for you. You don't deserve to have such true and loyal friends, Toad, you don't, really. Some day, when it's too late, you'll be sorry you didn't value them more while you had them!"

"I'm an ungrateful beast, I know," sobbed Toad, shedding bitter tears. "Let me go out and find them, out into the cold, dark night, and share their hardships, and try and prove by—Hold on a bit! Surely I heard the chink of dishes on a tray! Supper's here at last, hooray! Come on, Ratty!

The Rat remembered that poor Toad had been on prison fare for a considerable time, and that large allowances had therefore to be made. He followed him to the table accordingly, and hospitably encouraged him in his gallant efforts to make up for past privations.

They had just finished their meal and resumed their arm-chairs, when there came a heavy knock at the door.

Toad was nervous, but the Rat, nodding mysteriously at him, went straight up to the door and opened it, and in walked Mr Badger.

He had all the appearance of one who for some nights had been kept away from home and all its little comforts and conveniences. His shoes were covered with mud, and he was looking very rough and tousled; but then he had never been a very smart man, the Badger, at the best of times. He came solemnly up to Toad, shook him by the paw, and said, "Welcome home, Toad! Alas! what am I saying? Home, indeed! This is a poor home-coming. Unhappy Toad!" Then he turned his back on him, sat down to the table, drew his chair up, and helped himself to a large slice of cold pie.

Toad was quite alarmed at this very serious and portentous style of greeting; but the Rat whispered to him, "Never mind; don't take any notice; and don't say anything to him just yet. He's always rather low and despondent when he's wanting his victuals. In half an hour's time he'll be quite a different animal."

So they waited in silence, and presently there came another and a lighter knock. The Rat, with a nod to Toad, went to the door and ushered in the Mole, very shabby and unwashed, with bits of hay and straw sticking in his fur.

"Hooray! Here's old Toad!" cried the Mole, his face beaming. "Fancy having you back again!" And he began to dance round him. "We never dreamt you would turn up so soon! Why, you must have managed to escape, you clever, ingenious, intelligent Toad!"

The Rat, alarmed, pulled him by the elbow; but it was too late. Toad was puffing and swelling already.

"Clever? O no!" he said. "I'm not really clever, according to my friends. I've only broken out of the strongest prison in England, that's all! And captured a railway train and escaped on it, that's all! And disguised myself and gone about the country humbugging everybody, that's all! O no! I'm a stupid ass, I am! I'll tell you one or two of my little adventures, Mole, and you shall judge for yourself!"

"Well, well" said the Mole, moving towards the supper-table; "supposing you talk while I eat. Not a bite since breakfast! O my! O my!" And he sat down and helped himself liberally to cold beef and pickles.

Toad straddled on the hearth-rug, thrust his paw into his trouserpocket and pulled out a handful of silver. "Look at that!" he cried, displaying it. "That's not so bad, is it, for a few minutes' work? And how do you think I done it, Mole? Horse-stealing! That's how I done it!"

"Go on, Toad," said the Mole, immensely interested.

"Toad, do be quiet, please!" said the Rat. "And don't you egg him on, Mole, when you know what he is; but please tell us as soon as possible what the position is, and what's best to be done, now that Toad is back at last."

The position's about as bad as it can be," replied the Mole grumpily; "and as for what's to be done, why, blest if I know! The Badger and I have been round and round the place, by night and by day; always the same thing. Sentries posted everywhere, guns poked out at us, stones thrown at us; always an animal on the lookout, and when they see us, my! how they do laugh! That's what annoys me most!"

"It's a very difficult situation," said the Rat, reflecting deeply. "But I think I see now, in the depths of my mind, what Toad really ought to do. I will tell you. He ought to— "

"No, he oughtn't!" shouted the Mole, with his mouth full. "Nothing of the sort! You don't understand. What he ought to do is, he ought to—"

"Well, I shan't do it, anyway!" cried Toad, getting excited. "I'm not going to be ordered about by you fellows! It's my house we're talking about, and I know exactly what to do, and I'll tell you. I'm going to—"

By this time they were all three talking at once, at the top of their voices, and the noise was simply deafening, when a thin, dry voice made itself heard, saying, "Be quiet at once, all of you!" and instantly every one was silent.

It was the Badger, who, having finished his pie, had turned round in his chair and was looking at them severely. When he saw that he had secured their attention, and that they were evidently waiting for him to address them, he turned back to the table again and reached out for the cheese. And so great was the respect commanded by the solid qualities of that admirable animal, that not another word was uttered until he had quite finished his repast and brushed the crumbs from his knees. The Toad fidgeted a good deal, but the Rat held him firmly down.

When the Badger had quite done, he got up from his seat and stood before the fireplace, reflecting deeply. At last he spoke.

"Toad!" he said severely. "You bad, troublesome little animal! Aren't you ashamed of yourself? What do you think your father, my old friend, would have said if he had been here to-night, and had known of all your goings on?"

Toad, who was on the sofa by this time, with his legs up, rolled over on his face, shaken by sobs of contrition.

"There, there!" went on the Badger more kindly. "Never mind. Stop crying. We're going to let bygones be bygones, and try and turn over a new leaf. But what the Mole says is quite true. The stoats are on guard, at every point, and they make the best sentinels in the world. It's quite useless to think of attacking the place. They're too strong for us."

"Then it's all over," sobbed the Toad, crying into the sofa cushions. "I shall go and enlist for a soldier, and never see my dear Toad Hall any more!"

"Come, cheer up, Toady!" said the Badger. "There are more ways of getting back a place than taking it by storm. I haven't said my last word yet. Now I'm going to tell you a great secret."

Toad sat up slowly and dried his eyes. Secrets had an immense attraction for him, because he never could keep one, and he enjoyed the sort of unhallowed thrill he experienced when he went and told another animal, after having faithfully promised not to.

"There—is—an—underground—passage," said the Badger impressively, "that leads from the river bank quite near here, right up into the middle of Toad Hall."

"O, nonsense! Badger," said Toad rather airily. "You've been listening to some of the yarns they spin in the public-houses about here. I know every inch of Toad Hall, inside and out. Nothing of the sort, I do assure you!"

"My young friend," said the Badger with great severity, "your father, who was a worthy animal—a lot worthier than some others I know—was a particular friend of mine, and told me a great deal he wouldn't have dreamt of telling you. He discovered that passage—he didn't make it, of course; that was done hundreds of years before he ever came to live there—and he repaired it and cleaned it out, because he thought it might come in useful some day, in case of trouble or danger; and he showed it to me. 'Don't let my son know about it,' he said. 'He's a good boy, but very light and volatile in character, and simply cannot hold his tongue. If he's ever in a real fix, and it would be of use to him, you may tell him about the secret passage; but not before.'"

The other animals looked hard at Toad to see how he would take it. Toad was inclined to be sulky at first; but he brightened up immediately, like the good fellow he was.

"Well, well," he said; "perhaps I am a bit of a talker. A popular fellow such as I am—my friends get round me—we chaff, we sparkle, we tell witty stories—and somehow my tongue gets wagging. I have the gift of conversation. I've been told I ought to have a *salon*, whatever that may be. Never mind. Go on, Badger. How's this passage of yours going to help us?"

"I've found out a thing or two lately," continued the Badger. "I got Otter to disguise himself as a sweep and call at the back door with brushes over his shoulder, asking for a job. There's going to be a big banquet to-morrow night. It's somebody's birthday—the Chief Weasel's, I believe—and all the weasels will be gathered together in the dining-hall, eating and drinking and laughing and carrying on, suspecting nothing. No guns, no swords, no sticks, no arms of any sort whatever!"

"But the sentinels will be posted as usual," remarked the Rat.

"Exactly," said the Badger; "that is my point. The weasels will trust entirely to their excellent sentinels. And that is where the passage comes in. That very useful tunnel leads right up under the butler's pantry, next to the dining-hall!"

"Aha! that squeaky board in the butler's pantry!" said

Toad. "Now I understand it!"

"We shall creep out quietly into the butler's pantry—" cried the Mole.

"—with our pistols and swords and sticks—" shouted the Rat.

"—and rush in upon them," said the Badger.

"—and whack 'em, and whack 'em, and whack 'em!" cried the Toad in ecstasy, running round and round the room, and jumping over the chairs.

"Very well, then," said the Badger, resuming his usual dry manner, "our plan is settled, and there's nothing more for you to argue and squabble about. So, as it's getting very late, all of you go right off to bed at once. We will make all the necessary arrangements in the course of the morning to-morrow."

Toad, of course, went off to bed dutifully with the rest—he knew better than to refuse—though he was feeling much too excited to sleep. But he had had a long day, with many events crowded into it; and sheets and blankets were very friendly and comforting things, after plain straw, and not too much of it, spread on the stone floor of a draughty cell; and his head had not been many seconds on his pillow before he was snoring happily. Naturally, he dreamt a good deal; about roads that ran away from him just when he wanted them, and canals that chased him and caught him, and a barge that sailed into the banqueting-hall with his week's washing, just as he was giving a dinner-party; and he was alone in the secret passage, pushing onwards, but it twisted and turned round and shook itself, and sat up on its end; yet somehow, at the last, he found himself back in Toad Hall, safe and triumphant, with all his friends gathered round about him, earnestly assuring him that he really was a clever Toad.

He slept till a late hour next morning, and by the time he got down he found that the other animals had finished their breakfast some time before. The Mole had slipped off somewhere by himself, without telling any one where he was going. The Badger sat in the arm-chair, reading the paper, and not concerning himself in the slightest about what was going to happen that very evening. The Rat, on the other hand, was running round the room busily, with his arms full of weapons of every kind, distributing them in four little heaps on the floor, and saying excitedly under his breath, as he ran, "Here's-a-sword-for-the-Rat, here's-a-sword-for-the-Mole, here's-a-sword-for-the-Toad, here's-a-sword-for-the-Badger! Here's-a-pistol-for-the-Rat, here's-a-pistol-for-the-Mole, here's-a-pistol-for-the-Toad, here's-a-pistol-for-the-Badger!" And so on, in a regular, rhythmical way, while the four little heaps gradually grew and grew.

"That's all very well, Rat," said the Badger presently, looking at the busy little animal over the edge of his newspaper; "I'm not blaming you. But just let us once get past the stoats, with those detestable guns of theirs, and I assure you we shan't want any swords or pistols. We four, with our sticks, once we're inside the dining-hall, why, we shall clear the floor of all the lot of them in five minutes. I'd have done the whole thing by myself, only I didn't want to deprive you fellows of the fun!"

"It's as well to be on the safe side," said the Rat reflectively, polishing a pistol-barrel on his sleeve and looking along it.

The Toad, having finished his breakfast, picked up a stout stick and swung it vigorously, belabouring imaginary animals. "I'll learn 'em to steal my house!" he cried. "I'll learn 'em, I'll learn 'em!"

"Don't say 'learn 'em', Toad," said the Rat, greatly shocked. "It's not good English."

"What are you always nagging at Toad for?" inquired the Badger rather peevishly. "What's the matter with his English? It's the same what I use myself, and if it's good enough for me, it ought to be good enough for you!"

"I'm very sorry," said the Rat humbly. "Only I *think* it ought to be 'teach 'em', not 'learn 'em'."

"But we don't *want* to teach 'em," replied the Badger. "We want to *learn* 'em—learn 'em, learn 'em! And what's more, we're going to *do* it, too!"

"O, very well, have it your own way," said the Rat. He was getting rather muddled about it himself, and presently he retired into a corner, where he could be heard muttering, "Learn 'em, teach 'em, teach 'em, learn 'em!" till the Badger told him rather sharply to leave off.

Presently the Mole came tumbling into the room, evidently very pleased with himself "I've been having such fun!" he began at once; "I've been getting a rise out of the stoats!"

"I hope you've been very careful, Mole?" said the Rat anxiously.

"I should hope so, too," said the Mole confidently. "I got the idea when I went into the kitchen, to see about Toad's breakfast being kept hot for him. I found that old washerwoman-dress that he came home in yesterday, hanging on a towel-horse before the fire. So I put it on, and the bonnet as well, and the shawl, and off I went to Toad Hall, as bold as you please. The sentries were on the look-out, of course, with their guns and their 'Who comes there?' and all the rest of their nonsense. 'Good morning, gentlemen!' says I, very respectful 'Want any washing done to-day?'

"They looked at me very proud and stiff and haughty, and said, 'Go away, washerwoman! We don't do any washing on duty.' 'Or any other time?' says. I. Ho, ho, ,ho! Wasn't I *funny*, Toad?"

"Poor, frivolous animal!" said Toad very loftily. The fact is, he felt exceedingly jealous of Mole for what he had just done. It was exactly what he would have liked to have done himself, if only he had thought of it first, and hadn't gone and overslept himself.

"Some of the stoats turned quite pink," continued the Mole, "and the sergeant in charge, he said to me, very short, he said, 'Now run away, my good woman, run away! Don't keep my men idling and talking on their posts.' 'Run away?' says I; 'it won't be me that'll be running away, in a very short time from now!'"

"O, *Moly*, how could you?" said the Rat, dismayed.

The Badger laid down his paper.

"I could see them pricking up their ears and looking at each other," went on the Mole; "and the sergeant said to them, 'Never mind *her;* she doesn't know what she's talking about.'

"'O! don't I?' said I. 'Well, let me tell you this. My daughter, she washes for Mr Badger, and that'll show you whether I know what I'm talking about; and *you'll* know pretty soon, too! A hundred bloodthirsty badgers, armed with rifles, are going to attack Toad Hall this very night, by way of the paddock. Six boat-loads of rats, with pistols and cutlasses, will come up the river and effect a landing in the garden; while a picked body of toads, known as the Diehards, or the Death-or-Glory Toads, will storm the orchard and carry everything before them, yelling for vengeance. There won't be much left of you to wash, by the time they've done with you, unless you clear out while you have the chance!' Then I ran away, and when I was out of sight I hid; and presently I came creeping back along the ditch and took a peep at them through the hedge. They were all as nervous and flustered as could be, running all ways at once, and falling over each other, and everyone giving orders to everybody else and not listening; and the sergeant kept sending off parties of stoats to distant parts of the grounds, and then sending other fellows to fetch 'em back again: and I heard them saying to each other, 'That's *just* like the weasels; they're to stop comfortably in the banqueting-hall, and have feasting and toasts and songs and all sorts of fun, while we must stay on guard in the cold and the dark, and in the end be cut to pieces by blood-thirsty Badgers!'"

"O, you silly ass, Mole!" cried Toad. "You've been and spoilt everything!"

"Mole," said the Badger, in his dry, quiet way, "I perceive you have more sense in your little finger than some other animals have in the whole of their fat bodies. You have managed excellently, and I begin to have great hopes of you. Good Mole! Clever Mole!"

The Toad was simply wild with jealousy, more especially as he couldn't make out for the life of him what the Mole had done that was so particularly clever; but, fortunately for him, before he could show temper or expose himself to the Badger's sarcasm, the bell rang for luncheon.

It was a simple but sustaining meal—bacon and broad beans, and a macaroni pudding; and when they had quite done, the Badger settled himself into an arm-chair, and said, "Well, we've got our work cut out for us to-night, and it will probably be pretty late before we're quite through with it; so I'm just going to take forty winks, while I can." And he drew a handkerchief over his face and was soon snoring.

The anxious and laborious Rat at once resumed his preparations, and started running between his four little heaps, muttering. "Here's-a-belt-for-the-Rat, here's-a-belt-for-the-Mole, here's-a-belt-for-the-Toad, here's-a-belt-for-the-Badger!" and so on, with every fresh accoutrement he produced, to which there seemed really no end; so the Mole drew his arm through Toad's, led him out into the open air, shoved him into a wicker chair, and made him tell him all his adventures from beginning to end, which Toad was only too willing to do. The Mole was a good listener, and Toad, with no one to check his statements or to criticize in an unfriendly spirit, rather let himself go. Indeed, much that he related belonged more properly to the category of what-might-have-happened-had-I-only-thought-of-it-in-time-instead-of-ten-minutes afterwards. Those are always the best and the raciest adventures; and why should they not be truly ours, as much as the somewhat inadequate things that really come off?

CHAPTER 12

THE RETURN OF ULYSSES

When it began to grow dark, the Rat, with an air of excitement and mystery, summoned them back into the parlour, stood each of them up alongside of his little heap, and proceeded to dress them up for the coming expedition. He was very earnest and thorough-going about it, and the affair took quite a long time. First, there was a belt to go round each animal, and then a sword to be stuck into each belt, and then a cutlass on the other side to balance it. Then a pair of pistols, a policeman's truncheon, several sets of handcuffs, some bandages and sticking-plaster, and a flask and a sandwich-case. The Badger laughed good-humouredly and said, "All right, Ratty! It amuses you and it doesn't hurt me. I'm going to do all I've got to do with this here stick." But the Rat only said, "*Please*, Badger! You know I shouldn't like you to blame me afterwards and say I had forgotten *anything*!"

When all was quite ready, the Badger took a dark lantern in one paw, grasped his great stick with the other, and said, "Now then, follow me! Mole first, 'cos I'm very pleased with him; Rat next; Toad last. And look here, Toady! Don't you chatter so much as usual, or you'll be sent back, as sure as fate!"

The Toad was so anxious not to be left out that he took up the inferior position assigned to him without a murmur, and the animals set off. The Badger led them along by the river for a little way, and then suddenly swung himself over the edge into a hole in the river bank, a little above the water. The Mole and the Rat followed silently, swinging themselves successfully into the hole as they had seen the Badger do; but when it came to Toad's turn, of course he managed to slip and fall into the water with a loud splash and a squeal of alarm. He was hauled out by his friends, rubbed down and wrung out hastily, comforted, and set on his legs; but the Badger was seriously angry, and told him that the very next time he made a fool of himself he would most certainly be left behind.

So at last they were in the secret passage, and the cutting-out expedition had really begun!

It was cold, and dark, and damp, and low, and narrow, and poor Toad began to shiver, partly from dread of what might be before him, partly because he was wet through. The lantern was far ahead, and he could not help lagging behind a little in the darkness. Then he heard the Rat call out warningly, "*Come* on, Toad!" and a terror seized him of being left behind, alone in the darkness, and he "came on" with such a rush that he upset the Rat into the Mole and the Mole into the Badger, and for a moment all was confusion. The Badger thought they were being attacked from behind, and, as there was no room to use a stick or a cutlass, drew a pistol, and was on the point of putting a bullet into Toad. When he found out what had really happened he was very angry indeed, and said, "Now this time that tiresome Toad *shall* be left behind!"

But Toad whimpered, and the other two promised that they would be answerable for his good conduct, and at last the Badger was pacified, and the procession moved on; only this time the Rat brought up the rear, with a firm grip on the shoulder of Toad.

So they groped and shuffled along, with their ears pricked up and their paws on their pistols, till at last the Badger said, "We ought by now to be pretty nearly under the Hall."

Then suddenly they heard, far away as it might be, and yet apparently nearly over their heads, a confused murmur of sound, as if people were shouting and cheering and stamping on the floor and hammering on tables. The Toad's nervous terrors all returned, but the Badger only remarked placidly, "They *are* going it, the weasels!"

The passage now began to slope upwards; they groped onward a little further, and then the noise broke out again, quite distinct this time, and very close above them. "Ooo-ray-oo-ray-oo-ray-ooray," they heard, and the stamping of little feet on the floor, and the clinking of glasses as little fists pounded on the table. "*What* a time they're having!" said the Badger. "Come on!" They hurried along the passage till it came to a full stop, and they found themselves standing under the trap-door that led up into the butler's pantry.

Such a tremendous noise was going on in the banqueting-hall that there was little danger of their being overheard. The Badger said, "Now, boys, all together!" and the four of them put their shoulders to the trap-door and heaved it back. Hoisting each other up, they found themselves standing in the pantry, with only a door between them and the banqueting-hall, where their unconscious enemies were carousing.

The noise, as they emerged from the passage, was simply deafening. At last, as the cheering and hammering slowly subsided, a voice could be made out saying, "Well, I do not propose to detain you much longer"—(great applause)—"but before I resume my seat"—(renewed cheering)—"I should like to say one word about our kind host, Mr Toad. We all know Toad!"—(great laughter)—"*Good* Toad, *modest* Toad, *honest* Toad!"—(shrieks of merriment).

"Only just let me get at him!" muttered Toad, grinding his teeth.

"Hold hard a minute!" said the Badger, restraining him with difficulty. "Get ready, all of you!"

"—Let me sing you a little song," went on the voice, "which I have composed on the subject of Toad"—(prolonged applause).

Then the Chief Weasel—for it was he—began in a high, squeaky voice:

Toad he went a-pleasuring
Gaily down the street—

The Badger drew himself up, took a firm grip of his stick with both paws, glanced round at his comrades, and cried:

"The hour is come! Follow me!"

And flung the door open wide.

My!

What a squealing and a squeaking and a screeching filled the air!

Well might the terrified weasels dive under the tables and spring madly up at the windows! Well might the ferrets rush wildly for the fire-place and get hopelessly jammed in the chimney! Well might tables and chairs be upset, and glass and china be sent crashing on the floor, in the panic of that terrible moment when the four Heroes strode wrathfully into the room! The mighty Badger, his whiskers bristling, his great cudgel whistling through the air; Mole, black and grim, brandishing his stick and shouting his awful war-cry, "A Mole! A Mole!" Rat, desperate and determined, his belt bulging with weapons of every age and every variety; Toad, frenzied with excitement and injured pride, swollen to twice his ordinary size, leaping into the air and emitting Toad-whoops that chilled them to the marrow! "Toad he went a-pleasuring!" he yelled. "*I'll* pleasure 'em!" and he went straight for the Chief Weasel. They were but four in all, but to the panic-stricken weasels the hall seemed full of monstrous animals, grey, black, brown, and yellow, whooping and flourishing enormous cudgels; and they broke and fled with squeals of terror and dismay, this way and that, through the windows, up the chimney, anywhere to get out of reach of those terrible sticks.

The affair was soon over. Up and down, the whole length of the hall, strode the four Friends, whacking with their sticks at every head that showed itself; and in five minutes the room was cleared. Through the broken windows the shrieks of terrified weasels escaping across the lawn were borne faintly to their ears; on the floor lay prostrate some dozen or so of the enemy, on whom the Mole was busily engaged in fitting handcuffs. The Badger, resting from his labours, leant on his stick and wiped his honest brow.

"Mole," he said, "you're the best of fellows! Just cut along outside and look after those stoat-sentries of yours, and see what they're doing. I've an idea that, thanks to you, we shan't have much trouble from *them* to-night!"

The Mole vanished promptly through a window; and the Badger bade the other two set a table on its legs again, pick up knives and forks and plates and glasses from the debris on the floor, and see if they could find materials for a supper. "I want some grub, I do," he said, in that rather common way he had of speaking. "Stir your stumps, Toad, and look lively! We've got your house back for you, and you don't offer us so much as a sandwich."

Toad felt rather hurt that the Badger didn't say pleasant things to him, as he had to the Mole, and tell him what a fine fellow he was, and how splendidly he had fought; for he was rather particularly pleased with himself and the way he had gone for the Chief Weasel and sent him flying across the table with one blow of his stick. But he bustled about, and so did the Rat, and soon they found some guava jelly in a glass dish, and a cold chicken, a tongue that had hardly been touched, some trifle, and quite a lot of lobster salad; and in the pantry they came upon a basketful of French rolls and any quantity of cheese, butter, and celery. They were just about to sit down when the Mole clambered in through the window, chuckling, with an armful of rifles.

"It's all over," he reported. "From what I can make out, as soon as the stoats, who were very nervous and jumpy already, heard the shrieks and the yells and the uproar inside the hall, some of them threw down their rifles and fled. The others stood fast for a bit, but when the weasels came rushing out upon them they thought they were betrayed; and the stoats grappled with the weasels, and the weasels fought to get away, and they wrestled and wriggled and punched each other, and rolled over and over, till most of 'em rolled into the river! They've all disappeared by now, one way or another; and I've got their rifles. So *that's* all right!"

"Excellent and deserving animal!" said the Badger, his mouth full of chicken and trifle. "Now, there's just one more thing I want you to do, Mole, before you sit down to your supper along of us; and I wouldn't trouble you only I know I can trust you to see a thing done, and I wish I could say the same of every one I know. I'd send Rat, if he wasn't a poet. I want you to take those fellows on the floor there upstairs with you, and have some bedrooms cleaned out and tidied up and made really comfortable. See that they sweep *under* the beds, and put clean sheets and pillow-cases on, and turn down one corner of the bed-clothes, just as you know it ought to be done; and have a can of hot water, and clean towels, and fresh cakes of soap, put in each room. And then you can give them a licking apiece, if it's any satisfaction to you, and put them out by the back door, and we shan't see any more of *them*, I fancy. And then come along and have some of this cold tongue. It's first-rate. I'm very pleased with you, Mole!"

The good-natured Mole picked up a stick, formed his prisoners up in a line on the floor, gave them the order

"Quick march!" and led his squad off to the upper floor. After a time, he appeared again, smiling, and said that every room was ready, and as clean as a new pin. "And I didn't have to lick them, either," he added "I thought, on the whole, they had had licking enough for one night, and the weasels, when I put the point to them, quite agreed with me, and said they wouldn't think of troubling me. They were very penitent, and said they were extremely sorry for what they had done, but it was all the fault of the Chief Weasel and the stoats, and if ever they could do anything for us at any time to make up, we had only got to mention it. So I gave them a roll apiece, and let them out at the back, and off they ran, as hard as they could."

Then the Mole pulled his chair up to the table, and pitched into the cold tongue; and Toad, like the gentleman he was, put all his jealousy from him, and said heartily, thank you kindly, dear Mole, for all your pains and trouble to-night, and especially for your cleverness this morning." The Badger was pleased at that, and said, "There spoke my brave Toad!" So they finished their supper in great joy and contentment, and presently retired to rest between clean sheets, safe in Toad's ancestral home, won back by matchless valour, consummate strategy, and a proper handling of sticks.

The following morning, Toad, who had overslept himself as usual, came down to breakfast disgracefully late, and found on the table a certain quantity of egg-shells, some fragments of cold and leathery toast, a coffee-pot three-fourths empty, and really very little else; which did not tend to improve his temper, considering that, after all, it was his own house. Through the French windows of the breakfast-room he could see the Mole and the Water Rat sitting in wicker chairs out on the lawn, evidently telling each other stories; roaring with laughter and kicking their short legs up in the air. The Badger, who was in an arm-chair and deep in the morning paper, merely looked up and nodded when Toad entered the room. But Toad knew his man, so he sat down and made the best breakfast he could, merely observing to himself that he would get square with the others sooner or later. When he had nearly finished, the Badger looked up and remarked rather shortly: "I'm sorry, Toad, but I'm afraid there's a heavy morning's work in front of you. You see, we really ought to have a Banquet at once, to celebrate this affair. It's expected of you—in fact, it's the rule."

"O, all right!" said the Toad readily. "Anything to oblige. Though why on earth you should want to have a Banquet in the morning I cannot understand. But you know I do not live to please myself but merely to find out what my friends want, and then try and arrange it for 'em, you dear old Badger!"

"Don't pretend to be stupider than you really are," replied the Badger crossly; "and don't chuckle and splutter in your coffee while you're talking; it's not manners. What I mean is, the Banquet will be at night, of course, but the invitations will have to be written and got off at once, and you've got to write 'em. Now, sit down at that table—there's stacks of letter-paper on it, with 'Toad Hall' at the top in blue and gold—and write invitations to all our friends, and if you stick to it we shall get them out before luncheon. And *I'll* bear a hand, too, and take my share of the burden. *I'll* order the Banquet."

"What!" cried Toad, dismayed. "Me stop indoors and write a lot of rotten letters on a jolly morning like this, when I want to go around my property, and set everything and everybody to rights, and swagger about and enjoy myself. Certainly not! I'll be—I'll see you—Stop a minute, though! Why, of course, dear Badger! What is my pleasure or convenience compared with that of others! You wish it done, and it shall be done. Go, Badger, order the Banquet, order what you like; then join our young friends outside in their innocent mirth, oblivious of me and my cares and toils. I sacrifice this fair morning on the altar of duty and friendship!"

The Badger looked at him very suspiciously, but Toad's frank, open countenance made it difficult to suggest any unworthy motive in this change of attitude. He quitted the room, accordingly, in the direction of the kitchen, and as soon as the door had closed behind him, Toad hurried to the writing-table. A fine idea had occurred to him while he was talking. He *would* write the invitations; and he would take care to mention the leading part he had taken in the fight, and how he had laid the Chief Weasel out and he would hint at his adventures, and what a career of triumph he had to tell about; and on the flyleaf he would give a sort of programme of entertainment for the evening—something like this, as he sketched it out in his head:

SPEECH..BY TOAD

(There will be other speeches by Toad during the evening)

ADDRESS..BY TOAD

SYNOPSIS—Our Prison System—The Waterways of Old England—Horse-dealing, and how to deal—Property, its rights and its duties—Back to the Land—A Typical English Squire

(Composed by himself)

OTHER COMPOSITIONS..................BY TOAD
will be sung in the course of the evening by the . . . COMPOSER

The idea pleased him mightily, and he worked very hard and got all the letters finished by noon, at which hour it was reported to him that there was a small and rather bedraggled weasel at the door, inquiring timidly whether he could be of any service to the gentlemen. Toad swaggered out and found it was one of the prisoners of the previous evening, very respectful and anxious to please. He patted him on the head, shoved the bundle of invitations into his paw, and told him to cut along quick and deliver them as fast as he could, and if he liked to come back again in the evening perhaps there might be a shilling for him, or, again, perhaps there mightn't; and the poor weasel seemed really quite grateful, and hurried off eagerly to do his mission.

When the other animals came back to luncheon, very boisterous and breezy after a morning on the river, the Mole, whose conscience had been pricking him, looked doubtfully at Toad, expecting to find him sulky or depressed. Instead, he was so uppish and inflated that the Mole began to suspect something; while the Rat and the Badger exchanged significant glances.

As soon as the meal was over, Toad thrust his paws deep into his trouser-pockets, remarked casually, "Well, look after yourselves, you fellows! Ask for anything you want!" and was swaggering off in the direction of the garden where he wanted to think out an idea or two for his coming speeches, when the Rat caught him by the arm.

Toad rather suspected what he was after, and did his best to get away; but when the Badger took him firmly by the other arm he began to see that the game was up. The two animals conducted him between them into the small smoking-room that opened out of the entrance-hall, shut the door, and put him into a chair. Then they both stood in front of him,while Toad sat silent and regarded them with much suspicion and ill-humour.

"Now, look here, Toad," said the Rat. "It's about this Banquet, and very sorry I am to have to speak to you like this. But we want you to understand clearly, once and for all, that there are going to be no speeches and no songs. Try and grasp the fact that on this occasion we're not arguing with you; we're just telling you."

Toad saw that he was trapped. They understood him, they saw through him, they had got ahead of him. His pleasant dream was shattered.

"Mayn't I sing them just one *little* song" he pleaded piteously.

"No, not *one* little song," replied the Rat firmly, though his heart bled as he noticed the trembling lip of the poor disappointed Toad. "It's no good, Toady; you know well that your songs are all conceit and boasting and vanity; and your speeches are all self-praise and— and—well, and gross exaggeration and—and—"

"And gas," put in the Badger, in his common way.

"It's for your own good, Toady," went on the Rat. "You know you *must* turn over a new leaf sooner or later, and now seems a splendid time to begin; a sort of turning-point in your career. Please don't think that saying all this doesn't hurt me more than it hurts you."

Toad remained a long while plunged in thought. At last he raised his head, and the traces of strong emotion were visible on his features. "You have conquered, my friends," he said in broken accents. "It was, to be sure, but a small thing that I asked—merely leave to blossom and expand for yet one more evening, to let myself go and hear the tumultuous applause that always seems to me—somehow—to bring out my best qualities. However, you are right, I know, and I am wrong. Henceforth I will be a very different Toad. My friends, you shall never have occasion to blush for me again. But, O dear, O dear, this is a hard world!"

And, pressing his handkerchief to his face, he left the room with faltering footsteps.

"Badger," said the Rat. "*I* feel like a brute; I wonder what *you* feel like?"

"O, I know, I know," said the Badger gloomily. "But the thing had to be done. This good fellow has got to live here, and hold his own, and be respected. Would you have him a common laughing-stock, mocked and jeered at by stoats and weasels."

"Of course not," said the Rat. "And, talking of weasels, it's lucky we came upon that little weasel, just as he was setting out with Toad's invitations. I suspected something from what you told me, and had a look at one or two; they were simply disgraceful I confiscated the lot, and the good Mole is now sitting in the blue *boudoir*, filling up plain, simple invitation cards."

At last the hour for the banquet began to draw near, and Toad, who on leaving the others had retired to his bedroom, was still sitting there, melancholy and thoughtful. His brow resting on his paw, he pondered long and deeply. Gradually his countenance cleared, and he began to smile long, slow smiles. Then he took to giggling in a shy, self-conscious manner. At last he got up, locked the door, drew the curtains across the windows, collected all the. chairs in the room and arranged them in a semicircle, and took up his position in front of them, swelling visibly. Then he bowed, coughed twice, and, letting himself go, with uplifted voice he sang, to the enraptured audience that his imagination so clearly saw.

TOAD'S LAST LITTLE SONG!

The Toad—came—home!
There was panic in the parlour and howling in the hall
There was crying in the cow-shed and shrieking in the stall,
When the Toad—came—home!
When the Toad—came—home!
There was smashing in of window and crashing in of door,
There was chivvying of weasels that fainted on the floor!
When the Toad—came—home!

Bang! go the drums!
The trumpeters are tooting and the soldiers are saluting,
And the cannon they are shooting and the motor-cars are hooting,
As the—Hero-comes!
Shout—Hoo-ray!
And let each one of the crowd try and shout it very loud,
In honour of an animal of whom you're justly proud,
For it's Toad's—great—day!

He sang this very loud, with great unction and expression; and when he had done, he sang it all over again.

Then he heaved a deep sigh; a long, long, long sigh.

Then he dipped his hairbrush in the water-jug, parted his hair in the middle, and plastered it down very straight and sleek on each side of his face; and, unlocking the door, went quietly down the stairs to greet his guests, who he knew must be assembling in the drawing-room.

All the animals cheered when he entered, and crowded round to congratulate him and say nice things about his courage, and his cleverness, and his fighting qualities; but Toad only smiled faintly and murmured, "Not at all!" Or, sometimes, for a change, "On the contrary!" Otter, who was standing on the hearth-rug, describing to an admiring circle of friends exactly how he would have managed things had he been there, came forward with a shout, threw his arm round Toad's neck, and tried to take him round the room in triumphant progress; but Toad, in a mild way, was rather snubby to him, remarking gently, as he disengaged himself, "Badger's was the mastermind; the Mole and the Water Rat bore the brunt of the fighting; I merely served in the ranks and did little or nothing." The animals were evidently puzzled and taken aback by this unexpected attitude of his; and Toad felt, as he moved from one guest to the other, making his modest responses, that he was an object of absorbing interest to everyone.

The Badger had ordered everything of the best, and the banquet was a great success. There was much talking and laughter and chaff among the animals, but through it all Toad, who of course was in the chair, looked down his nose and murmured pleasant nothings to the animals on either side of him. At intervals he stole a glance at the Badger and the Rat, and always when he looked they were staring at each other with their mouths open; and this gave him the greatest satisfaction. Some of the younger and livelier animals, as the evening wore on, got whispering to each other that things were not so amusing as they used to be in the good old days; and there were some knockings on the table and cries of "Toad! Speech! Speech from Toad! Song! Mr Toad's Song!" But Toad only shook his head gently, raised one paw in mild protest, and, by pressing delicacies on his guests, by topical small-talk, and by earnest inquiries after members of their families not yet old enough to appear at social functions, managed to convey to them that this dinner was being run on strictly conventional lines.

He was indeed an altered Toad!

After this climax, the four animals continued to lead their lives, so rudely broken in upon by civil war, in great joy and contentment, undisturbed by further risings or invasions. Toad, after due consultation with his friends, selected a handsome gold chain and locket set with pearls, which he dispatched to the gaoler's daughter with a letter that even the Badger admitted to be modest, grateful, and appreciative; and the engine-driver, in his turn, was properly thanked and compensated for all his pains and trouble. Under severe compulsion from the Badger, even the barge-woman was, with some trouble, sought out and the value of her horse discreetly made good to her; though Toad kicked terribly at this, holding himself to be an instrument of Fate, sent to punish fat women with mottled arms who couldn't tell a real gentleman when they saw one. The amount involved, it was true, was not very burdensome, the gipsy's valuation being admitted by local assessors to be approximately correct.

Sometimes, in the course of long summer evenings, the friends would take a stroll together in the Wild Wood, now successfully tamed so far as they were concerned; and it was pleasing to see how respectfully they were greeted by the inhabitants, and how the mother-weasels would bring their young ones to the mouths of their holes, and say, pointing, "Look, baby! There goes the great Mr Toad! And that's the gallant Water Rat, a terrible fighter, walking along o' him! And yonder comes the famous Mr Mole, of whom you so often have heard your father tell!" But when their infants were fractious and quite beyond control, they would quiet them by telling how, if they didn't hush them and not fret them, the terrible grey Badger would up and get them. This was a base libel on Badger, who, though he cared little about Society, was rather fond of children; but it never failed to have its full effect.

CHILDREN'S CLASSICS

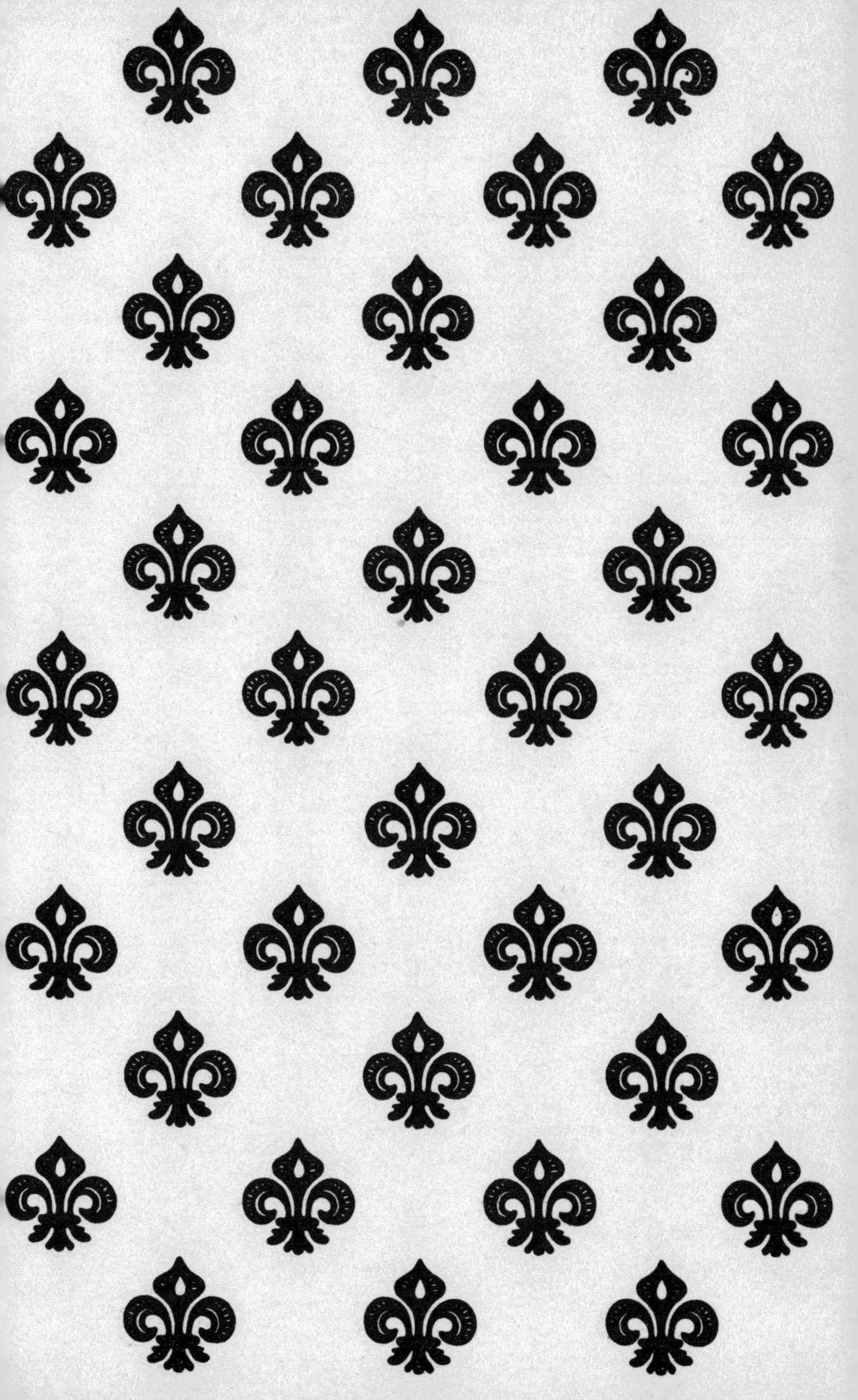

The Water-Babies

CHARLES KINGSLEY

The Water-Babies
A Fairy tale for a Land-Baby

Chapter 1

TOM SETS OUT WITH HIS MASTER, MR. GRIMES

Once upon a time there was a little chimney-sweep, and his name was Tom. He lived in a great town in the North country, where there were plenty of chimneys to sweep, and plenty of money for Tom to earn and his master to spend. He could not read nor write, and did not care to do either; and he never washed himself, for there was no water up the court where he lived. He had never been taught to say his prayers. He never had heard of God, or of Christ, except in words which you never have heard, and which it would have been well if he had never heard. He cried half his time, and laughed the other half. He cried when he had to climb the dark flues, rubbing his poor knees and elbows raw; and when the soot got into his eyes, or when his master beat him, or when he had not enough to eat, which happened every day in the week. And he laughed the other half of the day, when he was tossing halfpennies with the other boys, or playing leap-frog over the posts, and thought of the fine times coming, when he would be a man, and a master sweep, and sit in the public-house with a quart of beer and a long pipe, and keep a white bulldog with one grey ear, and carry her puppies in his pocket, just like a man. And he would have apprentices, one, two, three, if he could. How he would bully them, and knock them about, just as his master did to him; and make them carry home the soot bags, while he rode before them on his donkey, with a pipe in his mouth and a flower in his button-hole, like a king at the head of his army.

One day a smart little groom rode into the court where Tom lived. Tom was just hiding behind a wall, to heave half a brick at his horse's legs, when the groom saw him, and halloed to him to know where Mr. Grimes, the chimney-sweep, lived. Now Mr. Grimes was Tom's own master, so he put the half-brick down quietly behind the wall, and proceeded to take orders.

The groom said that Mr. Grimes was to come up next morning to Sir John Harthover's, at the Place, for the chimneys wanted sweeping.

His master was so delighted at his new customer that he knocked Tom down straight away, and drank more beer that night than he usually did in two. And when he got up at four the next morning he knocked Tom down again, in order to teach him that he must be an extra good boy that day, as they were going to a very great house, and might make a very good thing of it, if they could but give satisfaction.

And Tom thought so likewise, and would have behaved his best even without being knocked down.

Harthover Place was really a grand place, even for the rich North country; with miles of game-preserves, in which Mr. Grimes and the collier lads poached at times, and a noble salmon-river, and Sir John, a grand old man, whom even Mr. Grimes respected.

So Tom and his master set out; Grimes rode the donkey in front, and Tom and the brushes walked behind; out of the court, and up the street, past the closed window-shutters, and the winking weary policemen, and the roofs all shining grey in the grey dawn.

They passed through the pitmen's village, all shut up and silent now; and then they were out in the real country, and plodding along the black dusty road, between black slag walls, with no sound but the groaning and thumping of the pit-engine in the next field. But soon the road grew white, and the walls likewise; and at the wall's foot grew long grass and gay flowers, all drenched with dew; and instead of the groaning of the pit-engine, they heard the skylark saying his matins high up in the air, and the pit-bird warbling in the sedges, as he had warbled all night long.

All else was silent. For old Mrs. Earth was still fast asleep; and, like many pretty people, she looked still prettier asleep than awake. The great elm-trees in the gold-green meadows were fast asleep above, and the cows fast asleep beneath them; nay the few clouds which were about were fast asleep likewise, and so tired that they had lain down on the earth to rest, in long white flakes and bars, among the stems of the elm-trees, and along the tops of the alders by the stream, waiting for the sun to bid them rise and go about their day's business in the clear blue overhead.

On they went; and Tom looked, and looked, for he never had been so far into the country before; and longed to get over a gate, and pick buttercups, and look for birds' nests in the hedge; but Mr. Grimes was a man of business, and would not have heard of that.

Soon they came up with a poor Irishwoman, trudging along with a bundle at her back. She had a grey shawl over her head, and a crimson petticoat. She had neither shoes nor stockings, and limped along as if she were tired and footsore; but she was a very tall handsome woman, with bright grey eyes, and heavy black hair hanging about her cheeks. And she took Mr. Grimes' fancy so much, that when he came alongside he called out to her:

"This is a hard road; will ye up, lass, and ride behind me?"

But, perhaps, she did not like Mr. Grimes' look and voice; for she answered quietly:

"No, thank you: I'd sooner walk with your little lad here."

"You may please yourself," growled Grimes, and went on smoking.

So she walked beside Tom, and talked to him, and asked him where he lived, and what he knew, and all about himself, till Tom thought he had never met such a pleasant-spoken woman. And she asked him, at last, whether he said his prayers, and seemed sad when he told her that he knew no prayers to say.

Then he asked her where she lived, and she said far away by the sea. And Tom asked her about the sea; and she told him how it rolled and roared over the rocks in winter nights, and lay still in the bright summer days, for the children to bathe and play in it; and many a story more, till Tom longed to go and see the sea, and bathe in it likewise.

At last, at the bottom of a hill, they came to a spring. Out of a low cave of rock, at the foot of a limestone crag, the great fountain rose, and ran away under the road, a stream large enough to turn a mill.

And there Grimes stopped, and looked; and Tom looked too. Tom was wondering whether anything lived in that dark cave, and came out at night to fly in the meadows. But Grimes was not wondering at all. Without a word, he got off his donkey, and clambered over the low road wall, and knelt down, and began dipping his ugly head into the spring—and very dirty he made it.

Tom was picking the flowers as fast as he could. The Irishwoman helped him, and showed him how to tie them up; and a very pretty nosegay they had made between them. But when he saw Grimes actually wash, he stopped, quite astonished; and when Grimes had finished, and began shaking his ears to dry them, he said:

"Why, master, I never saw you do that before."

"Nor will again, most likely. 'Twasn't for cleanliness I did it, but for coolness."

"I wish I might go and dip my head in," said poor little Tom.

"Thou come along," said Grimes; "what dost want with washing thyself? Thou did not drink half a gallon of beer last night, like me."

"I don't care for you," said naughty Tom, and ran down to the stream, and began washing his face.

Grimes was very sulky, because the woman preferred Tom's company to his; so he dashed at him with horrid words, and tore him up from his knees, and began beating him. But Tom was used to that, and got his head safe between Mr. Grimes' legs, and kicked his shins with all his might.

"Are you not ashamed of yourself, Thomas Grimes?" cried the Irishwoman over the wall.

Grimes looked up, startled at her knowing his name; but all he answered was, "No, nor never was yet"; and went on beating Tom.

"True for you. If you ever had been ashamed of yourself, you would have gone over into Vendale long ago."

"What do you know about Vendale?" shouted Grimes: but he left off beating Tom.

"I know about Vendale, and about you, too. I know, for instance, what happened by night two years ago."

"You do?" shouted Grimes; and leaving Tom, he climbed up over the wall, and faced the woman. Tom thought he was going to strike her; but she looked him too full and fierce in the face for that.

"Yes; I was there," said the Irishwoman quietly.

"You are no Irish woman, by your speech," said Grimes, after many bad words.

"Never mind who I am. I saw what I saw; and if you strike that boy again, I can tell what I know."

Grimes seemed quite cowed, and got on his donkey without another word.

"Stop!" said the Irishwoman. "I have one more word for you both; for you will both see me again before all is over. Those that wish to be clean, clean they will be; and those that wish to be foul, foul they will be. Remember."

And she turned away, and through a gate into the

meadow. Grimes stood still a moment, like a man who had been stunned. Then he rushed after her, shouting, "You come back." But when he got into the meadow, the woman was not there.

Had she hidden away? There was no place to hide in. But Grimes looked about, and Tom also, for he was as puzzled as Grimes himself at her disappearing so suddenly; but look where they would, she was not there.

Grimes came back again, as silent as a post, for he was a little frightened; and, getting on his donkey, filled a fresh pipe, and smoked away, leaving Tom in peace.

CHAPTER 2

TOM'S EXPERIENCES AT HARTHOVER PLACE

And now they had gone three miles and more, and came to Sir John's lodge-gates.

Very grand lodges they were, with very grand iron gates and stone gate-posts, and on the top of each a most dreadful bogy, all teeth, horns, and tail.

Grimes rang at the gate, and out came a keeper on the spot, and opened.

"I was told to expect thee," he said.

The keeper went with them; and, to Tom's surprise, he and Grimes chatted together all the way quite pleasantly.

They walked up a great lime avenue, a full mile long, and between their stems Tom peeped trembling at the horns of the sleeping deer, which stood up among the ferns. Tom had never seen such large trees, and as he looked up he fancied that the blue sky rested on their heads. But he was puzzled very much by a strange murmuring noise, which followed them all the way. So much puzzled, that at last he took courage to ask the keeper what it was.

He spoke very civilly, and called him Sir, for he was very much afraid of him, which pleased the keeper, and he told him that they were the bees about the lime flowers.

"What are bees?" asked Tom.

"What make honey."

"What is honey?" asked Tom.

"Thou hold thy noise," said Grimes.

"Let the boy be," said the keeper. "He's a civil young chap now, and that's more than he'll be long if he bides with thee."

"I wish I were a keeper," said Tom, "to live in such a beautiful place, and wear green velveteens, and have a real dog-whistle at my button, like you."

The keeper laughed; he was a kind-hearted fellow enough.

By this time they were come up to the great iron gates in front of the house; and Tom stared through them at the rhododendrons and azaleas, which were all in flower; and then at the house itself, and wondered how many chimneys there were in it, and how long ago it was built, and what was the man's name that built it, and whether he got much money for his job?

But Tom and his master did not go in through the great iron gates, but round the back way, and a very long way round it was; and into a little back-door, where the ash-boy let them in, yawning horribly; and then in a passage the housekeeper met them, and she gave Grimes solemn orders about "You will take care of this, and take care of that," as if he was going up the chimneys, and not Tom. And then the housekeeper turned them into a grand room, all covered up in sheets of brown paper, and bade them begin; and so after a whimper or two, and a kick from his master, into the grate Tom went, and up the chimney, while a housemaid stayed in the room to watch the furniture.

How many chimneys Tom swept I cannot say; but he swept so many that he got quite tired, and puzzled too, for they were not like the town flues to which he was accustomed, but such as you would find in old country-houses, large and crooked chimneys, which had been altered again and again, till they ran one into another. So Tom fairly lost his way in them; but at last, coming down as he thought the right chimney, he came down the wrong one, and found himself standing on the hearthrug in a room the like of which he had never seen before.

Tom had never seen the like. He had never been in gentlefolks' rooms but when the carpets were all up, and the curtains down, and the furniture huddled together under a cloth, and the pictures covered with aprons and dusters; and he had often enough wondered what the rooms were like when they were all ready for the quality to sit in. And now he saw, and he thought the sight very pretty.

The room was all dressed in white—white window-curtains, white bed-curtains, white furniture, and white walls, with just a few lines of pink here and there. The carpet was all over gay little flowers; and the walls were hung with pictures in gilt frames, which amused Tom very much. There were pictures of ladies and gentlemen, and pictures of horses and dogs. But the two pictures which took his fancy most were, one a man in long garments, with little children and their mothers round him, who was laying his hand upon the children's heads. That was a very pretty picture, Tom thought, to hang in a lady's room. For he could see that it was a lady's room by the dresses which lay about.

The other picture was that of a man nailed to a cross, which surprised Tom much. He fancied that he had seen something like it in a shop window. But why was it there? "Poor man," thought Tom, "and he looks so kind and quiet. But why should the lady have such a sad picture as that in her room?" And Tom felt sad, and awed, and turned to look at something else.

The next thing he saw, and that too puzzled him, was a washing-stand, with pewters and basins, and soap and brushes, and towels, and a large bath full of clean water—what a heap of things all for washing! "She must be a very dirty lady," thought Tom, thinking of his master, "to want as much scrubbing as all that. But she must be very cunning to put the dirt out of the way so well afterwards, for I don't see a speck about the room, not even on the very towels."

And then, looking toward the bed, he saw that dirty lady, and held his breath with astonishment.

Under the snow-white coverlet, upon the snow-white pillow, lay the most beautiful little girl that Tom had ever seen. Her cheeks were almost as white as the pillow, and her hair was like threads of gold spread all about over the bed. She might have been as old as Tom, or maybe a year or two older; but Tom did not think of that. He thought only of her delicate skin and golden hair, and wondered whether she was a real live person, or one of the wax dolls he had seen in the shops. But when he saw her breathe, he made up his mind that she was alive, and stood staring at her, as if she had been an angel out of heaven.

No. She cannot be dirty. She never could have been dirty, thought Tom to himself And then he thought, "And are all people like that when they are washed?" And he looked at his own wrist, and tried to rub the soot off, and wondered whether it ever would come off. "Certainly I should look much prettier then, if I grew at all like her."

And looking round, he suddenly saw, standing close to him, a little ugly, black, ragged figure, with bleared eyes and grinning white teeth. He turned on it angrily. What did such a little black ape want in that sweet young lady's room? And behold, it was himself, reflected in a great mirror, the like of which Tom had never seen before.

And Tom, for the first time in his life, found out that he was dirty; and burst into tears with shame and anger; and turned to sneak up the chimney again and hide; and upset the fender and threw the fire-irons down, with a noise as of ten thousand tin kettles tied to ten thousand mad dogs' tails.

Up jumped the little white lady in her bed, and, seeing Tom, screamed as shrill as any peacock. In rushed a stout old nurse from the next room, and seeing Tom likewise, made up her mind that he had come to rob, plunder, destroy, and burn; and dashed at him, as he lay over the fender, so fast that she caught him by the jacket.

But she did not hold him. Tom had been in a policeman's hands many a time, and out of them too, what is more; and he would have been ashamed to face his friends for ever if he had been stupid enough to be caught by an old woman; so he doubled under the good lady's arm, across the room, and out of the window in a moment.

CHAPTER 3

TOM'S ESCAPE

He did not need to drop out, though he would have done so bravely enough. Nor even to let himself down a spout, which would have been an old game to him.

But all under the window spread a tree, with great leaves and sweet white flowers, almost as big as his head. Down the tree he went, like a cat, and across the garden lawn, and over the iron railings, and up the park towards the wood, leaving the old nurse to scream murder and fire at the window.

The undergardener, mowing, saw Tom, and threw down his scythe, and gave chase to poor Tom. The dairymaid heard the noise, got the churn between her knees, and tumbled over it, spilling all the cream; and yet she jumped up, and gave chase to Tom. A groom cleaning Sir John's hack at the stables let him go loose, ran out, and gave chase to Tom. Grimes upset the soot-sack in the new-gravelled yard, and spoilt it all utterly; but he ran out, and gave chase to Tom. The old steward opened the park-gate, and gave chase to Tom. The ploughman left his horses at the headland, and one jumped over the fence, and pulled the other into the ditch, plough and all; but he ran on, and gave chase to Tom. The keeper, who was taking a stoat out of a trap, let the stoat go, and caught his own finger; but he jumped up, and ran after Tom. Sir John looked out of his study window, ran out, and gave chase to Tom. The Irishwoman, too, was walking up to the house to beg; but she threw away her bundle, and gave chase to Tom likewise.

In a word, never was there heard such a noise, row, hubbub, babel, shindy, hullabaloo, as that day, when Grimes, gardener, the groom, the dairymaid, Sir John, the steward, the ploughman, the keeper, and the Irish woman, all ran up the park, shouting "Stop thief," in the belief that Tom had at least a thousand pounds' worth of jewels in his empty pockets; and the very magpies and jays followed Tom up, screeching and screaming, as if he were a hunted fox.

And all the while poor Tom paddled up the park with his little bare feet, like a small black gorilla fleeing to the forest.

Tom, of course, made for the woods. He had never been in a wood in his life; but he was sharp enough to know that he might hide in a bush, or swarm up a tree, and, altogether, had more chance there than in the open.

But when he got into the wood, he found it a very different sort of place from what he had fancied. He pushed into a thick cover of rhododendrons, and found himself at once caught in a trap. The boughs laid hold of his legs and arms, poked him in his face and his stomach, made him shut his eyes tight; and when he got through the rhododendrons, the hassock-grass and sedges tumbled him over, and cut his poor little fingers.

"I must get out of this," thought Tom, "or I shall stay here till somebody comes to help me—which is just what I don't want."

But how to get out was the difficult matter. And indeed I don't think he would ever have got out at all, if he had not suddenly run his head against a wall.

Now running your head against a wall is not pleasant, especially if it is a loose wall, with the stones all set on edge, and a sharp cornered one hits you between the eyes and makes you see all manner of beautiful stars. And so Tom hurt his head; but he was a brave boy, and did not mind that at all. He guessed that over the wall the cover would end; and up it he went, and over like a squirrel.

And there he was, out on the great grousemoors, which the country folk called Harthover Fell—heather and bog and rock, stretching away and up, up to the very sky.

Now, Tom was a cunning little fellow—as cunning as an old Exmoor stag.

He knew as well as a stag that if he backed he might throw the hounds out. So the first thing he did when he was over the wall was to make the neatest double sharp to his right, and run along under the wall for nearly half a mile.

Whereby Sir John, and the keeper, and the steward, and the gardener, and the ploughman, and the dairy-maid, and all the hue-and-cry together, went on ahead half a mile in the very opposite direction, and inside the wall, leaving him a mile off on the outside; while Tom heard their shouts die away in the woods and chuckled to himself merrily.

At last he came to a dip in the land, and went to the bottom of it, and then he turned bravely away from the wall and up the moor; for he knew that he had put a hill between him and his enemies, and could go on without their seeing him.

But the Irishwoman, alone of them all, had seen which way Tom went. She had kept ahead of every-one the whole time; and yet she neither walked nor ran. She went along quite smoothly and gracefully, while her feet twinkled past each other so fast that you could not see which was foremost; till every one asked the other who the strange woman was.

When she came to the plantation, they lost sight of her; for she went quietly over the wall after Tom, and followed him wherever he went, and Sir John and the rest saw no more of her.

And now Tom was right away into the heather, but instead of the moor growing flat as he went upwards, it grew more and more broken and hilly, but not so rough but that little Tom could jog along well enough, and find time, too, to stare about at the strange place, which was like a new world to him.

He saw great spiders there, with crowns and crosses marked on their backs, who sat in the middle of their webs, and when they saw Tom coming, shook them so fast that they became invisible. Then he saw lizards, brown and grey and green, and thought they were snakes, and would sting him; but they were as much frightened as he, and shot away into the heath. And then, under a rock, he saw a pretty sight—a great brown, sharp-nosed creature, with a white tag to her brush, and round her four or five smutty little cubs, the funniest fellows Tom ever saw. She lay on her back, rolling about, and stretching out her legs and head and tail in the bright sunshine; and the cubs jumped over her, and ran round her, and nibbled her paws, and lugged her about by the tail; and she seemed to enjoy it mightily.

And next he had a fright; for, as he scrambled up a sandy brow—whirr-poof-poof-cock-cock-kick—something went off in his face, with a most horrid noise. He thought the ground had blown up, and the end of the world come.

And when he opened his eyes (for he shut them very tight) it was only an old cock-grouse, who had been washing himself in sand, and who, when Tom had all but trodden on him, jumped up with a noise like the express train, and went off, screaming "Cur-ru-u-uck, cur-ru-u-uck—murder, thieves, fire—cur-u-uck-cock-kick—the end of the world is come—kick-kick-cock-kick."

So Tom went on and on, he hardly knew why; but he liked the great wide strange place, and the cool fresh bracing air. But he went more and more slowly as he got higher up the hill; for now the ground grew very bad indeed. Instead of soft turf and springy heather, he met great patches of flat limestone rock, with deep cracks between the stones and ledges, filled with ferns; so he had to hop from stone to stone, and now and then he slipped in between, and hurt his little bare toes; but still he would go on and up, he could not tell why.

What would Tom have said if he had seen, walking over the moor behind him, the very same Irish-woman who had taken his part upon the road? But whether it was that he looked too little behind him, or whether it was that she kept out of sight behind the rocks and knolls, he never saw her, though she saw him.

And now he began to get a little hungry, and very thirsty; for he had run a long way, and the sun had risen high in heaven, and the rock was as hot as an oven.

But he could see nothing to eat anywhere, and still less to drink.

The heath was full of bilberries and whimberries; but they were only in flower yet, for it was June. And as for water, who can find that on the top of a limestone rock? Now and then he passed by a deep dark swallow-hole, going down into the earth; and more than once, as he passed, he could hear water falling, trickling, tinkling, many many feet below. How he longed to get down to it, and cool his poor baked lips! But, brave little chimney-sweep as he was, he dared not climb down such chimneys as those.

So he went on and on, till his head spun round with the heat, and he thought he heard church bells ringing, a long way off.

"Ah!" he thought, "where there is a church there will be houses and people; and, perhaps, someone will give me a bit and a sup." So he set off again, to look for the church; for he was sure that he heard the bells quite plain.

And in a minute more, when he looked round, he stopped again, and said, "Why, what a big place the world is!"

And so it was; for, from the top of the mountain, he could see—what could he not see?

Behind him, far below, was Harthover, and the dark woods, and the shining salmon river; and on his left, far below, was the town, and the smoking chimneys of the collieries; and far, far away, the river widened to the shining sea; and little white specks, which were ships, lay on its bosom. Before him lay, spread out like a map, great plains, and farms, and villages, amid dark knots of trees. They all seemed at his very feet; but he had sense to see that they were long miles away.

And to his right rose moor after moor, hill after hill, till they faded away, blue into blue sky. But between him and those moors, and really at his very feet, lay something, to which, as soon as Tom saw it, he determined to go, for that was the place for him.

A deep, deep green and rocky valley, very narrow, and filled with trees; but through the wood, hundreds of feet below him, he could see a clear stream glance. Oh, if he could but get down to that stream! Then, by the stream, he saw the roof of a little cottage, and a little garden set out in squares and beds. And there was a tiny little red thing moving in the garden, no bigger than a fly. As Tom looked down, he saw that it was a woman in a red petticoat. Ah! perhaps she would give him something to eat. And there were the church bells ringing again. Surely there must be a village down there. Well, nobody would know him, or what had happened at the Place. The news could not have got there yet, even if Sir John had set all the policemen in the county after him; and he could get down there in five minutes.

Tom was quite right about the hue-and-cry not having got thither; for he had come, without knowing it, the best part of ten miles from Harthover; but he was wrong about getting down in five minutes, for the cottage was more than a mile off, and a good thousand feet below.

However, down he went, like a brave little man as he was, though he was very footsore, and tired, and hungry, and thirsty; while the church bells rang so loud, he began to think that they must be inside his own head, and the river chimed and tinkled far below; and this was the song which it sang:—

Clear and cool, clear and cool,
By laughing shallow, and dreaming pool;
Cool and clear, cool and clear,
By shining shingle, and foaming wear;
Under the crag where the ouzel sings,
And the ivied wall where the church bell rings,
Undefiled, for the undefiled;
Play by me, bathe in me, mother and child.

Dank and foul, dank and foul,
By the smoky town in its murky cowl;
Foul and dank foul and dank
By wharf and sewer and slimy bank;
Darker and darker the farther I go,
Baser and baser the richer I grow;
Who dare sport with the sin-defiled?
Shrink from me, turn from me, mother and child.

Strong and free, strong and free,
The floodgates are open, away to the sea,
Free and strong, free and strong,
Cleansing my streams as I hurry along,
To the golden sands, and the leaping bar,
And the taintless tide that awaits me afar.
As I lose myself in the infinite main,
Like a soul that has sinned and is pardoned again.
Undefiled for the undefiled;
Play by me, bathe in me, mother and child.

So Tom went down; and all the while he never saw the Irishwoman going down behind him.

Chapter 4

TOM REACHES THE DAME'S SCHOOL

A mile off, and a thousand feet down.

So Tom found it; though it seemed as if he could have thrown a pebble on to the back of the woman in the red petticoat who was weeding in the garden, or even across the dale to the rocks beyond. For the bottom of the valley was just one field broad, and on the other side ran the stream; and above it, grey crag, grey down, grey stair, grey moor walled up to heaven.

So Tom went to go down; and first he went down three hundred feet of steep heather, mixed up with loose brown gritstone, as rough as a file; which was not pleasant to his poor little heels, as he came bump, stump, jump, down the steep. And still he thought he could throw a stone into the garden.

Then he went down three hundred feet of limestone terraces, one below the other, as straight as if a carpenter had ruled them with his ruler and then cut them out with his chisel. There was no heath there, but—

First, a little grass slope, covered with the prettiest flowers, rock-rose and saxifrage, and thyme and basil, and all sorts of sweet herbs.

Then bump down a two-foot step of limestone.

Then another bit of grass and flowers.

Then bump down a one-foot-step.

Then another bit of grass and flowers for fifty yards, as steep as the house roof, where he had to slide down.

Then another step of stone, ten feet high; and there he had to stop himself, and crawl along the edge to find a crack; for if he had rolled over, he would have rolled right into the old woman's garden, and frightened her out of her wits.

Then, when he had found a dark narrow crack, full of fern, and had crawled down through it, with knees and elbows, as he would down a chimney, there was another grass slope, and another step, and so on, till—oh, dear me! I wish it was all over; and so did he. And yet he thought he could throw a stone into the old woman's garden.

At last he came to a bank of beautiful shrubs; whitebeam with its great silver-backed leaves, and mountain-ash, and oak; and below them cliff and crag, cliff and crag, with great beds of crown-ferns and wood-sedge; while through the shrubs he could see the stream sparkling, and hear it murmur on the white pebbles. He did not know that it was three hundred feet below.

You would have been giddy, perhaps, at looking down: but Tom was not. He was a brave little chimney-sweep; and when he found himself on the top of a high cliff, instead of sitting down and crying, he said, "Ah, this will just suit me!" though he was very tired; and down he went, by stock and stone, sedge and ledge, bush and rush, as if he had been born a jolly little black ape, with four hands instead of two.

And all the while he never saw the Irishwoman coming down behind him.

But he was getting terribly tired now. The burning sun on the fells had sucked him up; but the damp heat of the woody crag sucked him up still more; and the perspiration ran out of the ends of his fingers and toes, and washed him cleaner than he had been for a whole year. But, of course, he dirtied everything terribly as he went. There has been a great black smudge all down the crag ever since.

At last he got to the bottom. But behold, it was not the bottom—as people usually find when they are coming down a mountain. For at the foot of the crag were heaps and heaps of fallen limestone, with holes between them full of sweet heath-fern; and before Tom got through them, he was out in the bright sunshine again; and then he felt, once for all and suddenly, as people generally do, that he was b-e-a-t, beat.

He could not get on. The sun was burning, and yet he felt chill all over. He was quite empty, and yet he felt quite sick. There was but two hundred yards of smooth pasture between him and the cottage, and yet he could not walk down it. He could hear the stream murmuring only one field beyond it, and yet it seemed to him as if it was a hundred miles off.

He lay down on the grass till the beetles ran over him, and the flies settled on his nose. I don't know when he would have got up again, if the gnats and the midges had not taken compassion on him. But the gnats blew their trumpets so loud in his ear, and the midges nibbled so at his hands and face wherever they could find a place free from soot, that at last he woke up, and stumbled away, down over a low wall, and into a narrow road, and up to the cottage door.

And a neat pretty cottage it was, with clipped yew hedges all round the garden.

He came slowly up to the open door, which was all hung round with clematis and roses; and then peeped in, half afraid.

And there sat by the empty fireplace the nicest old woman that ever was seen, in her red petticoat, and short dimity bedgown, and clean white cap, with a black silk handkerchief over it, tied under her chin. At her feet sat the grandfather of all the cats; and opposite her sat, on two benches, twelve or fourteen neat, rosy, chubby little children, learning their letters; and gabble enough they made about it.

All the children started at Tom's dirty black figure—the girls began to cry, and the boys began to laugh, and all pointed at him rudely enough; but Tom was too tired to care for that.

"What art thou, and what dost want?" cried the old dame. "A chimney-sweep! Away with thee! I'll have no sweeps here."

"Water," said poor little Tom, quite faint.

"Water? There's plenty i' the beck," she said, quite sharply.

"But I can't get there; I'm most clemmed with hunger and drought" And Tom sank down upon the doorstep, and laid his head against the post.

And the old dame looked at him through her spectacles one minute, and two, and three; and then she said, "He's sick; and a bairn's a bairn, sweep or none."

"Water," said Tom.

"God forgive me!" and she put by her spectacles, and rose, and came to Tom. "Water's bad for thee; I'll give thee milk." And she toddled off into the next room, and brought a cup of milk and a bit of bread.

Tom drank the milk off at one draught, and then looked up, revived.

"Where didst come from?" said the dame.

"Over the Fell, there," said Tom, and pointed up into the sky.

"Over Harthover? and down Lewthwaite Crag? Art sure thou are not lying?"

"Why should I?" said Tom, and leant his head against the post.

"And how got ye up there?"

"I came over from the Place," and Tom was so tired and desperate he had no heart or time to think of a story, so he told all the truth in a few words.

"Bless thy little heart! And thou hast not been stealing, then?"

"No."

"Bless thy little heart! and I'll warrant not. Why, God's guided the bairn, because he was innocent! Away from the Place, and over Harthover Fell, and down Lewthwaite Crag! Who ever heard the like, if God hadn't led him? Why dost not eat thy bread?"

"I can't."

"It's good enough, for I made it myself"

"I can't," said Tom, and he laid his head on his knees, and then asked—

"Is it Sunday?"

"No, then; why should it be?"

"Because I hear the church bells ringing so."

"Bless thy pretty heart! The bairn's sick. Come wi' me, and I'll hap thee up somewhere. If thou wert a bit cleaner I'd put thee in my own bed, for the Lord's sake. But come along here."

But when Tom tried to get up, he was so tired and giddy that she had to help him and lead him.

She put him in an outhouse upon soft sweet hay and an old rug, and bade him sleep off his walk, and she would come to him when school was over, in an hour's time.

And so she went in again, expecting Tom to fall fast asleep at once.

But Tom did not fall asleep.

Instead of it he turned and tossed and kicked about in the strangest way, and felt so hot all over that he longed to get into the river and cool himself; and then he fell half asleep, and dreamt that he heard the little white lady crying to him, "Oh, you're so dirty; go and be washed"; and then that he heard the Irishwoman saying, "Those that wish to be clean, clean they will be." And then he heard the church bells ring so loud, close to him too, that he was sure it must be Sunday, in spite of what the old dame had said; and he would go to church, and see what a church was like inside, for he had never been in one, poor little fellow, in all his life. But the people would never let him come in, all over soot and dirt like that. He must go to the river and wash first. And he said out loud again and again, though being half asleep he did not know it, "I must be clean, I must be clean."

And all of a sudden he found himself, not in the outhouse on the hay, but in the middle of a meadow, over the road, with the stream just before him, saying, continually, "I must be clean, I must be clean." He had got there on his own legs, between sleep and awake, as children will often get out of bed, and go about the room, when they are not quite well. But he was not a bit surprised, and went on to the bank of the brook, and lay down on the grass, and looked into the clear, clear limestone water, with every pebble at the bottom bright and clean, while the little silver trout dashed about in fright at the sight of his black face; and he dipped his hand in and found it so cool, cool, cool; and he said, "I will be a fish; I will swim in the water; I must be clean, I must be clean."

So he pulled off all his clothes in such haste that he tore some of them, which was easy enough with such ragged old things. And he put his poor hot sore feet into the water; and then his legs; and the farther he went in, the more the church bells rang in his head.

"Ah," said Tom, "I must be quick and wash myself; the bells are ringing quite loud now; and they will stop soon, and then the door will be shut, and I shall never be able to get in at all."

And all the while he never saw the Irishwoman, not behind him this time, but before.

For just before he came to the river side, she had stepped down into the cool clear water; and her shawl and her petticoat floated off her, and the green water-weeds floated round her sides, and the white water-lilies floated round her head, and the fairies of the stream came up from the bottom and bore her away and down upon their arms; for she was the Queen of them all; and perhaps of more besides.

"Where have you been?" they asked her.

"I have been smoothing sick folks' pillows, and whispering sweet dreams into their ears; opening cottage casements, to let out the stifling air; coaxing little children away from gutters, and foul pools where fever breeds; turning women from the gin-shop door, and staying men's hands as they were going to strike their wives; doing all I can to help those who will not help themselves: and little enough that is, and weary work for me. But I have brought you a new little brother, and watched him safe all the way here."

Then all the fairies laughed for joy at the thought that they had a little brother coming.

"But mind, maidens, he must not see you, or know that you are here. He is but a savage now, and like the beasts which perish; and from the beasts which perish he must learn. So you must not play with him, or speak to him, or let him see you: but only keep him from being harmed."

Then the fairies were sad, because they could not play with their new brother, but they always did what they were told.

And their Queen floated away down the river; and whither she went, thither she came. But all this Tom, of course, never saw or heard; for he was so hot and thirsty, and longed so to be clean for once, that he tumbled himself as quick as he could into the clear cool stream.

And he had not been in it two minutes before he fell fast asleep, into the quietest, sunniest, cosiest sleep that ever he had in his life; and he dreamt about the green meadows by which he had walked that morning, and the tall elm-trees, and the sleeping cows; and after that he dreamt of nothing at all.

The reason of his falling into such a delightful sleep is very simple; and yet hardly any one has found it out. It was merely that the fairies took him.

Some people think that there are no fairies, but we will make believe that there are fairies in the world. There must be fairies; for this is a fairy tale: and how can one have a fairy tale if there are no fairies?

The kind old dame came back at twelve, when school was over, to look at Tom: but there was no Tom there. She looked about for his footprints; but the ground was so hard that there was not one to be seen anywhere.

So the old dame went in again quite sulky, thinking that little Tom had tricked her with a false story, and shammed ill, and then run away again.

But she altered her mind the next day. For, when Sir John and the rest of them had run themselves out of breath, and lost Tom, they went back again, looking very foolish.

And they looked more foolish still when Sir John heard more of the story from the nurse; and more foolish still, again, when they heard the whole story from Miss Ellie, the little lady in white. All she had seen was a poor little black chimney-sweep, crying and sobbing, and going to get up the chimney again. Of course, she was very much frightened: and no wonder. But that was all. The boy had taken nothing in the room; by the mark of his little sooty feet, they could see that he had never been off the hearthrug till the nurse caught hold of him. It was all a mistake.

So Sir John told Grimes to go home, and promised him five shillings if he would bring the boy quietly up to him, without beating him, that he might be sure of the truth. For he took for granted, and Grimes too, that Tom had made his way home.

But no Tom came back to Mr. Grimes that evening; and he went to the police-office, to tell them to look out for the boy. But no Tom was heard of. As for his having gone over those great fells to Vendale, they no more dreamed of that than of his having gone to the moon.

So Mr. Grimes came up to Harthover next day with a very sour face; but when he got there, Sir John was over the hills and far away; and Mr. Grimes had to sit in the outer servants' hall all day, and wait until Sir John came back.

For good Sir John had slept very badly that night; and he said to his lady, "My dear, the boy must have got over into the grouse-moors, and lost himself."

So, at five the next morning up he got, and into his bath, and into his shooting jacket and gaiters, and into the stable-yard, and bade them bring his shooting pony, and the keeper to come on his pony, and the huntsman, and the first whip, and the second whip, and the under-keeper with the bloodhound in a leash—a great dog as tall as a calf, of the colour of a gravel walk, with mahogany ears and nose, and a throat like a church bell. They took him up to the place where Tom had gone into the wood; and there the hound lifted up his mighty voice, and told them all he knew.

Then he took them to the place where Tom had climbed the wall; and they shoved it down, and all got through.

And then the wise dog took them over the moor, and over the fells, step by step, very slowly; for the scent was a day old, you know, and very light from the heat and drought. But that was why cunning old Sir John started at five in the morning.

And at last he came to the top of Lewthwaite Crag, and there he bayed, and looked up in their faces, as much as to say, "I tell you he is gone down here!"

They could hardly believe that Tom would have gone so far; and when they looked at that awful cliff, they could never believe that he would have dared to face it. But if the dog said so, it must be true.

"Heaven forgive us!" said Sir John. "If we find him at all, we shall find him lying at the bottom." And he slapped his great hand upon his great thigh, and said—

"Who will go down over Lewthwaite Crag, and see if that boy is alive? Oh that I were twenty years younger, and I would go down myself!" And so he would have done, as well as any sweep in the county. Then he said—

"Twenty pounds to the man who brings me that boy alive!" and, as was his way, what he said he meant.

Now among the lot was a little groom-boy, a very little groom indeed; and he was the same who had ridden up the court, and told Tom to come to the Hall; and he said—

"Twenty pounds or none, I will go down over Lewthwaite Crag, if it's only for the poor boy's sake. For he was as civil a spoken little chap as ever climbed a flue."

So down over Lewthwaite Crag he went: a very smart groom he was at the top, and a very shabby one at the bottom; for he tore his gaiters, and he tore his breeches, and he tore his jacket, and he burst his braces, and he burst his boots, and he lost his hat, and what was worst of all, he lost his shirt pin, which he prized very much, for it was gold: but he never saw anything of Tom.

And all the while Sir John and the rest were riding round, full three miles to the right, and back again, to get into Vendale, and to the foot of the crag.

When they came to the old dame's school, all the children came out to see. And the old dame came out too; and when she saw Sir John, she curtsied very low, for she was a tenant of his.

"Well, dame, and how are you?" said Sir John.

"Blessings on you as broad as your back, Harthover," says she—she didn't call him Sir John, but only Harthover, for that is the fashion in the North Country—"and welcome into Vendale: but you're no hunting the fox this time of the year?"

"I am hunting, and strange game too," said he.

"Blessings on your heart, and what makes you look so sad the morn?"

"I'm looking for a lost child, a chimney-sweep, that is run away."

"Oh, Harthover, Harthover," says she, "ye'll no harm the poor little lad if I give you tidings of him?"

"Not I, not I, dame. I'm afraid we hunted him out of the house all on a miserable mistake, and the hound has brought him to the top of Lewthwaite Crag, and—"

Whereat the old dame broke out crying, without letting him finish his story.

"So he told me the truth after all, poor little dear!" And then she told Sir John all.

"Bring the dog here, and lay him on," said Sir John, without another word, and he set his teeth very hard.

And the dog opened at once; and went away at the back of the cottage, over the road, and over the meadow, and through a bit of alder copse; and there, upon an alder stump, they saw Tom's clothes lying. And then they knew as much about it all as there was any need to know.

CHAPTER 5

TOM BECOMES A WATER-BABY

And Tom?

Ah, now comes the most wonderful part of this wonderful story. Tom, when he woke, for of course he woke—children always wake after they have slept exactly as long as is good for them—found himself swimming about in the stream, being about four inches long, and having round his neck a set of gills just like those of a sucking eft, which he mistook for a lace frill, till he pulled at them, found he hurt himself, and made up his mind that they were part of himself, and best left alone.

In fact, the fairies had turned him into a water-baby.

A water-baby? You never heard of a water-baby? Perhaps not. That is the very reason why this story was written. There are a great many things in the world which you never heard of; and a great many more which nobody ever heard of.

"But there are no such things as water-babies."

How do you know that? Have you been there to see? And if you had been there to see, and had seen none, that would not prove that there were none.

No water-babies, indeed? Why, wise men of old said that everything on earth had its double in the water. There are land-babies—then why not water-babies? Are there not water-rats, water-lilies, water-crickets, water-crabs, water-tortoises, water-scorpions, water-tigers and water-hogs, water-cats and water-dogs, sea-lions and sea-bears, sea-horses and sea-elephants, sea-mice and sea-urchins, sea-razors and sea-pens, sea-combs and sea-fans, and of plants, are there not water-grass, and water-crowfoot, water-milfoil, and so on, without end?

"But all these things are only nicknames; the water things are not really akin to the land things."

That's not always true. They are, in millions of cases, not only of the same family, but actually the same individual creatures. Do not even you know that a green drake, and an alder-fly, and a dragon-fly, live under water till they change their skins, just as Tom changed his? And if a water animal can continually change into a land animal, why should not a land animal sometimes change into a water animal?

But at all events, so it happened to Tom. And, therefore, the keeper, and the groom, and Sir John made a great mistake, and were very unhappy (Sir John at least) without any reason, when they found a black thing in the water, and said it was Tom's body, and that he had been drowned. They were utterly mistaken. Tom was quite alive; and cleaner, and merrier, than he ever had been. The fairies had washed him, you see, in the swift river, so thoroughly, that not only his dirt, but his whole husk and shell had been washed quite off him, and the pretty little real Tom was washed out of the inside of it, and swam away, as a caddis does when its case of stones and silk is bored through, and away it goes on its back, paddling to the shore, there to split its skin, and fly away as a caperer, on four fawn-coloured wings, with long legs and horns. They are foolish fellows, the caperers, and fly into the candle at night, if you leave the door open. We will hope Tom will be wiser, now he has got safe out of his sooty old shell.

But good Sir John did not understand all this, and he took it into his head that Tom was drowned. When they looked into the empty pockets of his shell, and found no jewels there, nor money—nothing but three marbles, and a brass button with a string to it—then Sir John did something as like crying as ever he did in his life, and blamed himself more bitterly than he need have done. So he cried, and the groom-boy cried, and the huntsman cried, and the dame cried, and the little girl cried, and the dairymaid cried, and the old nurse cried (for it was somewhat her fault), and my lady cried; but the keeper did not cry, though he had been so good-natured to Tom the morning before; for he was so dried up with running after poachers, that you could no more get tears out of him than milk out of leather: and Grimes did not cry for Sir John gave him ten pounds, and he drank it all in a week. And the little girl would not play with her dolls for a whole week, and never forgot poor little Tom. And soon my lady put a pretty little tombstone over Tom's shell in the little churchyard in Vendale, where the old dalesmen all sleep side by side between the limestone crags. And the dame decked it with garlands every Sunday, till she grew so old that she could not stir abroad; then the little children decked it for her. And always she sang an old old song, as she sat spinning what she called her wedding-dress. The children could not understand it, but they liked it none the less for that; for it was very sweet, and very sad; and that was enough for them. And these are the words of it:—

When all the world is young, lad,
And all the trees are green;
And every goose a swan, lad,
And every lass a queen;
Then hey for boot and horse, lad,
And round the world away;
Young blood must have its course, lad,
And every dog his day.

When all the world is old, lad,
And all the trees are brown;
And all the sport is stale, lad,
And all the wheels run down;
Creep home, and take your place there,
The spent and maimed among;
God grant you find one face there,
You loved when all was young.

Those are the words: but they are only the body of it: the soul of the song was the dear old woman's sweet face, and sweet voice, and the sweet old air to which she sang; and that, alas! one cannot put on paper. And at last she grew so stiff and lame, that the angels were forced to carry her; and they helped her on with her wedding-dress, and carried her up over Harthover Fells, and a long way beyond that too; and there was a new schoolmistress in Vendale.

And all the while Tom was swimming about in the river, with a pretty little lace-collar of gills about his neck, as lively as a grig, and as clean as a fresh-run salmon.

CHAPTER 6

TOM'S FIRST EXPERIENCES IN THE WATER

Tom was now quite amphibious, which means that he was both an animal and a fish: and what is better still, he was clean. For the first time in his life, he felt how comfortable it was to have nothing on him but himself. But he only enjoyed it: he did not know it, or think about it; just as you enjoy life and health, and yet never think about being alive and healthy.

He did not remember having ever been dirty. Indeed, he did not remember any of his old troubles, being tired, or hungry, or beaten, or sent up dark chimneys. Since that sweet sleep, he had forgotten all about his master, and Harthover Place, and the little white girl, and in a word, all that had happened to him when he lived before; and what was best of all, he had forgotten all the bad words which he had learned from Grimes, and the rude boys with whom he used to play.

That is not strange: for you know, when you came into this world, and became a land-baby, you remembered nothing. So why should he, when he became a water-baby?

But Tom was very happy in the water. He had been sadly over-worked in the land-world; and so now, to make up for that, he had nothing but holidays in the water-world for a long, long time to come. He had nothing to do now but enjoy himself, and look at all the pretty things which are to be seen in the cool clear water-world, where the sun is never too hot, and the frost is never too cold.

And what did he live on? Water-cresses, perhaps; or perhaps water-gruel, and water-milk.

Sometimes he went along the smooth gravel water-ways, looking at the crickets which ran in and out among the stones, as rabbits do on land; or he climbed over the ledges of rock, and saw the sand-pipes hanging in thousands, with every one of them a pretty little head and legs peeping out; or he went into a still corner, and watched the caddises eating dead sticks as greedily as you would eat plum-pudding, and building their houses with silk and glue. Very fanciful ladies they were; none of them would keep to the same materials for a day. One would begin with some pebbles; then she would stick on a piece of green wood; then she found a shell, and stuck it on too; and the poor shell was alive, and did not like at all being taken to build houses with; then she stuck on a piece of rotten wood, then a very smart pink stone, and so on, till she was patched all over like an Irishman's coat. Then she found a long straw, five times as long as herself, and said, "Hurrah! my sister has a tail, and I'll have one too"; and she stuck it on her back, and marched about with it quite proud, though it was very inconvenient indeed. And, at that, tails became all the fashion among the caddis baits in that pool, and they all toddled about with long straws sticking out behind, getting between each other's legs, and tumbling over each other, and looking so ridiculous, that Tom laughed at them till he cried.

Then sometimes he came to a deep still reach; and there he saw the water-forests. They would have looked to you only little weeds: but Tom, you must remember, was so little that everything looked a hundred times as big to him as it does to you, just as things do to a minnow, who sees and catches the little water-creatures which you can only see in a microscope.

And in the water-forest he saw the water-monkeys and water-squirrels (they had all six legs, though; everything almost has six legs in the water, except efts and water-babies); and nimbly enough they ran among the branches. There were water-flowers there too, in thousands; and Tom tried to pick them: but as soon as he touched them, they drew themselves in and turned into knots of jelly; and then Tom saw that they were all alive—bells, and stars, and wheels, and flowers, of all beautiful shapes and colours; and all alive and busy, just as Tom was. So now he found that there was a great deal more in the world than he had fancied at first sight.

There was one wonderful little fellow, too, who peeped out of the top of a house built of round bricks. He had two big wheels, and one little one, all over teeth, spinning round and round like the wheels in a threshing-machine; and Tom stood and stared at him, to see what he was going to make with his machinery. And what do you think he was doing? Brick-making. With his two big wheels he swept together all the mud which floated in the water: all that was nice in it he put into his stomach and ate; and all the mud he put into the little wheel on his breast, which really was a round hole set with teeth; and there he spun it into a neat hard round brick; and then he took it and stuck it on the top of his house-wall, and set to work to make another. Now was not he a clever little fellow?

Tom thought so: but when he wanted to talk to him the brick-maker was much too busy and proud of his work to take notice of him.

Now you must know that all the things under the water talk; only not such a language as ours; but such as horses, and dogs, and cows, and birds talk to each other; and Tom soon learned to understand them and talk to them; so that he might have had very pleasant company if he had only been a good boy. But I am sorry to say, he was too like some other little boys, very fond of hunting and tormenting creatures for mere sport. Some people say that boys cannot help it; that it is nature. But whether it is nature or not, little boys can help it, and must help it. For if they have naughty, low, mischievous tricks in their nature, as monkeys have, that is no reason why they should give way to those tricks like monkeys, who know no better. And therefore they must not torment dumb creatures; for if they do, a certain old lady who is coming will surely give them exactly what they deserve.

But Tom did not know that; and he pecked and hounded the poor water-things about sadly, till they were all afraid of him, and got out of his way, or crept into their shells; so he had no one to speak to or play with.

The water-fairies, of course, were very sorry to see him so unhappy, and longed to take him, and tell him how naughty he was, and teach him to be good, and to play and romp with him too: but they had been forbidden to do that. Tom had to learn his lesson for himself by sound and sharp experience.

At last one day he found a caddis, and wanted it to peep out of its house: but its house-door was shut. He had never seen a caddis with a house-door before: so what must he do, the meddlesome little fellow, but pull it open, to see what the poor lady was doing inside. What a shame! How should you like to have any one breaking your bedroom-door in, to see how you looked when you were in bed? So Tom broke to pieces the door, which was the prettiest little grating of silk, stuck all over with shining bits of crystal; and when he looked in, the caddis poked out her head, and it had turned into just the shape of a bird's. But when Tom spoke to her she could not answer; for her mouth and face were tight tied up in a new night-cap of neat pink skin. However, if she didn't answer, all the other caddises did; for they held up their hands and shrieked like the cats in Struwwelpeter: "Oh, you nasty horrid boy; there you are at it again! And she had just laid herself up for a fortnight's sleep, and then she would have come out with such beautiful wings, and flown about, and laid such lots of eggs: and now you have broken her door, and she can't mend it because her mouth is tied up for a fortnight, and she will die. Who sent you here to worry us out of our lives?"

So Tom swam away. He was very much ashamed of himself, and felt all the naughtier; as little boys do when they have done wrong and won't say so.

Then he came to a pool full of little trout, and began tormenting them, and trying to catch them: but they slipped through his fingers, and jumped clean out of the water in their fright. But as Tom chased them, he came close to a great dark hole under an alder root, and out floushed a huge old brown trout ten times as big as he was, and ran right against him, and knocked all the breath out of his body; and I don't know which was the more frightened of the two.

Then he went on sulky and lonely, as he deserved to be; and under a bank he saw a very ugly dirty creature sitting, about half as big as himself; which had six legs, and a big stomach, and a most ridiculous head with two great eyes and a face just like a donkey's.

"Oh," said Tom, "you are an ugly fellow to be sure!" and he began making faces at him; and put his nose close to him, and halloed at him, like a very rude boy.

When, hey presto; all the thing's donkey-face came off in a moment, and out popped a long arm with a pair of pincers at the end of it, and caught Tom by the nose. It did not hurt him much; but it held him quite tight.

"Yah, ah! Oh, let me go!" cried Tom.

"Then let me go," said the creature. "I want to be quiet. I want to split."

Tom promised to let him alone, and he let go. "Why do you want to split?" said Tom.

"Because my brothers and sisters have all split, and turned into beautiful creatures with wings; and I want to split too. Don't speak to me. I am sure I shall split. I will split!"

Tom stood still, and watched him. And he swelled himself, and puffed, and stretched himself out stiff, and at last—crack, puff, bang—he opened all down his back, and then up to the top of his head.

And out of his inside came the most slender, elegant, soft creature, as soft and smooth as Tom: but very pale and weak, like a little child who has been ill a long time in a dark room. It moved its legs very feebly; and looked about it half ashamed; and then it began walking slowly up a grass stem to the top of the water.

Tom was so astonished that he never said a word: but he stared with all his eyes. And he went up to the top of the water too, and peeped out to see what would happen.

And as the creature sat in the warm bright sun, a wonderful change came over it. It grew strong and firm; the most lovely colours began to show on its body, blue and yellow and black, spots and bars and rings; out of its back rose four great wings of bright brown gauze; and its eyes grew so large that they filled all its head, and shone like ten thousand diamonds.

"Oh, you beautiful creature!" said Tom; and he put out his hand to catch it.

But the thing whirred up into the air, and hung poised on its wings a moment, and then settled down again by Tom quite fearless.

"No!" it said, "you cannot catch me. I am a dragon-fly now, the king of all the flies; and I shall dance in the sunshine, and hawk over the river, and catch gnats, and have a beautiful wife like myself. I know what I shall do. Hurrah!" And he flew away into the air, and began catching gnats.

"Oh! come back, come back," cried Tom, "you beautiful creature. I have no one to play with, and I am so lonely here. If you will but come back I will never try to catch you."

"I don't care whether you do or not," said the dragon-fly; "for you can't. But when I have had my dinner, and looked a little about this pretty place, I will come back, and have a little chat about all I have seen in my travels. Why, what a huge tree this is! and what huge leaves on it!"

It was only a big dock: but you know the dragon-fly had never seen any but little water-trees; so it did look very big to him.

The dragon-fly did come back, and chatted away with Tom. He was a little conceited about his fine colours and his large wings; but you know, he had been a poor dirty ugly creature all his life before; so there were great excuses for him. He was very fond of talking about all the wonderful things he saw in the trees and the meadows; and Tom liked to listen to him, for he had forgotten all about them. So in a little while they became great friends.

And I am very glad to say, that Tom learned such a lesson that day, that he did not torment creatures for a long time after. And then the caddises grew quite tame, and used to tell him strange stories about the way they built their houses, and changed their skins, and turned at last into winged flies; till Tom began to long to change his skin, and have wings like them some day.

And the trout and he made it up (for trout very soon forget if they have been frightened and hurt). So Tom used to play with them at hare and hounds, and great fun they had; and he used to try to leap out of the water, head over heels, as they did before a shower came on; but somehow he never could manage it. He liked most, though, to see them rising at the flies, as they sailed round and round under the shadow of the great oak, where the beetles fell flop into the water, and the green caterpillars let themselves down from the boughs by silk ropes for no reason at all; and then changed their foolish minds for no reason at all either; and hauled themselves up again into the tree, rolling up the rope in a ball between their paws.

And very often Tom caught them just as they touched the water; and caught the alder-flies, and the caperers, and the cock-tailed duns and spinners, yellow, and brown, and claret, and grey, and gave them to his friends the trout. Perhaps he was not quite kind to the flies; but one must do a good turn to one's friends when one can.

And at last he gave up catching even the flies; for he made acquaintance with one by accident and found him a very merry little fellow. And this was the way it happened; and it is all quite true.

He was basking at the top of the water one hot day in July, catching duns and feeding the trout, when he saw a new sort, a dark grey little fellow with a brown head. He was a very little fellow indeed: but he made the most of himself, as people ought to do. He cocked up his head, and he cocked up his wings, and he cocked up his tail, and he cocked up the two whisks at his tail-end, and, in short, he looked the cockiest little man of all little men. And so he proved to be; for instead of getting away, he hopped upon Tom's finger, and he cried out in the tiniest, shrillest, squeakiest little voice you ever heard.

"Much obliged to you, indeed; but I don't want it yet."

"Want what?" said Tom, quite taken aback by his impudence.

"Your leg, which you are kind enough to hold out for me to sit on. I must just go and see after my wife for a few minutes. Dear me! what a troublesome business a family is!" (though the idle little rogue did nothing at all, but left his poor wife to lay all the eggs by herself). "When I come back, I shall be glad of it, if you'll be so good as to keep it sticking out just so"; and off he flew.

Tom thought him a very cool sort of personage; and still more so, when, in five minutes he came back, and said—"Ah, you were tired waiting? Well, your other leg will do as well."

And he popped himself down on Tom's knee, and began chatting away in his squeaking voice.

"So you live under the water? It's a low place. I lived there for some time; and was very shabby and dirty. But I didn't choose that that should last. So I turned respectable, and came up to the top, and put on this grey suit. It's a very business-like suit, you think, don't you?"

"Very neat and quiet indeed," said Tom.

"Yes, one must be quiet and neat and respectable,

and all that sort of thing for a little, when one becomes a family man. But I'm tired of it, that's the truth. I've done quite enough business, I consider, in the last week, to last me my life. So I shall put on a ball-dress, and go out and be a smart man, and see the gay world, and have a dance or two. Why shouldn't one be jolly if one can?"

"And what will become of your wife?"

"Oh! she is a very plain, stupid creature, and that's the truth; and thinks about nothing but eggs. If she chooses to come, why she may; and if not, why I go without her—and here I go."

And as he spoke he turned quite pale, and then quite white.

"Why, you're ill!" said Tom. But he did not answer.

"You're dead," said Tom, looking at him as he stood on his knee as white as a ghost.

"No, I ain't!" answered a little squeaking voice over his head. "This is me up here, in my ball-dress; and that's my skin. Ha, ha! you could not do such a trick as that!"

And no more Tom could, nor all the conjurers in the world. For the little rogue had jumped clean out of his own skin, and left it standing on Tom's knee, eyes, wings, legs, tail, exactly as if it had been alive.

"Ha, ha!" he said, and he jerked and skipped up and down, never stopping an instant, just as if he had St. Vitus's dance. "Ain't I a pretty fellow now?"

And so he was; for his body was white, and his tail orange, and his eyes all the colours of a peacock's tail. And, what was the oddest of all, the whisks at the end of his tail had grown five times as long as they were before.

"Ah!" said he, "now I will see the gay world. My living won't cost me much, for I have no mouth, you see, and no inside; so I can never be hungry nor have the stomach-ache neither."

No more he had. He had grown as dry and hard and empty as a quill, as such silly shallow-hearted fellows deserve to grow.

But, instead of being ashamed of his emptiness, he was quite proud of it, as a good many fine gentlemen are, and began flirting and flipping up and down, and singing—

"My wife shall dance, and I shall sing,
So merrily pass the day;
For I hold it quite the wisest thing,
To drive dull care away."

And he danced up and down for three days and three nights, till he grew so tired, that he tumbled into the water, and floated down. But what became of him Tom never knew, and he himself never minded; for Tom heard him singing to the last, as he floated down—

"To drive dull care away-ay-ay!"

And if he did not care, why nobody else cared either.

CHAPTER 7

TOM MEETS THE OTTER AND THE SALMON

But one day Tom had a new adventure. He was sitting on a water-lily leaf, he and his friend the dragon-fly, watching the gnats dance. The dragon-fly had eaten as many as he wanted, and was sitting quite still and sleepy, for it was very hot and bright, and kept on chatting to Tom about the times when he lived under the water.

Suddenly, Tom heard the strangest noise up the stream; cooing, and grunting, and whining, and squeaking.

He looked up the water, and there he saw a sight as strange as the noise; a great ball rolling over and over down the stream, seeming one moment of soft brown fur, and the next of shining glass: and yet it was not a ball; for sometimes it broke up and streamed away in pieces, and then it joined again; and all the while the noise came out of it louder and louder.

Tom asked the dragon-fly what it could be: but, with his short sight, he could not even see it, though it was not ten yards away. So he took the neatest little header into the water, and started off to see for himself; and, when he came near, the ball turned out to be four or five beautiful creatures, many times larger than Tom, who were swimming about, and rolling, and diving, and twisting, and wrestling, and cuddling, and kissing, and biting, and scratching, in the most charming fashion that ever was seen.

But, when the biggest of them saw Tom, she darted out from the rest, and cried, "Quick, children, here is something to eat, indeed!" and came at poor Tom, showing such a wicked pair of eyes, and such a set of sharp teeth in a grinning mouth, that Tom slipped in between the water-lily roots as fast as he could, and then turned round and made faces at her.

"Come out," said the wicked old otter, "or it will be worse for you."

But Tom looked at her from between two thick roots, and shook them with all his might, making horrible faces all the while, just as he used to grin through the railings at the old women, when he lived before.

"Come away, children," said the otter in disgust, "it is not worth eating, after all. It is only a nasty eft, which nothing eats."

"I am not an eft!" said Tom; "efts have tails."

"You are an eft," said the otter, very positively; "I see your two hands quite plain, and I know you have a tail."

"I tell you I have not," said Tom. "Look here!" and he turned his pretty little self quite round; and sure enough, he had no more tail than you.

"I say you are an eft, and therefore you are, and not fit food for me and my children. You may stay there till the salmon eat you (she knew the salmon would not, but she wanted to frighten poor Tom). Ha! ha! they will eat you, and we will eat them," and the otter laughed such a wicked cruel laugh.

"What are salmon?" asked Tom.

"Fish, you eft, great fish, nice fish to eat. We hunt them up and down the pools, and drive them up into a corner, the silly things; and we catch them, but we disdain to eat them all; we just bite out their soft throats and suck their sweet juice—Oh, so good!"—(and she licked her wicked lips)— "and then throw them away, and go and catch another. They are coming soon, children, coming soon; I can smell the rain coming up off the sea, and then hurrah for salmon, and plenty of eating all day long."

And the otter grew so proud that she turned head over heels twice, and then stood upright half out of the water, grinning like a Cheshire cat.

"And where do they come from?" asked Tom, who kept himself very close, for he was very frightened.

"Out of the sea, eft, the great wide sea, where they might stay and be safe if they liked. But out of the sea the silly things come, into the great river down below, and we come up to watch for them; and when they go down again we go down and follow them. And there we fish for the bass and the pollock, and have jolly days along the shore, and toss and roll in the breakers, and sleep snug in the warm dry crags. Ah, that is a merry life too, children, if it were not for those horrid men."

"What are men?" asked Tom; but somehow he seemed to know before he asked.

"Two-legged things, eft: and, now I come to look at

you, they are actually something like you, if you had not a tail, only a great deal bigger; and they catch the fish with hooks and lines, which get into our feet sometimes, and set pots along the rocks to catch lobsters. They speared my poor dear husband as he went out to find something for me to eat, and I saw them carrying him away upon a pole."

And the otter grew so sad that she sailed solemnly away down the burn, and Tom saw her no more for that time. And lucky it was for her that she did so; for no sooner was she gone, than down the bank came seven little rough terrier dogs, snuffing and yapping, and grubbing and splashing, in full cry after the otter. Tom hid among the water-lilies till they were gone; for he could not guess that they were the water-fairies come to help him.

But he could not help thinking of what the otter had said about the great river and the broad sea. And, as he thought, he longed to go and see them. He could not tell why; but the more he thought, the more he grew discontented with the narrow little stream in which he lived, and all his companions there; and wanted to get out into the wide wide world, and enjoy all the wonderful sights.

And once he set off to go down the stream. But the stream was very low; and when he came to the shallows he could not keep under water, for there was no water left to keep under. So the sun burned his back and made him sick; and he went back again and lay quiet in the pool for a whole week more.

And then, on the evening of a very hot day, he saw a sight.

He had been very stupid all day, and so had the trout; for they would not move an inch to take a fly, though there were thousands on the water, but lay dozing at the bottom under the shade of the stones; and Tom lay dozing too, for the water was quite warm and unpleasant.

But toward evening it grew suddenly dark, and Tom looked up and saw a blanket of black clouds lying right across the valley above his head. He felt not quite frightened, but very still; for everything was still. There was not a whisper of wind, nor a chirp of a bird to be heard; and next a few great drops of rain fell plop into the water, and one hit Tom on the nose, and made him pop his head down quickly enough.

And then the thunder roared, and the lightning flashed, and leapt across Vendale and back again, from cloud to cloud, and cliff to cliff, till the very rocks in the stream seemed to shake: and Tom looked up at it through the water, and thought it the finest thing he ever saw in his life.

But out of the water he dared not put his head; for the rain came down by bucketsful; and soon the stream rose, and rushed down, higher and higher, and fouler and fouler, full of beetles, and sticks, and straws, and worms, and addle-eggs, and wood-lice, and leeches, and other creatures that live in pools.

Tom could hardly stand against the stream, and hid behind a rock. But the trout did not; for out they rushed from among the stones, and began gobbling the beetles and leeches in the most greedy and quarrelsome way, and swimming about with great worms hanging out of their mouths, tugging and kicking to get them away from each other.

And now, by the flashes of the lightning, Tom saw a new sight—all the bottom of the stream alive with great eels, turning and twisting along, all down stream and away. They had been hiding for weeks past in the cracks of the rocks, and in burrows in the mud; and Tom had hardly ever seen them, except now and then at night: but now they were all out, and went hurrying past him so fiercely and wildly that he was quite frightened. And as they hurried past he could hear them say to each other, "We must run, we must run. What a jolly thunderstorm! Down to the sea, down to the sea!"

And then the otter came by with all her brood, twining and sweeping along as fast as the eels themselves; and she spied Tom as she came by, and said:

"Now is your time, eft, if you want to see the world. Come along, children, never mind those nasty eels: we shall breakfast on salmon tomorrow. Down to the sea, down to the sea!"

Then came a flash brighter than all the rest, and by the light of it—in the thousandth part of a second they were gone again—but he had seen them, he was certain of it—three beautiful little white girls, with their arms twined round each other's necks, floating down the torrent, as they sang, "Down to the sea, down to the sea!"

"Oh stay! Wait for me!" cried Tom; but they were gone: yet he could hear their voices clear and sweet through the roar of thunder and water and wind, singing as they died away, "Down to the sea!"

"Down to the sea?" said Tom; "everything is going to the sea, and I will go too. Goodbye, trout."

And now, down the rushing stream, guided by the bright flashes of the storm; past tall rocks; on through narrow strids and roaring cataracts, where Tom was deafened and blinded for a moment by the rushing waters; along deep reaches, where the white water-lilies tossed and flapped beneath the wind and hail; past sleeping villages; under dark bridge-arches, and away and away to the sea. And Tom could not stop, and did not care to stop; he would see the great world below, and the salmon, and the breakers, and the wide wide sea.

And when the daylight came, Tom found himself out in the salmon river.

Tom thought nothing about what the river was like. All his fancy was, to get down to the wide wide sea.

And after a while he came to a place where the river spread out into broad still shallow reaches, so wide that little Tom, as he put his head out of the water, could hardly see across.

And there he stopped. He got a little frightened. "This must be the sea," he thought. "What a wide place it is! If I go on into it I shall surely lose my way, or some strange thing will bite me. I will stop here and look out for the otter, or the eels, or someone to tell me where I shall go."

So he went back a little way, and crept into a crack of the rock, just where the river opened out into the wide shallows, and watched for someone to tell him his way: but the otter and the eels were gone on miles and miles down the stream.

There he waited, and slept too, for he was quite tired with his night's journey; and, when he woke, the stream was clearing to a beautiful amber hue, though it was still very high. And after a while he saw a sight which made him jump up; for he knew in a moment it was one of the things which he had come to look for.

Such a fish! ten times as big as the biggest trout, and a hundred times as big as Tom, sculling up the stream past him, as easily as Tom had sculled down.

Such a fish! shining silver from head to tail, and here and there a crimson dot; with a grand hooked nose and grand curling lip, and a grand bright eye, looking round him as proudly as a king. Surely he must be the salmon, the king of all the fish.

Tom was so frightened that he longed to creep into a hole; but he need not have been; for salmon are all true gentlemen, and they never harm or quarrel with anyone, but go about their own business, and leave rude fellows to themselves.

The salmon looked at him full in the face, and then went on without minding him, with a swish or two of his tail which made the stream boil again. And in a few minutes came another, and then four or five, and so on; and all passed Tom, rushing and plunging up the cataract with strong strokes of their silver tails, now and then leaping clean out of water and up over a rock, shining gloriously for a moment in the bright sun; while Tom was so delighted that he could have watched them all day long.

And at last one came up bigger than all the rest; but he came slowly, and stopped, and looked back, and seemed very anxious and busy, and Tom saw that he was helping another salmon.

"My dear," said the great fish to his companion, "you really look dreadfully tired, and you must not over-exert yourself at first. Do rest yourself behind this rock," and he shoved her gently with his nose, to the rock where Tom sat, for this was the salmon's wife.

Then he saw Tom, and looked at him very fiercely one moment, as if he was going to bite him.

"What do you want here?" he said, very fiercely.

"Oh, don't hurt me!" cried Tom. "I only want to look at you; you are so handsome."

"Ah?" said the salmon, very stately but very civilly. "I really beg your pardon; I see what you are, my little dear. I have met one or two creatures like you before, and found them very agreeable and well-behaved. Indeed, one of them showed me a great kindness lately, which I hope to be able to repay. I hope we shall not be in your way here. As soon as this lady is rested, we shall proceed on our journey."

What a well-bred old salmon he was!

"So you have seen things like me before?" asked Tom.

"Several times, my dear. Indeed, it was only last night that one at the river's mouth came and warned me and my wife of some new stake-nets which had got into the stream, I cannot tell how, since last winter, and showed us the way round them, in the most charmingly obliging way."

"So there are babies in the sea?" cried Tom, and clapped his little hands. "Then I shall have someone to play with there? How delightful!"

"Were there no babies up this stream?" asked the lady salmon.

"No! and I grew so lonely. I thought I saw three last night; but they were gone in an instant, down to the sea. So I went too; for I had nothing to play with but caddises and dragon-flies and trout."

"Poor little dear!" said the lady; "but how sad for him to live among such people as caddises, who have actually six legs, the nasty things; and dragon-flies, too! why, they are not even good to eat; for I tried them once, and they are all hard and empty; and, as for trout, every one knows what they are."

'Why do you dislike the trout so?" asked Tom.

"My dear, we do not even mention them, if we can help it; for I am sorry to say they are relations of ours who do us no credit. A great many years ago they were just like us: but they were so lazy, and cowardly, and greedy, that instead of going down to the sea every year to see the world and grow strong and fat, they chose to stay and poke about in the little streams and eat worms and grubs; and they are very properly punished for it; for they have grown ugly and brown and spotted and small; and actually will eat our children."

So the salmon went up, after Tom had warned them of the wicked old otter; and Tom went down, but slowly and cautiously, coasting along the shore.

Chapter 8

TOM'S ADVENTURES ON HIS WAY TO THE SEA

He was many days about it, for it was many miles down to the sea; and perhaps he would never have found his way, if the fairies had not guided him, without his seeing their fair faces, or feeling their gentle hands.

And, as he went, he had a very strange adventure. It was a clear still September night, and the moon shone so brightly down through the water, that he could not sleep, though he shut his eyes as tight as possible. So at last he came up to the top, and sat upon a little point of rock, and looked up at the broad yellow moon, and wondered what she was, and thought that she looked at him. And he watched the moonlight on the rippling river, and the black heads of the firs; and listened to the owl's hoot, and the fox's bark, and the otter's laugh; and smelt the soft perfume of the wafts of heather honey off the grouse-moor far above; and felt very happy, though he could not tell why. You, of course, would have been very cold sitting there on a September night, without the least bit of clothes on your wet back; but Tom was a water-baby, and therefore felt cold no more than a fish.

Suddenly, he saw a beautiful sight. A bright red light moved along the riverside, and threw down into the water a long taproot of flame. Tom, curious little rogue that he was, must needs go and see what it was; so he swam to the shore, and met the light as it stopped over a shallow run at the edge of a low rock.

And there, underneath the light, lay five or six great salmon, looking up at the flame with their great goggle eyes, and wagging their tails, as if they were very much pleased at it.

Tom came to the top, to look at this wonderful light nearer, and made a splash.

And he heard a voice say:

"There was a fish rose."

He did not know what the words meant: but he seemed to know the sound of them, and to know the voice which spoke them; and he saw on the bank three great two-legged creatures, one of whom held the light, flaring and sputtering, and another a long pole. And he knew that they were men, and was frightened, and crept into a hole in the rock, from which he could see what went on.

The man with the torch bent down over the water, and looked earnestly in; and then he said:

"Tak' that muckle fellow, lad; he's ower fifteen punds; and haud your hand steady."

Tom felt that there was some danger coming, and longed to warn the foolish salmon, who kept staring up at the light as if he was bewitched. But before he could make up his mind, down came the pole through the water; there was a fearful splash and struggle, and Tom saw that the poor salmon was speared right through, and was lifted out of the water.

And then, from behind, there sprang on these three men three other men; and there were shouts, and blows, and words which Tom recollected to have heard before; and he shuddered and turned sick at them now, for he felt somehow that they were strange, and ugly, and wrong, and horrible. And it all began to come back to him. They were men; and they were fighting; savage, desperate, up-and-down fighting, such as Tom had seen too many times before.

And he stopped his little ears, and longed to swim away; and was very glad that he was a water-baby, and had nothing to do any more with horrid dirty men, with foul clothes on their backs, and foul words on their lips; but he dared not stir out of his hole: while the rock shook over his head with the trampling and struggling of the keepers and the poachers.

All of a sudden there was a tremendous splash, and a frightful flash, and a hissing, and all was still.

For into the water, close to Tom, fell one of the men; he who held the light in his hand. Into the swift river he sank, and rolled over and over in the current. Tom heard the men above run along, seemingly looking for him; but he drifted down into the deep hole below, and there lay quite still, and they could not find him.

Tom waited a long time, till all was quiet; and then he peeped out, and saw the man lying. At last he screwed up his courage and swam down to him. "Perhaps," he thought, "the water has made him fall asleep, as it did me."

Then he went nearer. He grew more and more curious, he could not tell why. He must go and look at him. He would go very quietly, of course; so he swam round and round him, closer and closer; and, as he did not stir, at last he came quite close and looked him in the face.

The moon shone so bright that Tom could see every feature; and, as he saw, he recollected, bit by bit, it was his old master, Grimes.

Tom turned tail, and swam away as fast as he could.

"Oh dear me!" he thought, "now he will turn into a water-baby. What a nasty troublesome one he will be! And perhaps he will find me out, and beat me again."

So he went up the river again a little way, and lay there the rest of the night under an alder root; but, when morning came, he longed to go down again to the big pool, and see whether Mr. Grimes had turned into a water-baby yet.

So he went very carefully, peeping round all the rocks, and hiding under all the roots. Mr. Grimes lay there still; he had not turned into a water-baby. In the afternoon Tom went back again. He could not rest till he had found out what had become of Mr. Grimes. But this time Mr. Grimes was gone; and Tom made up his mind that he was turned into a water-baby.

He might have made himself easy, poor little man; Mr. Grimes did not turn into a water-baby, or anything like one at all. He could not know that the fairies had carried him away, and put him, where they put everything which falls into the water, exactly where it ought to be.

Then Tom went on down, for he was afraid of staying near Grimes: and as he went, all the vale looked sad. The red and yellow leaves showered down into the river; the flies and beetles were all dead and gone; the chill autumn fog lay low upon the hills, and sometimes spread itself so thickly on the river that he could not see his way. But he felt his way instead, following the flow of the stream, day after day, past great bridges, past boats and barges, past the great town, with its wharfs, and mills, and tall smoking chimneys, and ships which rode at anchor in the stream; and now and then he ran against their hawsers, and wondered what they were, and peeped out, and saw the sailors lounging on board smoking their pipes; and ducked under again, for he was terribly afraid of being caught by man and turned into a chimney-sweep once more. He did not know that the fairies were close to him always, shutting the sailors' eyes lest they should see him, and turning him aside from all foul and dangerous things. Poor little fellow, it was a dreary journey for him; and more than once he longed to be back in Vendale, playing with the trout in the bright summer sun. But it could not be. What has been once can never come over again. And people can be little babies, even water-babies, only once in their lives.

But Tom was always a brave, determined little English boy, who never knew when he was beaten; and on and on he held, till he saw a long way off the red buoy through the fog. And then he found, to his surprise, the stream turned round, and running up inland.

It was the tide, of course: but Tom knew nothing of the tide. He only knew that in a minute more the water, which had been fresh, turned salt all round him. And then there came a change over him. He felt strong, and light, and fresh; and gave, he did not know why, three skips out of the water, a yard high, and head over heels, just as the salmon do when they first touch the noble rich salt water.

He did not care now for the tide being against him. The red buoy was in sight, dancing in the open sea; and to the buoy he went. He passed great shoals of bass and mullet, leaping and rushing in after the shrimps, but he never heeded them, or they him and once he passed a great black shining seal, who was coming in after the mullet. The seal put his head and shoulders out of water, and stared at him. And Tom, instead of being frightened, said, "How d'ye do, sir; what a beautiful place the sea is!" And the old seal, instead of trying, to bite him, looked at him with his soft sleepy winking eyes, and said, "Good tide to you, my little man; are you looking for your brothers and sisters? I passed them all at play outside."

"Oh, then," said Tom, "I shall have play-fellows at last," and he swam on to the buoy, and got upon it (for he was quite out of breath) and sat there, and looked round for water-babies: but there were none to be seen.

The sea-breeze came in freshly with the tide and blew the fog away; and the little waves danced for joy around the buoy, and the old buoy danced with them. The gulls laughed like girls at play, and the sea-pies, with their red bills and legs, flew to and fro from shore to shore, and whistled sweet and wild. And Tom looked and looked, and listened; and he would have been very happy, if he could only have seen the water-babies. Then when the tide turned he left the buoy, and swam round and round in search of them: but in vain. Sometimes he thought he heard them laughing: but it was only the laughter of the ripples. And sometimes he thought he saw them at the bottom: but it was only white and pink shells. And once he was sure he had found one, for he saw two bright eyes peeping out of the sand. So he dived down, and began scraping the sand away, and cried, "Don't hide; I do want someone to play with so much!" And out jumped a great turbot with his ugly eyes and mouth all awry, and flopped away along the bottom, knocking poor Tom over. And he sat down at the bottom of the sea, and cried salt tears from sheer disappointment.

Tom sat upon the buoy long days, long weeks, looking out to sea, and wondering when the water-babies would come back; and yet they never came.

Then he began to ask all the strange things which came in out of the sea if they had seen any; and some said "Yes," and some said nothing at all.

He asked the bass and the pollock; but they were so greedy after the shrimps that they did not care to answer him a word.

And then there came by a beautiful creature, like a ribbon of pure silver with a sharp head and very long teeth; but it seemed very sick and sad. Sometimes it rolled helpless on its side; and then it dashed away glittering like white fire; and then it lay sick again and motionless.

"Where do you come from?" asked Tom. "And why are *you* so sick and sad?"

"I come from the warm Carolinas, but I wandered north and north, till I met with the cold icebergs, afloat in the mid ocean. So I got tangled amongst the icebergs, and chilled with their frozen breath. But the water-babies helped me from among them, and set me free again. And now I am mending every day; but I am very sick and sad; and perhaps I shall never get home again."

"Oh!" cried Tom. "And you have seen water-babies? Have you seen any near here?"

"Yes; they helped me again last night, or I should have been eaten by a great black porpoise."

How vexatious! the water-babies close to him, and yet he could not find one.

And then he left the buoy, and used to go along the sands and round the rocks, and come out in the night and sit upon a point of rock, among the shining seaweeds, in the low October tides, and cry and call for the water-babies; but he never heard a voice call in return. And at last, with his fretting and crying, he grew quite lean and thin.

But one day among the rocks he found a playfellow. It was not a water-baby, alas! but it was a lobster.

Tom had never seen a lobster before; and he was mightily taken with this one; for he thought him the most curious, odd, ridiculous creature he had ever seen.

He had one claw knobbed and the other jagged; and Tom delighted in watching him hold on to the seaweed with his knobbed claw, while he cut up salads with his jagged one, and then put them into his mouth, after smelling at them, like a monkey.

Tom asked him about water-babies. "Yes," he said. He had seen them often. But he did not think much of them. They were meddlesome little creatures, that went about helping fish and shells which got into scrapes. Well, for his part, he should be ashamed to be helped by little soft creatures that had not even a shell on their backs. He had lived quite long enough in the world to take care of himself.

He was a conceited fellow, the old lobster, and not very civil to Tom. But he was so funny, and Tom so lonely, that he could not quarrel with him; and they used to sit in holes in the rocks, and chat for hours.

Chapter 9

TOM SEES THE LITTLE WHITE LADY AGAIN

And about this time there happened to Tom a very strange and important adventure—so important, indeed, that he was very near never finding the water-babies at all; and I am sure you would have been sorry for that.

I hope that you have not forgotten the little white lady all this while. At least, here she comes, looking like a clean white good little darling, as she always was, and always will be. For it befell in the pleasant short December days, that Sir John was so busy hunting that nobody at home could get a word out of him. Whereon My Lady determined to go off and leave him, so she started for the seaside with all the children.

But where she went to nobody must know, for fear young ladies should begin to fancy that there are water-babies there!

Now it befell that, on the very shore, and over the very rocks, where Tom was sitting with his friend the lobster there walked one day the little white lady, Ellie herself, and with her a very wise man indeed—Professor Ptthmllnsprts.

He was a very worthy kind good-natured little old gentleman; and very fond of children. He had met Sir John somewhere or other, and had made acquaintance with him, and become very fond of his children.

Ellie and he were walking on the rocks, and he was showing her about one in ten thousand of all the beautiful and curious things which are to be seen there. But little Ellie was not satisfied with them at all. She liked much better to play with live children, or even with dolls, which she could pretend were alive; and at last she said, "I don't care about all these things, because they can't play with me, or talk to me. If there were little children now in the water, as there used to be, and I could see them, I should like that."

"Children in the water, you strange little girl?" said the professor.

"Yes," said Ellie. "I know there used to be children in the water, and mermaids too, and mermen. I saw them all in a picture at home, of a beautiful lady sailing in a car drawn by dolphins, and babies flying round her, and one sitting in her lap; and the mermaids swimming and playing, and the mermen trumpeting on conch-shells; and it is called "The Triumph of Galatea"; and there is a burning mountain in the picture behind. It hangs on the great staircase, and I have looked at it ever since I was a baby, and dreamt about it a hundred times; and it is so beautiful, that it must be true." But the professor would not agree to this, and said that no man was forced to believe anything to be true, but what he could see, hear, taste, or handle.

Now little Ellie was, I suppose, a stupid little girl; for, instead of being convinced by Professor Ptthmllnsprts' arguments, she only asked the same question over again.

"But why are there not water-babies?"

I trust and hope that it was because the professor trod at that moment on the edge of a very sharp mussel, and hurt one of his corns sadly, that he answered quite sharply:

"Because there ain't."

Which was not even good English, for the professor ought to have said, if he was so angry as to say anything of the kind—Because there are not: or are none: or are none of them; or because they do not exist.

And he groped with his net under the weeds so violently, that he caught poor little Tom.

He felt the net very heavy; and lifted it out quickly, with Tom all entangled in the meshes.

"Dear me!" he cried.

And he took him out.

"It has actually eyes!" he cried. "This is most extraordinary!"

"It is a water-baby!" cried Ellie; and of course it was.

"Water-fiddlesticks, my dear!" said the professor; and he turned away sharply.

There was no denying it. It was a water-baby: and he had said a moment ago that there were none. What was he to do?

He would have liked, of course, to have taken Tom home in a bucket. But what would Ellie say, after what he had just told her? He hesitated a moment. He longed to keep Tom, and yet he half wished he never had caught him; and at last he quite longed to get rid of him. So he turned away and poked Tom with his finger, for want of anything better to do; and said carelessly, "My dear little maid, you must have dreamt of water-babies last night, your head is so full of them."

Now Tom had been in the most horrible fright all the while; and had kept as quiet as he could; for it was fixed in his little head that if a man with clothes on caught him, he might put clothes on him too, and make a dirty black chimney-sweep of him again. But, when the professor poked him, it was more than he could bear; and, between fright and rage, he turned and bit the professor's finger till it bled.

"Oh! ah! yah!" cried he; and glad of an excuse to be rid of Tom, dropped him on to the seaweed, and thence he dived into the water and was gone in a moment.

"But it was a water-baby, and I heard it speak!" cried Ellie. "Ah, it is gone!" And she jumped down off the rock to try and catch Tom before he slipped into the sea.

Too late! and what was worse, as she sprang down, she slipped, and fell some six feet, with her head on a sharp rock, and lay quite still.

The professor picked her up, and tried to waken her, and called to her, and cried over her, for he loved her very much: but she would not waken at all. So he took her up in his arms and carried her to her governess, and they all went home; and little Ellie was put to bed, and lay there quite still; only now and then she woke up and called out about the water-baby: but no one knew what she meant, and the professor did not tell, for he was ashamed to tell.

And, after a week, one moonlight night, the fairies came flying in at the window and brought her such a pretty pair of wings that she could not help putting them on; and she flew with them out of the window, and over the land, and over the sea, and up through the clouds, and nobody heard or saw anything of her for a very long while.

And this is why they say that no one has ever yet seen a water-baby.

CHAPTER 10

TOM MEETS THE WATER-BABIES

But what became of little Tom?

He slipped away off the rocks into the water, as I said before. But he could not help thinking of little Ellie. He did not remember who she was; but he knew that she was a little girl, though she was a hundred times as big as he, and he thought about her all that day, and longed to have had her to play with; but he had very soon to think of something else. And here is the account of what happened to him, as it was published next morning in the Waterproof Gazette, on the finest watered paper, for the use of the great fairy, Mrs. Bedonebyasyoudid, who reads the news very carefully every morning, and especially the police cases, as you will hear very soon.

He was going along the rocks in three-fathom water, watching the pollock catch prawns, when he saw a round cage of green withes; and inside it, looking very much ashamed of himself, sat his friend the lobster, twiddling his horns, instead of thumbs.

"What, have you been naughty, and have they put you in the lock-up?" asked Tom.

The lobster felt a little indignant at such a notion, but he was too much depressed in spirits to argue; so he only said, "I can't get out."

"Why did you get in?"

"After that nasty piece of dead fish." He had thought it looked and smelt very nice when he was outside, and so it did, for a lobster: but now he turned round and abused it because he was angry with himself.

"Where did you get in?"

"Through that round hole at the top."

"Then why don't you get out through it?"

"Because I can't": and the lobster twiddled his horns more fiercely than ever, but he was forced to confess.

"I have jumped upwards, downwards, backwards, and sideways, at least four thousand times; and I can't get out: I always get up underneath there, and can't find the hole."

Tom looked at the trap, and having more wit than the lobster, he saw plainly enough what was the matter; as you may if you will look at a lobster-pot.

"Stop a bit," said Tom. "Turn your tail up to me, and I'll pull you through hindforemost, and then you won't stick in the spikes."

But the lobster was so stupid and clumsy that he couldn't hit the hole.

Tom reached and clawed down the hole after him, till he caught hold of him; and then, as was to be expected, the clumsy lobster pulled him in head foremost.

"Hullo! here is a pretty business," said Tom. "Now take your great claws, and break the points off those spikes, and then we shall both get out easily."

"Dear me, I never thought of that," said the lobster; "and after all the experience of life that I have had!"

But they had not got half the spikes away when they saw a great dark cloud over them: and lo, and behold, it was the otter.

How she did grin and grin when she saw Tom. "Yar!" said she, "you little meddlesome wretch, I have you now! I will serve you out for telling the salmon where I was!" And she crawled all over the pot to get in.

Tom was horribly frightened, and still more frightened when she found the hole in the top, and squeezed herself right down through it, all eyes and teeth. But no sooner was her head inside than valiant Mr. Lobster caught her by the nose and held on.

And there they were all three in the pot, rolling over and over, and very tight packing it was. And the lobster tore at the otter, and the otter tore at the lobster, and both squeezed and thumped poor Tom till he had no breath left in his body; and I don't know what would have happened to him if he had not at last got on the otter's back, and safe out of the hole.

He was right glad when he got out: but he would not desert his friend who had saved him; and the first time he saw his tail uppermost he caught hold of it, and pulled with all his might.

But the lobster would not let go.

"Come along," said Tom; "don't you see she is dead?" And so she was, quite drowned and dead.

And that was the end of the wicked otter.

But the lobster would not let go.

"Come along, you stupid old stick-in-the-mud," cried Tom, "or the fisherman will catch you!" And that was true, for Tom felt someone above beginning to haul up the pot.

But the lobster would not let go.

Tom saw the fisherman haul him up to the boat-side, and thought it was all up with him. But when Mr. Lobster saw the fisherman, he gave such a furious and tremendous snap, that he snapped out of his hand, and out of the pot, and safe into the sea. But he left his knobbed claw behind him; for it never came into his stupid head to let go after all, so he just shook his claw off as the easier method.

And now happened to Tom a most wonderful thing; for he had not left the lobster five minutes before he came upon a water-baby.

A real live water-baby, sitting on the white sand, very busy about a little point of rock. And when it saw Tom it looked up for a moment, and then cried, "Why, you are not one of us. You are a new baby! Oh, how delightful!"

And it ran to Tom, and Tom ran to it, and they hugged and kissed each other for ever so long, they did not know why.

At last Tom said, "Oh, where have you been all this while? I have been looking for you so long, and I have been so lonely."

"We have been here for days and days. There are hundreds of us about the rocks. How was it you did not see us, or hear us when we sing and romp every evening before we go home?"

Tom looked at the baby again, and then he said:

"Well, this is wonderful! I have seen things just like you again and again, but I thought you were shells, or sea-creatures. I never took you for water-babies like myself"

Now, was not that very odd? So odd, indeed, that you will, no doubt, want to know how it happened, and why Tom could never find a water-baby till after he had got the lobster out of the pot. And, if you will read this story nine times over, and then think for yourself, you will find out why.

"Now," said the baby, "come and help me, or I shall not have finished before my brothers and sisters come, and it is time to go home."

"What shall I help you at?"

"At this poor dear little rock; a great clumsy boulder came rolling by in the last storm, and knocked all its head off, and rubbed off all its flowers. And now I must plant it again with seaweeds, and coralline, and anemones, and I will make it the prettiest little rock-garden on all the shore."

So they worked away at the rock, and planted it, and smoothed the sand down round it, and capital fun they had till the tide began to turn. And then Tom heard all the other babies coming, laughing and singing and shouting and romping; and the noise they made was just like the noise of the ripple. So he knew that he had been hearing and seeing the water-babies all along; only he did not know them, because his eyes and ears were not opened.

And in they came, dozens and dozens of them, some bigger than Tom and some smaller, all in the neatest little white bathing dresses; and when they found that he was a new baby, they hugged him and kissed him, and then put him in the middle and danced round him on the sand, and there was no one ever so happy as poor little Tom.

"Now then," they cried all at once, "we must come away home, we must come away home, or the tide will leave us dry. We have mended all the broken seaweed, and put all the rock-pools in order, and planted all the shells again in the sand, and nobody will see where the ugly storm swept in last week."

And this is the reason why the rock-pools are always so neat and clean; because the water-babies come inshore after every storm to sweep them out, and comb them down, and put them all to rights again.

Chapter 11

THE HOME OF THE WATER-BABIES AND MRS. BEDONEBYASYOUDID

And where is the home of the water-babies? In St. Brandan's fairy isle.

Now when Tom got there, he found that the Isle stood all on pillars, and that its roots were full of caves. There were pillars of black basalt, like Staffa; and pillars of green and crimson serpentine, like Kynance; and pillars ribboned with red and white and yellow sandstone, like Livermead; and there were blue grottoes like Capri, and white grottoes like Adelsberg; all curtained and draped with seaweeds, purple and crimson, green and brown; and strewn with soft white sand, on which the water-babies sleep every night. But, to keep the place clean and sweet, the crabs picked up all the scraps off the floor and ate them like so many monkeys; while the rocks were covered with ten thousand sea-anemones, and corals and madrepores, who scavenged the water all day long, and kept it nice and pure. But, to make up to them for having to do such nasty work, they were not left black and dirty, as poor chimney-sweeps and dustmen are. No; the fairies are more considerate and just than that, and have dressed them all in the most beautiful colours and patterns, till they look like vast flower-beds of gay blossoms.

And, instead of watchmen and policemen to keep out nasty things at night, there were thousands and thousands of water-snakes, and most wonderful creatures they were. They were all named after the sea-fairies who took care of them. They were dressed in green velvet, and black velvet, and purple velvet; and were all jointed in rings; and some had eyes in their tails; and some had eyes in every joint, so that they kept a very sharp look-out; and when they wanted a baby-snake, they just grew one at the end of their own tails, and when it was able to take care of itself it dropped off; so that they brought up their families very cheaply. But if any nasty thing came by, out they rushed upon it; and then out of each of their hundreds of feet there sprang a whole cutler's shop of

Scythes,	*Billhooks,*	*Pickaxes,*
Forks,	*Penknives,*	*Swords,*
Lances,	*Fishhooks,*	*Gimblets,*
Corkscrews,	*Pins,*	*Needles,*
	And so forth,	

which stabbed, shot, poked, pricked, scratched, ripped, pinked, and crimped those naughty beasts so terribly that they had to run for their lives, or else be chopped into small pieces and be eaten afterwards.

And there were the water-babies in thousands, more than Tom, or you either, could count.

But I wish Tom had given up all his naughty tricks, and left off tormenting dumb animals now that he had plenty of playfellows to amuse him. Instead of that, I am sorry to say, he would meddle with the creatures, all but the water-snakes, for they would stand no nonsense. So he tickled the madrepores, to make them shut up; and frightened the crabs, to make them hide in the sand and peep out at him with the tips of their eyes; and put stones into the anemones' mouths, to make them fancy that their dinner was coming.

The other children warned him, and said, "Take care what you are at. Mrs. Bedonebyasyoudid is coming." But Tom never heeded them, being quite riotous with high spirits and good luck, till, one Friday morning early, Mrs. Bedonebyasyoudid came indeed.

A very tremendous lady she was; and when the children saw her they all stood in a row, very upright indeed, and smoothed down their bathing dresses, and put their hands behind them, just as if they were going to be examined by the inspector.

And she had on a black bonnet, and a black shawl; and a pair of large green spectacles, and a great hooked nose, hooked so much that the bridge of it stood quite up above her eyebrows; and under her arm she carried a great birch-rod. Indeed, she was so ugly that Tom was tempted to make faces at her: but did not; for he did not admire the look of the birch-rod under her arm.

And she looked at the children one by one, and seemed very much pleased with them, though she never asked them one question about how they were behaving; and then began giving them all sorts of nice sea-things—sea-cakes, sea-apples, sea-oranges, sea-bullseyes, sea-toffee; and to the very best of all she gave sea-ices, made out of sea-cows' cream, which never melt under water.

Now little Tom watched all these sweet things given away, till his mouth watered, and his eyes grew as round as an owl's. For he hoped that his turn would come at last; and so it did. For the lady called him up, and held out her fingers with something in them, and popped it into his mouth; and, lo and behold, it was a nasty cold hard pebble.

"You are a very cruel woman," said he, and began to whimper.

"And you are a very cruel boy; who puts pebbles into the sea-anemones' mouths, to take them in, and make them fancy that they had caught a good dinner! As you did to them, so I must do to you."

"Who told you that?" said Tom.

"You did yourself, this very minute."

Tom had never opened his lips; so he was very much taken aback indeed.

"Yes; everyone tells me exactly what they have done wrong; and that without knowing it themselves. So there is no use trying to hide anything from me. Now go, and be a good boy, and I will put no more pebbles in your mouth, if you put none in other creatures'."

"I did not know there was any harm in it," said Tom.

"Then you know now. People continually say that to me: but I tell them, if you don't know that fire burns, that is no reason that it should not burn you; and if you don't know that dirt breeds fever, that is no reason why the fevers should not kill you. The lobster did not know that there was any harm in getting into the lobster-pot; but it caught him all the same."

"Dear me," thought Tom, "she knows everything!" And so she did, indeed.

"And so, if you do not know that things are wrong, that is no reason why you should not be punished for them; though not as much, not as much, my little man" (and the lady looked very kindly, after all), "as if you did know."

"Well, you are a little hard on a poor lad," said Tom.

"Not at all; I am the best friend you ever had in all your life. But I will tell you; I cannot help punishing people when they do wrong. I like it no more than they do; I am often very, very sorry for them, poor things: but I cannot help it. If I tried not to do it, I should do it all the same. For I work by machinery, just like an engine; and am full of wheels and springs inside; and am wound up very carefully, so that I cannot help going."

"Was it long ago since they wound you up?" asked Tom. For he thought, the cunning little fellow, "She will run down some day: or they may forget to wind her up, as old Grimes used to forget to wind up his watch when he came in from the public-house; and then I shall be safe."

"I was wound up once and for all, so long ago, that I forget all about it."

"Dear me," said Tom, "you must have been made a long time!"

"I never was made, my child; and I shall go for ever and ever."

And there came over the lady's face a very curious expression—very solemn, and very sad; and yet very, very sweet. And she looked up and away, as if she were gazing through the sea, and through the sky, at something far, far off; and as she did so, there came such a quiet, tender, patient, hopeful smile over her face that Tom thought for the moment that she did not look ugly at all.

And Tom smiled in her face, she looked so pleasant for the moment. And the strange fairy smiled too, and said:

"Yes. You thought me very ugly just now, did you not?"

Tom hung down his head, and got very red about the ears.

"And I am very ugly. I am the ugliest fairy in the

world; and I shall be, till people behave themselves as they ought to do. And then I shall grow as handsome as my sister, who is the loveliest fairy in the world; and her name is Mrs. Doasyouwouldbedoneby. So she begins where I end, and I begin where she ends; and those who will not listen to her must listen to me, as you will see. Now, all of you run away, except Tom; and he may stay and see what I am going to do. It will be a very good warning for him to begin with, before he goes to school.

"Now, Tom, every Friday I come down here and call up all who have ill-used little children and serve them as they served the children."

And at that Tom was frightened, and crept under a stone; which made the two crabs who lived there very angry.

"These people," she said, "did not know that they were doing wrong: they were only stupid and impatient; and therefore I only punish them till they become patient, and learn to use their common sense like reasonable beings. And now do you be a good boy, and do as you would be done by, which they did not; and then, when my sister, Madame Doasyouwouldbedoneby, comes on Sunday, perhaps she will take notice of you, and teach you how to behave. She understands that better than I do." And so she went.

Tom determined to be a very good boy all Saturday; and he was; for he never frightened one crab, nor tickled any live corals, nor put stones into the sea-anemones' mouths, to make them fancy they had got a dinner; and when Sunday morning came, sure enough, Mrs. Doasyouwouldbedoneby came too. Whereat all the little children began dancing and clapping their hands, and Tom danced too with all his might.

And as for the pretty lady, I cannot tell you what the colour of her hair was, or of her eyes: no more could Tom; for, when any one looks at her, all they can think of is, that she has the sweetest, kindest, tenderest, funniest, merriest face they ever saw, or want to see. But Tom saw that she was a very tall woman, as tall as her sister; and she understood babies thoroughly, for she had plenty of her own, whole rows and regiments of them, and has to this day. And all her delight was, whenever she had a spare moment, to play with babies; for babies are the best company, and the pleasantest play-fellows, in the world. And therefore when the children saw her, they naturally all caught hold of her, and pulled her till she sat down on a stone, and climbed into her lap, and clung round her neck, and caught hold of her hands; and then they all put their thumbs into their mouths, and began cuddling and purring like so many kittens, as they ought to have done. While those who could get nowhere else sat down on the sand, and cuddled her feet—for no one, you know, wears shoes in the water. And Tom stood staring at them; for he could not understand what it was all about.

"And who are you, you little darling?" she said.

"Oh, that is the new baby!" they all cried, pulling their thumbs out of their mouths; "and he never had any mother," and they all put their thumbs back again, for they did not wish to lose any time.

"Then I will be his mother, and he shall have the very best place; so get out, all of you, this moment."

And she took up two great armsful of babies—nine hundred under one arm, and thirteen hundred under the other—and threw them away, right and left, into the water. They did not mind, but came paddling and wriggling back to her like so many tadpoles, till you could see nothing of her from head to foot for the swarm of little babies.

But she took Tom in her arms, and laid him in the softest place of all, and kissed him, and patted him, and talked to him, tenderly and low, such things as he had never heard before in his life; and Tom looked up into her eyes, and loved her, and loved, till he fell fast asleep from pure love.

And when he woke she was telling the children a story. And what story did she tell them? One story she told them, which begins every Christmas Eve, and yet never ends at all for ever and ever; and, as she went on, the children took their thumbs out of their mouths and listened quite seriously; but not sadly at all; for she never told them anything sad; and Tom listened too, and never grew tired of listening. And he listened so long that he fell fast asleep again, and, when he woke, the lady was nursing him still.

"Don't go away," said little Tom. "This is so nice. I never had anyone to cuddle me before."

"Don't go away," said all the children; "you have not sung us one song."

"Well, I have time for only one. So what shall it be?"

"The doll you lost! The doll you lost!" cried all the babies at once.

So the strange fairy sang:—

I once had a sweet little doll, dears,
The prettiest doll in the world;
Her cheeks were so red and so white, dears,
And her hair was so charmingly curled.
But I lost my poor little doll, dears,
As I played on the heath one day;
And I cried for her more than a week, dears,
But I never could find where she lay.

I found my poor little doll, dears,
As I played in the heath one day:
Folks say she is terribly changed, dears,
For her paint is all washed away,
And her arm trodden off by the cows, dears,
And her hair not the least bit curled:
Yet, for old sakes' sake she is still, dears,
The prettiest doll in the world.

"Now," said the fairy to Tom, "will you be a good boy for my sake, and torment no more sea-beasts till I come back?"

"And you will cuddle me again?" said poor little Tom.

"Of course I will, you little duck. I should like to take you with me and cuddle you all the way; only I must not"; and away she went.

So Tom really tried to be a good boy, and tormented no sea-beasts after that as long as he lived; and he is quite alive, I assure you, still.

Oh, how good little boys ought to be who have

kind mammas to cuddle them and tell them stories; and how afraid they ought to be of growing naughty, and bringing tears into their mammas' pretty eyes!

Chapter 12

TOM'S TEMPTATION AND PUNISHMENT

Now you may fancy that Tom was quite good, when he had everything that he could want or wish: but you would be very much mistaken. Being quite comfortable is a very good thing; but it does not make people good. Indeed, it sometimes makes them naughty, and I am very sorry to say that this happened to little Tom. For he grew so fond of the sea-bullseyes and sea-lollipops that his foolish little head could think of nothing else: and he was always longing for more, and wondering when the strange lady would come again and give him some, and what she would give him, and how much, and whether she would give him more than the others. And he thought of nothing but lollipops by day, and dreamt of nothing else by night—and what happened then?

He began to watch the lady to see where she kept the sweet things: and began hiding, and sneaking, and following her about, and pretending to be looking the other way, or going after something else, till he found out that she kept them in a beautiful mother-of-pearl cabinet away in a deep crack of the rocks.

And he longed to go to the cabinet, and yet he was afraid; and then he longed again, and was less afraid; and at last, by continual thinking about it, he longed so violently that he was not afraid at all. And one night, when all the other children were asleep, and he could not sleep for thinking of lollipops, he crept away among the rocks, and got to the cabinet, and behold! it was open.

But, when he saw all the nice things inside, instead of being delighted, he was quite frightened, and wished he had never come there. And then he would only touch them, and he did; and then he would only taste one, and he did; and then he would only eat one, and he did; and then he would only eat two, and then three, and so on; and then he was terrified lest she should come and catch him, and began gobbling them down so fast that he did not taste them, or have any pleasure in them; and then he felt sick, and would have only one more; and then only one more again; and so on till he had eaten them all up.

And all the while, close behind him, stood Mrs. Bedonebyasyoudid.

She took off her spectacles, because she did not like to see too much, and her eyes filled with great big tears, but all she said was:

"Ah, you poor little dear! you are just like all the rest."

But she said it to herself, and Tom neither heard nor saw her.

But what did the strange fairy do when she saw all her lollipops eaten?

She just said nothing at all about the matter, not even when Tom came next day with the rest for sweet things. He was horribly afraid of coming: but he was still more afraid of staying away, lest anyone should suspect him. He was dreadfully afraid, too, lest there should be no sweets—as was to be expected, he having eaten them all—and lest then the fairy should inquire who had taken them. But, behold! she pulled out just as many as ever, which astonished Tom, and frightened him still more.

And, when the fairy looked him full in the face, he shook from head to foot: however, she gave him his share like the rest, and he thought within himself that she could not have found him out.

But, when he put the sweets into his mouth, he hated the taste of them; and they made him so sick that he had to get away as fast as he could; and terribly sick he was, and very cross and unhappy, all the week after.

Then, when next week came, he had his share again; and again the fairy looked him full in the face; but more sadly than she had ever looked. And he could not bear the sweets: but took them again in spite of himself.

And when Mrs. Doasyouwouldbedoneby came, he wanted to be cuddled like the rest; but she said very seriously:

"I should like to cuddle you; but I cannot, you are so horny and prickly."

And Tom looked at himself: and he was all over prickles, just like a sea-hedgehog.

Which was quite natural; for you must know and believe that people's souls make their bodies just as a snail makes its shell. And therefore, when Tom's soul grew all prickly with naughty tempers, his body could not help growing prickly too, so that nobody would cuddle him, or play with him, or even like to look at him.

What could Tom do now but go away and hide in a corner and cry? For nobody would play with him, and he knew full well why.

And he was so miserable all that week that when the ugly fairy came and looked at him once more full in the face, more seriously and sadly than ever, he could stand it no longer, and thrust the sweetmeats away, saying, "No, I don't want any: I can't bear them now," and then burst out crying, poor little man, and told Mrs. Bedonebyasyoudid every word as it happened.

He was horribly frightened when he had done so; for he expected her to punish him very severely. But, instead, she only took him up and kissed him.

"I will forgive you, little man," she said. "I always forgive everyone the moment they tell me the truth of their own accord."

"Then you will take away all these nasty prickles?"

"That is a very different matter. You put them there yourself, and only you can take them away."

"But how can I do that?" asked Tom, crying afresh.

"Well, I think it is time for you to go to school; so I shall fetch you a schoolmistress, who will teach you how to get rid of your prickles." And so she went away.

Tom was frightened at the notion of a schoolmistress; for he thought she would certainly come with a birch-rod or a cane; but he comforted himself, at last, with thinking that she might be something like the old woman in Vendale—which she was not in the least; for, when the fairy brought her, she was the most beautiful little girl that ever was seen, with long curls floating behind her like a golden cloud, and long robes floating all round her like a silver one.

"There he is," said the fairy; "and you must teach him to be good, whether you like or not."

"I know," said the little girl; but she did not seem quite to like, for she put her finger in her mouth, and looked at Tom under her brows; and Tom put his finger in his mouth, and looked at her under his brows, for he was horribly ashamed of himself.

The little girl seemed hardly to know how to begin; and perhaps she would never have begun at all if poor Tom had not burst out crying, and begged her to teach him to be good and help him to cure his prickles; and at that she grew so tender-hearted that she began teaching him as prettily as ever child was taught in the world.

And what did the little girl teach Tom? She taught him, first, what you have been taught ever since you said your first prayers at your mother's knees.

She taught Tom every day in the week; only on Sundays she always went away home, and the kind fairy took her place. And before she had taught Tom many Sundays, his prickles had vanished quite away, and his skin was smooth and clean again.

"Dear me!" said the little girl; "why, I know you now. You are the very same little chimney-sweep who came into my bedroom."

"Dear me!" cried Tom. "And I know you, too, now. You are the very little white lady whom I saw in bed." And he jumped at her, and longed to hug and kiss her; but did not, remembering that she was a lady born; so he only jumped round and round her till he was quite tired.

And then they began telling each other all their story—how he had got into the water, and she had fallen over the rock; and how he had swum down to the sea, and how she had flown out of the window; and how this, that, and the other, till it was all talked out: and then they both began over again, and I can't say which of the two talked fastest.

And then they set to work at their lessons again, and both liked them so well that they went on well till seven full years were past and gone.

You may fancy that Tom was quite content and happy all those seven years; but the truth is, he was not. He had always one thing on his mind, and that was—where little Ellie went, when she went home on Sundays.

To a very beautiful place, she said.

But what was the beautiful place like, and where was it?

Ah! that is just what she could not say, save that it is the most beautiful place in all the world, and that it was worth all the rest of the world put together.

And of course that only made Tom the more anxious to go likewise.

"Miss Ellie," he said at last, "I will know why I cannot go with you when you go home on Sundays, or I shall have no peace, and give you none either."

"You must ask the fairies that."

So when the fairy, Mrs. Bedonebyasyoudid, came next, Tom asked her.

"Little boys who are only fit to play with sea-beasts cannot go there," she said. "Those who go there must go first where they do not like, and do what they do not like, and help somebody they do not like."

"Why, did Ellie do that?"

"Ask her."

And Ellie blushed, and said, "Yes, Tom; I did not like coming here at first; I was so much happier at home, where it is always Sunday. And I was afraid of you, Tom, at first, because—because—"

"Because I was all over prickles? But I am not prickly now, am I, Miss Ellie?"

"No," said Ellie. "I like you very much now; and I like coming here, too."

"And perhaps," said the fairy, "you will learn to like going where you don't like, and helping some-one that you don't like, as Ellie has."

But Tom put his finger in his mouth, and hung his head down; for he did not see that at all.

So when Mrs. Doasyouwouldbedoneby came, Tom asked her; for he thought in his little head, She is not so strict as her sister, and perhaps she may let me off more easily.

But when he asked the second fairy, she told him just what the first did, and in the very same words.

Tom was very unhappy at that. And, when Ellie went home on Sunday, he fretted and cried all day, and did not care to listen to the fairy's stories about good children, though they were prettier than ever. Indeed, the more he overheard of them, the less he liked to listen, because they were all about children who did what they did not like, and took trouble for other people, and worked to feed their little brothers and sisters instead of caring only for their play. And, when she began to tell a story about a holy child in old times, who was martyred by the heathen because it would not worship idols, Tom could bear no more, and ran away and hid among the rocks.

And, when Ellie came back, he was shy with her, because he fancied she looked down on him, and thought him a coward. And then he grew quite cross with her, because she was superior to him, and did what he could not do. And poor Ellie was quite surprised and sad; and at last Tom burst out crying; but he would not tell her what was really in his mind.

And all the while he was eaten up with curiosity to know where Ellie went to; so that he began not to care for his playmates, or for the sea-palace or anything else. But perhaps that made matters all the easier for him; for he grew so discontented with everything round him that he did not care to stay, and did not care where he went.

"Well," he said, at last, "I am so miserable here, I'll go; if only you will go with me?"

"Ah!" said Ellie, "I wish I might; but the worst of

it is, that the fairy says that you must go alone if you go at all. Now don't poke that poor crab about, Tom" (for he was feeling very naughty and mischievous), "or the fairy will have to punish you."

Tom was very nearly saying, "I don't care if she does"; but he stopped himself in time.

"I know what she wants me to do," he said, whining most dolefully. "She wants me to go after that horrid old Grimes. I don't like him, that's certain. And if I find him, he will turn me into a chimney-sweep again, I know. That's what I have been afraid of all along."

"No, he won't—I know as much as that. Nobody can turn water-babies into sweeps, or hurt them at all, as long as they are good."

"Ah," said naughty Tom, "I see what you want; you are persuading me all along to go, because you are tired of me, and want to get rid of me."

Little Ellie opened her eyes very wide at that, and they were all brimming over with tears.

"Oh, Tom, Tom!" she said, very mournfully—and then she cried, "Oh, Tom! where are you?"

And Tom cried, "Oh, Ellie, where are you?"

For neither of them could see each other—not the least. Little Ellie vanished quite away, and Tom heard her voice calling him, and growing smaller and smaller, and fainter and fainter, till all was silent.

Who was frightened then but Tom? He swam up and down among the rocks, into all the halls and chambers, faster than ever he swam before, but could not find her. He shouted after her, but she did not answer; he asked all the other children, but they had not seen her; and at last he went up to the top of the water and began crying and screaming for Mrs. Bedonebyasyoudid—which perhaps was the best thing to do—for she came in a moment.

"Oh!" said Tom. "Oh dear, oh dear! I have been naughty to Ellie, and I have killed her—I know I have killed her."

"Not quite that," said the fairy; "but I have sent her away home, and she will not come back again for I don't know how long."

And at that Tom cried bitterly.

"How cruel of you to send Ellie away!" sobbed Tom. "However, I will find her again, if I go to the world's end to look for her."

The fairy did not slap Tom, and tell him to hold his tongue: but she took him on her lap very kindly, just as her sister would have done; and put him in mind how it was not her fault, because she was wound up inside, like watches, and could not help doing things whether she liked or not. And then she told him how he had been in the nursery long enough, and must go out now and see the world, if he intended ever to be a man; and how he must go all alone by himself, as everyone else that ever was born has to go, and see with his own eyes, and smell with his own nose, and make his own bed and lie on it, and burn his own fingers if he put them into the fire. And then she told him how many fine things there were to be seen in the world, and what sort of a place it was, and then she told him not to be afraid of anything he met, for nothing would harm him if he remembered all his lessons, and did what he knew was right. And at last she comforted poor little Tom so much that he was quite eager to go, and wanted to set out that minute. "Only," he said, "if I might see Ellie once before I went!"

"Why do you want that?"

"Because—because I should be so much happier if I thought she had forgiven me."

And in the twinkling of an eye there stood Ellie, smiling, and looking so happy that Tom longed to kiss her; but was still afraid it would not be respectful, because she was a lady born.

"I am going, Ellie!" said Tom. "I am going, if it is to the world's end. But I don't like going at all, and that's the truth."

"Pooh! pooh! pooh!" said the fairy. "You will like it very well indeed, you little rogue, and you know that at the bottom of your heart. But if you don't, I will make you like it. Come here, and see what happens to people who do only what is pleasant."

And she took out of one of her cupboards (she had all sorts of mysterious cupboards in the cracks of the rocks) the most wonderful waterproof book, full of such photographs as never were seen.

CHAPTER 13

THE STORY OF THE DOASYOULIKES

The children looked with great delight for the opening of the book.

And on the title-page was written, "The History of the great and famous nation of the Doasyoulikes, who came away from the country of Hardwork, because they wanted to play on the Jews' harp all day long."

In the first picture they saw these Doasyoulikes living in the land of Readymade, at the foot of the Happy-go-lucky Mountains, where flapdoodle grows wild; and if you want to know what that is, you must read Peter Simple.

Instead of houses they lived in the beautiful caves of tufa, and bathed in the warm springs three times a day; and, as for clothes, it was so warm there that the gentlemen walked about in little beside a cocked hat and a pair of straps, or some light summer tackle of that kind; and the ladies all gathered gossamer in autumn (when they were not too lazy) to make their winter dresses.

They were very fond of music, but it was too much trouble to learn the piano or the violin; and as for dancing, that would have been too great an exertion. So they sat on ant-hills all day long, and played on the Jews' harp; and, if the ants bit them, why they just got up and went to the next ant-hill, till they were bitten there likewise.

And they sat under the flapdoodle-trees, and let the flapdoodle drop into their mouths; and under the vines, and squeezed the grape juice down their throats; and, if any little pigs ran about ready roasted, crying, "Come and eat me," as was their fashion in that country, they waited till the pigs ran against their mouths, and then took a bite, and were content, just as so many oysters would have been.

They needed no weapons, for no enemies ever came near their land; and no tools, for everything was readymade to their hand; and the stern old fairy Necessity never came near them to hunt them up, and make them use their wits, or die.

And so on, and so on, and so on, till there were never such comfortable, easy-going, happy-go-lucky people in the world.

"Well, that is a jolly life," said Tom.

"You think so?" said the fairy. "Do you see that great peaked mountain there behind," said the fairy, "with smoke coming out of its top?"

"Yes."

"And do you see all those ashes, and slag, and cinders lying about?"

"Yes."

"Then turn over the next five hundred years, and you will see what happens next."

And behold the mountain had blown up like a barrel of gunpowder, and then boiled over like a kettle; whereby one-third of the Doasyoulikes were blown into the air, and another third were smothered in ashes; so that there was only one-third left.

"You see," said the fairy, "what comes of living on a burning mountain."

"Oh, why did you not warn them?" said little Ellie.

"I did warn them all that I could. I let the smoke come out of the mountain; and wherever there is smoke there is fire. And I laid the ashes and cinders all about; and wherever there are cinders, cinders may be again. But they did not like to face facts, my dears, as very few people do; and so they invented a cock-and-bull story, which, I am sure, I never told them, that the smoke was the breath of a giant, whom some gods or other had buried under the mountain; and that the cinders were what the dwarfs roasted the little pigs whole with; and other nonsense of that kind. And, when folks are in that humour, I cannot teach them, save by the good old birch-rod."

And then she turned over the next five hundred years: and there were the remnant of the Doasyoulikes, doing as they liked, as before. They were too lazy to move away from the mountain; so they said, If it has blown up once, that is all the more reason that it should not blow up again. And they were few in number: but they only said, The more the merrier, but the fewer the better fare. However, that was not quite true; for all the flapdoodle-trees were killed by the volcano, and they had eaten all the roast pigs, who, of course, could not be expected to have little ones. So they had to live very hard, on nuts and roots which they scratched out of the ground with sticks. Some of them talked of sowing corn, as their ancestors used to do, before they came into the land of Readymade; but they had forgotten how to make ploughs (they had forgotten even how to make Jews' harps by this time), and had eaten all the seedcorn which they brought out of the land of Hardwork years since; and of course it was too much trouble to go away and find more. So they lived miserably on roots and nuts, and all the weakly little children had great stomachs, and then died.

"Why," said Tom, "they are growing no better than savages."

"And look how ugly they are all getting," said Ellie.

"Yes; when people live on poor vegetables instead of roast beef and plum-pudding, their jaws grow large, and their lips grow coarse."

And she turned over the next five hundred years. And there they were all living up in trees, and making nests to keep off the rain. And underneath the trees lions were prowling about.

"Why," said Ellie, "the lions seem to have eaten a good many of them, for there are very few left now."

"Yes," said the fairy; "you see it was only the strongest and most active ones who could climb the trees, and so escape."

"But what great, hulking, broad-shouldered chaps they are," said Tom; "they are a rough lot as ever I saw."

"Yes, they are getting very strong now; for the ladies will not marry any but the very strongest and fiercest gentlemen, who can help them up the trees out of the lions' way."

And she turned over the next five hundred years.

And in that they were fewer still, and stronger, and fiercer; but their feet had changed shape very oddly, for they laid hold of the branches with their great toes, as if they had been thumbs, just as a Hindoo tailor uses his toes to thread his needle.

The children were very much surprised, and asked the fairy whether that was her doing.

"Yes, and no," she said, smiling. "It was only those who could use their feet as well as their hands who could get a good living: or, indeed, get married; so that they got the best of everything, and starved out all the rest; and those who are left keep up a regular breed of toe-thumb-men."

"But there is a hairy one among them," said Ellie.

"Ah!" said the fairy, "that will be a great man in his time, and chief of all the tribe."

And, when she turned over the next five hundred years, it was true.

For this hairy chief had had hairy children, and they hairier children still; and every one wished to marry hairy husbands, and have hairy children too; for the climate was growing so damp that none but the hairy ones could live: all the rest coughed and sneezed, and had sore throats, and went into consumptions, before they could grow up to be men and women.

Then the fairy turned over the next five hundred years. And they were fewer still.

"Why, there is one on the ground picking up roots," said Ellie, "and he cannot walk upright."

No more he could; for in the same way that the shape of their feet had altered, the shape of their backs had altered also.

"Why," cried Tom, "I declare they are all apes."

"Something fearfully like it, poor foolish creatures," said the fairy. "They are grown so stupid now, that they can hardly think: for none of them have used their wits for many hundred years. They have almost forgotten, too, how to talk. For each stupid child forgot some of the words it heard from its stupid parents, and had not wits enough to make fresh words for itself. Beside, they are grown so fierce and suspicious and brutal that they keep out of each other's way, and mope and sulk in the dark forests, never hearing each other's voice, till they have forgotten almost what speech is like. I am afraid they will all be apes very soon, and all by doing only what they liked."

And in the next five hundred years they were all dead and gone, by bad food and wild beasts and hunters.

And that was the end of the great and jolly nation of the Doasyoulikes. And, when Tom and Ellie came to the end of the book, they looked very sad and solemn; and they had good reason so to do.

"But could you not have saved them from becoming apes?" said little Ellie, at last.

"At first, my dear; if only they would have behaved like men, and set to work to do what they did not like. But the longer they waited, and behaved like the dumb beasts, who only do what they like, the stupider and clumsier they grew; till at last they were past all cure, for they had thrown their own wits away. It is such things as this that help to make me so ugly, that I know not when I shall grow fair."

"And where are they all now?" asked Ellie.

"Exactly where they ought to be, my dear."

"Yes!" said the fairy, solemnly, half to herself, as she closed the wonderful book. "Folks say now that I can make beasts into men. Well, perhaps they are right; and perhaps, again, they are wrong. That is one of the seven things which I am forbidden to tell; and, at all events, it is no concern of theirs. Whatever their ancestors were, men they are; and I advise them to behave as such, and act accordingly. But let them recollect this, that there are two sides to every question, and a downhill as well as an uphill road; and, if I can turn beasts into men, I can, by the same laws, turn men into beasts. You were very near being turned into a beast once or twice, little Tom. Indeed, if you had not made up your mind to go on this journey, and see the world, like an Englishman, I am not sure but that you would have ended as an eft in a pond."

"Oh, dear me!" said Tom; "sooner than that, and be all over slime, I'll go this minute, if it is to the world's end."

CHAPTER 14

TOM'S JOURNEY TO SHINY WALL

And Nature, the old Nurse, took
The child upon her knee,
Saying, "Here is a story book
"Thy father hath written for thee.

"Come wander with me," she said,
"Into regions yet untrod,
And read what is still unread
In the Manuscripts of God."

And he wandered away and away
With Nature, the dear old Nurse,
Who sang to him night and day
The rhymes of the universe—

LONGFELLOW.

"Now," said Tom, "I am ready to be off, if it's to the world's end."

"Ah!" said the fairy, "that is a brave, good boy. But you must go farther than the world's end, if you want to find Mr. Grimes; for he is at the Other-end-of-Nowhere. You must go to the Shiny Wall, and through the white gate that never was opened; and then you will come to Peacepool, and Mother Carey's Haven, where the good whales go when they die. And there Mother Carey will tell you the way to the Other-end-of-Nowhere, and there you will find Mr. Grimes."

"Oh dear!" said Tom. "But I do not know my way to Shiny Wall, or where it is at all."

"Little boys must take the trouble to find out things for themselves, or they will never grow to be men; so that you must ask all the beasts in the sea and the birds in the air, and if you have been good to them, some of them will tell you the way to Shiny Wall."

"Well," said Tom, "it will be a long journey, so I had better start at once. Good-bye, Miss Ellie; you know I am getting a big boy, and I must go out and see the world."

"I know you must," said Ellie; "but you will not forget me, Tom. I shall wait here till you come."

And she shook hands with him, and bade him good-bye. Tom longed very much again to kiss her; but he thought it would not be respectful, considering she was a lady born; so he promised not to forget her.

He asked all the beasts in the sea, and all the birds in the air, but none of them knew the way to Shiny Wall. For why? He was still too far down south.

Then he met a ship, far larger than he had ever seen—a gallant ocean-steamer, with a long cloud of smoke trailing behind; and he wondered how she went on without sails, and swam up to her to see. A school of dolphins were running races round and round her, going three feet for her one, and Tom asked them the way to Shiny Wall: but they did not know. Then he tried to find out how she moved, and at last he saw her screw, and was so delighted with it that he played under her quarter all day, till he nearly had his nose knocked off by the fans, and thought it time to move. Then he watched the sailors upon deck, and the ladies, with their bonnets and parasols: but none of them could see him, because their eyes were not opened,—as, indeed, most people's eyes are not.

At last there came out into the quarter-gallery a very pretty lady, in deep black widow's weeds, and in her arms a baby. She leaned over the quarter-gallery, and looked back and back toward England far away; and as she looked she sang:

I

"Soft soft wind, from out the sweet south sliding,
Waft thy silver cloud-webs athwart the summer sea;
Thin thin threads of mist on dewy fingers twining,
Weave a veil of dappled gauze to shade my babe and me.

II

"Deep deep Love, within thine own abyss abiding,
Pour Thyself abroad, O Lord, on earth and air and sea;
Worn weary hearts within Thy holy temple hiding,
Shield from sorrow, sin, and shame my helpless babe and me."

Her voice was so soft and low, and the music of the air so sweet, that Tom could have listened to it all day. But as she held the baby over the gallery rail, to show it the dolphins leaping and the water gurgling in the ship's wake, lo! and behold, the baby saw Tom.

He was quite sure of that; for when their eyes met, the baby smiled and held out his hands; and Tom smiled and held out his hands too; and the baby kicked and leaped, as if it wanted to jump overboard to him.

"What do you see, my darling?" said the lady; and her eyes followed the baby's till she too caught sight of Tom, swimming about among the foam-beads below.

She gave a little shriek and start; and then she said, quite quietly, "Babies in the sea? Well, perhaps it is the happiest place for them"; and waved her hand to Tom, and cried, "Wait a little, darling, only a little: and perhaps we shall go with you and be at rest."

And at that an old nurse, all in black, came out and

talked to her, and drew her in. And Tom turned away northward, sad and wondering; and watched the great steamer slide away into the dusk, and the lights on board peep out one by one, and die out again, and the long bar of smoke fade away into the evening mist, till all was out of sight.

And he swam northward again, day after day, till at last he met the King of the Herrings, with a curry-comb growing out of his nose, and a sprat in his mouth for a cigar, and asked him the way to Shiny Wall; so he bolted his sprat head foremost, and said:

"If I were you, young gentleman, I should go to the Allalonestone, and ask the last of the Gairfowl."

Tom asked his way to her, and the King of the Herrings told him very kindly.

But just as Tom had thanked him and set off, he called after him: "Hi! I say, can you fly?"

"I never tried," says Tom. "Why?"

"Because, if you can, I should advise you to say nothing to the old lady about it. There; take a hint. Good-bye."

And away Tom went for seven days and seven nights due north-west, till he came to a great codbank, the like of which he never saw before. The great cod lay below in tens of thousands, and gobbled shell-fish all day long; and the blue sharks roved above in hundreds, and gobbled them when they came up. So they ate, and ate, and ate each other, as they had done since the making of the world; for no man had come here yet to catch them, and find out how rich old Mother Carey is.

And there he saw the last of the Gairfowl, standing

up on the Allalonestone, all alone. And a very grand old lady she was, full three feet high, and bolt upright, like some old Highland chieftainess. She had on a black velvet gown, and a white pinner and apron, and a very high bridge to her nose (which is a sure mark of high breeding), and a large pair of white spectacles on it, which made her look rather odd: but it was the ancient fashion of her house.

And instead of wings, she had two little feathery arms, with which she fanned herself, and complained of the dreadful heat; and she kept on crooning an old song to herself, which she learnt when she was a little baby-bird, long ago—

"Two little birds they sat on a stone,
One swam away, and then there was one,
With a fal-lal-la-lady.

"The other swam after, and then there was none,
And so the poor stone was left all alone;
With a fal-lal-la-lady."

It was "flew" away, properly, and not "swam" away: but, as she could not fly, she had a right to alter it. However, it was a very fit song for her to sing, because she was a lady herself.

Tom came up to her very humbly, and made his bow; and the first thing she said was—

"Have you wings? Can you fly?"

"Oh, dear, no, ma'am; I should not think of such a thing" said cunning little Tom.

"Then I shall have great pleasure in talking to you,

my dear. It is quite refreshing nowadays to see anything without wings. They must all have wings, forsooth, now, every new upstart sort of bird, and fly. What can they want with flying, and raising themselves above their proper station in life? In the days of my ancestors no birds ever thought of having wings, and did very well without; and now they all laugh at me because I keep to the good old fashion."

And so she was running on, while Tom tried to get in a word edgeways; and at last he did, when the old lady got out of breath, and began fanning herself again; and then he asked if she knew the way to Shiny Wall.

"Shiny Wall? Who should know better than I? We all came from Shiny Wall, thousands of years ago, when it was decently cold, and the climate was fit for gentlefolk; but now, I am the last of my family. A friend of mine and I came and settled on this rock when we were young, to be out of the way of low people. Once we were a great nation, and spread over all the Northern Isles. But men shot us so, and knocked us on the head, and took our eggs, until at last there were none of us left, except on the old Gairfowlskerry, just off the Iceland coast, up which no man could climb. Even there we had no peace; for one day, when I was quite a young girl, the land rocked, and the sea boiled, and the sky grew dark, and all the air was filled with smoke and dust, and down tumbled the old Gairfowlskerry into the sea. The dovekies and marrocks, of course, all flew away; but we were too proud to do that. Some of us were dashed to pieces, and some drowned; and those who were left got away to Eldey, and the dovekies tell me they are all dead now, and so here I am left alone. And soon I shall be gone, my little dear, and nobody will miss me; and then the poor stone will be left all alone."

"But, please, which is the way to Shiny Wall?" said Tom.

"Oh, you must go, my little dear—you must go. Let me see—I am sure—that is—really, my poor old brains are getting quite puzzled. Do you know, my little dear, I am afraid, if you want to know, you must ask some of these vulgar birds about, for I have quite forgotten."

And the poor old Gairfowl began to cry tears of pure oil; and Tom was quite sorry for her; and for himself too, for he was at his wits' end whom to ask.

But by there came a flock of petrels, who are Mother Carey's own chickens; and Tom thought them much prettier than Lady Gairfowl, and so perhaps they were; for Mother Carey had had a great deal of fresh experience between the time that she invented the Gairfowl and the time that she invented them. They flitted along like a flock of black swallows, and hopped and skipped from wave to wave, lifting up their little feet behind them so daintily, and whistling to each other so tenderly, that Tom fell in love with them at once, and called them to know the way to Shiny Wall.

"Shiny Wall? Do you want Shiny Wall? Then come with us, and we will show you. We are Mother Carey's own chickens, and she sends us out over all the seas, to show the good birds the way home."

Tom was delighted, and swam off to them, after he had made his bow to the Gairfowl. But she would not return his bow: but held herself bolt upright, and wept tears of oil as she sang:

"And so the poor stone was left all alone;
With a fal-lal-la-lady."

And now Tom was all agog to start for Shiny Wall; but the petrels said no. They must go first to Allfowlsness, and wait there for the great gathering of all the seabirds, before they start for their summer breeding-places far away in the Northern Isles; and there they would be sure to find some birds which were going to Shiny Wall: but where Allfowlsness was, he must promise never to tell, lest men should go there and shoot the birds, and stuff them, and put them into stupid museums, instead of leaving them to play and breed and work in Mother Carey's water-garden where they ought to be.

So where Allfowlsness is nobody must know; and all that is to be said about it is, that Tom waited there many days.

And after a while the birds began to gather at Allfowlsness, in thousands and tens of thousands, blackening all the air; and they paddled and washed and splashed and combed and brushed themselves on the sand, till the shore was white with feathers; and they quacked and clucked and gabbled and chattered and screamed and whooped as they talked over matters with their friends, and settled where they were to go and breed that summer, till you might have heard them ten miles off; and lucky it was for them that there was no one to hear them but the old keeper, who lived all alone upon the Ness, in a turf hut thatched with heather and fringed round with great stones slung across the roof by bent-ropes, lest the winter gales should blow the hut right away. But he never minded the birds nor hurt them: only, when all the birds were going, he toddled out, and took off his cap to them, and wished them a merry journey and a safe return; and then gathered up all the feathers which they had left, and cleaned them to sell down south, and make feather-beds for stuffy people to lie on.

Then the petrels asked this bird and that whether they would take Tom to Shiny Wall: but one set was going to Sutherland, and one to the Shetlands, and one to Norway, and one to Spitzbergen, and one to Iceland, and one to Greenland: but none would go to Shiny Wall. So the good-natured petrels said that they would show him part of the way themselves, but they were only going as far as Jan Mayen's Land; and after that he must shift for himself.

And then all the birds rose up, and streamed away in long black lines, north, and north-east, and north-west, across the bright blue summer sky; and their cry was like ten thousand packs of hounds, and ten thousand peals of bells. Only the puffins stayed behind, and killed the young rabbits, and laid their eggs in the rabbit-burrows.

And, as Tom and the petrels went north-eastward, it began to blow right hard, till you could not see where the sky ended and the sea began. But Tom and the petrels never cared, for the gale was right abaft, and away they went over the crests of the billows, as merry as so many flying-fish.

And at last they saw an ugly sight—the black side of a great ship, water-logged in the trough of the sea. Her funnel and her masts were overboard, and swayed and surged under her lee; her decks were swept as clean as a barn floor, and there was no living soul on board.

The petrels flew up to her, and wailed round her; for they were very sorry indeed, and also they expected to find some salt pork; and Tom scrambled on board of her and looked round, frightened and sad.

And there, in a little cot, lashed tight under the bulwark, lay a baby fast asleep; the very same baby, Tom saw at once, which he had seen in the singing lady's arms.

He went up to it, and wanted to wake it; but behold, from under the cot out jumped a little black and tan terrier dog, and began barking and snapping at Tom, and would not let him touch the cot.

Tom knew the dog's teeth could not hurt him: but at least it could shove him away, and did; and he and the dog fought and struggled, for he wanted to help the baby, and did not want to throw the poor dog overboard: but as they were struggling, there came a tall green sea, over the side of the ship, and swept them all into the waves.

"Oh, the baby, the baby!" screamed Tom: but the next moment he did not scream at all; for he saw the cot settling down through the green water, with the baby, smiling in it, fast asleep; and he saw the fairies come up from below, and carry baby and cradle gently down in their soft arms; and then he knew it was all right, and that there would be a new water-baby in St. Brandan's Isle.

And the poor little dog?

Why, after he had kicked and coughed a little, he sneezed so hard, that he sneezed himself clean out of his skin, and turned into a water-dog, and jumped and danced round Tom, and ran over the crests of the waves, and snapped at the jelly-fish and the mackerel, and followed Tom the whole way to the Other-end-of-Nowhere.

Then they went on again, till they began to see the peak of Jan Mayen's Land, standing up like a white sugar-loaf, two miles above the clouds.

And there they fell in with a whole flock of molly-mocks, who were feeding on a dead whale.

"These are the fellows to show you the way," said Mother Carey's chickens; "we cannot help you farther north. We don't like to get among the ice-pack, for fear it should nip our toes: but the mollys dare fly anywhere."

So the petrels called to the mollys: but they were so busy and greedy, gobbling and pecking and spluttering and fighting over the blubber, that they did not take the least notice.

"Come, come," said the petrels, "you lazy greedy lubbers, this young gentleman is going to Mother Carey, and if you don't attend on him, you won't earn your discharge from her, you know."

"Greedy we are," says a great fat old molly, "but

lazy we ain't; and, as for lubbers, we're no more lubbers than you. Let's have a look at the lad."

And he flapped right into Tom's face, and stared at him in the most impudent way, and then asked him where he hailed from, and what land he sighted last.

And, when Tom told him, he seemed pleased, and said he was a good plucked one to have got so far.

"Come along, lads," he said to the rest, "and give this little chap a cast over the pack, for Mother Carey's sake. We've eaten blubber enough for today, and we'll e'en work out a bit of our time by helping the lad."

So the mollys took Tom up on their backs, and flew off with him, laughing and joking—and oh, how they did smell of train oil!

And now they came to the edge of the pack, and beyond it they could see Shiny Wall looming, through mist, and snow, and storm. But the pack rolled horribly upon the swell, and the ice giants fought and roared, and leapt upon each other's backs, and ground each other to powder, so that Tom was afraid to venture among them, lest he should be ground to powder too. And he was the more afraid, when he saw lying among the ice pack the wrecks of many a gallant ship; some with masts and yards all standing, some with the seamen frozen fast on board. Alas, alas, for them! They were all true English hearts.

But the good mollys took Tom and his dog up, and flew with them safe over the pack and the roaring ice giants, and set them down at the foot of Shiny Wall.

"And where is the gate?" asked Tom

"There is no gate," said the mollys.

"No gate?" cried Tom, aghast.

"None; never a crack of one."

"What am I to do, then?"

"Dive under the floe, to be sure, if you have pluck."

"I've not come so far to turn now," said Tom; "so here goes for a header."

"A lucky voyage to you, lad," said the mollys; "we knew you were one of the right sort. So good-bye."

"Why don't you come too?" asked Tom.

But the mollys only wailed sadly, "We can't go yet, we can't go yet," and flew away over the pack.

So Tom dived under the great white gate which never was opened yet, and went on in black darkness, at the bottom of the sea, for seven days and seven nights. And yet he was not a bit frightened. Why should he be? He was a brave English lad, whose business is to go out and see all the world.

And at last he saw the light, and clear clear water overhead; and up he came a thousand fathoms, among clouds of sea-moths, which fluttered round his head. The dog snapped at them till his jaws were tired; but Tom hardly minded them at all, he was so eager to get to the top of the water, and see the pool where the good whales go.

And a very large pool it was, miles and miles across, though the air was so clear that the ice cliffs on the opposite side looked as if they were close at hand. All round it the ice cliffs rose, in walls and spires and battlements, and caves and bridges, and stories and galleries, in which the ice-fairies live, and drive away the storms and clouds, that Mother Carey's pool may lie calm from year's end to year's end. And the sun acted policeman, and walked round outside every day, peeping just over the top of the ice wall, to see that all went right; and now and then he played conjuring tricks, or had an exhibition of fireworks, to amuse the ice-fairies. For he would make himself into four or five suns at once, or paint the sky with rings and crosses and crescents of white fire, and stick himself in the middle of them, and wink at the fairies; and I daresay they were very much amused; for anything's fun in the country.

And there the good whales lay, the happy sleepy beasts, upon the still oily sea They were all right whales, you must know, and finners, and razor-backs, and bottle-noses, and spotted sea-unicorns with long ivory horns. But the sperm whales are such raging, ramping, roaring, rumbustious fellows, that, if Mother Carey let them in, there would be no more peace in Peacepool. So she packs them away in a great pond by themselves at the South Pole, two hundred and sixty-three miles south-south-east of Mount Erebus, the great volcano in the ice; and there they butt each other with their ugly noses, day and night from year's end to year's end.

But here there were only good quiet beasts, lying about, and blowing every now and then jets of white steam, or sculling round with their huge mouths open, for the sea-moths to swim down their throats. They were quite safe and happy there; and all they had to do was to wait quietly in Peacepool, till Mother Carey sent for them to make them out of old beasts into new.

Tom swam up to the nearest whale, and asked the way to Mother Carey.

"There she sits in the middle," said the whale.

Tom looked; but he could see nothing in the middle of the pool, but one peaked iceberg: and he said so.

"That's Mother Carey," said the whale, "as you will find when you get to her. There she sits making old beasts into new all the year round."

"How does she do that?"

"That's her concern, not mine," said the old whale; and yawned so wide (for he was very large) that there swam into his mouth 943 sea-moths, 13,846 jelly-fish no bigger than pins' heads, and forty-three little ice-crabs.

"I suppose," said Tom, "she cuts up a great whale like you into a whole shoal of porpoises?"

At which the old whale laughed so violently that he coughed up all the creatures; who swam away again very thankful at having escaped out of that terrible whalebone net of his, from which bourn no traveller returns; and Tom went on to the iceberg, wondering.

Chapter 15

TOM'S VISIT TO MOTHER CAREY

When he came near it, it took the form of the grandest old lady he had ever seen—a white marble lady, sitting on a white marble throne. And from the foot of the throne there swam away, out and out into the sea, millions of new-born creatures, of more shapes and colours than man ever dreamed. And they were Mother Carey's children, whom she makes out of the sea-water all day long.

He expected of course—like some grown people who ought to know better—to find her snipping, piecing, fitting, stitching, cobbling, basting, filing, planing, hammering, turning, polishing, moulding, measuring, chiselling, clipping, and so forth, as men do when they go to work to make anything.

But, instead of that, she sat quite still with her chin upon her hand, looking down into the sea with two great grand blue eyes, as blue as the sea itself Her hair was as white as the snow—for she was very very old—in fact, as old as anything which you are likely to come across.

And, when she saw Tom, she looked at him very kindly.

"What do you want, my little man? It is long since I have seen a water-baby here."

Tom told her his errand, and asked the way to the Other-end-of-Nowhere.

"You ought to know yourself, for you have been there already."

"Have I, ma'am? I'm sure I forget all about it."

"Then look at me."

And, as Tom looked into her great blue eyes, he recollected the way perfectly.

"Now, was not that strange?"

"Thank you, ma'am," said Tom. "Then I won't trouble your ladyship any more; I hear you are very busy."

"I am never more busy than I am now," she said, without stirring a finger.

"I heard, ma'am, that you were always making new beasts out of old."

"So people fancy. But I am not going to trouble myself to make things, my little dear. I sit here and make them make themselves."

"You are a clever fairy, indeed," thought Tom. And he was quite right.

"And now, my pretty little man," said Mother Carey, "you are sure you know the way to the Other-end-of-Nowhere?"

Tom thought; and behold, he had forgotten it utterly.

"That is because you took your eyes off me."

Tom looked at her again, and recollected; and then looked away, and forgot in an instant.

"But what am I to do, ma'am? For I can't keep looking at you when I am somewhere else."

"You must do without me, as most people have to do; and look at the dog instead; for he knows the way well enough, and will not forget it. Besides, you may meet some very queer-tempered people there, who will not let you pass without this passport of mine, which you must hang round your neck and take care of; and, of course, as the dog will always go behind you, you must go the whole way backward."

"Backward!" cried Tom. "Then I shall not be able to see my way."

"On the contrary, if you look forward, you will not see a step before you, and be certain to go wrong; but, if you look behind you, and watch carefully whatever you have passed, and especially keep your eye on the dog, who goes by instinct, and therefore can't go wrong, then you will know what is coming next, as plainly as if you saw it in a looking-glass."

Tom was very much astonished: but he obeyed her, for he had learnt always to believe what the fairies told him.

He was very sorely tried; for though, by keeping the dog to heels (or rather to toes, for he had to walk backward), he could see pretty well which way the dog was hunting, yet it was much slower work to go backwards than to go forwards. But, what was more trying still, no sooner had he got out of Peacepool, than there came running to him all the conjurers, fortune-tellers, astrologers, prophesiers, as many as were in those parts, all bawling and screaming at him, "Look ahead, only look ahead; and we will show you what man never saw before, and right away to the end of the world!"

But I am proud to say that Tom was such a little dogged, hard English boy, that he never turned his head round once all the way from Peacepool to the Other-end-of-Nowhere: but kept his eye on the dog, and let him pick out the scent, hot or cold, straight or crooked, wet or dry, up hill or down dale; by which means he never made a single mistake, and saw all the wonderful things, which it is my duty to relate to you in the next chapter.

Chapter 16

TOM'S JOURNEY TO THE OTHER-END-OF-NOWHERE, AND HIS ADVENTURES THEREIN

"Come to me, O ye children!
For I hear you at your play;
And the questions that perplexed me
Have vanished quite away.

"Ye open the Eastern windows,
That look towards the sun,
Where thoughts are singing swallows,
And the brooks of morning run.

"For what are all our contrivings
And the wisdoms of our books,
When compared with your caresses,
And the gladness of your looks?

"Ye are better than all the ballads
That ever were sung or said;
For ye are living poems,
And all the rest are dead."

LONGFELLOW

Here begins the account of the nine-hundred-and-ninety-ninth part of the wonderful things which Tom saw on his journey to the Other-end-of-Nowhere.

Now, as soon as Tom had left Peacepool, he came to the white lap of the great Sea-mother, ten thousand fathoms deep; where she makes world-pap all day long, for the steam-giants to knead, and the fire-giants to bake, till it has risen and hardened into mountain-loaves and island-cakes.

And there Tom was very near being kneaded up in the world-pap, and turned into a fossil water-baby.

For, as he walked along in the silence of the sea-twilight, on the soft white ocean floor, he was aware of a hissing, and a roaring, and a thumping, and a pumping, as of all the steam-engines in the world at once. And, when he came near, the water grew boiling-hot; not that that hurt him in the least: but it also grew foul; and every moment he stumbled over dead shells, and fish, and sharks, and seals, and whales, which had been killed by the hot water.

And at last he came to the great sea-serpent himself, lying dead at the bottom; and as he was too thick to scramble over, Tom had to walk round him three-quarters of a mile and more, which put him out of his path sadly; and, when he had got round, he came to the place called Stop. And there he stopped, and just in time.

For he was on the edge of a vast hole in the bottom of the sea, up which was rushing and roaring clear steam enough to work all the engines in the world at once; so clear, indeed, that it was quite light at moments; and Tom could see almost up to the top of the water above, and down below into the pit for nobody knows how far.

But, as soon as he bent his head over the edge, he got such a rap on the nose from pebbles, that he jumped back again; for the steam, as it rushed up, rasped away the sides of the hole, and hurled it up into the sea in a shower of mud and gravel and ashes; and then it spread all around, and sank again, and covered in the dead fish so fast, that before Tom had stood there five minutes he was buried in silt up to his ankles, and began to be afraid that he should have been buried alive.

And perhaps he would have been, but that while he was thinking, the whole piece of ground on which he stood was torn off and blown upwards, and away flew Tom a mile up through the sea, wondering what was coming next.

At last he stopped—thump! and found himself tight in the legs of the most wonderful bogy which he had ever seen.

It had I don't know how many wings, as big as the sails of a windmill, and spread out in a ring like them; and with them it hovered over the steam which rushed up, as a ball hovers over the top of a fountain. And for every wing above it had a leg below, with a claw like a comb at the tip, and a nostril at the root; and in the middle it had no stomach and one eye; and as for its mouth, that was all on one side. Well, it was a very strange beast; but no stranger than some dozens which you may see.

"What do you want here," it cried quite peevishly, "getting in my way?" and it tried to drop Tom: but he held on tight to its claws, thinking himself safer where he was.

So Tom told him who he was, and what his errand was. And the thing winked its one eye and sneered:

"I am too old to be taken in in that way. You are come after gold—I know you are."

"Gold! What is gold?" And really Tom did not know; but the suspicious old bogy would not believe him.

But after a while Tom began to understand a little. For, as the vapours came up out of the hole, the bogy smelt them with his nostrils, and combed them and sorted them with his combs; and then, when they steamed up through them against his wings, they were changed into showers and streams of metal. From one wing fell gold-dust, and from another silver, and from another copper, and from another tin, and from another lead, and so on, and sank into the soft mud, into veins and cracks, and hardened there. Whereby it comes to pass that the rocks are full of metal.

But, all of a sudden, somebody shut off the steam below, and the hole was left empty in an instant: and then down rushed the water into the hole, in such a whirlpool that the bogy spun round and round as fast as a teetotum. But that was all in his day's work, like a fair fall with the hounds; so all he did was to say to Tom—

"Now is your time, youngster, to get down, if you are in earnest, which I don't believe."

"You'll soon see," said Tom; and away he went, as bold as Baron Munchausen, and shot down the rushing cataract like a salmon.

And, when he got to the bottom, he swam till he was washed on shore safe upon the Other-end-of-Nowhere.

And first he went through Waste-paper-land, where all the stupid books lie in heaps, up hill and down dale, like leaves in a winter wood; and there he saw people digging and grubbing among them, to make worse books out of bad ones; and a very good trade they drove thereby, especially among children.

He came to the place where everyone knows his neighbour's business better than his own; and when he got into the middle of the town, they all set on him at once, to show him his way; or rather, to show him that he did not know his way; for as for asking him what way he wanted to go, no one ever thought of that.

But one pulled him hither, and another poked him thither, and a third cried—

"You mustn't go west, I tell you; it is destruction to go west."

"But I am not going west, as you may see," said Tom.

And another, "The east lies here, my dear; I assure you this is the east."

"But I don't want to go east," said Tom.

"Well, then, at all events, whichever way you are going, you are going wrong," cried they all with one voice—which was the only thing which they ever agreed about; and all pointed at once to all the thirty-and-two-points of the compass, till Tom thought all the signposts in England had got together, and fallen fighting.

And whether he would have ever escaped out of the town, it is hard to say, if the dog had not taken it into his head that they were going to pull his master in pieces, and tackled them so sharply about the legs, that he gave them some business of their own to think of at last; and while they were rubbing their bitten calves, Tom and the dog got safe away.

On the borders of that island he found Gotham, where the wise men live; the same who dragged the pond because the moon had fallen into it, and planted a hedge round the cuckoo, to keep spring all the year. And he found them bricking up the town gate, because it was so wide that little folks could not get through. He could not help saying that in his country, if the kitten could not get in at the same hole as the cat, she might stay outside and mew.

But he saw the end of such fellows, when he came to the island of the Golden Asses, where nothing but thistles grow. For there they were all turned into mokes with ears a yard long, for meddling with matters which they do not understand.

Then Tom came to a very famous island, the Isle of Tomtoddies, all heads and no bodies.

And when Tom came near it, he heard such a grumbling and grunting and growling and wailing and weeping and whining that he thought people must be ringing little pigs, or cropping puppies' ears, or drowning kittens: but when he came nearer still, he began to hear words among the noise; which was the Tomtoddies' song which they sing morning and evening, and all night too—

"I can't learn my lesson: the examiner's coming!"

And that was the only song which they knew.

And when Tom got on shore the first thing he saw was a great pillar, on one side of which was inscribed, "Playthings not allowed here"; at which he was so shocked that he would not stay to see what was written on the other side. Then he looked round for the people of the island: but instead of men, women, and children, he found nothing but turnips and radishes, without a single green leaf among them, and half of them burst and decayed, with toadstools growing out of them. Those which were left began crying to Tom, in half-a-dozen different languages at once, and all of them badly spoken, "I can't learn my lesson; do come and help me!"

"And what good on earth would it do you if I did?" quoth Tom.

Well, they didn't know that: all they knew was the examiner was coming.

Then Tom stumbled on the hugest and softest turnip you ever saw, and it cried to him, "Can you tell me anything at all about anything you like?"

"About what?" says Tom.

"About anything you like; for as fast as I learn things I forget them again. So my mamma says that my intellect is not adapted for science, and says that I must go in for general information."

Tom told him that he did not know general information: but he could tell him a great many strange things which he had seen in his travels.

So he told him prettily enough, while the poor turnip listened very carefully; and the more he listened, the more he forgot, and the more water ran out of him.

Tom thought he was crying: but it was only his poor brains running away, from being worked so hard; and as Tom talked, the unhappy turnip streamed down all over with juice, and split and shrank till nothing was left of him but rind and water; whereat Tom ran away in a fright, for he thought he might be taken up for killing the turnip.

Tom was so puzzled and frightened with all he saw, that he was longing to ask the meaning of it; and at last he stumbled over a respectable old stick lying half covered with earth. But a very stout and worthy stick it was.

"You see," said the stick, "there were as pretty little children once as you could wish to see, and might have been so still if they had been only left to grow up like human beings, and then handed over to me; but their foolish fathers and mothers, instead of letting them pick flowers, and make dirt-pies, and get birds' nests, and dance round the gooseberry bush, as little children should, kept them always at lessons, working, working, working, learning week-day lessons all week-days, and Sunday lessons all Sunday, and weekly examinations every Saturday, and monthly examinations every month, and yearly examinations every year, everything seven times over, as if once was not enough, and enough as good as a feast—till their brains grew big, and their bodies grew small, and they were all changed into turnips, with little but water inside."

"Ah!" said Tom, "if dear Mrs. Doasyouwouldbe-doneby knew of it she would send them a lot of tops, and balls, and marbles, and ninepins, and make them all as jolly as sandboys."

"It would be no use," said the stick. "They can't play now, if they tried. Don't you see how their legs have turned to roots and grown into the ground, by never taking any exercise, but sapping and moping always in the same place? But here comes the Examiner-of-all-Examiners. So you had better get away, I warn you, or he will examine you and your dog into the bargain, and set him to examine all the other dogs, and you to examine all the other water-babies. There is no escaping out of his hands, for his nose is nine thousand miles long, and can go down chimneys, and through key-holes, upstairs, downstairs, in my lady's chamber, examining all little boys, and the little boys' tutors likewise. But when he is thrashed—so Mrs. Bedonebyasyoudid has promised me—I shall have the thrashing of him: and if I don't lay it on with a will it's a pity."

Tom went off: but rather slowly and surlily; for he was somewhat minded to face this same Examiner-of-all-Examiners, who came striding among the poor turnips, binding heavy burdens and grievous to be borne, and laying them on little children's shoulders.

But when he got near, he looked so big and burly and dictatorial, and shouted so loud to Tom, to come and be examined, that Tom ran for his life, and the dog too. And really it was time; for the poor turnips, in their hurry and fright, crammed themselves so fast to be ready for the Examiner, that they burst and popped by dozens all round him, and Tom thought he should be blown into the air, dog and all.

He went down to the shore and jumped into the sea, and swam on his way, singing:—

"Farewell Tomtoddies, all; I thank my stars
That nought I know save those three royal r's:
Reading and riting sure, with rithmetick,
Will help a lad of sense through thin and thick."

Whereby you may see that Tom was no poet.

And next he came to Oldwivesfabledom, where the folks were all heathens.

And there he found a little boy sitting in the middle of the road, and crying bitterly.

'What are you crying for?" said Tom.

"Because I am not as frightened as I could wish to be."

"Not frightened? You are a queer little chap: but, if you want to be frightened, here goes—Boo!"

"Ah," said the little boy, "that is very kind of you; but I don't feel that it has made any impression."

Tom offered to upset him, punch him, stamp on him, fettle him over the head with a brick, or anything else whatsoever which would give him the slightest comfort.

But he only thanked Tom very civilly, in fine long words which he had heard other folk use, and which, therefore, he thought were fit and proper to use himself; and cried on till his papa and mamma came, and sent off for the Powwow man immediately. And a very good-natured gentleman and lady they were, though they were heathens; and talked quite pleasantly to Tom about his travels, till the Powwow man arrived, with his thunderbox under his arm.

And a well-fed, ill-favoured gentleman he was. Tom was a little frightened at first; for he thought it was Grimes. But he soon saw his mistake: for Grimes always looked a man in the face; and this fellow never did. And when he spoke, it was fire and smoke; and when he sneezed, it was squibs and crackers; and when he cried, it was boiling pitch.

"Here we are again!" cried he, like the clown in a pantomime. "So you can't feel frightened, my little dear—eh? I'll do that for you. I'll make an impression on you! Yah! Boo! Whirroo! Hullabaloo!"

And he rattled, thumped, brandished his thunder-box, yelled, shouted, raved, roared, stamped, and danced; and then he touched a spring in the thunder-box, and out popped turnip-ghosts and magic-lanthorns and pasteboard bogies and spring-heeled Jacks, with such a horrid din, clatter, clank, roll, rattle, and roar, that the little boy turned up the whites of his eyes, and fainted right away.

And at that his poor heathen papa and mamma were delighted; and fell down upon their knees before the Powwow man, and gave him a palanquin with a pole of solid silver and curtains of cloth of gold; and carried him about in it on their own backs: but as soon as they had taken him up, the pole stuck to their shoulders, and they could not set him down any more, which was a pitiable sight to see. But you see, they had chosen to do a foolish thing just once too often; so, by the laws of Mrs. Bedonebyasyoudid, they had to go on doing it whether they chose or not.

Ah! don't you wish that someone would go and convert those poor heathens, and teach them not to frighten their little children into fits?

"Now, then," said the Powwow man to Tom, "wouldn't you like to be frightened, my little dear? For I can see plainly that you are a very wicked, naughty boy."

"You're another," quoth Tom, very sturdily. And when the man ran at him, and cried "Boo!" Tom ran at him in return, and cried "Boo!" likewise, right in his face, and set the little dog upon him; and at his legs the dog went.

At which, if you will believe it, the fellow turned tail, thunderbox and all, and ran for his life, screaming.

"Help! thieves! murder! fire! He is going to kill me! I am a ruined man! He will murder me; and break, burn, and destroy my precious and invaluable thunderbox; and then you will have no more thunder-showers in the land. Help! help! help!"

At which the papa and mamma and all the people of Oldwivesfabledom flew at Tom, shouting, "Oh, the wicked, impudent, hard-hearted, graceless boy! Beat him, kick him, shoot him, drown him, hang him, burn him!" and so forth: but luckily they had nothing to shoot, hang, or burn him with, for the fairies had hid all the killing-tackle out of the way a little while before; so they could only pelt him with stones; and some of the stones went clean through him, and came out the other side. But he did not mind that a bit; for the holes closed up again as fast as they were made, because he was a water-baby. However, he was very glad when he was safe out of the country, for the noise there made him all but deaf.

Then he came to a very quiet place, called Leaveheavenalone. And there the sun was drawing water out of the sea to make steam-threads, and the wind was twisting them up to make cloud-patterns, till they had worked between them the loveliest lace, and hung it up in their own Crystal Palace; while the good old sea never grudged, for she knew they would pay her back honestly. So the sun span, and the wind wove, and all went well with the great steam-loom.

Chapter 17

TOM REACHES MR. GRIMES

At last, after innumerable adventures, each more wonderful than the last, Tom saw before him a huge building.

He walked towards this great building, wondering what it was, and having a strange fancy that he might find Mr. Grimes inside it, till he saw running toward him, and shouting "Stop!" three or four people, who, when they came nearer, were nothing else than policemen's truncheons, running along without legs or arms.

Tom was not astonished. He was long past that. Neither was he frightened; for he had been doing no harm.

So he stopped; and, when the foremost truncheon came up and asked his business, he showed Mother Carey's pass; and the truncheon looked at it in the oddest fashion; for he had one eye in the middle of his upper end, so that when he looked at anything, being quite stiff, he had to slope himself, and poke himself, till it was a wonder why he did not tumble over.

"All right—pass on," said he at last. And then he added: "I had better go with you, young man." And Tom had no objection, for such company was both respectable and safe; so the truncheon coiled its thong neatly round its handle, to prevent tripping itself up—for the thong had got loose in running—and marched on by Tom's side.

"Why have you no policeman to carry you?" asked Tom, after a while.

"Because we are not like those clumsy-made truncheons in the land-world, which cannot go without having a whole man to carry them about. We do our own work for ourselves; and do it very well."

"Then why have you a thong to your handle?" asked Tom.

"To hang ourselves up by, of course, when we are off duty."

Tom had got his answer, and had no more to say, till they came up to the great iron door of the prison. And there the truncheon knocked twice, with its own head.

A wicket in the door opened, and out looked a tremendous old brass blunderbuss charged up to the muzzle with slugs, who was the porter; and Tom started back a little at the sight of him.

"What case is this?" he asked in a deep voice, out of his broad bell-mouth.

"If you please, sir, it is no case; only a young gentleman from her ladyship, who wants to see Grimes, the master-sweep."

"Grimes?" said the blunderbuss. And he pulled in his muzzle, perhaps to look over his prison-lists.

"Grimes is up chimney No. 345," he said from inside. "So the young gentleman had better go on to the roof"

Tom looked up at the enormous wall, which seemed at least ninety miles high, and wondered how he should ever get up: but, when he hinted that to the truncheon, it settled the matter in a moment. For it whisked round, and gave him such a shove behind as sent him up to the roof in no time, with his little dog under his arm.

And there he walked along the leads, till he met another truncheon, and told him his errand.

"Very good," it said. "Come along: but it will be of no use. He is the most unremorseful, hard-hearted, foul-mouthed fellow I have in charge; and thinks about nothing but beer and pipes, which are not allowed here, of course."

So they walked along over the leads, and very sooty they were, and Tom thought the chimneys must want sweeping very much. But he was surprised to see that the soot did not stick to his feet, or dirty them in the least. Neither did the live coals, which were lying about in plenty, burn him, being a water-baby.

And at last they came to chimney No. 345. Out of the top of it, his head and shoulders just showing, stuck poor Mr. Grimes, so sooty, and bleared, and ugly, that Tom could hardly bear to look at him. And in his mouth was a pipe; but it was not alight; though he was pulling at it with all his might.

"Attention, Mr. Grimes," said the truncheon; "here is a gentleman come to see you."

But Mr. Grimes only said bad words; and kept grumbling, "My pipe won't draw. My pipe won't draw."

"Keep a civil tongue, and attend!" said the truncheon; and popped up just like Punch, hitting Grimes such a crack over the head with itself, that his brains rattled inside like a dried walnut in its shell. He tried to get his hands out, and rub the place: but he could not for they were stuck fast in the chimney. Now he was forced to attend.

"Hey!" he said, "why, it's Tom! I suppose you have come here to laugh at me, you spiteful little atomy?"

Tom assured him he had not, but only wanted to help him.

"I don't want anything except beer, and that I can't get; and a light to this bothering pipe, and that I can't get either."

"I'll get you one," said Tom; and he took up a live coal (there were plenty Iying about) and put it to Grimes' pipe: but it went out instantly.

"It's no use," said the truncheon, leaning itself up against the chimney and looking on. "I tell you, it is no use. His heart is so cold that it freezes everything that comes near him. You will see that presently, plain enough."

"Oh, of course, it's my fault. Everything's always my fault," said Grimes. "Now don't go to hit me again" (for the truncheon started upright, and looked very wicked); "you know, if my arms were only free, you daren't hit me then."

The truncheon leant back against the chimney, and took no notice of the personal insult, like a well-trained policeman as it was.

"But can't I help you in any other way? Can't I help you to get out of this chimney?" said Tom.

"No," interposed the truncheon; "he has come to the place where everybody must help themselves; and he will find it out, I hope, before he has done with me."

"Oh, yes," said Grimes, "of course it's me. Did I ask to be brought here into the prison? Did I ask to be set to sweep your foul chimneys? Did I ask to have lighted straw put under me to make me go up? Did I ask to stick fast in the very first chimney of all, because it was so shamefully clogged up with soot? Did I ask to stay here—I don't know how long—a hundred years, I do believe, and never get my pipe, nor my beer, nor nothing fit for a beast, let alone a man?"

"No," answered a solemn voice behind. "No more did Tom, when you behaved to him in the very same way."

It was Mrs. Bedonebyasyoudid. And, when the truncheon saw her, it started bolt upright—Attention!—and made such a low bow. And Tom made his bow too.

"Oh, ma'am," he said, "don't think about me; that's all past and gone, and good times and bad times and all times pass over. But may not I help poor Mr. Grimes? Mayn't I try and get some of these bricks away, that he may move his arms?"

"You may try, of course," she said.

So Tom pulled and tugged at the bricks: but he could not move one. And then he tried to wipe Mr. Grimes' face: but the soot would not come off.

"Oh, dear!" he said. "I have come all this way, through all these terrible places, to help you, and now I am of no use at all."

"You had best leave me alone," said Grimes; "you are a good-natured forgiving little chap, and that's truth; but you'd best be off. The hail's coming on soon, and it will beat the eyes out of your little head."

"What hail?"

"Why, hail that falls every evening here; and, till it comes close to me, it's like so much warm rain: but then it turns to hail over my head, and knocks me about like small shot."

"That hail will never come any more," said the strange lady. "I have told you before what it was. It was your mother's tears, those which she shed when she prayed for you by her bedside; but your cold heart froze it into hail. But she is gone to heaven now, and will weep no more for her graceless son."

Then Grimes was silent awhile; and then he looked very sad.

"So my old mother's gone, and I never there to speak to her! Ah! a good woman she was, and might have been a happy one, in her little school there in Vendale, if it hadn't been for me and my bad ways."

"Did she keep the school in Vendale.?" asked Tom. And then he told Grimes all the story of his going to her house, and how she could not abide the sight of a chimney-sweep, and then how kind she was, and how he turned into a water-baby.

"Ah!" said Grimes, "good reason she had to hate the sight of a chimney-sweep. I ran away from her and took up with the sweeps, and never let her know where I was, nor sent her a penny to help her, and now it's too late—too late!" said Mr. Grimes.

And he began crying and blubbering like a great baby, till his pipe dropped out of his mouth, and broke all to bits.

"Oh, dear, if I was but a little chap in Vendale again, to see the clear beck, and the apple-orchard, and the yew-hedge, how different I would go on! But it's too late now. So you go along, you kind little chap, and don't stand to look at a man crying, that's old enough to be your father, and never feared the face of man, nor of worse neither. But I'm beat now, and beat I must be. I've made my bed, and I must lie on it. Foul I would be, and foul I am, as an Irishwoman said to me once; and little I heeded it. It's all my own fault: but it's too late." And he cried so bitterly that Tom began crying too.

"Never too late," said the fairy, in such a strange soft new voice that Tom looked up at her; and she was so beautiful for the moment, that Tom half fancied she was her sister.

No more was it too late. For, as poor Grimes cried and blubbered on, his own tears did what his mother's could not do, and Tom's could not do, and nobody's on earth could do for him; for they washed the soot off his face and off his clothes; and then they washed the mortar away from between the bricks; and the chimney crumbled down; and Grimes began to get out of it.

Up jumped the truncheon, and was going to hit him on the crown a tremendous thump, and drive him down again like a cork into a bottle. But the strange lady put it aside.

"Will you obey me if I give you a chance?"

"As you please, ma'am. You're stronger than me—that I know too well, and wiser than me, I know too well also. And, as for being my own master, I've fared ill enough with that as yet. So whatever your ladyship pleases to order me; for I'm beat, and that's the truth."

"Be it so then—you may come out. But remember, disobey me again, and into a worse place still you go."

"I beg pardon, ma'am, but I never disobeyed you that I know of. I never had the honour of setting eyes upon you till I came to these ugly quarters."

"Never saw me? Who said to you, Those that will be foul, foul they will be?"

Grimes looked up; and Tom looked up too; for the voice was that of the Irishwoman who met them the day that they went out together to Harthover. "I gave you your warning then: but you gave it yourself a thousand times before and since. Every bad word that you said—every cruel and mean thing that you did—every time that you got tipsy—every day that you went dirty—you were disobeying me, whether you knew it or not."

"If I'd only known, ma'am—"

"You knew well enough that you were disobeying something, though you did not know it was me. But come out and take your chance. Perhaps it may be your last."

So Grimes stepped out of the chimney, and really, if it had not been for the scars on his face, he looked as clean and respectable as a master-sweep need look.

"Take him away," said she to the truncheon, "and give him his ticket-of-leave."

"And what is he to do, ma'am?"

"Get him to sweep out the crater of Etna; he will find some very steady men working out their time there, who will teach him his business: but mind, if that crater gets choked again, and there is an earthquake in consequence, bring them all to me, and I shall investigate the case very severely."

So the truncheon marched off Mr. Grimes, looking as meek as a drowned worm.

And for aught I know, or do not know, he is sweeping the crater of Etna to this very day.

"And now," said the fairy to Tom, "your work here is done. You may as well go back again."

"I should be glad enough to go," said Tom, "but how am I to get up that great hole again, now the steam has stopped blowing?"

"I will take you up the backstairs: but I must bandage your eyes first; for I never allow anybody to see those backstairs of mine."

"I am sure I shall not tell anybody about them, ma'am, if you bid me not."

"Aha! So you think, my little man. But you would soon forget your promise if you got back into the land-world. So come—now I must bandage your eyes." So she tied the bandage on his eyes with one hand, and with the other she took it off.

"Now," she said, "you are safe up the stairs." Tom opened his eyes very wide, and his mouth too; for he had not, as he thought, moved a single step. But, when he looked round him, there could be no doubt that he was safe up the backstairs, whatsoever they may be.

The first thing which Tom saw was the black cedars, high and sharp against the rosy dawn; and St. Brandan's Isle reflected double in the still broad silver sea. The wind sang softly in the cedars, and the water sang among the caves: the seabirds sang as they streamed out into the ocean, and the landbirds as they built among the boughs; and the air was full of song; but among all the songs one came across the water more sweet and clear than all; for it was the song of a young girl's voice.

And what was the song which she sang? Ah, my little man, I am too old to sing that song, and you too young to understand it. But have patience, and keep your eye single, and your hands clean, and you will learn some day to sing it yourself, without needing any man to teach you.

And as Tom neared the island, there sat upon a rock the most graceful creature that ever was seen, looking down, with her chin upon her hand, and paddling with her feet in the water. And when they came to her she looked up, and behold it was Ellie.

"Oh, Miss Ellie," said he, "how you are grown!"

"Oh, Tom," said she, "how you are grown too!"

And no wonder; they were both quite grown up—he into a tall man, and she into a beautiful woman.

"Perhaps, I may be grown," she said. "I have had time enough; for I have been sitting here waiting for you many a hundred years, till I thought you were never coming."

"Many a hundred years?" thought Tom; but he had seen so much in his travels that he had quite given up being astonished; and, indeed, he could think of nothing but Ellie. So he stood and looked at Ellie, and Ellie looked at him; and they liked it so much that they neither spoke nor stirred.

At last they heard the fairy say: "Attention, children. Are you never going to look at me again?"

"We have been looking at you all this while," they said. And so they thought they had been.

"Then look at me once more," said she.

They looked—and both of them cried out at once, "Oh, who are you, after all?"

"You are our dear Mrs. Doasyouwouldbedoneby."

"No, you are good Mrs. Bedonebyasyoudid; but you are grown quite beautiful now!"

"To you," said the fairy. "But look again."

"You are Mother Carey," said Tom, in a very low, solemn voice; for he had found out something which made him very happy, and yet frightened him more than all that he had ever seen.

"But you are grown quite young again."

"To you," said the fairy. "Look again."

"You are the Irishwoman who met me the day I went to Harthover!"

And when they looked she was neither of them, and yet all of them at once.

"My name is written in my eyes, if you have eyes to see it there."

And they looked into her great, deep, soft eyes, and they changed again and again into every hue, as the light changes in a diamond.

"Now read my name," said she, at last.

And her eyes flashed, for one moment, clear, white, blazing light: but the children could not read her name; for they were dazzled, and hid their faces in their hands.

"Not yet, young things, not yet," said she, smiling; and then she turned to Ellie.

"You may take him home with you now on

Sundays, Ellie. He has won his spurs in the great battle, and become fit to go with you and be a man; because he has done the thing he did not like."

So Tom went home with Ellie on Sundays, and sometimes on week-days, too; and he is now a great man of science, and can plan railroads, and steam-engines, and electric telegraphs, and rifled guns, and so forth; and knows everything about everything. And all this from what he learnt when he was a water-baby, underneath the sea.

"And of course Tom married Ellie?"

My dear child what a silly notion! Don't you know that no one ever marries in a fairy-tale under the rank of a prince or a princess.

"And Tom's dog?"

Oh, you may see him any clear night in July; for the old dog-star was so worn out by the last three hot summers that there have been no dog-days since; so that they had to take him down and put Tom's dog up in his place. And that is the end of my story.